THE
HOUSE
OF
FORTUNE

Jessie Burton is the author of the *Sunday Times* number one and *New York Times* bestsellers *The Miniaturist* and *The Muse*, as well as the *Sunday Times* bestseller *The Confession* and the children's books *The Restless Girls* and *Medusa*. In its year of publication *The Miniaturist* sold over a million copies world-wide, and in 2017 it was adapted into a major TV series for BBC One. Her novels have been translated into forty languages, and she is a regular essay writer for newspapers and magazines. She lives in London.

Also by Jessie Burton

Novels
The Miniaturist
The Muse
The Confession

Books for Children
The Restless Girls
Medusa

THE
HOUSE
OF
FORTUNE

Jessie Burton

PICADOR

First published 2022 by Picador
an imprint of Pan Macmillan
The Smithson, 6 Briset Street, London EC1M 5NR
EU representative: Macmillan Publishers Ireland Ltd, 1st Floor,
The Liffey Trust Centre, 117–126 Sheriff Street Upper,
Dublin 1, D01 YC43
Associated companies throughout the world
www.panmacmillan.com

ISBN 978-1-5098-8609-8

1 3 5 7 9 8 6 4 2

A CIP catalogue record for this book is available from the British Library.

Typeset by Palimpsest Book Production Ltd, Falkirk, Stirlingshire
Printed and bound by CPI Group (UK) Ltd, Croydon, CR0 4YY

Visit **www.picador.com** to read more about all our books
and to buy them. You will also find features, author interviews and
news of any author events, and you can sign up for e-newsletters
so that you're always first to hear about our new releases.

For my son,
to whom I read this story
before either of us understood it.

Contents

This captivity is long: build ye houses, and dwell in them; and plant gardens, and eat the fruit of them.

—Jeremiah, 29:28, as marked by Marin Brandt
in the Brandt family Bible

Every woman is the architect of her own fortune.

—motto, written by the miniaturist to Nella Brandt
in the autumn of 1686

The year 1705

An Inheritance

I

At eighteen, Thea is too old to be celebrating birthdays. Rebecca Bosman turned thirty in December and never mentioned it: that is sophistication. In bed, in the dark January dawn, Thea shivers under her sheets. She can hear her aunt and Cornelia bickering down in the salon, and her father dragging away the table for breakfast on the rug. They always start Thea's birthday sitting on that rug. Relentless tradition, the fun of pretending to be adventurers, making do with the provisions they have mustered. These days it's a pitiful conceit, because none of them have left the city walls for years. Also: what's wrong with a table? They've clung on to the good one: they should use it. Adults use tables. If Rebecca Bosman had to endure a birthday breakfast, *she* would have a table.

But Thea cannot tell them any of this. Cannot bear to go downstairs and see her Aunt Nella turn away, tugging the tatty paper chains she's surely hung off the huge iced windows. Her father, staring at the threadbare rug. Cornelia, her old nurse-maid, gazing forlornly at the little pufferts she's been up all night finessing. Thea has no wish to tip them into sadness, but she doesn't know how to extricate herself from this role they have put her in, their collective child. She might have become a woman today, but joy in this household is laced always with a fear of loss.

And here it comes, in the form of food, the sweet spiced waft from downstairs arriving underneath her bedroom door. The pufferts infused with rosewater, no doubt spelling Thea's name in case she should forget. Cornelia's fluffy cumin eggs to keep her prisoner, hot buttered rolls to warm her up. Delft butter, as a treat, and a thimble of sweet wine for the adults. Thea throws back the sheets, but still cannot bring herself to get up, feeling no lift of her spirits at the promise of special butter. The only thing she can hope for is that they have bought her tickets to the Schouwburg, so she can see Rebecca Bosman perform again. And afterwards, when the play is over, she can steal away to Walter, the only person who can propel her from her covers.

Soon, Thea thinks. Soon we will be together, and everything will feel right. But for now: prolonged and stale childhood.

Eventually mustering the will to put on her slippers and gown, moving slowly down the stairs in order not to be heard, Thea forces herself to be grateful. She must try not to disappoint them. Her family's over-the-top birthday cheer never used to bother her, but there is an ocean of difference between childhood and being eighteen. They are going to have to start treating her like an adult. And maybe this year, for the first birthday ever in Thea's life, someone will give her a present she really wants, and talk about her mother, give the gift of a story, or just an anecdote! Yes, we all know that today is the hardest day in the Brandt family calendar. Yes, eighteen years ago today, Marin Brandt died in this very house, giving Thea life. But who could find this day harder than me, Thea thinks as she moves across the hallway tiles – I, who have grown up motherless?

Every year, all they talk about is how much bigger Thea has grown in twelve months, how much bonnier, or cleverer, as if Thea is a brand-new person every time. As if, on every eighth day of January, which is always cold and always blue, she has come to them hatched from an egg. But Thea doesn't want to have her growth reflected back at her. She has the mirror for that. On her birthday, she wants to look into the glass and see her mother, to know who she was and why her father will never speak of her. Why almost all her questions are answered by the exchange of sombre looks and pursed lips. She hesitates, her back pressed against the wall. Perhaps even now they could be talking about Marin Brandt.

Expert eavesdropper, Thea waits in the shadows outside the salon, her breath held tight with hope.

No. They are squabbling about whether Lucas the cat will consent to wearing a birthday ruff. 'He hates it, Cornelia,' says her aunt. 'Look at his eyes. He'll vomit on the rug.'

'But it makes her laugh.'

'Not if she's eating pufferts by a pile of sick.'

Lucas, their yellow-eyed god of scraps, mewls in indignation. 'Cornflower,' Thea's father intervenes. 'Let Lucas go unclothed for breakfast. Allow him that. Maybe he can dress for dinner.'

'You two have no sense of occasion,' Cornelia retorts. 'He *likes* it.'

These familiar rhythms, these voices: Thea has known so very little else. She closes her eyes. She used to love to listen to Cornelia, her Aunt Nella, her father, to sit at their feet or to hang round their necks, being adored and petted, squeezed and teased. But these days, it is not the kind of music that interests her, it's not their necks she wants to hang around.

And this conversation about whether or not their enormous cat should wear a ruff gives Thea a fierce urge to be anywhere else. To be away from them, and start her own life, because not a single one of them knows what it is to be eighteen.

She takes a deep breath, exhales, goes in. As one, her family turn to her, and their eyes light up. Lucas trots over, dainty with his weight. The paper chains are strung along the windows, as she knew they would be. Like Thea, her family are still in their nightclothes – another Thea Birthday Tradition – and it is mortifying to see the contours of their old bodies. True enough, her Aunt Nella is clinging on fairly well at thirty-seven, but her father is forty-one, and a man of forty-one should be fully dressed before he comes to breakfast. Cornelia has such wide hips – is she not embarrassed by the way the light shines through her shift? I would be embarrassed, Thea thinks. I am never going to let my body flap about like that. Still, they cannot help it. Cornelia will always say: 'You get old, get wider hips, then die.' But Thea is going to be like Rebecca Bosman, who can fit into clothes she wore when she was Thea's age. The secret, Rebecca says, is to walk very quickly past any bakery. Cornelia would not agree.

'Happy birthday, Teapot!' Cornelia beams.

'Thank you,' Thea says, trying not to wince at the nickname. She scoops up Lucas and goes over to where they are all gathered on the rug.

'So tall!' says her father. 'When will you ever stop growing? I can't keep up.'

'Papa. I have been this height for two years.'

He takes her in his arms and gives her a long hug. 'You're perfect.'

'She's Thea,' says her aunt.

Thea meets her aunt's eyes and lets Lucas down. It's always Aunt Nella who tries to drag her father back from the brink of overpraise. Always Aunt Nella, the first to find fault.

'Let's eat,' Cornelia says. 'Lucas, no—' – for the cat, ruff-less and unencumbered, already has a piece of egg in his mouth. He skitters away to the corner, his back legs a pair of sandy pantaloons. It is common for Amsterdammers to dislike animals in their homes, fearing paw prints will mar new-scrubbed floors, droppings left in clean places, furniture massacred. But Lucas is indifferent to popular opinion. He has his private perfection and he is Thea's constant comfort.

'The greediest creature on the Herengracht,' says Aunt Nella. 'Won't catch mice, but happy to eat our breakfast.'

'Leave him,' Thea says.

'Teapot,' says Cornelia. 'Here are your birthday pufferts.' She presents them, THEA BRANDT spelled out in tiny pancakes. 'There's rosewater syrup, or if you'd like something more savoury with them—'

'No, no, this is fine. Thank you.' Thea sits down on the rug, folding her legs beneath her and popping two pufferts in quick succession into her mouth.

'Slowly!' Cornelia chides. 'Otto, a buttered roll with egg?'

'Please,' he replies. 'My knees won't take the rug. I'll sit on a chair, if no one minds.'

'You're not eighty,' says Aunt Nella, but Thea's father ignores her.

The women sit on the rug. Thea feels ridiculous and is glad no one looking in from the street can see. 'A thimble of wine for you?' Aunt Nella asks.

Thea sits up, resting her plate on her knee. 'Really?'

'You're eighteen. No longer a child. Here.' Aunt Nella hands over a small glass.

'From Madeira,' offers her father. 'They had an unaccounted barrel at the VOC, half-price.'

'Thank goodness it was,' says her aunt. 'We can't just be buying barrels of Madeira.'

Irritation flits across his face, and Aunt Nella flushes, staring down into the swirls of the rug.

'Let us make a toast,' Thea's father continues. 'To our Thea. May she always be safe—'

'—well fed,' says Cornelia.

'— and happy,' Thea adds.

'And happy,' echoes her aunt.

Thea swallows the wine, a bright hard shock glowing in her stomach to give her courage. 'What was it like,' she asks, 'the day that I was born?'

Silence on the rug, silence from the chair. Cornelia reaches for another roll and stuffs it with fluffy egg. 'Well?' Thea says. 'You were all there.'

Aunt Nella turns to Thea's father. Their eyes meet.

'You *were* there, weren't you, Papa?' Thea says. 'Or did I come into the world alone?'

'We all come into the world alone,' her aunt says. Cornelia rolls her eyes. Thea's father says nothing. It's always the same.

Thea sighs. 'You were not happy I was born.'

Her family comes alive and turns to her, aghast. 'Oh, no,' says Cornelia. 'We were so happy! You were a blessing.'

'I was the end of something,' says Thea.

Aunt Nella closes her eyes.

'You were a beginning,' her father says. 'The best beginning ever. Now: I think it's time for gifts.'

Thea knows she has been defeated, again. The easiest course of action is to eat another buttered roll and unwrap the gifts they have gathered. A box of her favourite cinnamon biscuits from Cornelia, and from her father and aunt – yes, they have been paying attention to some part of her soul at least – a pair of tickets for today's afternoon showing of *Titus*. 'Gallery seats?' she says, her heart rising. This is generous indeed. 'Oh, thank you!'

'Not every day you turn eighteen,' her father smiles.

'We can make a day of it,' Cornelia says. 'You and me.'

Thea looks at their brightened expressions. She can tell they have already planned who will accompany her – it makes sense, she supposes, for her father will have to leave soon for his clerking at the VOC, and her aunt dislikes the playhouse. 'Thank you, Cornelia,' she says, and her old nursemaid gives her hand a squeeze.

Titus is a violent play if ever there was, but Thea's favourites are the romances. Woodland idylls, island dreams, where everything is muddled before being put right. Since the age of thirteen Thea has been dragging either her aunt or Cornelia to the city playhouse. Arriving early, paying their entrance fees and the two-stuiver surcharge for standing seats, no hope of affording the dress circle, let alone a box, waiting for the place to fill with six hundred and ninety-nine other bodies. Her escapes into comedy or tragedy feel like a kind of homecoming. At the age of sixteen, after much begging and wheedling, and despite Cornelia's vehement reluctance, her family agreed she could occasionally make the five-minute walk to the playhouse on her own, as long as she came straight back home. Until meeting Walter backstage six months ago, Thea has kept her side of the bargain. But things are changing. Deceptions have been necessary. She has exaggerated the lengths of performances to steal the extra time with him. She has even fabricated play titles and show days to go backstage to find him. Her family have never doubted her. They have never checked whether this farce or that tragedy is being staged. And although at times Thea feels guilty, her and Walter's love is too important. Theirs is an unwritten romance performed in the back corridors of the Schouwburg, the words of which are indelible, inscribed as they are in the heart. Thea knows she will never give it up.

'Don't forget about this evening,' says her aunt.

Thea looks up from the pair of tickets in her hand. 'This evening?'

She sees it: the quick, shallow inhalation of breath that indicates her aunt's irritation. 'You had forgotten?' says Aunt Nella. 'The Sarragon Epiphany Ball. Thea, it's a miracle we were invited. I've been paying court to Clara Sarragon since Michaelmas to make it happen.'

Thea glances at her father's stony expression, and decides to risk it. 'You don't like those people. Why are we even going?'

'Because we have to,' Aunt Nella says, stalking towards the long, wide windows of the salon to look out across the stretch of the Heren canal.

'But why do we have to?' Thea presses.

No one answers. So Thea decides to play her last card. 'Doesn't Clara Sarragon own plantations in Surinam?'

The atmosphere in the room sharpens. Thea knows that her

father was taken to that colony and made a slave, and at the age of sixteen he was brought by her now-dead uncle to Amsterdam. She has been told just one story about that time by Cornelia, about how Amsterdam women would put songbirds in her father's hair, an image that has always made Thea feel a profound discomfort. But beyond that, a real knowledge of her father's past is hidden in a well she cannot dredge. Where her father was before that time in Surinam, or what shape his time in the colony took, Thea knows nothing. He never talks of it. It is a blank as profound as the silence around her white mother, another of the unspoken things which permeate this house like mist. Otto Brandt: he too might have hatched from an egg.

Thea is fed up with their silences. Whenever she pushes Cornelia, she receives the same response: 'I came from the orphanage,' Cornelia will say. 'And your father was taken from his first home. It is the way of things for us. This house is our harbour. It's where we stay. Where we belong.'

But what if you don't want to be in the harbour any more? Thea wonders to herself, but never dares to say out loud. What if you feel that you don't belong?

'What Clara Sarragon owns or does not own has nothing to do with you,' her aunt is saying in a hard voice. None of them look at Thea's father. 'Do not forget. Six o'clock tonight. We'll be ready in the hallway in our finery.'

'What's left of it,' says Thea.

'Precisely,' her aunt sighs.

'Go and dress, Teapot,' Cornelia says in a bright voice. 'I'll come up and help you with your hair.'

Thea glances at her father, who is now looking out of the window. Feeling a faint sheen of shame, she turns on her heel, leaving her family marooned inside the salon. As she ascends the staircase into the gloom of the upper corridor, Thea puts the Sarragon ball and her careless mention of Surinam out of her mind, and thinks about her real birthday treat. She will be happy to witness Rebecca creating magic on the stage, but behind those painted backdrops, something much more real waits. The love of Thea's life, her reason for living. No dreary party held by an Amsterdam grandee could ever ruin the promise of Walter Riebeeck.

II

By eleven thirty, Thea and Cornelia have left in a flurry of scarves and chatter, leaving Nella alone with Otto. Exhausted by the demands of the morning breakfast, the two of them, now dressed, reconvene in the salon to survey the debris of their earlier efforts. The house around them feels quiet and empty, whilst Lucas, full of egg, is fast asleep, a cushion against a cushion. Nella looks around the bare walls, the miserly fire. They haven't bothered with this room for months, being too large to heat, too many hard surfaces. Late in December the canals froze over, and a sense of the city's pinched withdrawal outside pervades the interior.

Going outside is an endurance, rain sopping wool hoods, the wind a frozen finger: Nella longs for lighter mornings, longer afternoons, to bury her threadbare fur collar in cedar for another year. The choicest firewood will be down to a small pile after this morning's little party, but only the working kitchen and their bedrooms usually see a fire. No point heating up this carcass of a building, too big, too full of echoes because they've thinned the furniture and sold the wall hangings. They've got peat supplies, but the smell is terrible. She yearns for spring.

'I can't see us doing this for her nineteenth,' she says. 'Did you see the expression on her face?'

'She liked it,' says Otto.

'We should be displaying ourselves more frequently in here,' Nella replies, changing the subject. She stares through the huge front windows. 'Reassuring the citizenry that everything inside is ticking over.'

'Such a performance is becoming wearisome.'

'I am well aware.'

'We need to be much more prudent with household supplies, Nella. Yet another guilder on beeswax candles?'

'It was her birthday,' Nella says, avoiding Otto's gaze, unwilling to admit those candles were for herself, to remember when the whole house was once filled with the hint of honey. 'Do you remember,' she says tentatively, for Otto doesn't like to reminisce, 'how we'd burn oil of rose?'

'Did we?'

'The best the city had, from a merchant who brought it from Damascus. We drenched the place.' Nella pauses. 'I don't regret it. Or maybe I do?' She gestures to the walls. 'Because now we are selling our paintings to pay the butcher.'

Otto sighs. Nella plumps one of the remaining cushions, swirling hidden dust up into the air. She sits, placing the cushion on her lap as if she might dandle it, curling her palms over the chair's carved lion heads, the familiar manes wreathed with leaves of acanthus. Closing her eyes, tracing the wooden muzzles, she shoots an upwards thought to God – but also, why not? – to Aphrodite: *Let tonight work. Let someone want her.*

She opens her eyes to find Otto regarding her. His look is disapproving. 'I know you don't want to go the ball,' she says.

'You surely cannot tell me you find the company of Clara Sarragon pleasurable.'

'What I find pleasurable is immaterial. As for Clara Sarragon, I will avoid her as much as I can. We are going on behalf of Thea.'

'For her to be stared at, whispered about behind people's hands? All my life I have tried to make sure my child was not a spectacle. They will make her one. And we will have put her there.'

'It might be a good thing that people notice her. Thea is beautiful, accomplished. She deserves a chance.'

'A chance at what?'

Nella doesn't dare say the big word: *marriage*. Otto stares into the empty grate, his mouth a line. 'You have no idea what it means to be noticed like I am noticed, like Thea is *noticed*,' he says. 'It is not what you think it is.'

Nella holds her tongue. Amsterdam is a port city, full of difference. There are the Huguenot French who have come fleeing Catholic murderousness: they had their weaving skills welcomed by this ever-pragmatic city, putting their hands to the silks that flowed from the East, making beautiful clothes for Amsterdammers to strut in. There are the itinerant workers from Germany and Sweden, Denmark, England, looking for work as maids or housebuilders. There are the rich Portuguese Hebrew merchants, arriving from their plantations in Brazil to buy houses nearby the Golden Bend, filling the streets with the incomprehensible, dancing melodies of two languages. Down at the docks reside men from Java and Japan: sailors, doctors, merchants, travellers, trinket-sellers. And in the Jewish quarter live the boys and girls who began their lives on the African continent, in places Nella has never been taught to name, now running errands on Dutch cobbles, or clutching instrument cases to play music at party after party, where they are considered exciting additions by the guests.

But despite this uneven multiplicity, for all of Thea's life, Nella has seen the darting stares, the lingering glances at Thea's head if her cap comes loose, the dark, coiled curls springing out, the bold and subtle assessments of her physical person. Thea, with her deep brown eyes, her ochre skin that the summer sun turns darker, while Nella and Cornelia flush pink. Nella has seen those stares, but she has not felt them, and this truth has drawn a line between her and Otto for eighteen years.

'This is a city of surveillance,' he says. 'Of keeping the peace with one hand and scratching what lies beneath the surface with the fingernails of the other. So remember how it is for her.'

'I *do* remember. We've done our best. What choice do we have, Otto? You want us to hide her forever? The only baby any of us have will ever have, and there was no paper and lace *kloppertje* on the front door, to say we'd had a girl.'

He looks at her. 'We?'

Nella ignores this. 'No paternity bonnet for you, to be teased and clapped on the back. No period of grace from city taxes. No feast, no dance, no music. No holding her up to the windows for neighbours to congratulate us on her fatness and bonniness. No mother, either.'

She's gone too far, and now Thea's mother is in the room with them. Marin, standing tall and erect, watching them with her mild grey eyes. Marin, who had died hours after Thea's birth, who left them stranded in the sea of a newborn, with no map, no compass, no sense of destiny. They have never spoken in mixed company about the identity of Thea's mother. As far as the city knows it, Thea is a motherless heiress of a darker hue, an enigma they would die for. They have never cared to elaborate further, and never had the need. But it remains astounding to Nella how Marin's imprints shift upon her niece's features, how a turn of Thea's head, the jut of her lip, the sound of a sigh, conjures her absent mother.

When Thea was about six months old, Nella, Otto and Cornelia agreed that the most sensible, most compassionate thing to do would be not to tell Thea too much about the forbidden manner of her conception, the details of her mother's death and her subsequent concealment. It was hard to speak to a child about such things, and as the years went by, they did not exercise that muscle. They did not want Thea to be associated with the guilt and shame of that time, or indeed, the horror of it. Whether it was right or not, Thea became solely her father's daughter, her aunt's niece and Cornelia's charge. She was *not* forbidden. She was Thea. Let Thea be Thea.

They learned to live around the unspoken subject of Marin until the silence shrank to nothing, vanishing into the panelling, subsumed into the furniture. They pushed Marin into the shadows. Thea briefly had a mother: now she was dead. No questions could be asked, because there was no focus for such inquiries. It was a decision formed from the panic of living in a judgemental society. Marin was unmarried when she gave birth. Marin and Otto could never have been married, not in that world, and they made a child the like of which few had seen on the Golden Bend. In the face of these impossibilities, they somehow had to make a robust and self-believing little girl.

What were we *thinking*? Nella wonders. You can't bury a mother and expect her never to rise up again. I should know.

Thea never asks her aunt directly: *What was my mother like?* Instead, she turns it on herself – *You didn't want me. You were not happy I was born.* In many ways, this is worse. In many ways, they have not succeeded at all.

'We did what we did to protect her,' Otto says, as if he is reading Nella's thoughts.

'And now she needs a different type of protection. Let me find it for her, Otto. Let me find her some feasts and music. It's taken us a long time to be re-admitted into this city. I have worked so hard in the last year, drinking tea with people I would rather push into the canal.'

Nella feels desperate. The two of them have been here so many times before. 'It's getting worse now she's older,' he says. 'People are bolder. There is less curiosity, more outright shock. She and I are not the only people in this city to look as we do. Far from it. But perhaps we are some of the few who dress so well, and that's what people hate.'

Nella remembers Thea at no more than six, clutching at Cornelia's skirts at the vegetable market. A woman shopping next to them had looked down, her expression of curiosity rapidly morphing into one of almost hunger. 'Oh, what a creature!' she had cried, plunging her fingers into the black corona of Thea's hair. 'I cannot place her. Is she – oh, she cannot be!' 'She's none of your business,' Cornelia had replied, moving Thea away and taking one of the cabbages in her hand like a grenade.

There have been many cabbage women and men over the last eighteen years: big-headed and pale, vegetative in intelligence. You could say the cabbage people have been legion. And then there are the girls and boys who are darker than Thea, the African Brazilian maids who stand outside the synagogues, waiting early to reserve a good seat for their mistresses, the Portuguese merchants' wives. As a child, Thea used to love to hear the girls calling to each other, their Portuguese or Hebrew-sounding names – *Francisca*, *Yizka*, *Gracia*. More than once, she had tugged on Nella's hand so that they might stop and look. As Thea got older, Nella saw her try to catch these maids' eyes, hoping for some recognition in turn. But bar one or two, the girls usually don't meet her gaze. They don't want trouble, Nella supposes. The whiteness from her mother marks her as not one of them. Or maybe it is Thea's clothes, as Otto says: simple in cut, but of finer, more durable quality. Or maybe it isn't either of those things at all. Nella has always felt so ignorant about these matters.

'Wealth, should Thea find it at the ball, would protect her,' Nella says. She hesitates. 'Marriage would protect her.'

'*Marriage*,' Otto says. 'Marriage is no guarantee of survival. You of all people should know that.'

Their eyes meet. They are entering dangerous territory. 'My daughter is better off staying here,' Otto says.

'And have you asked her if that's what she wants? You see our ledger books. You know how bad it is. You and I won't be here forever,' Nella pushes on. 'And then what? Do you want her here alone in this giant tomb, no income, no protection?'

He rises to his feet. 'Of course not.'

'Besides,' she continues, trying to break the tension, 'at least Cornelia's never going to die. Cornelia will outlive us all.'

Otto's reluctant smile gives them both a moment of relief.

She and Otto have carried the last eighteen years into their faces, but Cornelia clatters those pans in the kitchen as if she were still twenty, preparing to fight poultry and fish, any stubborn tuber. Cornelia's immortality actually feels plausible.

'Thea is not here to rescue us, Petronella,' Otto says. 'She owes no debt.'

'Good God. I know that.'

'Are you sure?' Otto looks her directly in the eyes. 'If you believe so deeply that marriage will secure her a future, why don't you do it yourself? You don't have to worry about raising her any more. You are thirty-seven, and she is just eighteen.'

'I was eighteen when I married.'

'And look how that went.'

'Otto—'

'You are a viable prospect. Sarragon has invited you to her ball. People see you as a rich widow, a dash of scandal, with a house on the Herengracht—'

'Which Johannes left to you! Personally, I have no wealth.'

Otto sighs. 'There will be someone who will give you what you want.'

He walks away to the window and Nella jumps up to join him. 'And what do I want?' she says.

Otto does not say it, but Nella knows what he is thinking. That she wants children. His presumption stings, as perhaps he knew it would. Nella knows what others in this city see of her: that she is not young, at thirty-seven. That she is long-widowed, unmarried, childless. Reserved, restrained, modest in dress. But in many ways, Nella has no clue who she is. She thought she would be earthbound, solid, sure of herself. Inwardly she is a watery person who could be swept away or dragged into a lake. Would a physician call her melancholic? Her age is liquid, running through her fingers. Her mind is dull, no delirious wonder. She used to feel her thoughts were held in a nautilus shell, infinite spirals shimmering, lifted from the bed of her skull.

'You want a home of your own,' Otto says.

'This is my home. Marriage to Johannes changed my life for the better.'

'That's not what you usually say.'

She ignores this. 'There is a man out there who will do the same for Thea.'

'He lied to you about what that life would be, and you've been dealing with that lie for the last eighteen years. Do you think he is the only man to do that?'

Nella absorbs the blow. 'Marin lied too. Yet you never blame her.'

Otto walks back into the centre of the salon. 'Why don't you just sell the wreck?' he says. 'We'd get some money from that.'

Nella feels a dark throbbing in her stomach. Not this. Not the wreck. Every now and then, Otto likes to summon up her childhood home in Assendelft, which she has never returned to since the day she was ordered to Amsterdam to become the wife of Johannes Brandt. Even after her sister, Arabella, her last remaining sibling, died four years ago, Nella has still resisted the journey into the past. Instead of going in person, she paid for an agent to visit the house and write up a report. What came back was damning, as Otto knows full well: large holes in the roof, the upper floor uninhabitable, the lake clogged with weeds and the orchards possibly barren. Cows had overtaken what once was the herb garden, and it looked to the agent as if a party of brigands had spent months holed up in the kitchen and ground-floor rooms, lighting fires in the middle of rugs, and smashing windows. Villagers nearby had claimed that it was haunted. Nella had read enough, and ordered the place to be boarded up. She has no intention of going back.

But even when she left her family home years before that, it was already a place of loss and fear and dereliction, and she has not told them why. She has worked hard to change herself from the Nella who lived there to the woman who lives here. The property is hers, indeed, hanging around her neck like a stone: her stone, and no one else's.

'I've told you before,' she says to him: 'Assendelft is not for sale.'

'Nella, you never go there.'

'It's not for sale.'

'Give me one reason why not.'

Nella sits in the chair and puts her head in her hands.

'I do not understand why you never speak of it,' Otto pushes.

She shoots her head up. 'Yet just as I will not speak of Assendelft, you will not speak of Marin. Nor of your days in Surinam. Nor your childhood in Dahomey. We both have our pasts, Otto. We both have things we do not speak of. I never ask you, so why do you ask me?'

He turns to her. 'These things are not the same. A house in the country, compared with my life?'

'We all have our stones,' she says.

'What do you mean?'

Nella bites her lip. 'Nothing.' His face closes. 'Otto,' she tries again. 'No one will buy it. No one can live in it. The land is dead.'

He walks towards the door. 'I have to go.'

'You're starting late.'

'Bert Schippers covered my shift so we could have the breakfast.'

'What are you working on at the moment?'

'Nutmeg consignment. Just in from the Moluccas.'

'And will you—'

But Otto has gone. Nella hears him in the hallway, gathering up his coat and hat, and then the sound of the front door, closing her in. 'Remember the ball,' she says, speaking to the empty walls.

She leans back, gathering a surprised Lucas into her arms. These conversations with Otto agitate, stirring up old memories she would prefer to lie dormant, but it seems impossible not to bring up the past when trying to wrangle a future.

Before her husband, Johannes, and his sister, Marin, died eighteen years ago, they had both written wills – because although they had their secrets, they were also sensible, upright citizens. The house on the Herengracht was left in Otto's name, and their VOC shares, their small parcels of land outside the city, and all their moveables were entrusted to Nella. It had seemed, for a while, as if Widow Brandt, Otto, Cornelia and Thea might survive the loss of Johannes and Marin in relative comfort. That hope was naive.

Despite the fact that Otto had worked by Johannes' side for nearly a decade, the merchants who had traded with Johannes, and the foreign and domestic clients who had relied on him, grew cold. Contacts and contracts expired. Fewer private dinners, no guild invitations. The manner of Johannes' death and Otto's perceived inferiority were disastrous to their finances. Perhaps, if her husband had been a different man, Nella could have been taken seriously as executrix of his financial legacies, as Amsterdam widows sometimes are. But her dead husband was disgraced, called a sodomite, publicly shamed, and shame is a shining thing. It reflected off them into the eyes of others, who abandoned them, blinded by its power.

By the third year of their abandonment, their status in the city drastically reduced, with Thea toddling around these polished floors, needing to be fed and clothed, their immediate funds had been used up. They sold off the land and the VOC shares, and eventually Cornelia said that the only recourse left was to pray. Otto found his inventory post at the VOC warehouse, offered to him by an officer there who remembered the plight of the Brandt family, and who was more sympathetic to Thea's father than the rest of the VOC and guilds put together. It was beneath Otto's abilities, but the only position he could find. Some of the boys he worked with were no older than thirteen: they must have looked at him and thought him a Methuselah. For what was he, but a storehouse of knowledge that they could use to promote their own interests? But the family was desperate, and in many ways, the money from Otto's salary has kept them afloat. Soon after he started his work, Otto began to suggest Nella marry again in the interest of future security. It's a refrain, over the past eighteen years, that he has returned to more times than Nella would like: 'Maybe Nella will have to marry a rich man.'

As the years have worn on and life has turned meaner and

narrower, Nella has begun to see all this in only one way: Marin had arranged her marriage with Johannes as a means to protect herself, treating Nella as an unwanted requirement. Johannes, too distracted and selfish to stand up to his powerful sister, had let his young wife love him with no consideration of the cost to her that such a love might contain. If Nella caught sleep in the months after Johannes' and Marin's deaths, her dreams were not of a drowning man plunging to the sea bed with a stone around his neck. The sensation of a stone was on her shoulders instead. With the arrival of Thea, her own life has been a sacrifice, one that Marin and Johannes were willing to make. What has she to show for these last eighteen years? Citizen of a nation that prides itself on self-construction, she has built nothing, inside or out. And yet it always hurts her, Otto's assumption that she would have been happy simply to walk away from the house on the Herengracht, to leave Thea behind. Why was he so sure that she'd be willing to start again?

The truth was, over the years following Johannes's death, it was the rich widows who caught Nella's attention. Women who chose not to marry again. They didn't have to. They had money of their own, and their dead husbands' fortunes. As widows, they were no longer legal entities controlled by a husband. Nella would pass them on the Golden Bend, or see them in their barges, pearls as large as hens' eggs round their necks or dangling from their ears, heading back to their softly perfect mansions and lack of obligations, their silent stocks buoying them in the choppy waters of Amsterdam till the day they too would meet their God. No man to please in the bed. No babies to risk dying for. Nella couldn't get those women out of her mind, even though she knew she had no giant pearls, no stocks, and a life which felt full of worry and obligation.

Why should I let another strange new man disembark upon the shore of my household, demanding I hand it over to him to manage? Nella had thought, watching another perfumed woman disappear behind her huge front door. And how would he treat Thea? How would he regard Otto, or Cornelia? Why take the risk? Her life was difficult, but it was hers. She had fought and paid the price for her tiny dominion.

But there is always the other side of the coin. The fact is, she has never encountered anybody else she might have wanted to marry. No decent man has crossed her path. With their reduced social life, and all her attention given to Thea, potential husbands over the intervening years have been scarce, and scarcer still as she grows older, with a surname like hers and its legacy of shame and financial decline. What she owns is a private loneliness, no future for her that she can see. Otto assumes her desire for children, but what does he know of the things she desires? She barely knows them herself.

Nella places Lucas on her chair and moves swiftly into the echoing hallway and up the staircase, and up again, to the narrower top floor and the steps to the attic. Taking care not to stand on her skirts, with a candle in one hand, she half-crouches in the darkness, enveloped by the cold and damp. No one knows she comes up here, every anniversary of Marin's death. It is another secret.

In the corner, in the shadows, sits Marin's travelling chest. Cornelia would probably think it morbid and damaging to open it. Otto would say it was not her right. Thea is not even aware this chest exists, how the mystery of her mother is so nearly embodied in its hidden artefacts. Nella and Cornelia had planned to show her, to tell her – but somehow, they have never found the right time. It comforts Nella, to be the only one to kneel before Marin's chest, to unclasp the old locks either side, to lift the lid.

The scent of cedar shavings rises up, and Nella's heart beats hard. Looking into Marin's chest is like peering into a small coffin except the body has fled, and instead of a winding sheet are several rolled-up scrolls. Holding her candle aloft, Nella sees the familiar scattered seeds and bright feathers that once adorned Marin's private room. Her dried petals, her animal skulls. Here are Marin's books, their boards pressed together and tied with string. Nella sees the top title: *The Unfortunate Voyage of the Ship Batavia*, one of Marin's favourites, a story of travel and mutiny, blood thirst and enslavement. She takes out the most-thumbed volume, *The Memorable Accounts of the Voyage of the Nieuw Hoorn*, and tracing her finger over the woodcuts of old familiar shipwrecks and shorelines, she imagines Marin's slender hand on her shoulder. *Spying again, are we, Petronella? These things aren't for you.*

Marin's voice lies beyond these walls, yet somehow she always feels buried deep inside Nella's body.

Here are Marin's maps: Nella unfolds every one, covering the floorboards with the world. In the quiet of the attic here is Africa, and here Molucca. Here, Java and Batavia. Here England, Ireland, France, North and South America. And there are Marin's handwritten words: *Weather? Food? God?* Questions to which Marin never found her answers.

Nella stares hard into the continent of Africa, into the

crenellations of the cartographer's pen that indicate rocky coasts and mountains, deserts and lakes, looking at this unfamiliar territory in search of a solution to Otto's enduring silence, of where he came from before he arrived in Amsterdam. She moves to the map of Surinam, running her finger over the name, thinking of him, of sugar caramelizing the air, of a ball tonight full of heat and music. *Doesn't Clara Sarragon own plantations in Surinam?*

Placing down her candlestick, Nella plunges her hand into the cedar shavings and touches what she has really been looking for.

She has kept these miniatures neat, over the years. These three dolls of Otto and Marin, and the little wax baby she stole from a workshop, that day eighteen years ago when her life turned upside down. She lifts them out, one by one. Time has been kind to their small bodies. In keeping Otto so pristine, Nella wonders if she has kept his life safe. She has always believed there was power in the miniaturist's work, but with the passing of eighteen years, it feels presumptuous, and he would say as much. Otto's existence has been like Nella's; far from secure.

The miniature of Marin has also been preserved to perfection. She stares up at her sister-in-law, her face slim and pale, her eyes grey, that high forehead, that held and slender neck. She looks so lifelike. She's been shrunk, that's all: her death mistaken. Marin's dress is sober but expensive, black wool and velvet. Nella touches the fabric, lined with a pelt of sable, edged at the neck with a large plain collar of lace, its fashion long out of date. She cannot pull away from the penetrating gaze. These dolls were always too well made, too meticulously observed, too lovingly created to be disregarded. She feels a shiver running up her back.

'What are we going to do, Marin?' she whispers.

She waits, but the miniature is mute.

Undaunted, Nella places Otto and Marin gently near the bottom of the chest, where she found them. She puts in the maps and the skulls, the shining black seeds, the dried flowers, the misshapen pods, the iridescent blue and ruby-red feathers. She returns Marin's books, checking the strings on all of them to make sure the covers are well secured.

But when it comes to replacing the baby, Nella waits. She holds it in her palm. This tiny thing has always represented Thea to her, and for all its weightlessness, it seems to hum against Nella's skin, so perfectly, painstakingly crafted, the child's clothes made from slender offcuts of the finest bleached cambric. Nella loves to hold it. When Thea was born, it was a sign to her that Thea was always meant to be. A kernel of hope. A reassurance. An exemplar of the miniaturist's skill. A promise that things might renew.

Nella squeezes the newborn gently, as if to press upon the secret of its power. So small, so swaddled, half the length of Nella's little finger, its face peering through the white bandages like a nut. Thea stopped being a baby so long ago, but it feels to Nella as if this is all she has, this stolen offering of comfort and guidance, a sense of being seen.

'Come back to me,' she speaks into the dark.

But the baby lies in her hand, unmoved. The attic is silent. The only sound is the scratching of Lucas at the bottom of the attic stairs, concerned as to what his mistress might be doing in the shadows. Nella moves towards the window and gazes down on the frozen canal, but there's no sign of a solitary woman, watching the house, no sign of a bared blonde head. Although the miniaturist's hair might be grey by now. Eighteen years is a long time. Too long. It can never happen again how it happened back then. There is no one on the canal path at all.

Yet without further hesitation, because if she stops to think about what Cornelia and Otto might say if they find out what she's doing, she'll lose her nerve, Nella slips the baby into her pocket. She closes Marin's lid and moves slowly by the light of her single candle down the attic steps. She dusts the cobwebs off her skirts, and Lucas circles her. He is a wise cat, for all his foolish gluttony. He knows there has been a disturbance, another theft, a change. But like his mistress, he cannot tell their consequence.

III

Thea is pinioned by the scenes unfolding in the candlelight. *Titus*, it is called in Dutch: based on the play by William Shakespeare, and Rebecca plays Lavinia. The audience does not see Lavinia's rape by the brothers, Demetrius and Chiron, but it does see how afterwards her hands and tongue are cut off. How the emperor Titus, played by a burly actor, stuffs other people's children into a pie. All of it is horrible to watch, and the audience groans and sighs. When Lavinia's tongue is cut out, her mouth vomiting red ribbon – and later, when the characters begin to eat the child pie, holding aloft a bleeding organ before gobbling it down, Cornelia drops her head and whispers: 'I can't bear much more of this. I think I'm going to be sick.'

'It isn't real,' Thea whispers back, but she rolls her tongue against the inside of her mouth, checking an attachment at the root. Because despite what Thea says to Cornelia, it does feel real to her. All of it. It feels more real than life. Rebecca Bosman is the best actress in the whole of the United Provinces and beyond. There is no one to touch her. She makes it seem as if what is happening down there, away from the audience, is the true world, and what is up here, among the sweaty bodies and the beating fans, is merely an interlude, a limbo, a sad pause in the face of colour and passion. Some people come to the Schouwburg to lose themselves for a couple of hours, but Thea comes to discover herself, to build her soul with words and light. She has seen Rebecca lose her tongue four times, and every time it happens, it feels like a surprise.

Tears come to Thea's eyes as Lavinia, righteous and vengeful, tells of her ordeal without the use of speech. She feels that she is inside Rebecca, that Rebecca is inside her. She feels emboldened, transported to a more truthful place, where a woman has refused the shackles of silence. When the play is over and the actors have taken their bows, the audience begins to funnel out of the auditorium, streaming under the three arches of the Schouwburg into the darkening afternoon on the Keizersgracht. Cornelia rises, pallid in her cheek, but Thea tugs at her to sit back down. 'Wait a moment, will you?' she asks. Her mind is on Walter, how she might be able to contrive to get backstage and see him. 'I want to savour it.'

'I don't,' says Cornelia. 'That was a nightmare from start to finish.' But because it is her beloved nurseling's birthday, she sits back down. 'Why couldn't it have been a comedy?'

'Because the world is very cruel.'

Cornelia rolls her eyes. 'I don't need two hours in the playhouse to tell me that.'

'But doesn't it make you feel alive?'

Cornelia shudders, the residue of gore and sorrow, of violation, hanging on her face. 'It just made me think of death. Please, Teapot. Let's go.'

Thea takes a deep breath. 'It made *me* think about my mother.'

Cornelia stiffens: she cannot make the connection, but still Thea waits. Cornelia has been the only one over the years to offer titbits of Marin Brandt and her brother. Because of Cornelia, Thea knows how her mother used to make her family eat herring when they could afford better meat. How her skirts had hidden linings of the finest sable. How good she was with numbers. Yet enjoyable as these fragments are, they fail to make a fuller portrait.

Why did she make you eat herring? Why did she keep the softness of her skirts a secret? Thea will ask, and Cornelia will clam up, as if the original fact was enough, as if subsequent information is not hers to give. And yet Thea has often sensed in Cornelia an urge to say more, as if she wants to talk about her dead mistress, to gossip about her, even – and no one will let her.

'Cornelia, I'm a woman now,' Thea says, as if explaining to a simpleton.

Cornelia raises her eyebrows.

'Why can't I know who she was? Papa tells me nothing. What were he and my mother *like* together?'

Cornelia looks stricken. 'Thea, we're in public.'

'No one's listening.'

Cornelia glances over her shoulder. 'If your mother and father conducted themselves behind closed doors, what makes you think I'll talk about them in the open air?'

Thea leans forward. 'Tell me something of my uncle, then. Were you there when he was drowned?' Cornelia begins to twist the strings of her purse. She looks angry, but Thea won't give up. 'Was anyone there?'

Cornelia chews her lip. 'This is entirely not a conversation for a birthday.'

'I know what he was,' Thea whispers.

Cornelia lifts her hand, placing it slowly on the side of Thea's face. Her palm is cool and slim and the shock of it forces Thea to meet her old nurse's eye. 'He was a man,' Cornelia says. 'He loved his family. People respected him. And we have worked hard to bring ourselves back to that place of respectability. We no longer live with fear or shame, because your father and aunt have pushed those imps away.'

'By courting the likes of Clara Sarragon?' Thea curls her lip.

Cornelia shrugs. 'You do what you must. Reputation matters, in a city like this.'

'Then why do we live in a city like this?'

'Because there is nowhere else in the world to live.'

Thea sighs. 'Cornelia, how can you have sat with me through play after play, looking at the tropical backdrops, or the suggestions of a London street, a Parisian palace – and say there is nowhere else in this world that a woman may lay down her hat and call it home?'

'London is a filthy place,' says Cornelia. 'And Paris is even worse.'

'But why should everything depend on what people like Clara Sarragon think of us?' Thea protests. 'Clara Sarragon has no *gift*. She is not someone I respect. She's rich, that's all.' Thea gestures to the empty seats. 'Sarragon could never fill a theatre like this. She is no Rebecca Bosman. She has no soul.'

'Everyone has a soul.'

'She could never inspire love. She can offer me nothing.'

But Cornelia is used to these outbursts and will not be fazed. 'Thea, you're still going to that ball. No speeches to me will change that. And I don't think Clara Sarragon wants your love. She's in the business of money and power, and according to your aunt, proper young girls of the city do well under her patronage.'

'The proper young girls of the city,' Thea repeats with scorn. 'I know them well.'

Cornelia looks away. She knows them too; the white-necked girls with rosy cheeks at the school Thea attended until the age of twelve. Hard to find one among them who would bring Thea close. 'Thea,' she says. 'We need to go home.'

'There's plenty of time. I promised Rebecca I'd go backstage and visit her. She told me to, next time I was here.'

Cornelia sighs. She does not like broken promises, and Thea knows this. 'Then I shall come too.'

'You don't have to do that.'

Cornelia rises to her feet, straightening her skirts. 'Maybe I'd like to meet a famous actress? See what she's like up close?'

'We're not in a menagerie.'

Cornelia, on her free days, will often be found at Blue John's menagerie on the Kloveniersburgwal, where she likes to meander with a glass of beer and a morsel, surrounded by forlorn-looking birds and creatures of the most extraordinary shapes and sizes from the Americas and Indies, most of which end up displayed more dead than alive. She sniffs. 'I dare say she's not as interesting as the seahorse I saw at Christmas.'

'We'll see about that,' Thea says.

※

Six months ago, on a warm July afternoon, Thea had attended a performance of *The Farce of Pyramus and Thisbe*. She'd been giddy with laughter throughout, her joy bubbling up inside her and spilling into the auditorium. Rebecca was playing the hunter-goddess Diana, a silver moon on her head so large that Thea marvelled at its staying power. Afterwards, she'd been slow to leave, unwilling to return to the sombre atmosphere of the house on the Herengracht, and as she was dawdling through the front courtyard of the Schouwburg before making the ten-minute walk home, Rebecca Bosman, no less, had crossed her path.

'You were so wonderful, Madame,' Thea had said. The urge to speak had been overwhelming; she might never get another chance. 'Your speech to the lovers was the best I've ever seen it done.'

Rebecca, no longer in her huntress outfit, but with something of that other world still about her, had stopped and turned, taking in the sight of Thea: a girl who did not look like the women who came to preen in the boxes, to titter and spy on the rest of the city's inhabitants. 'You have seen it before?' she asked.

'Several times,' Thea replied, even giddier now that the goddess had stopped to talk. 'But the others never quite made it believable. It must be hard to play Diana. I mean to say – not hard for *you*, obviously – but when one is trying to communicate such difference, it doesn't always work.'

A light of merriment had entered Rebecca's eyes. 'Your name, Madame?' she asked.

No one had ever called Thea *Madame*. 'I'm Thea Brandt,' Thea replied, curtseying deep.

'And I'm Rebecca.'

'I know.'

Rebecca asked her if she'd come to the Schouwburg alone,

and Thea's delight vanished into embarrassment. 'I have,' she replied, staring at her feet. 'I would have come with a friend, but—'

'Oh, I always go to the playhouse alone,' Rebecca had replied. 'A few hours of private peace. You're quite right.'

'I am? I was supposed to be going to the fish market.'

'I'm sure the cod will understand.'

And so it had begun. Rebecca invited Thea backstage to meet the other actors. Thea saw how all the props were put back together again in the places they needed to be for the start of the next performance, as if nothing had happened, as if everything was happening for the first time, everyone allowed to begin again, all mistakes forgotten. It was a revelation, to see the mechanics of the mystery, the exquisite, mundane professionalism of it. Rebecca took her into her private dressing room, and Thea was entranced by its particularity, the scent of sandalwood, the ewer of lemon water, the little dog which Rebecca told her she had named Emerald in honour of her eyes. Rebecca was an artist, living according to the tides of her talent rather than the demands of a society that would normally have her married off, hiding her gift in the dark. She was magnetic to Thea. She asked Thea's opinion on the plays she'd seen, the books she'd read. She was humane and generous. It felt like a dream that Thea had no wish to wake from.

Now, in the cold air of January, Rebecca comes to the back door of the playhouse with her arms out, still stained with blood from the performance, her mouth and chin still smeared. It is an arresting sight, but she smiles at Thea and Cornelia, happy to see her most ardent supporter. She is handsome, in her thirties, short and neat, with a sure step, long red hair flowing loose around her shoulders. Still dressed in her costume, her skirt is that extra bit wider, the material shot with much more silk than the average woman's, its crushes and planes designed to capture every flicker of candlelight.

'Come in!' she says, her tongue restored.

Thea rushes towards her. 'How do you do it, every time? You're magical.'

'Not magic, sweetheart. Practice,' Rebecca says with a red grin.

'This is our maid, Cornelia,' Thea says. Cornelia steps forward, looking suddenly very small.

Rebecca smiles again, proffering both palms. 'Welcome, Cornelia. Were you in the audience too?'

'Good afternoon, Mrs Bosman,' Cornelia replies, looking at Rebecca's hands, then up to her stained face. Thea has to push down her irritation: doesn't Cornelia end up almost daily with blood to her elbows, gutting a fish, beheading a chicken? Why not take the woman's reddened hands and be done?

'*Miss* Bosman,' Rebecca says, dropping her hands. 'Been enough wives on the stage to never want to be one in real life.'

She laughs. Cornelia does not. Thea wants the earth to split apart and swallow her. 'Miss Bosman,' Cornelia corrects herself, stiffly.

Rebecca turns on her heel and walks into the bowels of the playhouse, and Thea and Cornelia trot to keep up. 'It's only pig's blood,' she says over her shoulder. 'Every day I have to scrub my hands and face, as if I've spent hours in the shambles, pulling guts. Let's go to my room. It's much warmer there. This weather will be the death of us all.'

She walks Cornelia and Thea past a large room where several of the cast are relaxing, peeling off their wigs, wiping rouge from their faces. Thea cannot help slowing down, in the hope that Walter might be in there. A coffee-pot warms on a stove and the smell wafts through the corridor. Copies of the *Amsterdam Courant* are scattered over a table, one in the large hands of Titus himself, who raises his eyebrows over the top on seeing the women pass. In a corner sit the two young boys who sing in the musical intervals, hired to lift the tension of *Titus* with their unbroken voices. They can't be older than seven or eight. One of them looks up at Thea, taking her in with reciprocated, unbridled curiosity. They sit with a guardian of sorts, a white woman, busy unpacking them some bread and cheese. Walter is nowhere to be seen.

In Rebecca's room, a handsome fire is well into its burning, and there are rugs and chairs, and Emerald is so deeply asleep in her basket that she does not even raise her head. There are scripts piled on tables and the floorboards. A coat and bonnet hang on the door, and three costumes swing neatly on a wooden rail screwed between the walls of an alcove. On the table is a small picnic of food, a cup of coffee, a decanter of red wine. The room has a homely, neat feel to it, and Thea can see Cornelia beginning to relax, impressed to see no dust, clean windows, the fragrance of lemon and rosewater. She can almost sense the grudging approval coming off the maid in waves.

'It's a mess,' Rebecca says, striding over to the ewer and basin and beginning to soap and scrub away the blood on her face and hands.

'Far from it,' Cornelia demurs.

'It's small, but it's mine,' Rebecca replies, drying herself on a strip of pristine linen. She gestures to the two spare chairs. 'Please, sit,' she says. 'I've heard so much about you, Mistress Cornelia. Your pufferts, your *hutspots*. I want to winkle the recipes from you.'

Cornelia blushes. 'They can all be found in *The Sensible Cook*, Madame.' She hesitates, daring to offer a connection. 'I am not magical either. I have been cooking them for thirty years.'

Rebecca beams. 'The perfect argument in favour of practice.'

'I am sure anyone could do it.'

'But few are prepared to put in the hours,' Rebecca replies, and Cornelia's ears turn pink.

It is astonishing: Cornelia is never modest about her cooking, she marinades in confidence nearly every time she serves a dish. But here she is, bashful, eager to talk, Rebecca's generosity and openness disarming her in minutes. Few people can live up to Cornelia's high standards, but it would appear that Rebecca has managed it. Cornelia looks as if she cannot bear to exist in the beam of such sunshine, but also as if she cannot countenance the thought of leaving it. She seems on the point of saying something more, but she wrenches herself away and walks to the door. 'I must return home,' she says. 'Work to do.'

'Now?' says Rebecca, looking genuinely disappointed.

'Always,' says Cornelia. 'Thea, you must be back no later than five o'clock. Otherwise –' she glances at Rebecca – 'your aunt will put you in a pie.'

Rebecca laughs. Thea boggles at the success of Cornelia's joke. 'I promise,' she says.

'You might be a woman now, Thea, but we'll all pay the

price if you don't go to the Sarragon ball.' Cornelia turns to Rebecca. 'Thank you for this afternoon, Madame. Most enjoyable. I know a good recipe for a soap that can get out the more stubborn blood, should you require it.'

Before Rebecca can reply, Cornelia tightens her scarf around her neck, and disappears into the corridor.

Thea watches the door close. 'You impressed her. It's why she couldn't stay. She never knows what to do if she's impressed about something.'

Rebecca pours them both a small glass of wine. 'I like her very much. You're lucky. A toast: to still having nursemaids at eighteen.'

'I don't need a nursemaid.'

Rebecca shrugs. 'Personally, I'd love one.'

'But you have everything.'

'I have a lot of things. A loving nursemaid is not one.' Rebecca sighs. 'The Sarragon ball? Quite the invitation.'

'If you like that sort of thing.'

Rebecca's eyes widen. 'It will be exciting. I wish I could come.'

Thea feels a little dart of hope. 'Were you invited?'

'Yes. But I have a performance. I choose pig's blood over pearls. Anyway, by the time I'd be able to get there, all the best people would have probably left. But, Thea, listen—' She walks over to her rail of dresses and flourishes a gold silk gown from amidst the material. 'Take this to wear.'

Thea's eyes drink in the golden dress her friend is holding up. 'I couldn't.'

'You could.'

'My legs will stick out of the bottom.'

Rebecca shrugs. 'It's been hemmed for me. There's a swathe of material under there. I'll ask Fabritius to let it down and press it. It'll suit you better. I wore it for Juliet, but the colour of it swamped.'

Thea walks over to the gown and touches the material. 'You are so kind to me. I wish you were coming to the ball.'

'I doubt your aunt would approve. You said she didn't like actors. Why, when we're perfectly harmless?'

'Rebecca,' Thea says, dropping her hands from the dress and going back to the table. 'You heard I don't have much time. Is he here?'

A shadow crosses Rebecca's features. She places the gold dress over the back of a chair. 'Tell me, Thea Brandt: why do you come to the playhouse? Do you think you come for him?'

'I love him.'

Rebecca looks grave. 'I know you do. And Walter's a good painter.' She reaches for the bread on the table and pulls off a chunk. 'But he's not a god, Thea. He's just a man.'

'And yet he deserves my worship.'

Rebecca runs her hand through her hair, her expression one of discomfort. 'I know that time for you feels finite. But you'll see it will stretch out. There's so much more to come.'

'What do you mean?'

'I don't want to tell you what to do, but—'

'Exactly.' Thea cannot help rolling her eyes. You're not my mother.'

'I want you to be happy.'

'I've never felt happier.'

'All I mean to say is: be careful.'

'Of what?'

Rebecca sighs. 'I promised myself I wouldn't interfere. I know you're happy. But Walter is what – twenty-five, six?'

'He'll be twenty-six in April.'

'Nearly eight years your senior.'

'Eight years is nothing. Age is immaterial. You don't know him as I do. You don't understand.'

'I understand that you are a Brandt. And that means something.'

'Maybe in the past it did,' Thea says. 'It means nothing now. I thought you didn't care about the rules of society? You never married. You have your own room here. Your freedom.'

'There are still rules for me, whether I like them or not,' Rebecca says. 'Just – tread carefully with yourself. With him. You are more of a prize than you think, and you deserve only the best.'

'And the best is what she'll get,' says a voice at the door.

The women turn as one and Thea's heart soars into her mouth. Rebecca looks away but Thea rises to her feet. He has come for her, the chief set-painter of the Schouwburg. She is a falcon to his wrist, flying to the sight of her love.

IV

Walter Riebeeck is not the first man Thea has gathered up into her imagination. When she was sixteen, she was convinced that Robert Hooft, who dropped off hens' eggs for Cornelia, was the most beautiful man in the world. And before him, Abraham Molenaar, the spring broom-seller – he was also the most beautiful man in the world. And before him, when she was fifteen, Dirk Sweerts, the one who cleaned the salon windows: he was also beautiful. When she was fourteen, there was Geert Brennecke, who delivered the salted piglets from Claes the butcher: he too was what your eyes might call a blessing. Thea could not help it, seeing beauty in boys everywhere, boys who didn't realize she saw it, boys who didn't care. These were the eyes God gave her, but the gaze only went in one direction. From these creatures she never received glances in return.

But Walter was different, from the very beginning. It was Thea who stumbled into the painting-room one day, exploring the corridors whilst Rebecca was having her silver moon re-fitted for the evening's performance. And there was Walter, standing in the late summer afternoon light that flooded the floor from the high windows, meditating upon a towering flat of bucolic beauty, his brush in hand, touching up a strawberry bush.

He turned at the sound of the door, and Thea froze. He

frowned, as if he had no wish to be interrupted, but on seeing her his expression changed. He looked at her with surprise, then interest, and Thea, who had never been looked at in that way by a man, was glued to the spot.

'You have a good face,' he said. 'Are you new?'

All thoughts of Robert Hooft and his hens' eggs were forgotten.

Walter noticed her, as Rebecca had noticed her. Walter's approval of Thea somehow enfolds with Rebecca's affection. It is all happening under the same roof, inside the infinite possibility of the Schouwburg. Walter's backdrops and constructions are extraordinary. You could pluck his fruit and live inside his landscapes. There's not a more talented man on God's earth, but it isn't just his beauty, his voice, his hands or talent. It's everything he is, even the parts Thea cannot reach yet. He is blue-eyed and twenty-five, a man with dreams to travel the cities of Europe, to build sets the like of which Drury Lane and the Opéra have never seen, his Dutch feats of paint and wood.

Thea listens to Walter's speeches of escape, of new beginnings where he will earn the highest respect, and between these lines she sees a space for her body in his Parisian bed, a hook for her clothes on the back of his London door. It is easy to garland Walter with his future, because the brush is already in his hand. It is easy to imagine him painting a world from nothing. Thea knows his dreams will happen, by the way his brush dabs the flats, by how trees and beaches, woodland groves, Venetian palazzi and humble farmhouses grow from nothing through the magic of his skill. Her admiration for his talent is indivisible from her anticipation for him as a man. Thea cannot unpick these two feelings, she cannot unweave what is spinning together faster than she can measure, and nor does she want to. There are days when she feels possessed by all the futures inside him that will be promised to her too, if things carry on as they are. Even the clouds in the sky when she walks home afterwards hold wisps of the shape of his face. Her deepest joy is that Walter feels exactly the same. They are fixed in their orb as a pair, forever, tight and loving.

❦

Leaving Rebecca in her dressing room, Thea follows Walter through the gloom of the Schouwburg corridors, over coiled ropes and costumes discarded from the earlier performance, as if the characters have evaporated. She knows the route to the painting-room so well that she could do it with her eyes closed. Walter pushes open the door and stands aside to usher her in. She loves this room, the smell of linseed and paint, the recently sawn wood. She likes to wander in and out of the half-made sets, under an arch that is yet to be painted, or through a little door that leads to nowhere except a bundle of rags. It feels like an antechamber to their life ahead. One day soon, she can feel it in her blood: they will step out of this room and something will change. Something will have been constructed, painted, made to stand on its own two feet.

'I'm doing palm trees,' Walter says. 'A new set. *Life Is a Dream* by Calderón.'

'Oh yes,' Thea says, although she has never read this play. She makes a note to do so.

'The director wants to put it in a hot place, so I suggested palms. Make the audience feel like they need to peel off their woollens.'

46

Thea stands before Walter's three towering stretched canvases. The coast Walter has painted is nothing like a Netherlands seascape – no dark-brown or slate-coloured waters, no sandbar full of stones. The water is almost turquoise, spanning endlessly to a distant horizon. Huge conches have been washed up along the shoreline, and they rest like almost animate objects, their mysterious insides hinting at invisible intimacy. The pale yellow sand leads up to a fringe of enormous trees, captured in various states of incline, their palms casting shadows.

Walter points towards the tops of the flats. 'Those are coco-nut trees,' he says. 'Apparently, if you stand under one and the nut falls onto your head, you'll probably die. Can you imagine? I don't know if I've got them right yet. I've never seen one.'

Walter is so gifted at creating another reality that Thea might truly be murdered by these delicacies, concealed in his painted branches. 'How pitiful, to be killed by a tree,' she observes, 'even if it was you who painted it. They look wonderful.'

He turns to her and scoops her into his arms. He likes to hear her praise. 'Not as wonderful as you,' he says, burying his face in the side of her neck. Thea's entire body starts to buzz from deep within. He pulls her scarf over her head. 'Let me peel off *your* woollens,' he murmurs.

'*Walter*,' she says, but she is delighted to let him unhook her coat, to feel him run his fingers up and down her spine. It feels as if he is touching her entire body at once and it turns her skin to gooseflesh. The sensation that lies within that sensation: there are no words for it.

Sometimes, Thea thinks that perhaps she could stop at this:

the caressing of her spine on the surface of her blouse. It could be enough. But part of her knows there is so much more of her body for Walter to touch. Before her there must have been other women, as much as it pains Thea to consider their superior experience. It can only be a matter of time before the sides of Thea's neck and the stretch of her back are not enough for him. For her too, maybe. Thea wants everything from him, she wants him to be hungry for her, but she also wants her time with him to contain only this. The pleasure of having her spine stroked does strange things to the soles of her feet, to the secret place between her legs.

'We can't just have these snatched moments,' she whispers. 'I'm always worried someone will burst in. Rebecca says—'

'Rebecca Bosman just likes to make trouble,' says Walter, irritation flitting across his face. 'She's a strange, lonely woman. She can't tell the difference between the parts they pay her to play and the life she lives outside.'

'Walter! That is not kind.'

He pulls away, looking down at her. 'And you believe Rebecca is kind? She thinks only of her performances.'

'But—'

'Shh,' Walter says, tipping Thea's chin and bringing his mouth to hers. All speech vanishes. Thea is mute with pleasure, her tongue against his. She presses herself tighter to him, kissing him more deeply, and he wraps his hands around her waist, lifting her to the tips of her toes.

'I could come to your lodging,' she whispers. 'Why meet at the playhouse when I can come to your lodging?'

'I'd love that. But my landlady won't let me have visitors,' he murmurs. 'I'd lose the place. And there's nothing wrong with here, is there? We have privacy. I have you to myself, and you have me. We're each other's secret.'

'We are.'

'Would you like me to make it more comfortable? I'll fetch cushions—'

'Walter, it's perfect. And I suppose here at least, we can trust everyone to keep our secret.'

'I hope that's true.' He looks away, almost shy. 'Do you . . . think you will ever tell your family about me?'

'Oh, I want to,' Thea says. 'I want to, very much. But how will I ever start such a conversation? My father, my aunt . . . it would be very hard. You're Pyramus and I'm Thisbe, and we're trapped in fate's cold grip, separated by a thick wall.'

Walter laughs.

'It's not funny,' Thea protests. 'You know I love you so much.'

'And I love you. More than anything.'

'More than painting?'

'That's a cruel question. You don't keep me in bed and board.'

'I know.' Thea hesitates. 'But you could keep me in your bed.'

Walter looks at her and begins to kiss her again, deeper than ever, his hand running under her blouse onto her breasts. His fingers are warm and certain. Thea thinks if he went under her skirts she would let him; there would be nothing else for her to do. They stagger back to prop themselves against the whitewashed wall, partly hidden by an old flat of a Greek temple. 'What do you do to me?' he whispers.

'This,' she whispers back, her hand creeping down to the

hardness in his breeches. He moans, pressing himself closer, and at that moment the door bangs. They spring apart, still hidden.

'Your dress for tonight,' says a clear voice, used to making itself heard across large spaces. It is Rebecca. 'Fabritius let it down for you.'

Thea clamps her hand to her mouth to stop the giggle bursting out. Walter, dishevelled and flushed, glances at her with lust.

'I assume you're in here, Thea,' Rebecca says. Her voice is tighter now. 'And it's half-past four. In case you didn't know.'

Thea can hear the other woman's skirts moving as she lays the dress over Walter's chair. 'I hope you have a very enjoyable night tonight,' Rebecca says. 'That you make the most of it. Come and see me soon? And, Thea?' There is a pause. 'Take care of the dress.'

The painting-room door closes once again. 'What's all this?' Walter asks. 'What dress?'

Thea rolls her eyes and pushes herself off the wall, their moment of intimacy broken. 'Clara Sarragon's Epiphany Ball,' she says. 'My aunt has schemed for us to attend.'

Walter's eyes widen. 'That's one of the most famous parties in the city. I knew you lived on the Herengracht, but is your family that well connected?'

'Of course we aren't,' Thea says. 'My aunt is trying to be. I don't know why: it'll just be full of merchant bores with nothing better to do. Rebecca was invited, but she's performing tonight, of course. Did you get an invitation?'

'Oh, yes. Stacked up amongst all the others I receive from the regentesses of this city.'

'Well, why wouldn't they invite you? You are a famous artist of this city.'

'I am a set-painter.'

'You are *chief* set-painter.'

'It's not my world,' he says shortly. 'They do not understand the likes of me.'

'Or me,' Thea says, but Walter doesn't reply. 'Walter, they would be lucky if you came even for fifteen minutes.'

'I am not interested,' he says. 'I'm only sorry that you have to go.'

'So am I,' Thea sighs. She begins to readjust her blouse, tucking it in, straightening her cap.

'Wait,' he says. 'Don't think I've forgotten it's your birthday. I had something planned.'

Thea thrills inwardly with delight. Suddenly, Walter drops to his knees and lifts up her skirts. 'What are you doing?' she says.

He stops, pulling his head out from under her petticoats. 'You don't want me to?'

'But what are you going to do?'

He grins. 'Wait and see,' he says, and vanishes again.

Suddenly Thea feels his tongue upon her. 'Oh, sweet Jesu,' she whispers, as an indescribable warmth spreads inside her. 'Walter, someone might come in.'

'I'm hidden,' he murmurs. 'I don't know about you.'

'But—'

'Do you want me to stop?'

'*Don't.*'

Thea feels as if her body is melting onto his mouth, as if Walter is revealing to her both a vulnerability she had no idea she possessed, as well as incredible strength. 'Tell me that you love me,' she whispers.

'I love you,' he whispers into her. She shudders and cries out as he holds her tightly. In that moment, Thea has never felt so sure that someone is telling her a truth.

Walter emerges, a mischievous, pleased look in his eye. 'This is the best birthday I've ever had,' Thea says. 'And it's all because of you.'

He kisses and kisses her, on her eyelids, her mouth, her cheeks, her neck. She kisses him back, and they hold each other tight. 'Shall I come here next Wednesday?' she whispers.

'I'll be waiting,' he whispers back.

Reluctantly, Thea leaves their little world of the painting-room. Rebecca's right: she's going to be late. She runs from Walter's palm trees, his tongue, his hands, Rebecca's gold dress tight against her arm. Her body is singing, and the place between her legs singing most of all. She cannot believe what has just happened, that such a degree of sophistication now belongs to her, too, and that it happened on her birthday. Finally, finally, she has waved childhood goodbye.

Up the Keizersgracht Thea runs, and down Leidsegracht towards her home. She runs the canal paths against the weight of her skirts. Thea has been told that she knows nothing of the world, and yet she knows so much. She knows about places her feet haven't even trod. The inside of her head is a lagoon, and the stars above its surface are still unnamed. She is a light in herself, and the love she feels for Walter ignites her as she runs into the gathering dark.

V

Thea knows something is wrong the moment she steps through the front door. She is expecting Cornelia to appear, chiding her for being late, but no one comes. The atmosphere is thick, not with the bustle you might expect when preparing for a ball, but with something heavy, almost ominous.

'Hello?' she calls, standing in the hallway, unable to locate by instinct the rest of her family.

The salon door opens and Cornelia hurries out, closing it quickly behind her. 'Come,' she says, crossing the black and white tiles. 'Upstairs. We need to get you ready.' She looks at Thea's borrowed dress, the lowered hem trailing on the tiles. 'You're not wearing that, are you? I've prepared what you're going to wear—'

'Cornelia.' Thea inclines her head in the direction of the salon. 'What's happening in there?'

'Nothing for you to worry about.' But Cornelia's face, pale and drawn, says otherwise.

Thea strides over to the salon door. 'Wait,' Cornelia hisses, with such urgency and authority that Thea obeys. A beat of dread begins in her stomach, spreading upwards to her chest. She thinks, for a moment, that perhaps she and Walter have been discovered, that she's in more trouble than she could ever imagine. But surely by now her aunt would have come flying out at her, her father close behind in a state of muted horror.

'There's been some news,' Cornelia says.

'What news? We never have news.'

Cornelia runs a work-worn hand over her brow. 'If you must go in, and I know I can't stop you—'

'You can't. I'm eighteen now—'

'I *know*. But if you must go in, be gentle.'

This is a surprising instruction. Why should Thea be gentle, when she is the one in the dark? 'When am I not gentle?' she asks.

Cornelia gives her a hard look.

'Is someone dead?' Thea says, beginning to lose patience. Although she cannot imagine who it might be. Apart from Walter, there's no one to lose.

Briefly, Cornelia closes her eyes. 'Just go in,' she says. 'Though I doubt your father will thank me.' She hurries off, down the stairs towards her kitchen.

The giddying sensations of the last hours at the playhouse have sunk away to nothing. Thea wants to cling on to them, but it's impossible in a house like this. It's almost like the birthday present from Walter never happened. She cannot stand it. Why do her family always have to ruin everything?

She leaves Rebecca's gold dress on the chair outside the salon and goes in. Her father is sitting on one side of the empty grate, and the cavernous room is very cold. Her aunt stands at the other side of the mantelpiece, her expression pinched. She glances up in surprise. 'Thea? Why are you not ready?'

'Who's died?' Thea says. 'We can't go to a ball if someone's died.'

'No one's died,' says her father. 'At least,' he sighs, 'not yet.'

'Papa?' Thea asks, more softly now, remembering Cornelia's advice.

'Come here, child.' He offers his hand. Thea goes towards him and takes it. 'It's nothing for you to worry about.'

'Cornelia said that, and I don't believe her.'

'You're right not to,' says her aunt, taking a seat on the other side of the fireplace. 'Otto, tell her. You can't hide it from her.'

'I had no intention of hiding it,' Thea's father snaps. 'But it's my daughter's birthday, Petronella.'

'Papa, you're frightening me.'

He looks up at her. 'Nothing to be frightened of. It is a resolvable matter. What is? Regrettably, I have lost my position in the VOC.'

'What? You left?'

Her father looks pained. 'I have been dismissed.'

For a moment, Thea cannot understand. Dismissed? How is that possible? Her father has worked at the city's most famous company for as long as she can remember. He is a good clerk, a very good one, fifteen years registering inventories of cargo coming in from the East. Nutmeg, salt, cinnamon, cloves, silk and cotton, copper, porcelain, silver, gold and tea – Thea knows them all, a particularly Amsterdammish lexicon, those many luxuries and novelties flooding in under his nose, committed by his hand. This is what her father does.

She looks down at him, her hard-working and dedicated father, who has opened out his hands, as if to see the answer in the lines of his palms. 'I don't understand,' she says.

'They said that I'm too old.'

'Too *old*?' Thea recalls guiltily her morning thoughts upon seeing him in his nightclothes. She wishes she could take them back. 'You're not too old.'

'They say that I am slower than the others.'

Aunt Nella makes a noise of disgust.

Thea feels a stricture on her own throat, a slight dizziness. Her father has become something other than her father: he is now a man to be criticized. It is an appalling realization. She wants to run to the VOC and shout at someone. She looks towards her aunt, who appears more resigned than Thea, but grim.

'But some of the men you work with are the same age as you,' Thea says. 'Bert Schippers – he's ancient. There are men working there in their sixties.'

'A point I also made,' her aunt replies.

Cornelia comes in, standing miserably in the corner. 'Is anyone hungry?'

'I didn't think it would happen,' her father says. 'I should have seen it. They've been putting me in charge of only the smallest transactions. The most inconsequential deliveries. Nothing of importance, despite my experience.'

'Men at the VOC come and go like the tides,' Cornelia says. 'You have stayed the duration.'

He looks over at her. 'Until now.'

'It's outrageous,' Aunt Nella says, rising to her feet again and slamming her hand onto the mantel edge. 'All the professed rewarding of ambition and grit that the VOC – and indeed, our entire republic – like to harp on about, when really this city only elevates a few men from the right families.'

'The right families,' says Thea's father. 'That's one way of putting it.'

There is a long silence. The four of them contemplate a future that has suddenly become yet more uncertain. It's as if the ropes that were tethering them have been severed, and are snaking away, and Thea and her family are drifting into unknown waters with no sense of where they might go. She knows what her father will not say to her – that perhaps this dismissal has nothing to do with his age, nor the speed with which he can do his job, nor coming from the right family. *That's one way of putting it.* His expression, so tired, communicates everything to Thea. She knows her family have believed in shielding her from the stares and comments over the years. Their hope that Thea will not notice them herself is almost pitiful. Sometimes, she wishes they had just stated the obvious, rather than pretending that people didn't mean to reach out for her hair, or ask where she was from, and why she looked like she looked, when her accent was pure Amsterdam. It might not have been Otto Brandt's age that put a thick line through his name, in the big book of the VOC. They will probably never know.

'Well,' she says. 'I am sure you will find another position.'

No one replies. Her father stares into the grate.

'Thea, your dress is laid on your bed,' says her aunt in a tight voice. 'Go and get ready.'

Cornelia opens the salon door and gestures Thea to follow. Thea looks at her aunt in disbelief. 'We're really still going?'

'We need the Sarragon network even more.'

'But—'

'Thea, please. Do as your aunt requests,' says her father.

Thea hates it when they take the same side. She cannot believe he is willing to put himself, and her, through the farce of this evening. Inwardly fuming, but remembering again Cornelia's exhortation to gentleness, she leans over and kisses him on the cheek. Closing the door behind her, she pretends to follow Cornelia, who has already moved quickly up the stairs towards Thea's room, no doubt to prepare the beeswax pomade between her fingers for the tips of her nurseling's curls. But Thea tiptoes back to the keyhole and bends down to hear what her father and aunt will not say in her presence.

'But why now?' Aunt Nella is saying. 'After all these years? It's criminal. To think they can treat you in this manner.'

'There's a new foreman. There's a mood in the water. They've been waiting to do it. It could be any number of reasons. None of them interest me. None of them are valid.'

'Otto, what are we going to do? Without your income, I do not—'

'I will think of something.' Her father sounds as if he wants Aunt Nella to stop talking.

'It is good we're going to the ball,' her aunt says. Her pattens clack loudly on the salon floorboards, as she paces up and down. 'You do agree, do you not? You see the sense in it, particularly after a day like this?'

'Petronella, do not use this loss to promote your intentions. My situation with the VOC has nothing to do with Thea.'

'It has everything to do with her.'

Thea watches miserably through the keyhole as her father puts his head in his hands. 'On days like this,' he says, 'I will be punished for saying it, but I'm glad Marin never lived to see such shame.'

Thea grips the doorframe. It's unbearable to see them like

this, sniping at each other over her, for her father to say such a thing about her own mother. She had wanted to hear them speak of Marin Brandt, but not like this. Her birthday wish has now been granted, but in such a twisted way. And what exactly are these so-called intentions of her aunt?

Thea wants to run to her father, to promise him that she will find him another job herself, that she will get a job of her own. But in her heart she knows that none of this is true. These things are not in her control. Her sense of powerlessness is overwhelming. She's looking through a keyhole at an underwater world. She cannot go inside this room and help, because she would not be able to breathe.

A hand on her arm. Thea turns to find Cornelia, her face much more severe, taking up Rebecca's gold dress from the chair where Thea dropped it. 'Thea, come,' she whispers.

'But—'

'No. It's time to get ready. You've heard enough.'

VI

Clara Sarragon's mansion is the newest on the Prinsengracht, only completed at the end of 1704, in time for the family to move in for Christmas. It is enormous. Double-fronted, black-bricked, carved bouquets of stone flowers slung under every towering window, and cherubim above. Chandeliers blaze from every pane, and huge torches flame either side of the open double doors, flanked by a pair of liveried footmen, whose skin shines in the light of the fires.

Nella, Otto and Thea hesitate at the foot of the stone staircase. They are standing on the edge of a precipice and yet the only way is up.

'An hour,' Otto says. 'I will do this for an hour.'

'You might enjoy yourself, once you're inside,' Nella replies. 'Think how good the food will be. She probably has a battalion down in her kitchens.'

'We have perfectly good food at home,' he says. 'Why has she even invited us? To gawp?'

'Otto, please. Not *now*. Come: we look ridiculous, hovering around outside.'

The three of them make their way up the nine steps, past the footmen, who stare ahead as if the trio are invisible. 'What is the point of them?' Otto murmurs as they enter the main hallway. 'Living statues? Part of the entertainment?'

'Are you going to be like this all night, or the just for the hour you've promised me?' Nella hisses back.

She regrets her words immediately. His face closes: what a day he has had, first the VOC, and now this: an evening with Clara Sarragon. Thea scowls at her, but Nella knows already that she's been too harsh. 'I'm sorry,' she whispers. 'Otto, forgive me. Nerves.'

He pretends not to hear. The entrance where they stand feels as high as a cathedral, gleaming with a thousand honeyed candles. The walls are covered in brand-new red leather, pigskin by the look of it, no doubt thick to touch and smothering. Two gargantuan paintings hang on either side of the hallway. From what Nella can tell of the subject matter, before another footman approaches them to take their hats and cloaks, they depict the Annunciation and the Resurrection. The paintings are dizzying in scale, brimming with figures, the details suggesting the hand of a master rather than a workshop. Between them loom two enormous closed doors.

The footman returns with a numbered copper token for their belongings. Nella thanks him, slipping it into her little velvet pouch. She eyes her companions. Otto, in his finest black wool waistcoat and brocaded shirt, and his broad and shining collar, looks elegant, but his expression is uncomfortable. And well it might be, for she feels discomfort too. The muffled roar of the ballroom beyond the sealed doors, hundreds of voices rising and falling above the strains of an orchestra, is intimidating. Otto and Marin might have accompanied Johannes to parties like this on occasion, but Nella never did. The gatherings Johannes took her to were smaller, just for merchants and guildsmen and their wives, where the talk of the night was business. She remembers the silversmiths' ball, held in a tiny building compared to this. Now there is no Johannes to protect her. Nella steadies herself. She is eighteen years older now. She is not a little girl.

She glances at Thea, and sees how completely indifferent her niece seems to the splendour of the Sarragon mansion. It's as if Thea looks upon these dazzling things and does not see them. She's wearing a gold dress, apparently borrowed from the playhouse actresses – and she shines like treasure for an altarpiece. Her straight posture, her youth and beauty, this shimmering garment: Thea suits this setting much better than her aunt or father.

Nella pushes down a dart of jealousy, a pang of regret for her own youth. She herself is in her best dress – a silver one that Johannes ordered for her long ago. She has not lost or gained a figure in that time, but it seems wrong that it should still fit, that she should be wearing the same gown she wore in a different life. She wishes, briefly, that she *was* eighteen again, and in a gold dress, not a silver.

No, she tells herself. You are here for Thea, not old memory.

'Heads up,' she whispers, although Thea barely needs the instruction. 'We are just as entitled to be here as everyone else.'

A swell of people arriving behind them pushes them onwards to the ballroom doors, which swing open as they approach. The heat hits like a wave, and for a moment Nella forgets to breathe. If the facade of the house and the entrance hall were impressive, then this room is spectacular.

'The preachers will be rolling in their pulpits,' Otto murmurs, surveying the mirrored walls. There are mirrors everywhere, around the sides, and to their disbelief, above their heads. The ceiling has no *trompe l'oeil*, no cornicing, no frescoes – just enormous gilded panels of mirrored glass. The guests' voices are a cacophony, blending and clashing then blending again with the strains of violins. Servants with their trays aloft, laden with ewers of wine and crystal glasses, duck and weave round large skirts and staggering men.

The most honoured guests are the regents and regentesses, high, deep dynasties of families who have long held the purse strings of this city – not the merchants who put the money in those purses for them. Nella wonders about Otto's questions – *Why has she even invited us? To gawp?* and for a moment she is filled with regret that she has made them come – for apart from the footmen and a few musicians, she cannot see anyone who looks like Otto and Thea. Perhaps he is right: they have they been invited for a little thrill of scandal, the black man who lives on the Herengracht, his mixed daughter, and the widow of the man drowned by the city for his supposed sins. Coming here was a terrible idea.

She is about to back away, to grab them by the hand and return to the Herengracht – when from out of the crowd looms Clara Sarragon, dressed head to toe in bright turquoise silk. 'Aha!' says Clara, her voice piercing, rich. 'Madame Brandt. You are most welcome. But you have no refreshment?'

Nella curtseys deeply. 'Madame Sarragon. I'm sure I'll find one.'

'No: refreshment will find *you*.' Clara waves her hand in the direction of one of her footmen. 'Their job, after all.' She smiles, two rows of neat teeth. They can't be real, Nella thinks. The woman's easily fifty. Rumour has it she eats candied fruit from dawn to dusk.

Clara turns to Otto and Thea. 'Finally, we meet,' the woman says, offering her hand to Otto. 'I've heard much about you.'

Nella feels her lungs contract. She doesn't want Otto to think she talks about him behind his back. Otto takes the woman's hand, lifting it to touch it with a kiss. 'Madame Sarragon,' he says. 'And I you.'

Something flickers in Clara's face, which she quickly buries. 'This is your daughter, Thea?'

'It is.'

Clara's gaze travels down Thea's body, and back up to her face. 'Do you have sisters, or brothers?' she asks.

'I do not, Madame Sarragon,' Thea replies.

'Why, then, everything's pinned on you.'

'I beg your pardon?'

Clara laughs. 'That's why people come here, girl. Didn't your family tell you? You're here to find a husband.'

Thea turns to her aunt, speechless. She stares at her father, who looks away. Before Nella can say anything, can explain, Clara Sarragon carries on. 'You really didn't tell her?' she says. 'You have not *prepared* her? Oh, cruel trick!' She lets out a tinkling laugh. 'You should have said something. For here I come, crashing in.' She turns to Thea. 'Well, Thea Brandt, you'll learn quickly. My daughters here will guide you.'

Clara wafts her hand again, and as if summoned from thin air, two young women make their approach. 'This is a place where power is brokered,' Clara says. 'Where marriages are made. Where those who have long enjoyed a sense of belonging come to face the *arrivistes*.' She throws a glance sideways at Nella. 'It's merely my job to make it all work.' She stands back, taking them in as a group. 'I can't always offer a guarantee.'

Although his expression remains neutral, Nella can tell that Otto is incandescent with rage. We should never, ever have come, she thinks. Despite the warmth of the room, Thea looks drained, but there is nothing to be done, because suddenly the Sarragon daughters are upon them.

'These are my girls, Catarina and Eleonor,' their mother explains. 'Girls, do you know Thea Brandt?'

Catarina and Eleonor turn to Thea. 'I don't think so,' says Catarina. 'I would have remembered.'

But a sharp light comes into Eleonor's eye. 'I have!' she says. 'I've seen you from our box in the playhouse, Miss Brandt. You are often in the daily seats. Indeed –' the older girl casts her gaze over Thea's shining dress – 'I seem to remember this was a costume for one of the courtesans in *The Duchess of Malfi*. Did you have it made after you were inspired?'

Nella feels her insides beginning to fold up. The chink of glasses, the mirrors, the hysteria of voices speaking all at once, churn together to make her feel dizzy. She wishes she was alone in her room, with a fire, a book. It is hard to tell, with these daughters, whether their comments are deliberately viperish. She wants to believe they are not, that this is just the tone of society conversation, but she doesn't dare meet Otto's eye. She is to blame for this: she alone.

In that moment, Nella's sole wish is to take Thea out of here. But to her surprise, her niece stands firm and unsmiling in the face of the girls' simpers.

'Not quite correct,' Thea says. 'The play was *Romeo and Juliet*, and the dress was lent to me by Rebecca Bosman, when she played the title character.'

The mere mention of this name impresses the Sarragon

girls, outweighing their shock at being corrected. Their eyes bulge, but like their mother, they quickly hide their feelings. 'So you have come as a tragic heroine?' Eleonor says. Catarina titters.

Thea stares at Eleonor as if she is one of the strange creatures to be found in Cornelia's menagerie. 'It is not a tragedy to die for love.'

Clara's eyebrows reach her hairline, but Thea isn't finished. 'Juliet lived truly. And besides, I do not see the point in wasting guilders on dresses that will only get trodden on.' She looks towards the sweaty crowd then back to the girls, as if to say: *Is this your idea of fun?*

'The Brandt family know a great deal about thrift,' says Clara. 'I'm sure they could teach us a lot.'

Before Nella can make their excuses, Clara spies something over her shoulder. 'Ah! Here, you! Come here.'

The group turns to see a man in the crowd, frozen on the spot. If Thea is dazzling, straight from the Schouwburg stage, this man is the opposite. He is scruffy, about Nella's age, with wild, dark-brown hair that stands on its ends, his shirt well made but hanging off him. He has a stork's look, thin and rangy. Knees that might snap. He looks tired, and as if he would rather be anywhere else, as if this summoning from Madame Sarragon is the last nail in his coffin. He appears to be carrying a silver tray of food, yet he does not seem to be a serving-man. In such a place as this, he looks too clumsy and unkempt.

'Madame Sarragon,' he says, approaching. His accent is educated, his manner wary.

'This is Caspar Witsen,' Clara says, barely able to conceal her self-satisfaction. 'My personal botanist. Aren't you, Witsen?'

Caspar Witsen briefly looks at Clara, before settling his gaze on the platter. 'That I am, Madame.'

'I insist you try his jam. Or *my* jam, really.' Clara chivvies Caspar Witsen with her hand. 'Well, Witsen? Give them some. But don't tell them what it is!'

Nella glances at the platter that this Caspar person is offering, as the hostess herself lifts off one of the morsels and pops it in her mouth. Fearing that this entire exchange has ruined Thea's chances of Clara's help in the marriage market, she takes one off the platter. It is a square of toast, smeared with something alarmingly yellow, but she will do anything to improve this situation, so she eats it. Reluctantly, Otto and Thea do the same.

Whatever this jam is, it is sweeter and zestier than strawberry or greengage. It feels as if tiny bubbles are bursting upon Nella's lips. The flavour is more intense than lemon, yet somehow fuller and lighter at the same time. Nella is not sure if she likes it, but Otto has closed his eyes. When he looks at her, she feels rooted to the spot by his expression of shock.

'Pineapple!' Clara crows in triumph. 'You didn't guess! So I have told you. Have you ever tasted pineapple before, Madame Brandt?'

'I have not,' Nella replies, swallowing down the last of the unwelcome acidity. Thea declines another, and Clara smiles, once more revealing her perfect teeth. 'And would it *amaze* you if I told you it grew not in Surinam, where I first tasted it, of course – but on our own shores, a few miles from here?'

'It definitely would,' says Nella obediently, hating herself. 'I am all astonishment.' She has met Sarragon enough times over the past few months to be accustomed to this pattern of questioning, of Clara's need for a chorus rather than a conversation companion, someone to whom she can boast.

Clara leans in. 'I found him grubbing around in the garden of the university,' she murmurs, although despite the clamour around them, Nella is sure Caspar Witsen can hear every word. 'My son is studying there, and I was paying a visit to his tutors to see whether they were doing anything useful for him. There was Witsen, handling some of the most beautiful flowers I've ever seen. I quickly realized he was being underused – I have a sense for these things. It turns out I was right. Witsen has the most *alchemical* green fingers.'

Nella cannot help glancing down at Caspar Witsen's fingers, almost expecting them to be the colour of grass. All she sees is how dirty they are under the nails. He notices and she blushes as he holds his right hand up to her, nails forward. 'Hazard of the job,' he says. 'It's just soil, Madame, nothing to be scared of.'

'I am not scared of soil,' Nella replies. She feels foolish at speaking such a sentence. He drops his hand quickly, as if realizing the gesture's intensity.

'It adds to his authenticity,' Clara interrupts. 'It's like having my own farmer, except a clever one. Witsen now works on my estate out in Amersfoort. We're building a much larger pineapple stove than the university has. We're considering also harvesting mango and guava. I dream of them! The fruits of the colony – on my doorstep, and at my party!'

'And what do you plan to do with all your bounty, Madame?' Otto asks. 'Will you hold a party like this every week, for marriage contracts and pineapple jam?'

Caspar Witsen turns to him sharply, but Clara laughs, fixing her gaze on Otto. 'Marriage is a young woman's game,

Seigneur,' she says, glancing at Nella. 'Pineapples, on the other hand? I am going to make money. I'm patenting the recipes, and selling them into Europe.'

'Are they your recipes?' Otto asks.

Clara bats the air with her hand, as if the morality of possession is beneath her. 'I've had a sample batch sugared, preserved and bottled here – the stuff you've been enjoying right now – and with Witsen's expertise and my husband's connections, we're already securing several contracts. The English in particular love jam. Forget opium – they're quite ridiculous about it.'

'And all without having to go to Surinam,' says Otto.

'Exactly,' Clara replies, her eyes shining. 'It cuts out an inconvenient journey.'

'Indeed it does,' Otto says. He turns to Caspar Witsen. 'Seigneur: how did *you* first come to discover the properties of the pineapple?'

For the first time this evening, Caspar Witsen looks enthused. Still holding the tray, he begins to tell Otto of his early encounters with the fruit, but Nella is distracted by the undercurrents of the previous conversation about Thea's marriage prospects. After mustering so much effort to get here, she is depleted by Clara's barbs and boasting, and worried that Otto will say something they may all, in time, regret. Still: Thea has handled herself with great strength, a quality that reminds Nella of Marin. She has to admit that it was not something she was expecting.

I am not like that, she thinks. How can it be that the spirit of Marin is within her, when the two of them never met properly at all?

She tries to meet her niece's eye to make peace, but Thea determinedly will not do it. Nella had planned to introduce Thea to the idea of her destiny slowly. First: seeing how she took to the hierarchies of such a ball. But now, with her father's depressing VOC news and Clara's indiscretion about the actual purpose of this night, the shape of Thea's future has been pushed roughly into the open. Thea is eighteen. A beneficial marriage for her must be spotted on the horizon. This evening could unfold many ways, but eventually, Thea will have to realize that her story can end in only one.

Nella could slap Clara Sarragon, reach out right now to land a flat hard palm upon the woman's self-satisfied cheek. And yet, despite this ambush and the sudden precariousness of her family's position, Thea has gathered herself. Compared with the Sarragon girls, who giggle behind their hands at the eccentric appearance of Caspar Witsen, Thea is detached, her gaze distant, and Nella watches with fascination the small smile growing on her niece's lips, as if all around her is gossamer, and she herself is far away.

Watching Thea, Nella feels a sudden tightness under her sternum, a swift and fluttering forgetfulness of how to breathe. It feels, at first, like panic. The sense of fear is unnameable, constricting, and she cannot hang it on anything. Despite the heat of this crowded room, a cold chill comes to her neck, running down her back, her hairs on end, her skin prickling, damp beneath her silver dress. Not caring how odd she must appear, Nella whirls around, pinioned by her disbelief. But no – that old, familiar feeling she hasn't had for eighteen years is gripping her body and mind, just as it did whenever she was close to the miniaturist.

It cannot be possible. But as Nella turns back to the group, a presence brushes behind her, almost touching her waist. She's come. She's *here*. Even though part of Nella knows the thought is ridiculous, she wonders if her plea in the attic did not go unheard.

She swears she hears a woman say her name, and she whips around again to face the swarm of the ballroom, scanning the crowd for the one face she knows she would recognize, even now, all these years later. Those light-brown, almost orange eyes, that fair hair—

'Nella? Are you all right? You're very pale.'

She turns back, dazed, and it is Otto who is asking her, Otto who is speaking her name, and Clara Sarragon, who has a look of distaste on her face, and her daughters, goggling – and here is Caspar Witsen with his tray of pineapple jam, and Thea, staring at her in bewilderment. Nella swallows, trying to compose herself. The last thing she wants to do is cause a scene. But she cannot resist her own urge. After all these years, she cannot lose sight of the only person who can raise the hairs on the back of her neck.

'I'm quite all right,' she replies, her voice far away from her body. She smiles tightly, the blood rushing out of her head, so much so she almost loses balance. 'Will you excuse me?'

Before Otto can protest, Nella abandons him and Thea to the claws of Clara, who will no doubt delight in picking apart her strange behaviour. She pushes forward into the swirl of silks. She is elbowed, almost winded, and someone treads on her hem, splashing wine on her front, but Nella doesn't care. The noise of the crowd rises more chaotic in her head, but she keeps her eye on every corner for the sight of the miniaturist's cloak.

She's here, Nella's sure of it. The heat from hundreds of candles presses into her body. The music surges within her like a wave, but she won't give up. On she goes, against the flow of drunken people, deep into the heart of the ballroom.

'Allow me,' says a man's voice.

Nella comes to, finding herself seated on a chair, in a small wood-panelled antechamber adjoining the ballroom. 'You were lucky I was standing behind you,' he says.

'You were? When?' Nella scrutinizes his face. The sense of cold has vanished. Only heat and sweat remains, and a clamminess, a faint rind of shame. She feels exhausted, as if she has been running too fast. She knows the miniaturist has gone.

'You fainted against me,' the man says. 'I put you by a window.'

'I *fainted*?'

He is a young man. Short, in his twenties, a neat, dark suit, dashes here and there of a mustard-yellow brocade. Shoulder-length brown hair. Thick eyebrows, brown eyes. A pleasant enough expression.

She exhales. 'I did not eat enough, that's all. How long was I—?'

'A mere matter of a minute.'

'And did anyone—?'

'No one saw,' he replies, smiling, understanding her Amsterdammer's preoccupation. 'I was by the wall. You collapsed a little against me, and I propped you in this chair. Nothing dramatic. Appearances were maintained.'

She blushes. 'Thank you.'

The young man looks over his shoulder through the

doorway, where the ballroom continues to heave. 'It is a very hot room,' he says. 'In fact, I fear that with the volume of candles Clara Sarragon burns, and the amount of flammable silks, any moment we're all going to go up in flames. Can I fetch you someone?'

'No thank you,' Nella replies. She thinks quickly. 'May I ask your name?'

'Jacob van Loos. Happy to be of service.'

'I'm Petronella Brandt,' she replies.

Even in her compromised state, Nella sees how her name has an effect. Her unease grows. Jacob van Loos goes very still, looking down at her with renewed interest. 'Van Loos is a Leiden family, is it not?' she says, making a monumental effort to pull herself together, a true Amsterdam merchant's widow, dressed in her finest silver. 'Are you part of that illustrious branch?'

He smiles. 'How is it that all women of our class can tell the families and their cities as quickly as if they were reciting the alphabet?'

Our class: those two words give Nella such relief. They hold warmth, a sense of inclusion! They make her feel as if all her efforts and doubts about coming have been worth it. Jacob van Loos has seen something familiar in her. She laughs, determined not to lose him. 'We are not trained for much, Seigneur,' she says. 'Our minds are never put to such good use as yours.'

'Well, you're right, nevertheless,' he replies. 'My family resides in Leiden, but I work in Amsterdam. The third son of a family is not so illustrious that he can afford not to work.'

'Spoken like a true Dutchman.'

A third son. Not as wealthy as a first born, but maybe a more likely match for Thea, given that the Brandts are a long way from the grandest families in this city, for all that they live on the Herengracht. Nella wants to keep him here as long as she can. 'You work on your family's behalf?'

'I manage their affairs in the city. I'm a lawyer. My middle brother is the soldier, and the eldest runs our estate.'

'A very efficient machine,' Nella replies.

'As was my father's intention.'

He is well versed in presenting himself. But despite the noise from the ballroom, Nella hears a note in his voice – bitterness, perhaps, or maybe resignation? He seems to realize this slip, and focuses once more on her. 'I, too, have heard of your family,' he says. 'Are you Petronella Brandt, wife of Johannes?'

When he asks her this, Nella feels as if everything is about to be pulled from under her. This man is young: it would probably flatter him to be direct. 'The correct term is widow,' she replies. 'And don't believe everything you hear.'

'I don't,' he says. 'I know of your family, because I studied the case at university.'

She cannot hide her surprise. 'The case?'

'Your husband's case. His trial.'

She is speechless. No one has talked publicly to her of Johannes's trial since it took place eighteen years ago. The mention of it – and of Johannes – *here*, in a small antechamber alongside the furnace of the Sarragon ball, in the mouth of this young man, is almost too much.

Jacob van Loos frowns. 'I shouldn't have spoken. I am sorry—'

'No,' she says. 'It's . . . I didn't realize one was able to do such a thing. Study the case.'

'Oh yes,' he says. 'The republic keeps a record of everything, Madame.'

'Of course it does.' Nella stares into the polished wooden floor. We will never be free of the past, she thinks. Ever.

'It was a miscarriage of justice,' Jacob says. He does not speak to her gently, but with the confident detachment of the lawman, as if Johannes were nothing more than a name scribbled in the archives, not a real man the state let fall between its fingers.

Nella pictures her husband as he was alive. Sea-salted, standing in the shadows of the hallway, his beloved dog Rezeki at his side. She thinks of him with his lover, Jack, the one who lied in the courtroom to see him ruined. She remembers the damp of the Stadhuis cell. Johannes's broken body. These old traumas, which a place like the Sarragon ball is supposed to annihilate.

'Your husband did not receive a fair trial,' Jacob continues. 'And in point of the evidence, he should never have been put on trial at all.'

Nella is glad her head is bowed, that he cannot see her expression. Words won't bring Johannes back from the dead. She forces the threat of tears away, and straightens up. 'The thing is,' she says, 'it was a very long time ago.'

Jacob van Loos looks almost severe. 'I cannot imagine such a loss to feel so distant—'

'There you are!' says a voice at the doorway. Both Jacob and Nella turn to see Thea, backlit by the glow of the ballroom, shining in her golden dress. Thea hurries over, ignoring

Jacob van Loos entirely. Nella watches this man's reaction: he is looking at Thea with barely concealed surprise. Nella cannot help herself: she begins to calculate the risks of keeping them both here, of introducing them to each other, to see what might happen. It is, after all, the point of this ball. She has never done this before, normally keeping the stares at bay, but Jacob must be a gentleman if he saved her from falling.

'Are you well?' Thea asks her aunt. 'We've been worried where you were.'

'I'm very well,' Nella replies. She smiles brightly. 'Thea, this is Seigneur van Loos. You could say he rescued me.'

'From what?' Thea barely glances at him.

From what indeed? Nella wonders, thinking about how close she has come to the miniaturist, and how, once again, she has lost her. But she feels her irritation rising: if she can endure the talk of Johannes's trial, Thea can tolerate a simple greeting. *Look at this young man!* she wants to shout.

'I don't know,' she says, attempting a laugh. 'It was so hot in there, I suppose. I took a bad turn.'

'Did you faint?'

Nella hesitates. 'No.' Next to her, Jacob shifts on his feet, as if to tread her lie into the floorboards.

Thea sighs, looking through the doorway to the far side of the ballroom. 'Papa's still talking to that pineapple man. They've had their heads together since you left.'

Jacob van Loos addresses Thea. 'Mistress, I will go and fetch your mother some water.'

Thea snaps her head round. 'She's not my mother.'

Nella sees how angry Thea is with her, for bringing her here, for forcing her to confront Clara Sarragon's marriage revelations. 'I can go for myself,' she says, beginning to rise from her chair. 'You two stay—'

'*I'll* go,' Thea interrupts, and is gone before Nella can stop her.

Nella sighs. 'Thea's mother is dead,' she says. She is surprised to be making this revelation to a man she's barely met, but she wants to offer Jacob pieces of this family, to see how he might take them. Still, she must be careful.

'I am sorry,' says Jacob.

'She's eighteen years today,' Nella continues, as if this might excuse Thea's monumental indifference to Jacob's presence. 'She's very distracted. She's great friends with the Sarragon girls, and – well, Seigneur – young women have such a particular energy, don't you think?'

She trails off, as if the words do not belong in her mouth.

Jacob van Loos smiles. 'Thea is very beautiful.'

'And very accomplished.'

'Does she know the lists of all the best families, and the cities in which they reside?'

Nella begins to scramble a reply, when she realizes Jacob is teasing. Teasing is good. It suggests a fondness already – or a tolerance, at the very least. Jacob van Loos has noticed Thea, and called her beautiful.

'She plays the lute,' Nella says. 'And enjoys the Schouwburg very much.'

'Indeed?'

'You may think this forward, Seigneur. But would you accept an invitation to our house on the Herengracht, for supper?' Nella asks. 'Next Wednesday night? As a means to thank you for rescuing me.'

'The rescue was mild, Madame. You were in no danger.'

'Do come. Our cook, Cornelia, is one of the best in the city.'

Jacob van Loos, this man who has appeared to Nella from nowhere, continues to look at her. What is he thinking? What is it that he is weighing up? He is already aware of the scandal at the head of their tree, the famed merchant, Johannes Brandt, Nella's three-month husband, executed by the state eighteen years ago. He has read the trial papers, after all. But until he laid eyes on Thea, did he know about her, too? Does he hear the speculations about the identity of her mother? Jacob called Thea beautiful. But would he sit opposite Otto and find it within his faculties to fathom how, in this new year of our Lord, 1705, an African man with an Amsterdam accent holds the deeds to a house on the Herengracht, and his daughter stands beside him, her pale white mother buried unknown in the floor of the Old Church? It has to be a risk Nella is willing to take.

'I would like to come,' he says, and he smiles, and Nella feels her heart lift for the first time all day.

Strange Gifts

VII

The morning after the Sarragon ball, Thea sleeps late, woken only by Lucas barrelling open her door and leaping up to sit on her pillow. The golden gown borrowed from Rebecca has been draped over the chair by Cornelia. It hangs limp, no longer glowing, as if all the magic in the fabric was stolen by the effort of the night before. At least she did not spill any wine on it, nor smear pineapple jam upon its panels. She closes her eyes again, glad to be away from the heat of the place, those stupid Sarragon girls, their viper mother, her father's discomfort, her aunt vanishing like a lunatic into the crowd. And well might Aunt Nella have run away – for shame, for lying to Thea in the way she has. She thinks of Clara Sarragon's words: *You have not prepared her? Oh, cruel trick!*

How could her aunt not tell Thea the purpose of taking her to such a party? How dare she? It is humiliating. Yes, her father might have lost his position at the VOC, but she is not some calf to be sold off at the market to put money in the coffers.

They do not love me, Thea thinks. They care so little for me that they would barter me off to the first bidder.

They had left the party at about ten, her aunt with a quiet look of triumph, her father preoccupied with his own thoughts, and Thea so angry that she could have beaten her fists on the canal path and not cared who saw. As they entered their own house, Aunt Nella looked over her shoulder as if in search of someone. *There's no one there*, Thea wanted to shout. *Who would ever be waiting for you?*

They stood in their hallway, and it was impossible not to notice the difference from the Sarragon residence. The plain black and white tiles, the sturdy but naked panelling, the lack of ornaments and giant paintings, the chill in the air. Cornelia the solitary servant, waiting in the shadows to take their coats and give them warm blankets. You would never be able to host an Epiphany ball in this house. A funeral, perhaps, but never a ball. And yet her aunt had been buoyant, despite the cold, despite the tired hour.

Thea just wants to stay in bed, to think of Walter in the painting-room, his hands upon her, his tongue – their life ahead, image upon image building until she falls asleep again. But her wish is not to be granted, for Cornelia comes in and stands at the foot of her bed. 'Ah, a little toe,' Cornelia says, reaching down and holding Thea's foot like a fishwife inspecting shrimp at the market. 'I heard there was an ankle under here. Maybe if I'm lucky, a nice young leg?'

It's one of their old games, the piecing together of Thea's limbs into the comfort of a body. But Thea doesn't want old games, and her body is no longer a child's. She pulls her foot back sharply under the covers. Lucas leaps to the floor in shock.

'Not so fast,' says Cornelia. 'What happened last night? I'm waiting here until you wake up and eat breakfast with us as a fully-fledged person. It might take a while, but that's the burden God gave me.'

'Not hungry,' Thea mumbles into her pillow. The touch of linen on her lips makes her think of Walter's mouth on hers; the remembrance of being kissed moves up her legs into her stomach, pulsing in her throat. What they did in the painting-room yesterday was scandalous, truly. No one in that ballroom would believe it, and Thea wants more. Her lack of hunger is a lie. She is ravenous, for everything. But if she turns over and faces the day, Cornelia might see.

'Tell me about the party,' Cornelia says. 'Heaven, or hell?'

Thea arranges her face and looks up. 'Hell, hell, hell. Far too many people, and Clara Sarragon hates us.'

'Hates you? She invited you.'

'Exactly. We were just there to be laughed at. I don't know how Aunt Nella couldn't see it.' Thea sits up. 'Did you know she was planning to marry me off?'

Cornelia seems surprised. 'She wouldn't do that.'

'That's why she took me. She didn't tell me because she knew I wouldn't go. It was bad enough with Papa's news, but within five minutes of us arriving, Sarragon told me that I was there to find a husband. Papa said *nothing*.'

Cornelia looks stricken. 'Well, I don't suppose it was the time or the place for an argument. Your father and your aunt only ever do things in your best interest.'

'They don't know anything about my best interest. They know nothing about me! I would never marry anyone she chooses.'

Cornelia sighs, walking over to the windows to draw apart the curtains. 'Thea, she's doing her best.'

Finally, Cornelia leaves, and Thea pulls on some woollen stockings, throws a bed gown over her nightshirt, and makes her way down the main staircase, towards the top of the stairs that lead to the working kitchen. She hesitates. In the basement, she can hear her father and aunt arguing.

'If Thea is going to have children one day, they will be legitimate,' Aunt Nella is saying. 'If she's going to declare her love for someone, it will be from inside a church.'

'Petronella, these fantasies you speak of are years away.'

'Fantasies? These are normal things, Otto. We've slid away from wealth, but Thea will rise again to riches. She impressed people last night. She impressed me. She might share her mother's streak of stubbornness, but history is not going to repeat itself.'

'And what does that mean?'

'You know what it means. No more illegitimacy. No more hidden affairs that end up leading to all sorts of trouble.'

Thea can hardly believe her ears. In the brief silence that follows, she holds her breath.

'I haven't even met him,' her father says, his voice tight. 'And you've asked him to our home?'

'Otto, however much we want to keep her near, Thea cannot waste away inside this house, into her twenties, her thirties maybe, and beyond. And there is a chance that might happen, given the shade of her skin and the emptiness of our coffers.'

'You need not remind me either of her colour or our coffers.'

'Loneliness and poverty are miserable!'

'I am aware of that.'

'Then how can you be unaware that there is no future in this house for our child?'

'*My* child.'

There is a long pause. 'That is very unfair,' says Aunt Nella.

Her voice is constricted, too. 'I have been here from the very beginning. And now I'm simply trying to find Thea a future.'

'I understand your concern.'

'Then I marvel that you do not share it. What do you think is going to happen, some sort of miracle? This family has always been short on those. Toot,' she sighs, using his old nickname. 'We *have* to do this. Our choices . . . may be limited.'

'Who says they will be limited?'

'You have lived for twenty-five years in this city. The VOC dismisses you, and you ask me that question? Thea needs to be safe.' She lowers her voice. 'Money is safety. And who with money might marry her, Otto? *Who?*'

'We do not know the first thing about this man's intentions. Why are you so convinced he has marriage on his mind? It was you he talked to, not her.'

'All the more reason to invite him. He was at the Sarragon ball, wasn't he? Everyone knows the purpose of these things.' Everyone except Thea, perhaps.

'And I was there too, Nella, but I wasn't looking for a wife. You have lived outside the world of men for so long. You are naive.'

Thea cannot bear to hear them any more. She clomps down the stairs, and predictably enough, the conversation stops. They turn to greet her. Her father looks tired. Her aunt is already dressed, neat in a deep-black gown and pristine white collar.

'Thea,' says Aunt Nella, smiling. 'You look very well. Good dreams?'

'I dreamed you were getting married, Aunt Nella.'

Her aunt's smile freezes. 'You did?'

'Yes. And the only thing to eat was a wall of pineapples.'

'You mock me.'

'The truth is,' Thea says, 'I do not remember my dreams.'

'Lucky you,' her aunt sighs.

'Come,' says her father. 'Eat some porridge.'

Thea pulls herself to the trestle table and spoons a bowl of oats and honey.

'Thea,' begins her aunt. 'I understand that what Clara Sarragon said to you last night must have come as a surprise. I regret that she broached the subject in such a fashion.'

'I regret that she broached the subject at all,' says Thea. 'She has the largest house on the Golden Bend, and the goodwill of a flea. She was laughing at us. I am glad *I* did not dance to her tune.'

Aunt Nella looks uncomfortable. 'It is true that she is no great friend of ours. But one good thing *did* come out of our visit to the ball. You remember the young man who helped me?'

'No.'

'The lawyer from Leiden, Jacob van Loos. The coat with the mustard threads?'

'I don't remember his coat. Oh: you mean the one who thought you were my mother?'

'Well, we can all make mistakes on first impressions, Thea. But I've invited him to supper, to thank him for attending to me. He's coming next Wednesday, and we shall all eat together.'

'Wednesday night?' Thea says, unable to hide her distress. Wednesdays are for Walter, but with a dinner like this, she will be expected to be close at hand all day. Both her father and aunt turn in surprise at her vehemence, and Thea busies herself with her porridge.

'You have a prior engagement on Wednesday night?' her

aunt asks. 'A guild dinner we didn't know about? A VOC banquet you were going to attend?'

'No,' Thea mutters. 'Of course I don't. I never do anything.'

'It's just a dinner,' Aunt Nella says, massaging her temples. 'With an erudite, thoughtful young man—'

'I will never marry him,' Thea says. She stares at them both. 'Because when I marry, it will be for love.'

Her father looks stupefied. At first, Thea feels a thrill at shocking him, and then she fears she's said too much.

'Love,' Aunt Nella says, sounding exhausted. 'Love is all very well. But what is the harm in speaking with Jacob van Loos, over a delicious supper, in making a better acquaintance?'

'You don't know a thing about love,' says Thea.

There is a painful silence.

'I don't?' says her aunt.

'*True* love springs from the earth, fully formed.'

'I see.'

'It's not found during tedious suppers, or sitting on chairs having collapsed against the nearest available man.'

'Thea,' her father warns. 'Enough.'

Aunt Nella stares into the old kitchen table. 'I do not profess to be an expert in love,' she says. 'But I do know something about it. More than you think. More than your playwrights' love, spoken for just two hours and dissolved into applause.'

'It does not dissolve,' says Thea. 'It *lasts*.'

Aunt Nella picks up her porridge spoon and begins pointing it for emphasis. 'Love is something that is learned in far less alluring settings, Thea, than playhouses and ballrooms. It is earned in the deeds you do. The words you speak. It takes practice. Patience. Time.' She puts her spoon back into her porridge. 'You will learn about love, I am sure. But it might not take the form you originally expected.'

Thea grips her own spoon. 'I care nothing for your cold philosophy of love. Your banker's love.'

Aunt Nella laughs. 'I wish I were a banker. Then we wouldn't even be having this foolish conversation.'

The women's words run from their mouths like butter off a heated pan. 'You talk of accumulating lessons,' Thea says with scorn. 'Of the forced practice of love. It is *disgusting* to me. Unnatural.'

'Given your youth, I wonder how you are such an expert in it?' Aunt Nella says, the colour rising in her cheeks. 'You are a gentleman's daughter on the Herengracht, yet you talk like a poet in the coffeehouses. How *do* you know so much about love, Thea?'

Thea feels pinioned. 'It is a subject that interests me,' she says. 'When love comes to us, when we choose to give it—'

'Enough,' says her father. 'Enough!'

'Papa! Tell her that it is pointless this lawyer should come.'

The two women turn to him. Thea's father runs a hand slowly over his head, as if under the ministrations of his palm he will locate the right thought. 'I do not like having strangers in my house,' he says, and Thea's heart lifts. 'One dinner,' he adds, and she feels her happiness sink back down. 'Just one. On the condition that I never have to see Clara Sarragon again. And if Thea doesn't like this van Loos fellow, then we never have to see him again, either.'

❧

If Thea cannot see Walter next Wednesday, she must warn him. She must share with him the torture of Jacob van Loos – and there is no better excuse to go back to the playhouse than to return the gold dress. 'I have to do it this morning,' she tells Cornelia an hour after breakfast, in her bedroom being dressed. Her head is singing with the worries and insults of the morning – *Who with money might marry her, Otto? Who? We've slid away from wealth . . . the emptiness of our coffers.* But Thea is also fearful. Marriage to the wrong man happens all the time in this city, and not just in plays. Her true love might be snatched away. She needs to see Walter.

Cornelia moves round Thea, undoing her bound-up hair to check it, dipping her fingers in the beeswax pomade, curling the last strands of Thea's front curls tighter round her index finger to check they are well coiled, and not too shrunken. She tuts. 'This weather,' she says. 'What the mist does and then the warmth! We only treated it last night.'

'Just tie it back today,' Thea says, impatient. 'Tuck it under my cap, I need to go.'

'I could come with you.' Cornelia ties Thea's hair, so practised she barely even looks at what she does. Sometimes, Thea thinks, Cornelia treats her hair as if it were her own personal challenge against the world.

'You can't,' says Thea. 'I would like you to come, of course. But won't you want to discuss Wednesday's dinner with Aunt Nella?'

'What's he like?' Cornelia frowns, finishing the last of the tucking and firmly tying the strings of Thea's cap.

'Who?'

'This Jacob person?'

'Oh. I don't know. I'm sure we'll find out.' Thea takes Cornelia's hand and squeezes it. 'Just one of your excellent suppers will reveal all, I promise. And then he'll be gone.'

'This family strikes strange bargains with each other,' Cornelia sighs.

◈

Aunt Nella is resting in her bedroom – probably licking her wounds, despite the fact it is Thea who is hurt. Her father is in his counting room. Thea passes his open door: he looks absorbed, his pen aloft, turning the pages of the family ledger. If what Aunt Nella says about their money is true, how long can they last here? All they have is this house and their frac-tured reputation, which she is supposed to reinstate to a glory she has never known.

Cornelia has pressed Rebecca's dress and sprinkled it with lavender water. It looks as good as new. Thea covers it in her spare cloak and pulls open the heavy front door. She will probably never wear a dress like it again, like Juliet at her Capulet ball. She must admit it was exhilarating to shine so brightly, to draw so many glances, whether critical or not. She looked spectacular last night, and her only regret is that the one person she wanted to witness her fleeting majesty wasn't there. She will tell him: he can paint it in his mind's eye.

The prospect of seeing Walter invigorates her, and Thea steps into the cold air. The canal is far from busy – fewer barges and passers-by at this time of year. Those who are on the water or hurrying along the canal paths have their heads down against the wind. Now is not the time to meander. There are no celebrations to look forward to for weeks; the spring harvest is far away, the summer festivities even farther.

But with her back to the house, Thea feels hopeful. She has never been further than the boundaries of this city, but every now and then, she feels a conviction that one day she will break out of these narrow streets with their tall, thin houses. One day, for her, the canal will open onto the sea. The story of her family is not her story, however much they keep insisting that it is.

Thea is so absorbed with these thoughts, that she steps on the parcel that has been left at the top of their stone stairs. She jumps back, swiftly lifting her foot. The package is half the length of her boot, plain brown paper, tied with string. To her amazement, she sees her full name written in neat black capital letters along the top right corner. No one has ever sent her a parcel before. Unhesitating, Thea scoops it up. It is light, compact, and the surprise of it thrums in her fingers.

If she goes back into the relative warmth of the hallway to open it, Cornelia will ask what she is up to. Or worse, her aunt or father. She looks up and down the canal for anyone who seems like they might have just delivered something. But there is no one.

Thea closes the front door and leans against it in the cold air, placing the golden dress on the step in order to rip apart the paper. When she sees what is lying inside, she lets out a gasp of delight. It seems impossible, but it's true.

Here is Walter, miniaturized to absolute perfection. He has been turned into an extraordinary little doll, and he fits inside her palm.

Astonished, Thea drinks up every detail of her love's face,

his arms, his boots. Easy, one might say, to miniaturize perfection when a man is already perfect. But this little puppet is something else. Here is her Walter with his shoulder-length dark-blond hair, his sheen of stubble, his blue eyes held in a moment of merriment, that strong jaw. His lips are closed, and it is hard to tell whether he is smiling or smirking. It is the only minor chord of this living picture resting in Thea's hand; it's as if Walter is still holding back his truest happiness, and her challenge is to find it. He is wearing his painter's smock, and he holds a brush in his right fist like a tiny spear. The tips of the bristles have been dipped in red paint – red like blood, like his strawberries, the red of life. In his other hand is a palette, but there are no paints upon it: just empty, colourless, naked wood.

It has to be a present from Walter. Only an artist of his skill could make such a thing, and be thinking of her when he made it. But when Thea presses on his handsome biceps, she realizes the figure is not carved from wood, but cast in wax. Does Walter know how to work in wax, as well? Can his large hands make this tiny brush, this palette no larger than a coin? Has he really sewn this shrunken smock? Of course he has, Thea tells herself. There is no end to Walter's talents.

It's like a treasure clue, an invitation to go and seek out the real version. Thea turns the doll over, in search of a message – *meet me at my lodging*, or some such instruction. But there is nothing. Just the back of Walter's head, his body, which she gently touches. When Thea lifts his smock, expecting to find underclothes, she discovers that Walter is naked. She stares at this nakedness, at his beautiful body cast with thought and knowledge, the attention deep, anatomical yet artistic.

Only he could have done this, she thinks. No one could have seen him as purely as he might see himself.

The present of this doll excites Thea, but it also makes her feel furtive. To be standing out here, in the cold, looking at naked beauty. Walter has given her the private gift of himself. Quickly, she wraps the paper round his precious body and puts him in her pocket. A miniature is all very well, but Thea wants the real thing, and she must have it.

VIII

Having bribed the Schouwburg's back-door guard with a couple of stuivers to let her through, Thea finds Walter in his painting-room. As she opens the door, Walter, brushing a palm tree and with his back to her, throws words over his shoulder. 'I requested that you leave me alone.' His voice is hard with irritation.

'It's me,' says Thea.

Walter turns, any trace of disgruntlement gone. 'Thea? This is a surprise – I thought you wouldn't be able to come until Wednesday?'

'I had to return Rebecca's dress.' She waits for him to ask her about the surprise on her doorstep, but he does not. She locks his door, not wanting interruptions.

'Ah,' says Walter. 'The dress. And how was the Sarragon spectacular?'

Thea lays the gown over the back of a chair and drapes her arms over Walter's shoulders. She wants to talk about the miniature, to take out the doll and admire it with him, to praise Walter for his ingenuity, his playfulness, to tell him that she has not rushed here for the dress, but to his summons. 'The ball was horrible,' she says.

'I don't believe it.'

'Full of over-perfumed matrons. Old men in wigs. Pine-apple jam everywhere. The sweat and desperation of the unmarried.'

Walter laughs, putting his arms around her waist. 'Heavenly. And did you dazzle them, my angel?'

Thea thinks of Clara Sarragon, eyeing her up and down. Of Eleonor and Catarina, sniggering behind their hands at her borrowed dress. Of Jacob van Loos, appearing from nowhere to rescue her aunt. She remembers the way she'd caught Aunt Nella gazing at her, admiration undercut by envy. 'I'm sure I didn't,' she says.

'In a dress like that?'

'Everybody there was fake.'

He raises his eyebrows. 'Fake?'

'I've seen truer performances inside this building. Pretending all the time is so exhausting.'

'And what were you pretending?'

'That I wanted to be anywhere else but here.'

Walter runs the fabric of the dress between his fingers. 'Put it on for me.'

Thea feels a little dart of shock, because it is more trans-gressive to wear Rebecca's Juliet dress in the actual playhouse it's supposed to be worn in, than at a ball run by a mercenary social climber. 'I can't do that.'

'Why ever not? Let me paint you in this dress.'

Walter has never offered to paint her before. 'You would really do that?'

'I want to. But it might be like trying to paint the sun.'

Imagine what Catarina and Eleonor Sarragon would give, to be dressed in this golden gown belonging to Rebecca

Bosman, to be sitting for a portrait by someone as gifted as Walter Riebeeck. There are moments in Thea's life right now that she cannot believe are real. She smiles, carrying the dress behind a tall, unpainted flat, and begins to untie the laces of her overclothes. She thinks again about the miniature in her pocket, how much she wants to tell him about it. But Walter's offer might not last and she must take it while she can.

Besides, there is another matter she needs to discuss. 'Walter,' she says. 'I won't be able to see you next Wednesday. My aunt is holding a supper at our house. I wish you could come, but . . .' She trails off, unsure how to finish the sentence.

There is a brief silence. 'What sort of dinner?' he asks.

Thea steps into the dress, pushing her arms into the neatly pressed sleeves. She imagines that through the fabric, some of Juliet's self-possession has passed into her skin. 'She has invited a man who she met at the ball.'

'A man?'

'Yes. A Jacob someone.'

'A Jacob Someone?' Walter repeats. 'Oh, I think I've heard of the Someones. Illustrious family. In shipping.'

Thea laughs. 'I don't know him. He's a lawyer.'

'A rich one?'

'I don't want to go, Walter—'

'—but it's time to snag a husband?'

His bitterness, and his interpretation of the situation, shocks her. What will it take for her to convince Walter that she is his, and always will be? Thea steps out from behind the screen, the stays at the back of the borrowed dress still undone. 'I don't want any old husband,' she says. 'Lawyer or not.'

Walter takes a step away, assessing how the light falls on the golden silk. Thea comes towards him, her arms out, taking up both of his hands. 'Are you listening?' she says. 'The only person I want is you.'

He meets her gaze. 'How can I be sure? You go to these balls—'

'I went to *one*! And I didn't even want to.'

He sighs. 'I suppose your family just want what's best for you.'

'You're what's best for me. My family don't even know me.'

Walter removes his hands from hers and goes to the table where his brushes are laid out in perfect lines. 'Jacob, and Thea Someone. A grand life. I can see it.' He pauses, lifting one of the brushes into his right fist. 'I can see you leaving me.'

Thea feels a rising desperation. She should never have mentioned this dinner. Now she has worried the one person whose happiness means most to her. She closes her eyes, and when she does, it isn't Walter she sees, and it is certainly not Jacob. It's Aunt Nella, expectant, full of assumption that Thea Brandt will do as she is told.

'Walter,' she says, opening her eyes. 'As I love you, and you love me, why shouldn't you and I be married?'

Walter's hand is suspended in the air. She wants him to speak, to break this strange spell, with words that will move them out of this room and into the real world.

Walter's eyes widen. 'What did you say?'

'I said, why shouldn't you and I be married?'

He looks shocked. 'Is that what you want?'

'Of course. Isn't it what you want? The last six months have been the happiest of my life.'

When he doesn't reply, Thea feels uneasy. 'Walter – it *is* what we both want, eventually – isn't it?'

He appears to gather himself. 'Of course it is. I just wasn't sure of your feelings.'

Thea is astonished. 'Are they not obvious?'

He frowns. 'Women are not always obliged to be constant.'

It is such a naive thing to say it makes her laugh. 'Well, I am constant. You know I am. And just imagine, Walter. We wouldn't need to skulk around like this, like thieves, as if we were doing something bad.'

'I suppose we can't hide in here forever, can we?' he says, looking around the painting-room.

'No, we can't.'

Walter clears his throat. 'It's normally the man who asks these things,' he says. 'You've taken me by surprise. Your father, your aunt. They won't approve.'

'They won't be the ones marrying you. And I know as soon as they meet you, Walter – as soon as they see us together – they'll understand. They will see our happiness and be happy too.'

Walter appears to be thinking. 'A betrothal, then? You'd like a betrothal?'

A warmth spreads over Thea's chest. She comes over to the brush table and squeezes Walter's hands. 'Let us be betrothed,' she whispers.

'But we don't need to marry immediately,' he says. 'We should plan for a proper ceremony.'

'The sooner the better, Walter. Because then my aunt can stop her fool's errand, and you and I can begin our life out of the shadows.'

He runs his hand through his hair. 'I think I should finish my contract at the Schouwburg before we marry. Because then we will have more money. And that will settle any concerns your family might have.'

'That's a good idea. In three months, then.' Thea knows everything about Walter's work: there are twelve weeks left before a new freedom is his – and now, hers too.

'Then I may work anywhere I wish,' he says.

'London? Paris?'

'If you like.'

'But which?'

'Let's pull the city out of a hat,' Walter says, grinning.

'And we would go as husband and wife.'

'We couldn't go otherwise,' he replies, putting his arm round her waist.

Thea holds him tightly. Her beloved – her betrothed! – smells of painting oils and soap, and his own indefinable scent, clean cotton and Walter-ness, and it stops the breath in her throat. 'Sweet Jesu,' she murmurs, her mouth against his chest. 'I'm so happy. I didn't know it was *possible* to feel this happy.'

'I know,' he says, kissing her on the top of the head. He holds her apart for a moment, cupping her face in his hands. 'So you understand: if we're betrothed, we are in a marriage contract.'

She looks into his eyes. 'I may not be a notary or priest, Walter, but I believe that is the case.'

'So we are, in a way, already husband and wife.'

'Well. I haven't been a bride yet, and we haven't been married in front of the altar.'

'No, but in the eyes of God, we are married. We have

plighted our troth,' he says, and she laughs at the rightness of it.

Walter draws her to himself. 'Which means there is nothing stopping us,' he says, 'if you should wish, from lying as man and wife.'

Inside the tight circle of his embrace, Thea doesn't move, the knot of his painting smock pressed on her cheek. There is a line here, she thinks: a line drawn at my feet, invisible on the floorboards of this painting-room. From the moment Thea set eyes on Walter she has, one way or another, envisaged this line, this blurred streak that someday would solidify itself beneath her. She and Walter, naked, together, as one. And now he is asking her to step over it.

She thinks, in this moment, not of Walter, nor even of herself, but of Cornelia, carefully pressing the sleeves of this golden dress, bunched right now in Walter's fists. What would Cornelia say if she could hear Walter's words?

Cornelia would not have Thea married to a man she does not love. Cornelia would understand her desperation to secure Walter's promise.

As for her father or her aunt, Thea pushes them deep below the floorboards of this painting-room, as she slips off the golden dress Walter had said he wants to paint. She leans backwards in his embrace and looks him in the eye. 'In the eyes of God,' she says, 'I am your wife.'

Slowly, Walter lowers her to the floor. 'Are you going to do to me what you did yesterday?' she asks.

Walter grins. 'And what did I do yesterday?'

Thea swats lightly him on the shoulder. 'Walter Riebeeck. You know what you did.'

He kisses her. 'You're perfect, Thea Brandt,' he whispers. 'You are more than just a Someone.'

The lovers lie on paint-spattered dust sheets, surrounded by forest and beach, and fake crumbling castles, looming over their heads. At times, the physical sensations are painful to Thea. Walter stops to let her relax and resume, holding her, caressing her, reassuring her. And when she lies back again, Thea closes her eyes on the myriad worlds around her, trying to focus only on him, on his body loving hers, wanting her, this man to whom she has promised the rest of her life. Because to open her eyes, to see Walter doing what he is actually doing might be almost too much to take in. She will never forget this first time, but there are moments when Walter is moving over her that Thea feels as if this is all make-believe, as if she never came to the playhouse today at all, as if she never found his doll, nor locked herself inside his room.

When Walter pulls out of her with an odd, wheezing cry, a mix of anguish and pleasure, he spills himself all over Rebecca's dress, and before Thea can protest, saying they must get some water for it – for what if Rebecca sees! – Walter begins kissing her between her legs, over and over. Soon, Thea forgets the stain on the dress, and the sensations from what he is doing build inside her until she too cries out, a gasp of astonishment that this could happen again, and even better, that a miracle can be found more than once.

Afterwards, they lie on the dust sheets, staring up into the high ceiling.

'Do husbands and wives do this every day?' she asks.

Walter laughs, doing up his breeches. She could spend her

life working out ways to make him laugh: the funny girl, not born from an egg, but from a secret, deep in the city of money.

'Without fail they do,' he says. He reaches for a wet rag and begins to sponge Rebecca's dress.

Thea rolls on her side to face him. She feels womanly, in control of her own destiny. 'Will we live together in your lodgings?'

Walter, frowning, keeps dabbing at his stain. 'We can't yet. You know that, don't you?'

Thea thinks of her family. How on earth is she ever going to tell them that she has found a husband for herself, without their help? 'Of course I do. I'm simply thinking about the future. Or perhaps we could find another lodging? A new one, new for the both of us?'

Walter leans over and kisses her gently on the mouth. 'We can do whatever you want.'

Thea sits up, pulling on her shift. 'Fabritius will wonder what that puddle is.'

'Don't worry about Fabritius. I'll leave it to dry by my fire and he'll never be the wiser.'

'A pair of deceivers,' she says, grinning. She tries not to think how carefully Cornelia pressed the dress for Rebecca's return.

'White lies,' says Walter. 'Not hurting anyone.'

'I want to show you something.' Thea gets up to rifle though the pocket of her skirt. She holds out the doll of her lover, expecting Walter to grin in complicity. *You found it!* he'll say. *You understood it, and you came.*

But Walter is not grinning. In fact, he stares at the puppet in horror. 'What's that?' he says. 'Is that supposed to be me?'

'Of course it is. Stop teasing, Walter. You made it for me.' But Walter rears back and Thea begins to feel uneasy. 'Didn't you?'

'Where did you get it?' he says.

'It was on my doorstep this morning. In a package, with my name on the front.'

'Do you really think I'd make an image of myself and put it on your doorstep?'

Thea falters. 'I – I don't know. I thought it was a present from you. It was a message that you wanted me to come and see you.'

'A present?'

Walter appears mesmerized by the sight of his own doll. Gingerly, he approaches it, still in Thea's grasp. He lifts the arm that holds the empty palette. 'I would not send such a thing. And I certainly never have an empty palette. Mine is always full.'

Thea tries to pull him back to soft affection, to intimacy. 'Of course it is. It's a very beautiful puppet, whether you made it or not.'

Walter stares at the doll again. 'I don't like it,' he says, his eyes darting to the door. 'Is someone watching us? Who made it?' He throws the miniature onto the dust sheet, scrambling to his feet, pulling on his boots and smock. He looks agitated, younger than his twenty-five years. 'Have you told anyone about us?'

'Of course I haven't.'

'No slip of the tongue at the Sarragon ball? Did you drink wine last night, boasting of your playhouse lover?'

'Walter, *no*. And even if I were to speak of you, why is that such a bad thing? We're betrothed now. We are to be married.'

When Walter doesn't reply, and because he seems so agitated, Thea decides to lie. '*I* made it,' she says.

He stares at her. 'What?'

'I confess: it was me.' Thea feels very naked without her overclothes. She wishes she could slip behind the painted scenery and put on the dress in which she came. 'This is just a joke that's gone wrong,' she says. 'It's nothing.'

'You made this?' says Walter. 'Are you telling the truth?'

'I thought you'd like it.'

From the door comes the sound of footsteps passing, a shuffling, then a fall to quiet. 'Well, I don't,' Walter says quietly.

'I'm sorry,' Thea replies. She is mystified at his agitation, and shaken by his distaste. She feels cold.

'All right,' he says. 'I believe you. But now I need to carry on with that beach.'

They come together, eye to eye, a husband and wife of sorts, without marriage papers or a ring, in this room of make-believe. But when they kiss, and hold each other tight, Thea feels a little better. This happens all the time with lovers, she supposes. Misunderstandings simply make reconciliation more pleasant.

'I'm glad we did what we did,' she whispers.

'Me too,' says Walter, kissing her forehead. 'And I'll see you soon. Have a good dinner next Wednesday, won't you? Think of me.'

'I'm always thinking of you.'

Walter points to the miniature still discarded on the dust sheet. 'Well in that case, maybe he can keep you company.'

Thea leaves the playhouse feeling possessed with a potent secret. Something in her life has shifted, and she wants to hold on to it. She's glad not to have seen Rebecca Bosman, for fear she would have to explain the damp circle, spreading on the golden dress. She takes a longer route home, wanting to be alone with her thoughts, to gather herself so that no one in her family might suspect what she has done.

The city is well awake by now: all the boards have been taken down from the shop windows, and the sellers of Amsterdam are filling their displays. Amsterdam prides itself on cleanliness, the broom and the cloth instruments to show one's perfected morality, or at least your intentions in that direction.

Thea wanders past pristine stoops, windows sparkling, all paths clean of any ordure. *No sin here!* these houses and thoroughfares say. She dawdles outside a haberdasher's, staring into shots of silk and cotton, the threads of dyed madder, saffron and black, spread against whitewashed boards to magnify their shades. A cheesemonger slowly places his heavy rounds of vintage Gouda in the window like giant suns, rearranging them with a quiet smile, as if inviting passers-by to play a game to which he alone understands the rules.

Can't *any* of them tell what she has done? Can they not see the light in her eyes? The cheesemonger looks up and startles at the sight of her, eyes widening in his red-cheeked face. It is hard in that moment, through the glass, for Thea to be sure he hasn't jumped like this because he'd simply been lost in concentration and she'd appeared to him from nowhere, or if it's because he has never seen someone who looks like her. What does his shock not bother to hide – benign curiosity, suspicion, fear?

I'm not going to steal your cheese, Thea thinks, and she turns away quickly, unwilling to let herself be scrutinized, unwilling to let her new thoughts about the painting-room turn into this old preoccupation.

Maids scurry past, indifferent, muffled in scarves, their wicker baskets swinging empty on their arms, heading to the markets, to fetch the shiniest sole and whiting just hooked from the freezing sea, or the plumpest beetroot for their idle masters to chew on and complain. Thea meanders on, lost in her thoughts.

She had believed, after such intimacy, such an act of trust, that she would feel light and happy. She has made love with Walter; she is not a virgin. Some might call it a scandal, but hers is a true betrothal. But what was supposed to be such a loving morning, both a reunion and a beginning, has taken a strange turn, and the doll is entirely to blame. The canal ways back to the Herengracht, usually so familiar, seem to have altered in quality. Under the ice, the water looks deeper, and even the house fronts seem less welcoming, their windows huge and blank. Thea feels the miniature of Walter buried deep in her pocket, and as she turns back in the direction of home, she cannot help looking over her shoulder, scanning the faces of the Amsterdammers all around her for signs of unnatural, hostile scrutiny.

It is simply *impossible* that someone knows about her and Walter: is watching them. Thea cannot tell where the truth of it lies. Momentarily, she considers throwing the doll onto the ice. It has hurt and offended her love, and she cannot fathom the purpose of its sudden appearance on her doorstep. It must be true that he didn't make it. As Walter says, he is an artist of many colours. Not just one paintbrush, dipped in red.

They have spoken of shared lodgings, they have seen each other naked. But now Walter is back to work, painting his scenes, as if it never happened. Thea's lower stomach aches and her heart feels stoppered. That she loves Walter, she knows. That he loves her, she's sure. He wishes to marry her – this wonderful fact! – and Aunt Nella is right about one thing at least: in Amsterdam, a marriage is everything. Their betrothal is a sign not just of Walter's desire for Thea, but his *belief* in her, his willingness to make their future a public reality. But Thea wants time to stop for a while, to crawl inside it like a rabbit in a burrow, to think about all the things that have happened this morning.

She feels in her pocket for her miniature lover, sensing power in his little form. But who's to say that's only because she loves the real man so much, and is pouring her heart into his replica? It is, after all, just a doll. Still: she feels it is not to be discarded – not yet, wherever it came from. She will put this Walter in the small locked box she keeps beneath her bed, the key always round her neck. She will protect him from her aunt, from her father and Cornelia, until the time is right.

When she reaches her front door, Thea takes a deep breath, to swallow down this unprecedented day, to clear the secrets of her body from her face. But as she enters the hallway, one thought roils in particular. If *she* didn't make this miniature, and Walter didn't either then who, in this city of secrets, did?

IX

They will begin this supper with egg fritters, garnished with hot-house-grown fennel and dill, an unseasonal, added extra from the market. To add: a hen, wrapped in smoked bacon with mace, saffron and white wine sauce. The hen will be chased by a side of venison, which itself will be flanked by cold capons in lemon juice. Many extra guilders they cannot spare will be spent on this battalion of food, but Jacob van Loos needs to understand that the Brandts know how to entertain, and Cornelia's cooking is key.

'And I thought,' Cornelia says, heading out to the vegetable market the day before Jacob's visit, looking both sheepish (the expense) and vindicated (the cause) – 'that I'll make some Savoy cabbage in the Spanish manner.'

'Does it come with a side of pickled rosary?' Nella asks, but Cornelia is unfazed: when she has it in her mind to cook something, mockery is immaterial. Hanna and Arnoud Maakvrede's famous cinnamon biscuits (*gratis*, but don't tell Arnoud) will adorn the assembled meal. Otto has been to a vintner he knows through his clerking at the VOC, and bargained three stone flasks of Bordeaux which had been rolling their way to Sweden. They have searched their house for the best carved chairs, the sofa under the dust sheet. They have hung their remaining pictures on the salon walls, and unrolled the choicest rug upon its floor. Otto has lugged the firewood. Nella has plumped their cushions. From the morning to the evening of the supper, Cornelia has stayed in the kitchen, wrestling her capons.

And as for Thea, her only job is to practise the lute, and to put on her best dress, sewn when she was fifteen, a ruby-coloured damask that she claims is these days too short in the sleeve. Still; youth and beauty. Once Cornelia has gone upstairs to fold Thea's curls into two voluminous plaits, finishing the ends with black ribbons, it takes Thea less than ten minutes to be dressed, and now, in the semi-lit arena of the hallway, with Jacob surely mere minutes away, she half-turns towards her aunt, a vision in red, her pearl earrings glinting through the shadows. True, her wrists are a little exposed, but Thea stands so sure of herself, like a Venetian courtesan posing for her portrait. Nella feels a mixture of awe and irritation, and under that, a current of fear. This girl is running from her reach.

'You will remember your lute pieces?' she asks.

'My lute pieces?'

Nella suppresses a sigh. Since the Sarragon ball, whenever she asks her niece what's on her mind, what music plays in her head instead of the notes on the page before her, Thea claims she is thinking of nothing. It's an obvious lie. Often, Nella catches Thea staring into space, wearing a dreamy almost-smile that she takes off her face when she realizes she's being observed. She does not address the issue of her ambush by Clara Sarragon, which surprises Nella, who had expected anger, given the way the evening had unfolded. But Thea's answers to any question posed her are diffuse, and the stories behind her eyes and on her lips Nella knows she can no longer access, cannot even begin to guess at.

And at other times since the ball, Thea has been irreverent, self-important, her spiritedness spilling over, running circles round her aunt. It's hard to know what version you might get. On every occasion that Nella has tried to make a conversation, the endeavour flounders. She has forgotten how to talk to this mysterious young woman – that, or she has not learned a new way to speak to her. Vanished is the child who Nella once read to and taught to read, whose hand she held at the spring and winter *kermisses*, watching flower-girls and skaters, offering hot, caramelized nuts out of her free palm for Thea's chubby fingers.

'Thea,' she says, trying to be gentle. 'This evening is important.'

'Important for whom? Why do you cling to this man, even though I am the one who would be taken away?'

Nella falters. 'It's just a supper. An introductory supper.'

'But you said it was important.'

'Well, yes, because—'

'He might be a brute. He might beat me, starve me.'

'He's not that type of man,' Nella says, her voice rising despite her best intentions.

'How do you know?'

'He set me on a chair,' says Nella, feeling ridiculous. 'Does that not suggest a good nature?'

Thea looks incredulous. 'You would marry me to the first man who sets you on a chair?'

Nella takes a deep breath. '*If* one day you married a man who – God forbid – ever hurt you, Thea – then you would come back home to us, sit around a tallow candle, eat a slender herring and bemoan your fate. Divorce is well within your rights, but I suggest you attempt a marriage first. This family is running out of money, and you can save yourself.'

'You are so hard,' Thea says, tears springing to her eyes.

Nella pushes down her anger. 'If I'm hard it's because you are stubborn. You seek freedom, I know that. I was the same—'

'You were never like me.'

'Believe me when I tell you that marriage could be your means to it.'

'But you never married again.'

No. Because you were here, Nella wants to say, but she bites her tongue.

Thea tips her chin in the air: here it comes, the imperious side. 'You know very little of men, as far as I can see,' her niece declares.

They both know this is a comment too far, but Jacob must be nearly round the corner and Nella will not be broken. 'I have enjoyed a different type of freedom,' she replies tightly. 'Besides I never met anybody who came close.'

'So if you have never met anybody who came close, why are you so keen on selling me short?'

'To become a wife is your only option,' Nella snaps, and Thea's eyes shine with triumph that she has pushed her aunt to anger. 'Or would you go and ask Hanna Maakvrede to apprentice in her bakery? We did not raise you to cut shapes in gingerbread.'

'That man coming here tonight will not be the means to my freedom. I don't need his marriage or his money.'

'I would suggest that you do. You have a long life ahead of

you, Thea, God willing, and if Jacob van Loos is prepared to share his fortune—'

'You mean if he's prepared to overlook the colour of my complexion.'

'That is not what I said.'

Thea laughs. 'Just you wait.'

'What do you mean?'

'Nothing,' says Thea, her face closed again.

⋘ ⋙

Jacob arrives on a fine barge, long, low-slung, painted in black with surprising accents of buttercup, glinting in the light from the hallway. Nella and Otto wait, Thea at their side. Nella's heart hammers. She keeps shifting from foot to foot, but Otto and Thea stand poised like statues, refusing to show their thoughts.

On entering the house, the guest hands his hat to Cornelia without looking at her. 'Seigneur Brandt,' he says, bowing low. 'Madame Brandt. Thea.'

'Seigneur van Loos,' says Nella. 'Welcome.'

Curtseys, bows, moments of nervousness between them all. Cornelia, slightly crunching his hat brim, closes away the cold night air, and the hallway intensifies in its golden light. Every beeswax candle they could find is burning.

Jacob is impressed by the house, Nella can tell. Its flesh might be scanter these days, but the bones are strong. He cranes his head back to admire the *trompe l'oeil* on the ceiling. He stares at the *grisailles* on the wall with the same intensity he focused upon Thea in Clara Sarragon's antechamber. Reaching into his coat pocket to hold aloft a long-stemmed clay pipe, he says: 'You do not object?'

112

'Of course not,' says Nella. 'You have time for a pipe before we eat.'

'Thank you.' Jacob feels deeper in his pocket. 'And I nearly forgot: Mistress Thea, I have brought you a present.' He pulls out a slim volume, wrapped in a sheet of stiff paper. Thea comes forward and takes it from his outstretched hand. She stares down at it, unmoving. From the shadows, Cornelia watches. Nella wishes she would busy herself elsewhere.

'Aren't you going to see what it is?' Nella says.

Thea, exchanging a brief glance with her father, opens the book and stands for a moment, reading the half-title. Nella sees the almost imperceptible tightening of Thea's jaw and her own throat constricts. *Look at him*, she urges her niece silently. *Thank him. Speak!*

'*A Critical Argument on Theatrical Performances* by Voetius,' Thea reads, keeping her voice low, not raising her eyes from the book. Nella is sure she hears a tut in the shadows, but Jacob seems not to have noticed.

'I haven't read it myself,' Jacob says. 'I don't have much time to read. But I thought it might interest you.'

He removes his coat and Cornelia comes forward to take it, disappearing into the dark to hang it with his hat. Underneath, Jacob reveals himself to be wearing an expensive jerkin, black hose and, on his feet, the most extraordinary pair of slippers. They look so soft, so entirely unsuitable for the Amsterdam cobbles.

Thea looks at the slippers first, before her gaze travels up to rest briefly on his face. 'Thank you, Seigneur,' she says smoothly. 'I am sure I will learn a great deal from its pages.'

'I am sure you will.'

'Come,' Nella says. 'Let us sit in the salon.'

The salon glows with a large fire, and even though there are no footmen waiting in the shadows, no maids scurrying around the panelling, Nella knows the house looks beautiful. She is not too concerned about their lack of staff, for it is not uncommon even for wealthy merchant families to keep a slim group of servants. Marin always said it was foolish to fill your house with strangers: it was prudent and godly to keep a small house. If Nella ever refers to this, Cornelia will raise her brows and hold up a pair of chapped hands.

But we don't keep a small house, do we? Nella thinks, closing the door of the salon with a smile. We keep a giant mausoleum, with the names of the dead wreathed upon the air.

'I declare: this is one of the most wonderful houses in the city,' Jacob says. 'A hidden gem.'

Nella gently elbows Thea. 'Thank you, Seigneur,' Thea murmurs. For someone so keen to sound her opinions, she has turned demurely mute.

'Other households drape themselves in gold and velvet, marble, ivory, everywhere you look. Like living in a jewel box. No air holes to breathe,' Jacob says.

'You do not like ornament?' asks Nella, taking a seat and gesturing for him to do the same.

'The right ornament, in the right place, is incomparable,' Jacob replies, settling down by their fire as if he does this every day. He reaches into his jerkin pocket and brings out a small ivory box, from which he proceeds to fill the pipe with dark bits of leaf, which Nella assumes must be tobacco. 'But too many ornaments,' he continues, 'and my cuff will catch one and smash it on the floor. Here is a godly observance of the beauty of essentials. Have you held many parties?'

'Not too many, Seigneur,' she says. Behind Jacob's back, Otto throws Nella a glance. 'We have lived many happy years in this house,' she continues, her smile tight. Down here in the salon, the hallway and the dining room, they can just about keep up the act, cleverly concealing the true emptiness of the place, the sense of abandonment from room to room – but what if he realizes how desperate they are?

'Seigneur Brandt,' says Jacob, turning to Otto. 'I did not see you at the Sarragon ball.'

'I was there,' Otto says. 'But not for long.'

'Not your preferred entertainment?'

Otto gives a thin smile. 'I prefer quieter gatherings, with real friends. You are a lawyer, I'm told?'

'I am. I look after my family's interests in the city. New contracts, trading opportunities and the like.'

'And your family trust you to do that? You are still young.'

'My father died ten years ago. That takes your youth. My mother returned to Leiden, and charged me with the responsibility of handling matters in Amsterdam.'

'A dutiful son,' says Otto.

'You would have to ask my mother.' Jacob grins, dipping a spill from the mantelpiece into the fire to light the end of his pipe. They watch him bring the smoke into his mouth. It shoots out of his nostrils, the room filled with a choking wood scent, a lemony aftertaste. 'I'm experimenting with citron and fennel,' he says, sitting down again. 'I buy the tobacco from a trader in Virginia.'

'Have you been to Virginia?' Otto asks.

Jacob shakes his head. 'I have not left Europe.'

'I see.'

'And you, Seigneur Brandt. Are you a man of leisure, or profession?'

Otto catches Nella's eye. Prepared to lie, he looks into the firelight. 'I control the flow of arrivals to the VOC warehouses. In charge of distribution.'

Jacob nods, taking another drag on the mouthpiece. He does not notice Otto's ripple of discomfort. 'With our turnover, that must be a demanding job.'

Otto pours Jacob a glass of Bordeaux and takes a seat. 'Indeed.'

'Thea,' says Nella: 'perhaps, before eating, we could hear a pavane?'

Before Thea can respond, there is a loud knock at the front door. All of them turn, and Thea begins to make her way to the salon door, clearly eager for escape into the hallway.

Nella stops her. 'Cornelia will go,' she says, fixing Thea with a stare. 'Stay. Play us something.'

Thea scowls and walks to the lute case. Nella wills herself not to jump up and answer the knock herself. There was no second guest in her plan for tonight, and as cold air seeps in at the bottom of the salon door, over Thea's lukewarm lute-plucking, Nella longs to hear the muted conversation in the hallway. She half-hopes, half-prays that the miniaturist has come. After the re-emergence of the baby from the attic, and the strange presence in the ballroom, surely now is the time.

Surely the miniaturist will leave something on the doorstep, just like all those years ago.

The salon door opens. Otto rises to his feet. Nella's heart beats hard. 'Caspar Witsen!' he cries, all geniality. 'Come in, come in!'

Nella plunges into confusion as she takes in Clara Sarragon's botanist. Caspar Witsen, with his wild hair, his sagging woollen scarf around his neck, the battered satchel thrown across his body, standing on the threshold of the salon. In his hands he cradles, of all things, a pineapple. Thea has stopped plucking the lute, and stares at the new arrival with a barely concealed expression of amusement.

'Go in properly, Mr Witsen,' Cornelia scolds. 'You're letting in the night.'

Caspar Witsen stalks onto the middle of the rug, and Cornelia, throwing a look of despair at Nella, disappears behind the closing door, back to the safety of her kitchen. The newcomer stares around the room, his initial expression of excitement fading to uncertainty. The fire continues to crackle, and for a moment, Nella is speechless. Again, she wonders what this man is doing here, with his spindly, soiled fingers, his air of intensity, this spiny fruit on his palms like a strange creature he has rescued from the cold.

She glances over at Jacob, who puffs on his pipe by the fire with a look of detached amusement. He must think we run our evenings like a tavern, she thinks. An open door, through which anyone can swing.

Otto refuses to meet her gaze, and Nella feels her confusion turning to ire. He *knew* how important this evening was. How precious a presence a man like Jacob could be to them – and yet here is this pineapple man who hasn't seen a comb since Michaelmas, and Otto, welcoming him with open arms.

'It was kind of you to ask me to sup,' Caspar says.

Nella feels her cheeks burn. Ask him to *sup*? After all the planning she and Cornelia have put into the food, all the hours spent making this house sparkle, their dresses, their hair, whilst Otto did nothing but chat with a vintner, whilst Thea dawdled in her room? There will be enough food for him, because Cornelia always makes too much, but that isn't the point. The point is, Otto has deliberately sabotaged tonight. She calls upon her remaining serenity. Jacob cannot see her flustered.

Caspar turns to Nella. 'Madame,' he says, offering the pineapple: 'a gift of thanks.'

'Thank you, Mr Witsen.' Nella arranges her face as she takes the weight of the fruit.

'Have you ever held one before?'

'I confess not. It is heavier than I anticipated.' She looks up at Caspar. 'A little rough to touch.'

He smiles. Nella looks down at her gift, tempted to throw it in the fire, to see what it might do. She forces herself to appear unruffled, as indulgent of this eccentric gardener as Clara Sarragon had been. If Clara Sarragon can have a pineapple man at her party, then so can Nella Brandt. She walks to the fireplace and places the fruit gently on the mantel, and the group stands back to assess it.

'What a curious shape,' says Jacob.

'A beautiful shape,' says Caspar.

'It looks half like something you'd see in a jungle,' Jacob says. 'And half what a group of boys might kick on the grass.'

'We met Mr Witsen at Clara's ball,' Nella explains to Jacob.

'It appears that the night was a veritable trove of gentlemen,' Jacob replies. Her lute now totally abandoned, Thea appears to choke behind her hand. Otto takes another sip of wine, and Nella's spirits sink further. *Just one evening*, she thinks. *All I wanted was one normal dinner.*

Caspar fumbles in his satchel and produces a jar. 'I brought this too,' he says. 'The jam you tried. But maybe you will not want it?'

'Of course we do,' says Otto, retrieving the pot from Caspar's fingers. 'I thoroughly enjoyed it.' He sets it on the mantel by the pineapple. 'Now we are assembled,' he says, turning to smile at Nella. 'I think it's time to eat.'

⋞§.❧

The table is a sea of white damask covered with the remainder of Johannes's glinting crystal. Nella withdraws into herself as the men speak of trading, of pineapples, of the English and the French. Otto is at the head of the table, Thea to his left, Jacob to his right. Nella and Caspar are further down. She stares at the painting behind Jacob's head, the last of Marin's favourites, a shipwreck by Bakhuizen. She can hear the creak of masts, the howl of a tropical wind, the cries of drowning sailors, only their arms visible under thick spray. She has always hated this picture. Only Marin would have bought a painting of a shipwreck, she thinks: and stuck it above our heads in the dining room. A reminder of the peril of overreaching, inside a room of pleasure.

Soon, all the fritters have gone, the hen and the venison. The capons have been vanquished, their remains scattered on plates like shot, small blood-like splashes of Bordeaux upon the damask. Seated next to her aunt, Thea simulates docility, but inside her Nella sees a fire is burning. Thea stares into her glass, as if the dregs of her wine are an unfathomable ocean.

I was never like that at her age, Nella thinks. I did what I was told. Does she actually think I have arranged all this for my own amusement? Does she not think that I would rather be downstairs with Cornelia and Lucas, warming myself by the fire? Thea behaves as if she's the one doing us a favour. She's interested in nothing but herself, has no idea how the years will come upon her like a cat, waiting slyly round the corner.

Nella balls her fists in her lap, telling herself to be calm, be generous: *Remember what the girl was born into. She's not a bad child, just a bored one who doesn't have a clue how the world works.*

'A stove-house for the perfect pineapple, that is my dream,' says Caspar, and Otto's eyes are bright as he follows the botanist's movements with the salt cellar and water ewer he is using for some sort of demonstration. 'There are good ones on private estates already. There's Clara Sarragon and her husband. And those at Leeuwenhorst and Sorgvliet. Clingendael and Vijverhof, of course.'

Otto smiles. 'Petronella always tells me there is nothing to do in the country. Perhaps she's wrong.'

That wasn't me. That was Marin, Nella wants to say. But the last thing she is going to do right now is bring up Thea's mother.

Caspar looks surprised. He peers down the table. 'You know the countryside, Madame?'

'I did.'

Otto and Thea also turn towards her, as if expecting her to defend the longueurs of a country childhood. 'But my time in Assendelft was spent gathering apples,' she says. 'We knew nothing of these things. They were not for us.'

Jacob juts out his lower lip. 'But the world moves on.'

Nella feels rigid in her corset, mechanical in her mind. The dining room is glowing, but it feels like a prison. She has pulled her hair too tight under her cap and she wants to rip it off. After all her planning, all her work, she wants to yank the tablecloth past her waist. She wants to see the last of Johannes's crystal, his fine Delft bowls, his silver forks, tumble to the floor, to bounce or shatter on the pristine boards. To run upstairs and pull her hair pins. To blow out her candle and get under the covers. And yet the men keep talking.

'You have a point, I think, van Loos,' says Caspar. 'It moves on, and there's so much more to do. What one really needs is a stove-house for two hundred plants. Warmth in the winter, day and night. You could grow more than pineapples. Guava, mango. Passion flower, banana.'

'Think of the jam. The candied pieces. The flavoured rum. It would make a fortune,' Jacob says.

'But what you need for all of that,' Caspar says, lifting the salt cellar up, 'apart from the land, of course – is a connection to the VOC and the WIC.'

'Why?' asks Thea.

'Because both companies have a great advantage over these amateur aristocrats on their country estates,' Caspar replies. He speaks to her equally, as if she were a man. 'Most seeds and flowers enter this city through their trading routes. They hold the monopoly on what comes in and out. It's up to those who stay at home, as to whether they flourish or die. But it's expensive. Hence the aristocrats.' He sighs. 'Hence Clara Sarragon.'

'And how expensive *is* it, approximately?' Otto asks.

'Oh, thousands of guilders,' Caspar replies. 'And we need to do better than the orangery models and stove systems we already have. We need to secure soil and air temperatures, just as hot as they are in the Indies. We need to discover whether steam will work best. Whether it's tanner's bark that will stay hottest longer and keep the fruits growing.'

Nella has no concept of these wealthy private estates, these gardens, these plots to grow unfamiliar fruits. This ambition. *Tanner's bark* are not words in her lexicon. *Why are you here?* she wants to scream at Caspar. Pineapples and mangoes have conquered Cornelia's capons. Otto likes the disruption such a fanatic might bring to a supper with a suitor for his daughter, but Nella will not give in. And Jacob, despite the dominance of this talk of cultivation and cross-continent pollination, does seem to be enjoying himself. He takes out the small ivory box again and pinches out more tobacco, placing it delicately into the bowl of his pipe. He is going to cover us with clouds of smoke while we eat, Nella thinks. And we are going to let him.

Clutching at conversational straws, she says: 'I have often wondered how one keeps tobacco dry on board. How is it done?'

She has never wondered such a thing at all, yet prim, solic-itous, the question comes from her mouth. She is a woman, so she must enquire, must set up questions so a man might demonstrate his knowledge. Thea suppresses a yawn.

'It is a long and arduous process,' Jacob replies, reaching to the candle with a spill and lighting the contents of his bowl. 'Damp and salt, sunshine, darkness. Impossible at times.' He points behind him to the painted shipwreck. 'Have *you* any wish to travel abroad, Mistress Thea?'

Thea looks startled, but she pauses, appearing to think. 'I should like to see Paris and London,' she says. 'To go to Drury Lane, to see the actresses there. I should like to visit the Opéra.' Then she cuts the last of her fritter with concentration, eyes cast down, as if she has revealed something of herself she had been unwilling to give.

Paris, London, Drury Lane. They never speak of these places, and yet to Thea they seem so familiar. I think of shipwrecks and dead husbands, Nella muses, and Thea dreams of Paris? 'What's wrong with Amsterdam?' she asks, sounding far harsher than she intended. The party turns to her in surprise. She falters, glancing at Jacob. 'After all, in Amsterdam, any man can rise to brilliance.'

'Quite right,' says Jacob.

Caspar laughs. 'You really believe that?'

'It was true of my husband,' Nella says, trying not to bristle.

'Madame Brandt,' says Caspar, banging his long thighs on the underside of the table in his excitement, 'this is a city where about five families occupy every position of influence. They make sure their sons and nephews inherit all. They marry each other's daughters. The gold circle of power remains impenetrable and perpetual.'

Jacob makes another long exhalation of his pipe, the room filling with the scent of smoke and fennel. Nella is at the end of her patience. 'Well, you should know all about that, Mr

Witsen, working as you do for Clara Sarragon. Perhaps you enjoy the reflection of that gold circle very much?'

Caspar laughs. 'Oh, but that is not true.' Nella sees him glance at Otto. 'As of yesterday, I am no longer in her employ.'

'What?' she says, unable to conceal surprise. Clara Sarragon had seemed so sure of her possession.

'Yes, Madame. I've set myself free.'

'Free? To do what?'

'Seigneur van Loos,' Otto intervenes, before Caspar can reply. 'Tell us: how long have you had your house on the Prinsengracht? Is it one of those handsome new ones?'

Jacob takes a swig of wine. 'It's four years old, which is how long ago I purchased it. And yet it remains large and empty, except for myself and Mrs Lutgers, my housekeeper.' Hearing that Jacob himself has such a small staff, Nella feels relief. 'But I should like to fill it,' he goes on. 'Have a table like this one. Lots of faces around it, as when I was a boy. Good food and good cheer. I'm quite determined to make my own family tree. My own pedigree – however little a man like Witsen thinks it might count for.'

Jacob smiles, an honorary Amsterdammer: speaking his dream into being, declaring his purpose, speaking of his house therefore himself. Nella watches as Thea bows her head, smoothing the folds of her ruby dress, detaching once again from the evening.

Caspar laughs good-naturedly at the barb, but Nella thinks of the branches of Jacob's tree, sprouting higher to the sun, leaves dappling this shaky ground which they will finally cast off. They can begin again with a seedling. They *will* begin again, couched in Jacob's dream. Jacob van Loos is a rare specimen and they must keep him. Better still: they must make him want to stay.

'Let us retire to the salon,' she says. Enough of pineapples, of stove-houses, of allusions to her childhood in Assendelft. Nella looks up once more at the painted shipwreck. Marin would want me to fight for her daughter, even if her daughter doesn't like it, she thinks. She turns to the company with a new smile. 'A little lute before the gentlemen take their leave?'

'Excellent,' says Jacob. 'I always love to hear the lute.'

X

That night, Nella dreams of Assendelft.

Her childhood home shows no signs of life as she stands before its two broad storeys, red brickwork rising against white skies, the wind whipping loose her cap. The old trees of her father's house are withered sentinels, barren orchards that once held apple and cherry, now an army with no battle to fight. Her family's graves are in the apple orchard: Geert Oortman, her father; Petronella, her mother. Arabella and Carel, her siblings. All dead, as in real life, but she turns her back on them and walks round the house, pausing by the lake.

The body of water is large and murky, both on the surface and underneath. The Muscovy ducks have gone, but in the middle Nella spies her childhood boat, rotten, peeling, gliding towards her of its own accord. She knows that something terrible will happen when the boat touches the shore, that it must never reach her, and she whirls back towards the house.

The blank windows look down upon her, gaping holes with missing panes where sinuous vegetation writhes its way inside. It seems to be falling apart in front of her eyes, the holes in the roof widening as she stares up in horrified wonder. Surely she cannot go in there; but she can't stay by the lake. Above the room where Geert Oortman died, dissolved once and for all in his drink, the chimneys begin to crumble. Next to that is where her mother wept, hitting the walls with bruised fists, her mind unravelling. Down there is the room in which Nella met Johannes Brandt, and was married to him, so her life and his might begin again. The brickwork seems to ripple, each room barely holding in its sorrow.

Behind her, the boat bumps repeatedly against the edge of the shore. The horror of it chokes her. There is the sloshing sound of a body dragging itself from the lake, a pair of feet shifting on the gravel, and the footsteps grow louder. Finally, Nella springs to life, racing round the side of the house. The shadow is close at her heel, sopping wet, a wetness trying to lay a hand on her waist, sodden fingers fumbling for her skirts. Nella runs through the trees, tripping on roots, her cap strings flying, her bare feet sinking into the boggy earth, freezing cold and covered in dirt. She can barely move, but she must keep on. Screaming, she reaches for the door, and against her will she turns the handle, falling into whatever lies behind.

Nella wakes with a gasp. Lying in the dark in Amsterdam, her heart pounding, her sweat sticks her to the sheets. She lies there in silence. Has she actually screamed? She waits for a real door to open, for Cornelia's footsteps, an old friend poking round her head, candlelight flickering her concern. But no one comes. The dark flower that has bloomed inside her ribs begins to close, and her breath returns to normal.

Nella sits up in the bed where eighteen years ago she was supposed to begin again, and shakily puts a taper to a candle.

When you dream of childhood rooms, you are dreaming of your self. Or looking for her, at least. She lies back on her bed, staring into the cracks in the ceiling. It is the middle of the night: no sounds from the canal.

There was a Nella who existed before Amsterdam: before her dead husband, Johannes Brandt, and his dead sister, Marin. Before a family of gravestones under the Oortman trees. There was a person before all these ghosts who want something from her. A girl whose vision unspooled over a span of fields, who picked strawberries from the bushes at the door, who roamed under the vast skies of Assendelft, where cattle grazed on a horizon so low it looked as if God was driving them beneath it.

But even though these are facts, that child did exist, so did that house, those cows, those strawberries, Nella also knows how memory will prune your life, enlarge, diminish it. None of what you recall is exact. You may find yourself believing that there was beauty and bravery, certain that once you had it. But you cannot be sure.

From her linen drawer, Nella takes out the miniature baby and holds it tight. She puts her head on the pillow, willing herself to have peace. Till dawn, she tosses in her sheets, worrying about money, about whether Jacob will want to see Thea again, and why the windows of Assendelft moved, in her mind, like gaping maws.

❧

Later the following morning, exhausted, Nella eats alone in the working kitchen. Thea, already dressed, comes down the stairs and falters, as if she had been hoping to find Cornelia, or no one at all – to eat in peace, as Nella has been doing. It hurts to see how wary Thea looks, and when she makes as if to turn away, Nella calls her back.

'Thea? Wait.'

'I'm tired, Aunt Nella.'

'So am I. Can we talk about last night?'

But Thea stands on the stairs, refusing to move. 'Is Papa awake?'

'Not as far as I know.' Nella gazes at her niece's neat black dress, the scarf already round her neck. Lucas trots down the stairs and settles himself between two folds of Thea's skirts. 'It's not like you to be dressed this early.'

'My room's cold. There's never enough warmth in this house.'

'Some breakfast?'

'I'm not hungry.'

'I can cook some bacon, griddle a—'

'I'm not hungry.'

So Nella is not forgiven for last night. Neither for the ball, most likely. Nor for any of the past eighteen terrible years of Thea's life. She tries to gather herself. She says: 'I dreamed I was in Assendelft.' Thea looks up in surprise. Nella sees the spark of curiosity in her niece's eyes, which the girl quickly extinguishes. 'Well,' she adds. 'More a nightmare, really.'

Thea comes to sit opposite her aunt, her expression blank. She leans over and takes Nella's bacon rind. Nella lets her do it.

'It wasn't like the houses Caspar Witsen was describing,' Nella says. 'The opposite, in fact. Although I barely remember what it looks like in real life.'

It feels as if she has carried the fallen leaves of her father's dream orchards down from her bedroom into this warm room. Black and wet from the rain, they almost stick to her skin. Thea rips the bacon rind in two, dropping half of it on the floor for Lucas. She stuffs the other half into her mouth, chewing in unladylike fashion. Again, Nella passes no comment. She reaches down and pats Lucas's head.

'I do remember there were lots of animals where I grew up,' she says.

Still, Thea says nothing: Nella will have to work harder.

'Then again, none of the barns in Assendelft could compare to the creatures of Blue John's menagerie. Has he brought in new creatures this year, do you know? Have you been with Cornelia?'

Thea shrugs, remaining silent. They listen to the sounds of Lucas and his bacon.

'I think you're very lucky to have a place to escape to like that,' Thea says suddenly, with vehemence. 'A country house.'

Marry Jacob and you might get one yourself, Nella wants to say. But she is keen not to provoke, pleased to have finally extracted two full sentences. She never likes talking or thinking about Assendelft, and begins to regret even mentioning what she saw in her sleep last night. But here they are, talking civilly to one another, as other things rise up, dark shapes among her father's leaves.

'It was more of a farming place than a countryside idyll,' she says. 'But it fell apart.'

Thea frowns. 'Fell apart?'

Nella hesitates. 'To live there became difficult.'

'It couldn't have been any harder than living here,' Thea says.

'There was a lake.' Nella finds the breath in her throat running out. She cannot say more.

'I should like to see a lake,' Thea says. 'We don't even have a barge.'

Jacob could give you a barge. 'But sweeting,' Nella says: 'you cannot swim.'

'I can learn. Just because you can't do something *now* doesn't mean you won't be able in the future.'

'My brother and sister knew how to swim. Carel and Arabella.'

'Did they ever come to this house?'

'No. They were quite a bit younger than me. I was sent away to marry Johannes and set up my life in Amsterdam. From the beginning, I had so much to learn.' Nella thinks of how unwelcoming Marin was in the first few weeks, how hard she made it for Nella to feel she might fit in. 'I was learning how to be a wife,' she says. 'Trying to run a household. All that sort of thing.'

Nella looks at her niece. *All that sort of thing.* Her husband's secret male lover. Marin and Otto's secret connection. The efforts to sell sugar to keep the family afloat – and threaded through it all, the miniaturist. The miniaturist, always on the edge of her life, and living in its heart. Thea has no idea how it was and how much easier it could be for her! But Nella knows that she must always present a positive portrait of her marriage, otherwise Thea will never want to do it herself.

'I didn't think having them hanging on my skirts would be very helpful.'

'But what about when they were older? Didn't you want to see them?' Thea, sensing blood, leans forward. 'Didn't you *like* them?'

'Carel left home when he was thirteen. I would have liked to see him again. But I didn't.'

Thea's eyes widen. 'You never saw him again? Where did he go, Molucca?'

'Antwerp.'

Thea cannot help herself. She snorts. 'Just the edge of the world, then. And what happened to Arabella?'

Nella takes a deep breath. Arabella is a subject she enjoys thinking about even less than her parents. 'Our father died when I was seventeen, and I had to marry in order to secure a future. Arabella stayed in Assendelft with my mother,' she says, as if this is a sufficient summary of the life of Arabella. Catching Thea's expression, she adds: 'It was quite usual, what happened – the eldest daughter, leaving to marry. The boy, striking out alone to seek his fortune.'

But Nella knows that it is not usual for a boy from such a 'good' family to take to the road at thirteen, for his eldest sister to never communicate with the home she'd left behind. She thinks of Jacob, of the neat little trio of van Loos brothers. Landowner, soldier, lawyer, such easy archetypes, still orbiting round their mother. It is not the family life she has known, but then again: nor has anyone who has grown up in this house on the Herengracht.

'And what happened to them?' Thea asks. 'After you married my uncle, and Carel ran away?'

Nella wants Otto to wake up, to come downstairs and pull her out of these uncomfortable memories. But in her mind she is confronted with an image of her mother. Mrs Oortman had once been an attractive, plump and competent woman, but all Nella can see is the sight of her mother, driving her head against her bedroom wall. She feels the click inside herself, when the moment came to take her by the arms, her dead eyes fixated upon the Assendelft lake. She recalls the softness of her mother's skin, the dabbing of her broken, bleeding forehead with a square of cotton. The endless guiding her into that unmade bed. Arabella, too young, wide-eyed at the door, watching her sister avoid their mother's snagged fingernails, her sour breath. The guttural recriminations in the woman's throat. At times, it was like being children of an animal.

To avoid Thea's enquiring gaze, Nella looks down at the remains of her breakfast. They did not look after themselves in Assendelft. The tattered reputation of their father worked its way inside them, and when her mother hurt herself to let his demon out, it was Arabella who saw that demon most of all.

The guilt surges inside Nella, so unbearable that she has to move away to the fire under the pretence of fetching more hot water for her coffee-pot.

'My mother had good days,' she says, trying to control her shaking voice.

She realizes that Thea has no conception of what she's talking about. How could she even begin to catalogue for Thea what it was like to live in a world made entirely of your mother's fantasies? The accusations, the fabrications of a world that wasn't there? No descriptions, no account, could ever encompass the degradation and powerlessness that permeated Assendelft, a reality they kept so well hidden in order to get Nella married, to get her to Amsterdam, to restore at least some degree of normality to the Oortman name, whether Nella wanted to or not.

'My mother wasn't well,' she tries again. 'She found it hard to hold on . . . to what was real.'

Her mother, staring out at the lake, something inside its currents taking its message towards her, in a language only she could understand. 'She died about a year after I came to Amsterdam,' Nella says.

Thea places her palms face down on the table. 'And . . . how did she die?'

Nella feels a blockage, somewhere in her ribs. 'She drowned in the lake.'

Thea is silent for a moment. Her gaze slides away, as if she is picturing this scene of loss, piecing together a place she has never visited, with a woman she will never meet.

Underneath her reluctance to talk of all these things, Nella cannot help registering a guilty sliver of satisfaction. So now you know, she thinks. You're not the only one with a missing mother. This is what you get when you ask questions.

'We don't know if she meant to drown,' she says. 'But she did. They buried her in the apple orchard, beside my father.'

Thea is astounded. 'But – what happened to Arabella? Why didn't she come and live here?'

Nella feels her hands twist together, almost of their own accord. 'I didn't know for quite a while that my mother was dead.'

'*What?*'

'Carel was away. I had no correspondence with Assendelft.'

'But why?'

'I just didn't,' Nella snaps. She takes a deep breath, turning round to the kitchen table. 'Not everyone is close to their family.'

'But Arabella would have been very young!'

'And you were even younger, Thea. You were so little.'

'And Arabella?'

'She was nine. But you were my purpose.'

134

Thea looks agog. 'Are you saying it was my fault?'

'Of course I'm not.' Nella feels almost breathless.

'But she was your sister,' Thea says. 'She was nine. If I had a sister, *I* would have gone back.'

'How do you know what you would have done? Arabella was perfectly happy.'

'How do *you* know, if you never went to see her?'

Nella grips the edge of the kitchen table. 'She loved Assendelft. I arranged it so that she stayed in the house with our last remaining servant. She grew up looking after the animals and gardens.'

'I can't believe you never went back.'

'There was so much going on in Amsterdam – it was what happened, Thea. That's what happens in life, you know. You can't always squeeze it into a neat, three-act play. You can't be in two places at once.'

Thea is silent, but Nella knows that her niece is marinating in the ecstasy and outrage of rich new information.

She feels a little dizzy, as if she's come down here to confess, to cast herself in a poor light. She has failed to give Thea her side of things – what it was like to grow up amongst that army of her father's trees, encircled by her parents' marriage. And what happened after, with her mother. She has made herself look heartless, a survivor at others' cost. Perhaps this is the lesson she is trying to impart: what Thea needs to do in this life to make it better for herself. But all she has succeeded in doing is make herself seem monstrous.

Before Nella can spill open any more, pulling those awful days out of herself – the letter that had come from Arabella, detailing the final hours of their mother's life before the drowning, the description of her body after, and Nella's decision not to tell Otto and Cornelia a word of it – there are footsteps, finally, at the top of the kitchen stairs.

Nella turns, grateful that Otto has risen and they can begin the real day. She can banish that boggy lake from her mind, the mutating windows of that house, the image of her bloated mother, and Arabella, left behind. But it's Cornelia who descends into the warmth of the kitchen, wearing a look of concern, clutching a small envelope.

Nella's whole body thrills with excitement, almost a conviction, that she will see that old, familiar handwriting, finally addressed to her. Another miniature, after all these years. But she notices how Thea gets to her feet, how, on seeing the note in Cornelia's outstretched hand, Thea seems riven with expectation. From whom could Thea be expecting a note?

'It's from van Loos,' Cornelia says. She looks at Nella. 'Addressed to you.'

Thea sits back down and Nella feels a similar deflation. 'You were expecting something?' Nella asks.

'No,' says Thea. 'Were you?'

'A message from Jacob.'

'Well then. Your wish is granted. Aren't you going to open it?'

Nella breaks open the seal and scans the message, unable to hide a smile. Her plan is working, after all. 'Oh, Thea,' she says. 'Jacob has invited us to the playhouse, in a week's time. To seats in a *box*.'

Cornelia narrows her eyes. 'You don't like the playhouse.'

'Jacob is taking us to the playhouse?' Thea looks stricken.

'Yes. What's wrong with that?'

'He doesn't like the playhouse either,' says Thea. 'If that terrible book he bought me is anything to go by.'

'He brought you a *gift*,' Nella says, trying to control her irritation.

'All things considered, I'd have preferred a pineapple. What did you do with the one that Caspar gave you? I haven't seen it in the salon.'

'Don't mention pineapples to me,' Nella says. 'Ask Cornelia. It was hardly my area of expertise.'

Cornelia flushes. 'It's in the pantry with the potatoes,' she says. 'I don't know what to do with it.'

Thea sighs. 'According to Jacob's book, girls who attend the playhouse suffer shamelessness and looseness of speech.'

'Perhaps he has a point.'

Thea folds her arms. 'Cornelia can use his pages to wrap her cheese, for all I care. That *gift* put a cold finger down my back. Why did Jacob think I might like it?'

'It put a what?' says Nella sharply.

Thea sighs. 'Nothing.'

'This invitation is good news, Thea. Very good news! The dinner worked.'

'I wonder why you sound so grateful, Aunt. You and I could have always seen a play together, if that was what you wanted.'

Nella chooses to disregard Thea's face of rage. She ignores Cornelia's expression of discomfort. She clutches Jacob's note tightly in her fist, and the bricks of her childhood turn once more to dust.

XI

It explains so *much*, Thea fumes, as she hurries towards the Schouwburg. Aunt Nella always talks as if she was dragged from the countryside and forced to marry Johannes Brandt. But she couldn't wait to get away! It means *nothing* to her to have abandoned her poor family. No wonder she never talks about her childhood. The morning's conversation has showed Thea nothing but Aunt Nella's typical ruthlessness, and it makes Thea sick. No wonder she has no quibbles about ordering me off to be married, Thea thinks: nor cares about telling me anything about Marin Brandt! Why would she, having being so willing to let her own mother drown and never talk about it, and to abandon her child of a sister to live with some cowhand?

I would have taken Arabella under my wing, Thea tells herself, walking so fast her boots hit hard against the cobbles. Held her tight. *And* I would have been there to rescue my mother from the lake.

She makes her way onto the Keizersgracht, wanting Walter close, wanting her own secrets. Even alone she can physically feel the miracle of him – in her belly, in her throat, in the tips of her fingers. To think that they should be tied together in these invisible ways, and not a single person around them can see! She wants Walter so much that she wishes she could climb into his head, take up space inside his ribs. She wants nothing between their bodies; she doesn't want him to do anything without her.

As she approaches the back of the playhouse, Thea can't help looking around, her neck prickling as if someone might be watching. She stands for a moment, scanning the flow of citizens, but no one has their eyes upon her. When she turns back towards the playhouse, the sensation fades: Amsterdam is busy with its own affairs as usual, a sweet relief.

But at the back door, the guard is new. When Thea makes to move past him with a nod, he stops her. 'Where are you going?' he asks.

She stares at him. 'Is Rebecca Bosman here?'

'What's it to you?'

'I'm Thea.' She feels hot, a little foolish. 'I'm her friend.'

'If I let everyone in who says they're Madame Bosman's friend.' The guard lands heavily on the last word, as if the notion of such a friendship for Thea is dubious.

'Is it money you want?' Thea asks, drawing herself up to full height. The guard narrows his eyes, but before he can say any more, she spies Walter walking down the corridor behind him. 'Walter!' she calls. 'There's been a misunderstanding.'

Walter turns. For a strange, fleeting moment, it's as if he doesn't recognize her. Thea feels weightless, vaguely sick, but the guard breaks the spell. 'You know this young lady?'

'I do,' says Walter.

'*Really?*'

'Really. You can let her through.'

Grudgingly, the guard steps aside. Thea moves past him without a second glance. Once they have turned the corner, she throws her arms around Walter's neck.

'Thea. Not here.'

'But aren't you pleased to see me?'

'You can't hang about me like that in public.'

'This isn't public. There's no one here,' she says, but she drops her arms and walks alongside him as Walter paces the labyrinth of corridors towards his room.

'*Life Is A Dream* opens in a week,' he says. 'You can't be here too long. I'm sorry.'

'Of course,' she says. 'I understand.' But she doesn't, not really: not when she knows she could be perfectly silent, sitting in the corner, watching him paint. She wants to confess to him that she will be there when the play opens, but Walter doesn't like it when she mentions Jacob Someone, so she says nothing. Walter cannot be pushed. He needs to honour his contract with the Schouwburg. She must be patient: the tropical beaches need their time.

Just as they near the painting-room door, Thea slips her hand into Walter's, and Rebecca turns the corner. The actress breaks into a smile, but Thea sees her momentary blink of dismay, her eyes on their entwined hands. Walter drops her hand, but the actress's discontent with what she's seeing is palpable.

'Thea!' Rebecca says. 'How lovely it is to see you. I hope the dress worked well?'

Walter takes up her hand again, squeezing it tightly in collusion, and Thea thinks of the stain spreading on Rebecca's gold fabric, Walter, his torso bare, dabbing at her dress with a rag. 'Oh, yes. Yes it did,' she says. 'Thank you. It was so kind of you and Fabritius.'

There is a brief, awkward silence. 'Are you rehearsing?' Thea asks.

'I am,' says Rebecca. 'But a small respite for a quarter-hour. Come and join me in my room?'

'I should like that. Walter was just going to show me his new sets. Then I could knock on your door?'

But Rebecca turns to Walter. 'May I borrow her now? Fifteen minutes is not that long.'

Walter stiffens. He and Rebecca face each other, their eyes locked. Rebecca smiles and Walter turns the door handle of his painting-room. 'Of course,' he says, pushing open the door. 'You're free to do whatever you wish.'

In Rebecca's room, Thea hovers at the threshold, worried at having to be in two places at once. 'So,' Rebecca says gently, closing the door and leading Thea to a chair. 'How was the ball?'

Thea shrugs. 'Tiring.'

'You didn't meet any good young men?'

'I didn't need to. But my aunt found one she liked, although she says she wants him for me. His name is Jacob.'

Rebecca sits opposite Thea and pours them both small glasses of wine. 'Do you like him?'

'No.'

Rebecca takes a sip. She places her glass down and reaches out for Thea's hand. 'Thea,' she says. 'I want to give you some advice. About Walter.'

Thea pulls her hand away. 'I don't need it.'

Rebecca sighs, running a hand over her neatly pressed russet hair. 'Thea,' she says, lowering her voice, 'I know you love him. I know yours is an honourable love. And I have enjoyed seeing you so happy. But . . . I feel that I must speak.'

'It is not your place to speak,' Thea says. 'You are not on stage now.'

Rebecca's eyes widen. 'But—'

'I'm old enough to know my own heart!'

'But are you old enough to know his?'

This question, uttered so gently, stings. It hurts to have her lover and herself so doubted, by Rebecca, of all people. Thea recalls the hostility in Walter's voice when speaking of her – the only time she has heard such a tone from him. *She's a strange, lonely woman.* What does he know, that Thea does not? Rebecca has never seemed strange to Thea, but perhaps she *is* lonely. Walter has seen more of the world than Thea has, and he sees these things more clearly.

'I'm not trying to ruin this for you,' Rebecca says. 'I'm trying to protect you.'

Thea stares at her in disbelief. 'From what?'

'What do you truly know of him?' Rebecca urges. 'What has he promised?'

'I know he loves me. And I know things you can only pretend onstage.'

'Thea—'

'Stop it, Rebecca. We are betrothed.'

The actress looks stunned. '*What?* How far has this gone?'

For a moment, Thea wants to tell Rebecca everything. She wants to boast and crow and strut, to give her friend the full picture so that she might finally understand. But then she thinks of Walter's anger over the doll, his intense discomfort at the thought that anyone but them should know their business. She thinks of how she has felt so watched throughout her life, along these canals. She takes a deep breath. 'I know he can be difficult sometimes. But that's only because he wants to do things the right way.'

'The right way,' Rebecca scoffs. 'For whom?'

'For *us*.'

Rebecca closes her eyes.

'You know nothing of him,' Thea snaps. She feels miserable; she did not come here to argue with her only friend.

Rebecca's eyes are hard. '*Exactly*. He doesn't mix with us here.'

'Because he's busy! And he's not an actor, Rebecca – he's an artist, and you should respect that. I thought you were different. I thought you looked at me and saw a woman, an equal—'

'I *do*. Which is why I'm talking to you—'

'You're talking to me as if I'm a child. As if I do not know my own mind. You're no better than my aunt. You cannot see what true love is. I pity you.'

Rebecca raises her hands in surrender. 'Enough,' she says. The atmosphere between them is so sour, Thea can almost taste it. 'Very well: if that is what you wish. I'll speak no further. Believe it or not, I am capable of that.'

Thea rises to her feet and makes her way to Rebecca's door. She opens it and stands in the corridor, her head turned in the direction of Walter's painting-room.

'Soon it won't be a secret,' she says. 'And *then* you'll see. This isn't make-believe.'

'I know it's not,' says Rebecca. 'And that is the real pity.'

Arriving home an hour later, Thea is startled to find Cornelia in the hallway. 'Where have you been?' the maid says, her tone almost rough.

'For a walk. That's allowed, isn't it?'

As Cornelia approaches, Thea can see how pale her old nursemaid is, how she wrings her hands, her eyes darting back and forth along the canal path behind Thea's head. Cornelia closes the door. 'And where did you walk?'

'Nowhere far.' The maid's expression is haunted. 'Cornelia, what *is* it?'

Cornelia hurries over. 'A little parcel came addressed to you,' she whispers.

A dark thrill runs through Thea's body. 'A little parcel?'

'I found it when I was mopping the front step,' Cornelia says. 'Who would be leaving a parcel for you on the front step, without knocking?'

'Where is it?'

'It's over here,' Cornelia hisses, wiping her hands on her apron and stalking over to a hall chair.

A little parcel rests on the seat, smaller and even more compact than the first one. It looks as if there is something hard inside it, the shape of a small box. Cornelia picks the parcel up as if it might be contaminated, and Thea feels a rush of possessiveness. She wants to be the only one to hold it, to rip open the paper, to reveal its insides. She wants to be alone with it. She remembers Walter's horror at the doll of himself and feels a faint beat of dread in her veins.

She comes forward to take it but Cornelia snatches it to her chest. 'I shouldn't give it to you,' she says.

'I beg your pardon?'

'Who might be sending you parcels?'

Thea thinks quickly. 'Eleonor Sarragon.'

'Why would she be sending you anything?' Cornelia asks, making a face.

'It's *mine*, Cornelia. Hand it to me. It's got my name on it, see?' Still, Cornelia grips tightly to this little offering. 'Sweet Jesu, what's wrong with you?'

'There's nothing wrong with me.'

'Then why are you so frightened? It's just a ring Eleonor was going to lend me,' Thea says, smoothly. 'I didn't think she was serious.' She smiles. 'But here we are.'

Cornelia stares down at the parcel. Plausibly, Thea supposes it *could* contain a ring inside a box, but she knows that Eleonor would never inconvenience herself this way, nor ever be that generous, and Cornelia must know that.

'Eleonor Sarragon has lent you a ring?' says Cornelia.

'Just to borrow. Just for a bit.' Lightly, Thea prises the parcel from the claw of her nursemaid's fingers. Immediately, she feels a sort of promise in her fingertips, a hidden allure.

'Open it then,' Cornelia says. 'I'd like to see this ring.'

Thea is shocked at this directness. 'Not if you speak like that.'

'You don't *understand*,' says Cornelia, looking stricken. 'When packages come like this, little ones, unmarked . . . you have to be careful.'

'You're not making sense!'

Cornelia twists her fingers together. 'There are . . . *things* that have happened in this house, Thea. Before you were born.'

'*Everything* happened before I was born. Tell me what exactly, and I will show you the ring.'

Cornelia stares at the parcel. 'Your father, your aunt – they would be angry if I—'

'Fine. Keep their secrets. We're a family who lives for them. We love to hide ourselves away, so that means I too am allowed to open a gift in privacy, seeing as we value it so much.'

'But not if . . .' Cornelia grabs Thea by her arms and Thea is shocked by her strength. 'Thea, we've worked so hard to protect you.'

'Don't worry about me. I can assure you, it would take more than a little ring to turn my head. I know what a viper Eleonor Sarragon is.'

Cornelia lets Thea go. 'If you're certain it's from her,' she says, sounding miserable.

By now, Thea is so impatient to be upstairs alone, that she almost believes that they live in a world where Eleonor Sarragon might bother to send her a friendship ring. 'I am,' she says, moving away as carelessly as she can up the staircase, towards her bedroom.

'Teapot?'

Thea takes a deep breath and turns round. 'Yes?'

Cornelia is almost tearful. 'Just be careful. *Promise* me you'll be careful.'

'I will.'

Mystified by Cornelia's intensity, Thea locks her bedroom door, climbs onto her bed and sits with the parcel on her lap. Until this month, she has never received presents from anyone outside her family, and she wonders, with a brief sinking of her heart, whether it might be a second gift from Jacob van Loos. Eleonor Sarragon was a weak story. Jacob would have been a better excuse to use to push Cornelia away. Maybe this time it could be a book of homilies on how a woman can be a good wife.

But it isn't a book. It's far too small. Slowly, Thea unties the string and unfolds the paper.

She blinks, dazzled by the beauty before her.

There, resting in cushions of sheep's wool, is a most exquisite tiny golden house. It is the size of a large peach stone, glimmering up at her from its protective bed. But when Thea lifts it up, she realizes that it has not been cast from gold, but rather carved in wood and gilded with gold leaf. It is lighter than she had imagined, and as she shakes it, she suspects it's been hollowed out. The house has a large front door, with windows either side. On the first floor are three more windows. It has a tiled roof and six chimneys, and as Thea rotates it, she sees there are windows on all four sides of the piece. The brickwork and the tiles of the roof have been carved into the wood. The door has tiny hinges and a handle, but however hard Thea tries to pull it, it will not budge.

She puts it on the table beside her, mesmerized by its enigma. It's not as alarming to her as the doll of Walter. It is purely enchanting. It is not a house she has seen before. But it has been so carefully made, as if it should be stored already in her memory.

Thea sits back against her pillows and stares at this empty, beautiful, inaccessible house, and is reminded of the stark surprise of Walter's miniature palette. Reaching for the box under her bed, she unlocks it and lifts out his doll.

She has been doing this every night, a ritual of devotion and assurance, and by now she has memorized the proportions of his minimized limbs. Walter stares up at her, her lover: her husband to be. Thea keeps switching her attention between Walter and the house. Their sizes are not equivalent. She can see no connection between them. Who is sending her these things, and why? Who in this city, apart from Walter, could be capable of such suggestive detail and artistry?

She considers Cornelia's paranoid behaviour downstairs, her feverish urges for Thea to confess who the sender might be. *There are . . . things that have happened in this house, Thea. Before you were born.*

No, Thea tells herself: you're not Cornelia. You don't live in the past, and you're not scared.

Rebecca once told Thea that when she was a young actress, she would often become frustrated with audiences. They would laugh when she wanted them to be moved. They would come together and weep over a piece she was approaching with levity. She told Thea that she realized that she had no control over them at all. If they saw her as evil, it came from their own fear. If they sympathized, that came from their own hearts, not from anything she did.

It had seemed strange to Thea, hearing that. She had assumed that Rebecca was someone with great power to influence, and a retainer of that power. The secret is to hand the audience the power, Rebecca had told her. Give them a mirror. Show them themselves, and they will be greedy for it.

Thea holds the doll of Walter in one hand, and in the other the shining house. She has experienced a lifetime of being looked at in this city, but there has never been a mirror; the staring people of Amsterdam look at Thea until she feels everything except her own self. That is why this attention, the offering of these miniatures, feels different. Personal. Solidifying. It feels just as Rebecca said: as if they are a glass in which Thea is gazing into herself. And just like Rebecca's captivated audience, Thea is greedy to know more.

A Hot-House

XII

There are several reasons why Nella does not like the play-house. The price of the tickets, for one. The heat from the candles. The air-sawing, the declamatory pomp – and that is just the audience, so often smug and self-satisfied, pretending to be edified when really it just turns up to spy on itself, to feel naughty in the face of the preachers' consternation. But in Jacob's box, with a fine view of the stage, and at a remove from the bodies who make her nervous, Nella thinks she might be contented enough, if it brings them a step closer to a potential marriage. She peers over the balcony: the way money elevates you, literally, metaphorically! She feels like a hawk in her nest, looking down at the little heads beneath.

Her husband's lover was an actor, and Nella has had a prejudice against them ever since. Jack Phillips had been a young man from England, pretending to die on their hallway tiles, before using his wound to accuse Johannes of an attempt at murder. His involvement with Johannes's execution might have been enough cause for Nella to hate anyone who makes a living deceiving others for their own gain, but she suspects she cannot generalize. Jack was Jack. And actors are not deceivers, Thea insists: they are fabricators of truth.

Nella looks to the stage. This Rebecca Bosman, for example: now, she is good. Subtle, musical, very alluring. Nella steals a glance at Thea, expecting her to look enraptured by her favourite actress, but Thea is stone-faced. There are dark circles under her eyes. She could at least put on a performance to half-match what's unfolding on the stage, but she has been this way all week, ever since they received Jacob's invitation.

And as for Jacob, Nella can't lean forward to check. She can see only his hands in his lap, still as caught fishes, glinting with three gold rings. Otto does not care to adorn himself, save for an earring now and then, but here is a man in favour of rubies.

Nella closes her eyes, imagining the wedding: Thea, radiant, Jacob, steadfast and pleased; a goodly spread of food but nothing boastful, a new beginning but a final sense of safety.

She feels buoyant, proud of herself. She has schemed since before last winter that they might be sitting here, on the cusp of February, with a man so eligible that all the merchant daughters of Amsterdam would want him. Those little bitches will have to slink off unsatisfied, in their new skirts and courting bonnets, for Jacob has chosen Thea Brandt. A new play at the Schouwburg, and he has chosen Thea to put on show in his box.

Occasionally from below, or from the other boxes, someone might peer at them, one of whom looks decidedly like Clara Sarragon, fluttering her fan – and although Nella and Thea are used to being looked at, this time it's different. It's different when you're sitting next to Jacob van Loos.

Thea appears to be scanning those below her, as though in search of someone. Who is it she seeks, when Rebecca is so masterfully commanding their attention? Before Nella can whisper the question, Thea turns to her aunt and asks quietly:

'Do you not think it has been so prettily set, Aunt Nella? Do you see those individual conches, scattered on the shore?'

Nella peers at the stage. It is a wondrous scene of a beach: the painter – or painters? she knows nothing of these things, but there is an awful lot of painting down there – have outdone themselves. The backdrops seem to have advanced somewhat from her memory of bringing Thea here as a child. The palm trees and shores look disturbingly lifelike, not that Nella would be able to compare them to any lived reality she has known. Only apple trees grow in her memories, and the spread of a dark black lake. She cannot see the conches, and is surprised that Thea can be so specific. Maybe her eyes are weakening? 'I see them,' she lies. 'The whole scene is beautiful. It's extraordinary what they can do these days. Whoever made them has a talent.'

She is rewarded by the unexpected sight of Thea's serious face breaking open into a bright smile. The little pearls in Thea's ears shake as she turns back with delight to the story on the stage. She really does love the playhouse.

Within five minutes the end of the act is upon them. Soon the space is full of noise, the orchestra making merry music to encourage the audience to good cheer. The three of them shift in their seats, and Jacob turns to Thea. 'Are you enjoying it?'

Thea looks suffused with delight. Nella's heart swells: such a look always shows Thea at her best. 'Oh, very much, Seigneur,' Thea says. 'I think Madame Bosman is over-acting a little. But I am enraptured by the settings.' She looks back down to the sets, and Jacob looks enchanted.

'I know you have expressed a desire to visit London and

Paris, Mistress Thea –' *He remembered*, Nella thinks – 'but might you ever wish to visit a scene like the one before us now? Not under the cloak of tragedy, of course.'

Thea looks at him blankly, and Jacob sweeps his arm over the edge of the box, towards the painted flats. 'I refer to the setting that enraptures you so much. The hot beach.'

Thea's former effusion is so vanished as to make her look severe. 'No,' she says. 'For me those palm trees are real. I have no need to see their likeness elsewhere.'

Jacob smiles, glossing over her froideur. 'But the colour of the sky? None of that tempts you? I have heard of such places. Hot places, strange places. I would see them myself.'

Nella holds her breath. Thea places a hand on her heart. 'You don't understand, Seigneur. I have seen them here.'

Now it is Jacob's turn to look at her blankly. Thea rises to her feet. 'Would you please excuse me? I must . . .' She trails off, as if embarrassed in front of Jacob to hint at feminine needs. The young man jumps to his feet and bows, but Thea has already moved towards the curtains covering the door to their box. In seconds, she has gone.

Nella, unsure of what has just happened, but keen to regain the atmosphere of intimacy, of talk of travel and pleasure, reaches for the decanter of punch for which Jacob has paid. She pours him a glass, smiling as she does, offering reassurance that this is all very normal behaviour from their beloved young woman, who sees palm trees in her heart.

'I haven't seen Thea this animated in many months,' she says. 'You inspire it in her.'

Jacob sips at his punch. 'You have raised her since she was a baby, have you not?'

His question settles on her oddly, coming from nowhere, delving all the way back to the beginning of things, whereas Nella would rather dwell on the minutes at hand. But she must be accommodating, must show that nothing he asks is beyond her composure.

'I have,' she says. Nella thinks briefly of the baby hidden in her bedroom, stolen from the miniaturist's workshop on the Kalverstraat eighteen years ago, the tiny baby that wasn't hers. Would things have been different if she'd left it behind? There is no way to tell. No way to ask the miniaturist, to force her to explain. 'But I have not done it alone,' she adds. 'Thea's father has been instrumental. And Cornelia, who still lives with us.'

'But it is very sad that she should not have a mother. Was the lady a gentlewoman?' Jacob asks, drawing the question down swiftly on the heels of his sympathy.

Nella feels her head swim. That Thea's mother is sadly dead, has become easy enough to say. That Thea never knew her, also consigns Marin to a dark part of their memories that supposedly has no bearing on the present day. But these descriptors are the thin end of the wedge. Marin's name is never mentioned in public. Gentlewoman, yes. Merchant's sister, businesswoman, too. Also, a sphinx. Cruel when she wanted to be. Clever, and also caring. She endured until she did not. A woman who shared her bed with her brother's manservant, and kept their dealings secret. It's impossible to begin.

Jacob wonders about it, Nella realizes. He wonders who this missing woman is who left behind her child.

Does it matter? she wants to say, feeling exhausted. Does it matter if Marin was a laundress, or a pastry-maker, or the illegitimate child of the city's richest regent? Marin isn't here. But I've been here, for eighteen years.

'She was a gentlewoman,' she says.

There is a long silence. 'You are a close family,' he observes.

'Well. There are no secrets between us.'

Jacob looks back to the stage and takes another sip of his punch. 'Thea has a great deal of passion.'

Nella cannot divine his tone. 'Haven't all eighteen-year-old women?'

'No,' Jacob says, so bluntly that it shocks her. How many eighteen-year-old women has he known? 'Thea has an excess of spirit,' he says.

Nella absorbs what feels like a blow to her own body. Thea's spirit is in fine balance, she wants to say, although over these past weeks, it can hardly be claimed as true. She pours herself a drink, sipping it gingerly as if tasting the currents of this conversation. 'Her mother was a very active person.'

Jacob turns to her, curious. 'Active?'

'I always think it is far better to have a woman who is active. Healthy, interested. Such qualities also could be termed an excess of spirit. But they are required in our world, our city, Seigneur. One would not want a weak, sick sort of woman.'

'One would not,' Jacob replies. 'And yet she died in child-birth.'

Nella grips the edge of the balcony. The callousness of it makes her want to snap the stem of her glass. She wills herself into serenity.

'It was very unfortunate,' she says. Suddenly, she is in that dying room with Cornelia, eighteen years ago, watching in horror as Marin slipped from their grasp. 'Her mother was older than the usual woman.'

Forgive me, Marin, she says silently. *Forgive me, forgive me. You would do the same.*

And as Nella sits there, in the luxury of this man's playhouse box, so ashamed of the things she is saying, she realizes that she does often sound like Marin in these instances. As if she is drawing her bucket from deep in the well of what Marin has left behind. That persistence, that cold-eyed realism, under which Marin buried such flights of fancy.

Does Jacob want me to carry on? Nella wonders. Is he really interested? Or does he want me to close my fishwife's mouth and let him drink his punch in peace?

She shivers, as if the draughts of the Herengracht mansion are on her skin. Perhaps it is obvious to Jacob van Loos – the pitiful way they must scrabble together a stage-set to impress a suitor, out-dazzled by the real show below. But Jacob seems unfazed, as if this is just any other conversation. Nella admonishes herself silently and sits up straight, thinking of their ledger books, of the sums that have dwindled now they can no longer even rely on the salary from the VOC. The options are narrowing. Again; Marin would do the same.

'Thea is too special to moulder away on the Herengracht,' she says bluntly.

Her words are as direct as his. They hold truth. They force Jacob to turn to her and she pushes on. 'I have noticed,' she says, drawing her skirts around her, 'that Thea is always delighted to come and see the plays which end in marriage.'

'Is that so?'

'Yes. And she is ready, I believe. It is what she desires. Thea will not say it herself, but for the right man, she will marry. And he will be a lucky man.'

'He will.'

Nella's mind is racing. Where has Thea got to? She remembers how Jacob had walked into their hallway, how he'd tipped his head back with pleasure, staring into their *trompe l'oeil*. 'Of course, Thea is the sole heir to everything,' she says.

There is another long silence. She waits, hardly able to breathe properly. Is it enough to convince him, a house with one of the best addresses in the city?

'So the property on the Herengracht will be hers,' he says.

'Yes.'

'I assumed no less.' Jacob stares out into the auditorium. His expression is unreadable. 'But what do you think would keep her happy, Madame Brandt, other than her trips to the playhouse?'

Nella hesitates. It has been a few years too long since she could tell what would make Thea happy. 'I think the gentleman in question would have to ask Thea herself.'

Jacob glances at Thea's vacated seat. She has been gone a long time, and it makes Nella uncertain. 'I do not like the playhouse much,' he replies. 'I prefer the blood and guts of real life. And yet I see how much Thea enjoys it.' He pauses. 'Would you say she is a . . . fanciful person?'

'Far from it. You are perceptive enough to see that yourself. Thea may love the playhouse, but she is sensible. She has experienced, perhaps more than other girls her age, the potential abrasiveness of society.'

He looks thoughtful. 'And the playhouse is her escape?'

Nella closes her fan and uses it to indicate what is left of the audience. 'In this city, is it not everyone's, who can afford it?'

'I suppose.'

'But Thea understands life in a way these people do not. Her understanding is a great asset. And so it would be, to any husband.'

Jacob frowns. 'I don't want a wife who is too worldly.'

Nella forces herself not to look at him. Jacob, not she, has uttered the word *wife*, and it hovers between them, like a column of light, of life. A world of marriage, and Jacob has stepped inside it.

'Thea is not worldly,' she says. 'She sees the world, but does not immerse herself in it. As is right for the daughter of a gentleman and a lady. That is why she comes to the playhouse. She is at one remove, raised with dignity.'

Jacob says nothing. Nella holds fast, waiting to see what will come. She knows that there are easier brides out there. Those obvious daughters, with their families long enmeshed in the nets of Amsterdam's elites – but remember, Nella, she tells herself: it is your niece he has invited.

'It's strange,' Jacob observes after a while. 'When your niece has gone, things do seem a little less bright.'

⋖§⋗

After the play is over, he insists on walking them back along the Keizersgracht. Nella makes sure that she is on the edge of the party, a few steps behind, allowing the pair to speak alone but with decorum. Jacob is attendant to whatever it is Thea is saying, and for all the world they seem like a married couple already, walking with leisure, wrapped in furs against the night.

At the playhouse, Thea had returned to Jacob's box, blushing, hurried, taking her seat with a quick smile in his direction before the action began again. Her flushed cheeks suggested that she knew they'd been talking about her: maybe that had been her purpose in leaving them alone in the first place? And here she is, post-performance, gesticulating with her hands into the cold air of the Golden Bend, enthused by something, at least. Jacob, looking up at her, listening to her fluency, acknowledging her passion. Nella has not given up hope: not at all.

At their front door, candlelight glows through the salon windows, and Nella cannot understand it. Otto never sits in there alone, and Cornelia does not like the room. For a moment, it seems as if someone else lives in her house, and its rhythms and routines are unknown to her. Jacob hands Thea up the front steps, and Nella notices the way her niece inclines her head briefly to examine the doorstep. Their step is bare, but at least here is other bounty, their potential future, in the shape of this young lawyer.

'Good night, ladies,' he says. 'A very pleasant evening.'

Nella comes to join them on the step. 'Thea, did you enjoy it?'

Thea fixes a serene gaze upon her aunt. 'It was special to be able to see the entire stage from such advantage. It helped me better understand the story.' She tips her chin, smiling. 'I feel extremely clarified.'

It is an odd word to choose. Thea delivers it with a flourish, turning to lift the dolphin knocker before letting it drop with a heavy thud. Nella falters, turning to Jacob, desperate to sew the evening up with grace, a promise of more to come, before Cornelia opens the door.

'Seigneur van Loos, we have been honoured tonight,' she says.

Jacob removes his hat and waves her words away. A play-house box is nothing to him, Nella supposes, financially, or spiritually. She wonders if he, too, sitting through this evening, now understands this story better. She herself feels as if she's missing some of the threads. A sudden worry washes over her that they might never see him again.

The front door remains inexplicably closed, and for a mad moment Nella thinks that this house is indeed not their house: Cornelia will not come. Jacob will witness their finery fading, standing on a bare doorstep, with nowhere to go, Thea the heir of nothing. He bows, and begins to move away down the steps.

'We will see you soon, I hope,' Nella calls just as Cornelia pulls open the door. The hallway in semi-darkness looms and Nella feels both a sense of loss that the evening is dissolving, and a relief that soon she'll be in bed.

'You surely will,' Jacob replies. 'Come for dinner next Sunday, to my house on the Prinsengracht.'

Nella feels such relief she almost wants to rush down the steps towards him. 'Thank you,' she says.

'I'll send a note. And Mistress Thea? I enjoyed your lecture on our walk tonight. I, too, feel clarified.'

Thea says nothing. Jacob has taken Thea's word from her, only to hand it back, slightly out of shape. He smiles and turns away, and they listen to his boots on the cobbles, quiet then quieter, leaving them in silence.

'*Lecture*?' Nella whispers as they bustle inside, but she is hardly angry, for a dinner invitation has been issued. She still has her hands on the threads of this story. 'What on earth were you lecturing him about?'

Thea sighs. 'It was a conversation. I was merely telling him about the play. Its meanings, the making of it.'

'What do you know of the making of it?'

Thea closes the front door and turns back to her aunt. 'Rebecca Bosman told me. It can take a great deal of time to put together something that we enjoy for a couple of hours and then discard even more quickly,' she says. 'Perhaps Seigneur van Loos is not used to hearing a woman string more than one sentence together?'

'Seigneur van Loos is a gentleman, and listened most attentively to what I had to say,' Nella replies. 'And he has invited us to dinner, Thea. Think what that might mean.'

Thea bites her lip. 'What did you two talk about exactly, when I wasn't there?'

Nella tries to change the subject. 'Is Otto in the salon?' she asks Cornelia, as they hand the maid their scarves and coats.

'Yes, Madame.'

'What is he doing? Has he lit a fire in there?'

'Perhaps best to ask him yourself,' Cornelia replies, her expression inscrutable. She folds the coats over her arm. 'Thea, come,' she adds. 'I've run you a bath.'

The women gaze at Cornelia in confusion. Cornelia hates running baths. The endless heating of the water, carrying the ewers, cumbersome and slopping, from the kitchen all the way upstairs. It is the one portion of domestic life where she finds herself content with a little dirt. But Cornelia takes Thea by the upper arm and begins to steer her with determination to the staircase. 'Come, sweeting,' she says. 'I don't want the water to get cold.' She leaves the coats draped over the bottom of the banister, and practically bundles Thea upwards.

Nella, mystified, stands at the foot of the staircase, watching the two of them disappear. She glances at the bar of buttery light under the salon door, but something stops her going in. She walks instead towards one of the hall windows, to look out at the night sky. *I would quite like a bath myself*, she thinks, drawing her arms around her, staring into the inky black velvet. Her breath steams the window and she makes a spiral in the mist with her index finger. *Perhaps I shall slip into Thea's water when she is finished.*

From the shadows, Lucas emerges, brushing himself round and round her skirts, making his incongruous squeak. 'Are you pretending that you haven't eaten tonight?' Nella asks him quietly. She sighs, having no desire to enter the salon and explain the evening to Otto, to defend her 'intentions', as he puts it. She begins to move towards the downstairs staircase to find the relentless cat a sliver of something in the kitchen. But the hard, sudden sound of men's laughter from behind the salon door stops her in her path. She turns, surprised: she had assumed Otto was alone. *Who is here with him, so late in the evening?*

Lucas's treat forgotten, Nella moves silently across the tiles, lowering her eye to the salon keyhole. There, with his long stork legs and his mane of hair, with papers scattered all over the rug, sits Caspar Witsen. He seems at home, in front of the fire. He laughs again at something Otto, sitting in the chair opposite, has just said. They look like old friends, as they dip their heads towards the endless papers between them on the floor. Nella is not in the playhouse now, but she feels like she could be watching a scene whose plot is far beyond her.

'It could be spectacular,' Caspar says. 'But more importantly: sustained. If the cultivation works.'

Otto looks up. 'You think it won't?'

'There will need to be margin for error. It might not. But I am an optimistic man, so I don't see why it won't. I have experience already to build on.'

'The place has not been used well for a long time,' says Otto.

Caspar leans back. 'Still. It has all our requirements. But I find it strange that you have never been there. Have you never been curious?'

Otto sighs. 'Naturally.'

'Then surely you would have gone to inspect it, even once?'

It is Otto's turn to lean back. 'Not mine to visit,' he says. 'Only this house is in my name, Witsen. I can do what I wish with this house, but that's all.'

'You are proposing such an undertaking,' Caspar says, shaking his head.

'You've read the report,' Otto replies. 'It is full of promise, and we're pioneers.'

'Or pineappleers,' says Caspar.

Otto makes a face. 'One other thing to put in our contract: the cessation of your jokes.'

Caspar raises his hands in apology. 'But in all seriousness. We cannot do this without her.'

'I know.'

'I won't be a trespasser.'

'I understand.'

'You said you would speak to her.'

'I just need to find the opportune moment.'

Nella pushes open the door and stands on the threshold. The two men stare at her. They look entirely caught.

'Now is as opportune a time as any, gentlemen,' she says. 'Who is this woman you must speak to? And what exactly is it that you cannot do without her?'

There is nowhere for Otto and Caspar to run. No way to deny the papers at their feet, their air of excited, pleased complicity, glowing in the firelight. What do they think Nella is going to do? Chase them up the chimney and scramble them over the roof?

'Now you have both gone quiet,' she says.

'Witsen is here as my guest,' Otto replies.

Swiftly, Caspar rises to his feet, and bows. 'Madame Brandt. Good evening.'

'Mr Witsen. I see you have not brought a jar of pineapple jam this time. Instead, a deluge of papers.'

Caspar, as if in the presence of a dangerous beast, slowly leans down, gathering leaf by fluttering leaf.

'No need,' Nella says, walking towards the fireplace. The men lean away from the papers. Caspar's face is etched with worry, but there is a spark of defiance in Otto's eye, as if he is preparing himself. Nella thinks of the perfection of Rebecca Bosman's timing, striding the stage tonight. She will not wait for the moment – a day, a week, a month from now, when this pair will be better prepared, ready with the upper hand. She will have her own clarification, and command it, right now.

She approaches the rug and looks down at the papers. At first glance, the top items look easy enough to understand. Diagrams of orangeries and stove-houses, engineering cross-sections of contraptions and machines, bird's-eye plans of laid-out gardens and conservatories. She reaches for them, and as she does, she sees the agent's written report on Assendelft tucked beneath, which she had long locked away in Johannes's counting room. She doesn't even need to read it to remember everything it says: the acreage, the barn use, the state of the house: *uninhabitable*.

She stares at them. Otto glances at Caspar, who avoids his gaze, guilty schoolboys, all bravado and chit-chat gone.

'Why, *exactly*, are you looking at the report on Assendelft?' she says. Still, they do not speak. 'Otto? What are you planning?'

As if to answer, Otto reaches to the rug and hands her up a different piece of paper, covered in numbers. '*Assendelft*,' she reads out loud: '*Calculations and Projections*.' Her eye runs down the column. She cannot believe her eyes. The men have estimated profits for the next ten years.

She feels light-headed. Their eyes are on her, she can sense it, their held breath, but she refuses to look at them. 'That's my home,' she says.

'This is your home,' says Otto.

Nella ignores this. 'Why are you turning my home into a counting exercise?'

But she knows the answer. She nudges the papers with the toe of her boot and cries out at the map of her childhood. Snatching it up, her knuckles turn white as she grips the diagram. It was drawn up years ago, and the proportions of the house are not accurate. But here are the orchards at the front and back. Here is the herb garden, the vegetable patch. The fruit wall, facing south, that let them grow peach and fig trees this far north. Here is the lake. And all over it, notes in

Otto's hand and what must be Caspar's, arrows shooting left and right and questions covering it – *Reposition. Remove and rebuild. Extend fruit wall here?*

Nella stares at what they have done for some minutes, stupefied. These two have had the gall to conquer her childhood with their pencils, then drop it, carelessly, on the rug.

She looks up at Otto. 'What have you *done*?'

'I haven't done anything, Nella. Let me explain—'

'How long have you been planning? Since the Sarragon ball?'

Caspar rises to his feet. 'Perhaps I should go.'

'You will stay exactly where you are,' Nella says, and he obeys.

'I lost my position, Petronella,' Otto says. 'You have no idea how— I was only trying—'

'But this is mine,' Nella replies, hitting the map with one hand. 'It's *mine*. Not yours.'

She looks into the apple trees under the lines of the men's arrows. She sees the bare black branches, the mud underfoot in her terrible dream, those empty rooms of sorrow. How easily people think they can inscribe upon and change a place of which they know nothing.

She begins to crumple the plan and Caspar leaps to his feet. 'Madame! I have spent much time on that!'

Nella glares at him. If Caspar tussles with her for possession, she won't have any hesitation to rip it in half.

'Witsen, it's all right,' Otto says. Caspar sits back down.

'You were going to ambush me,' she says Otto.

'I wasn't.'

'You spoke of me just now as if I were an obstacle.'

'I would not expect you to understand,' Otto replies, his voice cold.

'You never do. But at least I understand that a pineapple is not going to save us.'

'And neither will the third son of a Leiden family, who fancies he can educate my daughter on the playhouse. Nella, the land there—'

'Jacob is the future. And *this*,' Nella says, holding up the map of her childhood in her fist, 'is the past. And believe me, Otto, Mr Witsen: I will not let either of you drag me back.'

She storms out of the salon, leaving the men stranded, two islands in their paper sea.

XIII

The first thing Thea notices, once Cornelia has bundled her into her bedroom, is that there is no bath at all. Her room, in fact, doesn't even have a fire. The shutters are closed. The space is almost completely dark, illuminated only by one dim tallow candle, its flame guttering with the motion of their bodies.

'What's the matter?' Thea whispers. 'What's going on?'

Cornelia closes the door and turns the key in the lock. She plunges her hand into the pocket of her apron. For a moment Thea thinks that she has found the doll of Walter and the little gold house, and her panic begins to rise. How will she explain her tiny lover with his empty palette, and the hollow house, no bigger than a peach stone? She will not be able to give any answer that might keep her secret safe.

'This came for you when you were at the playhouse,' Cornelia says, thrusting a small envelope towards her. It is too flat to contain a miniature, Thea is sure of it. She feels a little calmer, affecting indifference, deliberately not taking it from Cornelia's outstretched hand.

'Another present from Eleonor Sarragon?' Cornelia asks, her voice hard.

'Most probably. Where was it?'

'On the doorstep. Again. Strange how we never see who delivers these things, don't you think?'

'It's just a note,' Thea says. 'Why are you behaving this way over a note?'

Cornelia runs a hand over her eyes. 'Please, give it to me,' Thea goes on, as reasonably as she can. 'I've spent this evening exchanging courtesies with a dull man in whom I have no interest, merely to satisfy the whims of my aunt. I will not satisfy yours also.'

Cornelia looks shocked, but Thea firmly takes the note from her fingers and ushers her to the door. 'You worry too much,' she says to her old nursemaid, giving her a kiss on her cheek, where the skin is hot and damp.

'I don't worry enough.'

'Cornelia,' Thea says, before closing the door, 'I am not a little girl.'

Finally alone, Thea lights two more tallow candles and studies the envelope. She cannot tell if it has the same handwriting as the two miniatures, because this time her name has been written in cursive letters, not capitals. It might be from Walter, still hungry from their rushed encounter at the Schouwburg earlier, between the acts. Thea can hardly believe her daring, leaving her aunt and Jacob like that in the box, to caress her lover and be caressed by him in turn. She yearns for it to be from him, and hurriedly, she opens it.

Thea Brandt, it begins.

It is odd that Walter should address her with her full name. Then she reads the second sentence.

I know what you have been doing with Walter Riebeeck.

Thea stares at these words, her stomach beginning to contract.

You have been in congress with him, the note continues. *Have given yourself wantonly to him. And I have seen it. If you do not follow these instructions, I will tell all of Amsterdam what a whore you are.*

Her mouth goes dry.

Everyone will know what you are. You will never recover; shame will be yours again and you its author. Think of the cost to your family, but one hundred guilders will buy my silence. Leave the money under the third misericord, to the left of the altar in the Old Church. It will be checked each day, but if the money is not placed by Sunday, then the Brandt reputation will fall beyond repair.

There is no signature, no sign on the envelope. Thea grips the paper as if it is an evil she cannot get rid of, and then, her hand slightly trembling, she lays it on her bedcover and lowers herself to the floorboards. Reaching for her empty chamber pot, she begins to retch. This cannot be happening. This is a living nightmare.

Thea stays crouched, so shocked that no tears come. No sob, nothing but this retching, as if maybe she could bring up one hundred guilders, could turn herself inside out and vanish, her body transformed into the sum of money required to protect her.

She curls up into a ball. One hundred guilders. She knows that her father and aunt pay Cornelia a salary of sixty guilders for the whole year, and that Cornelia considers this generous. But one hundred guilders, to be handed over in a single day? Thea's not seen such a sum in her life. She closes her eyes. She has never felt such terror.

❦

At three o'clock the next morning, Thea is finally convinced that her family is fast asleep. When she had risen from her knees and managed to get back into bed, she had heard arguing downstairs in the salon, her aunt's voice rising and falling, her father's too. But it seems unlikely that Cornelia made any report of the note that was delivered, because no one rushed into her room. Cornelia still has some discretion, at least. Her father and her aunt were arguing about something else, and for once, Thea does not care to know what it is. She had heard the door to her aunt's room shut, then the familiar sound of her father moving around the ground floor, closing the down-stairs shutters, drawing his family into this house's safety that for Thea is suddenly nothing but illusion.

She's so cold she can barely move. Her kneecaps are drawn up beneath her chin like two saucers of bone, her neck sore from hunching, her eyes staring into the ever-dimming room. She thinks of Cornelia, sitting next to her in the playhouse for her birthday. 'We have worked hard,' Cornelia had said to her. 'We no longer live with fear or shame.' And all Thea could think of in that moment was seeing Walter.

And it's not true, what Cornelia said. Shame is still a dark imp, sitting in every corner of this house. Her father, embarrassed by his joblessness. Cornelia, paranoid over notes and packages. Her aunt, desperate to climb away from the past, willing to have Thea endure a marriage without love if it means she can cling to a sliver of respectability. And the ghosts of shame are here too. An uncle, executed by the state for the crime of sodomy. An unmarried mother, dying in childbirth. And now, a note, in which the child who was born to her is called a whore.

Nothing in that note matches how Thea's love for Walter has blossomed. How in her heart it reaches for the sky. She takes up the note again, breathing it in for a hint of scent, but there is nothing but the bland resistance of milled paper. She cannot see the words in the darkness, but has already committed them to memory. What is a whore, really? Thea wonders, closing her eyes. What does it mean, and who would call me that? I love Walter Riebeeck, and we are betrothed.

There is one person Thea can think of who might have written this, the only person who knows about them both. It's too painful to contemplate – that Rebecca, her one friend, might do this to her, might call her these names. It seems impossible.

She's a strange, lonely woman, Walter said. But Thea's sure this is not Rebecca's doing. However much Rebecca dislikes Walter, and on whatever bad terms she and Thea parted last time they saw each other, Rebecca would not stoop to this. For a start, the most successful actress of the Schouwburg doesn't need the money. More than once, Rebecca has told Thea of her investments she has made in the VOC, and of the house she rents on the Leidsegracht which costs her four hundred guilders a year. Nor would Rebecca do something so cruel. She has already expressed her dislike of Walter, so it's hardly likely she'd undertake all this without fear of Thea questioning her.

Thea puts her knees down and lies back on her bed, still in her clothes. So who does need such funds? Who would do this to her?

Be practical, she tells herself, trying to be braver than she feels, as she tucks the note under her pillow. Although Thea does not wish for such poison to lie so close to the seat of her thoughts, she dare not allow this correspondence to stray beyond arm's length. The defence of love, for a hundred guilders: where can she get such a sum? For get it she must, to buy away her shame. To push it back into the water. And now is the hour, when the house feels dead.

She sits up again, and manages to tiptoe to the threshold of her door. Her feet are like ice, shoeless in order to move unheard. She stands in the corridor, concentrating only on the minutes in hand. What can she sell, that no one else will notice is missing? So much of their precious cargo has gone already, keeping the family in beeswax and good firewood, fine slices of bacon, and dinners with unwanted suitors. All but one of the paintings her uncle and her mother accrued have gone. So have the finest rugs, the most ornate silver-work. Thea herself has nothing of value; her skirts and bodices, her cloak, her boots – all these are made of good material, but she cannot sell them, because what then for a whore in hiding?

She stands at the foot of the attic ladder. Since she was little, she's been forbidden to go up there alone, in case she might fall: but no one can stop her now. Thea grips either side of the ladder and begins to climb. At the top, it is colder than a tomb and she cannot see much. A little moonlight, glowing from an uncovered window in the centre of the gable, lends a gauzy sheen to bulky boxes and dust sheets, and she uses it to navigate her way across the gritty floorboards.

There must be something here she can sell, something no one has wanted for decades. She moves around, lifting up the sheets to reveal a chair with three legs, and an old games table from better days. One box contains threadbare blankets. No one will buy those, not for the money she needs. In the corner of the attic, her eye is caught by a chest wedged under a beam.

She moves slowly towards it, and kneels down, running her hands over the old wood. It looks like another blanket box, but this one is sturdier, more reinforced. In the semi-darkness, she can feel a pair of latches on either side, and she frees them, wincing as rusted metal grates on metal. But the lid lifts with surprising ease, and the pleasant aroma of cedar wood rises to her nose. Angling herself so that the moonlight might help her, Thea looks down at her treasure.

Resting on cedar shavings are books, tied together in blocks. Whose are they? There aren't books in the house, given how expensive they are. Her father and aunt prefer to read the heavy ledgers of house accounts, and there's the old family Bible, of course – but these, hidden away in the top of the house – these look different. Thea lifts a block out, pulling the string apart, opening the book that sits on top. This volume is well bound and substantial. Inside it are woodblock illustrations of a shipwreck, and underneath it there is another of similar quality, and another and another.

It's tempting to carry off a whole block, but even though Thea never sees anyone climbing into the attic, she does not want to make it obvious that she has chipped into this surprising hoard. Shifting her position, she pushes her hand deeper into the shavings of cedar wood. Her fingers touch a small animal skull, which she quickly drops. There are feathers here too, long plumes not belonging to any birds she has seen in her lifetime. There are pod-like shapes, seeds like jewels pinched between her fingers.

Suddenly, Thea touches something yielding but substantial. Material of some sort, soft like sable. To her astonishment, her hand finds a pair of legs, and then a pair of arms, and her heart beats hard as she pulls out a miniature woman. She takes the doll to the window, and sees by the moonlight a pair of grey eyes, an elegant neck, an old-fashioned collar. An expression of restraint and a familiar, strong mouth.

The breath stops in her lungs. She knows who this is. It's her mother. She runs her hands over Marin's skirts. Her sleeves, her slender hands. She holds this person in her palm. It seems strange to meet her mother finally, when she can't talk, and Thea can hardly raise her voice above a whisper, both of them bound by different types of silence. Thea stares at the doll, sensing in the level of detail, the fineness, the thrum of potential inside each limb, the similar marks of the maker of the doll of Walter. Can it be possible they are made by the same person, and if so, how? What is a miniature of her mother doing up in this attic, and who put it there? And why has no one ever told her it existed?

The doll continues to stare up blindly at her living daughter, mute and secretive despite the promise of that potent mouth. Her heart racing, and with the doll of Marin still in one hand, Thea goes back to the chest and keeps rummaging, until her spare hand lights on another figure hidden in the cedar. Carrying it back to the window, she knows immediately that she's holding her father. Here is his suit of black, and his open gaze is unmistakable. 'Papa?' she whispers, unable not to greet this strange likeness. But Thea's father is fast asleep below her feet. This is just his uncanny double.

Thea holds them together by the light of the moon: her parents, suspended in her fingers. She wills them to yield their answers. As she looks at them, together again but in such a compromised fashion, Thea feels again how little she knows of their story, how it will forever be locked behind silence and the inexorability of death. However hard she tries, she will not taste the love between them. These dolls, as beautiful and delicate as they are, will tell her nothing.

But for a moment, she considers taking them to her room. They could join with Walter and the tiny gold house, her hoard where her past meets her future, shrunken to a manageable size beneath her bed. Yet something stops her. These miniatures belong alone, up here, together. They are not hers to take. Quite whose they are, Thea doesn't know, but she cannot displace them. She must not take them into her possession. If her own living, breathing father will not speak to her about the past, about private things, then how can she expect any more from a puppet?

And, if she is honest with herself: they are a little eerie. To be confronted with her mother's face like this, after all these years: Thea doesn't know what to feel. She had thought she might be elated, or feel a sense of closeness. But perhaps it is enough to know that her simulacrum is up here, nourished in cedar wood, existing on in this impenetrable form, whilst her bones turn to dust in the Old Church floor.

'I'll come back and visit,' Thea whispers into her mother's ear – Marin's ear, lifelike as it is, hearing nothing. Her eyes, seeing nothing. Thea lays her mother and father back into the shavings, covering them over, her heart strangely sad. She holds on to her mother for one last second, and as she pulls away, her hand touches what feels like a scroll.

She grips it, assuming it's a rolled-up painting. Everyone knows how much Amsterdammers love a painting, whether it's in a frame or not. *This* is the sort of thing you can sell, she thinks. The cold and dark of the attic are becoming too overwhelming, and the discovery of the dolls has unnerved her, so without further consideration, she plucks out this rolled piece, closes the lid and replaces the latches. A sudden wave of determination washes up her body. Slowly, silently, the scroll still rolled up in her fist, Thea moves away from her tiny parents, tiptoeing across the floor, filigreed with silver patches of moonlight. Taking one last look at the chest, she descends the ladder, away from the land of the dead.

In her room, she lights the stubs of her candles and unrolls what she has found, but is surprised to discover not a genteel landscape of a watermill or a farm, nor one of those peasant tavern scenes that seem so numerous when she passes them at the markets. It is, instead, a detailed map of Africa. Someone has written on it, *Weather? Food? God?*

Thea does not recognize the hand. Nor does she recognize the place name on the bottom west coast of the continent, where the questions hover, which has been labelled *Dahomey*. But it is a fine map, she can see that even by her weak candlelight. It has been carefully drawn, with much thought put into the topography of all the parts of the landmass and the coasts. Her excitement rises: this will fetch a good price, even with the three inked questions. The questions might even make it more valuable. She could conjure a story about those questions. 'We are a family of adventurers,' she imagines herself saying to the cartographers on Raamstraat. We have voyaged beyond our rug, after all.

Thea rolls up the map and tucks it down the back of her bed, in case Cornelia should come in next morning and spy it. Her rest, until dawn, is short and fitful. She dreams of her mother's hand reaching out from inside the attic chest, slender, waxen palm opening to offer a bouquet of writhing spiders. The spiders tumble, their upturned black legs liquefying into the ink lines of a map, running into mountains and lakes Thea does not recognize, a new and hostile world.

XIV

The art dealer stands in the dining room before the shipwreck by Bakhuizen. He is not the same man who has purchased their other paintings. Nella has divided that embarrassment up, choosing several dealers over the past few months through the pages of *Smit's List*. This one, de Vries, is a tall young man with the air of someone used to sitting for his own portrait, rather than being the one to sell them. He knows nothing of the many other artworks that have left this house, wrapped in silk and sacking. At least, Nella hopes he doesn't, because then he will smell her desperation. He has eyes, of course. He can see the walls are bare.

'It's a good one,' he says, and she's surprised: not that she didn't expect it to be of high quality – because Marin purchased it, after all – but rather that de Vries would confess to it. She is used to demurrals from these men: reductions, grimaces, anything to guarantee a cheaper sale. She knows their tricks and prides herself that for the most part she has resisted them, securing good prices for the pieces that have adorned her existence for eighteen years.

As de Vries assesses the painting, Nella wonders: what does it do to a person to have their fantastical views removed, these visual stories contained within heavy oak frames? Do you make up more in your head in place of the want? She has become so accustomed to these various pictures, even the ones she didn't like – the dead hares, the bloodied birds, the rotting fruit, Marin's relentless reminders of the drip of time and the inevitability of death. And although she has never liked those masts like keeling crucifixes, the whites of the sailors' eyes, the tedious message that travel is peril, whilst also making it look exciting – she will miss it. It was Marin's favourite. And their walls, after this one, will be entirely naked.

'The frame's gold leaf,' she says. 'I assume you will want the frame too.'

De Vries blinks slowly. His sandy eyelashes and pink cheeks remind Nella of a young pig. There is a movement at the door and Thea appears, unaware that Nella is not alone. She looks oddly guilty, and startles at the presence of de Vries. Nella notes his familiar moment of surprise, before it sinks smoothly back underneath his features. Everything he does in his work must be smooth, she supposes, everything unruffled. It is the most normal thing in the world for a widow to live in a house this grand, on the Herengracht canal, and have nothing on her walls. It is the most normal thing to have Thea turn up like this, not dressed as a servant, but as a gentlewoman, in her sober black skirts, her neat cap the colour of a perfect onion. De Vries looks at Thea as if she is a still life.

'Where's Papa?' Thea says.

'Out,' replies Nella. 'This is Seigneur de Vries. He is assessing this painting for me.'

De Vries bows, but Thea does not move. 'Does Papa know you're selling it?' she asks, and the question spreads hot anger in Nella's body. Why does Thea assume she needs Otto's permission to sell a painting? These paintings were entrusted to my wardenship, Nella wants to say: I do not need to answer to your father, nor to an eighteen-year-old. I can do with this painting what I want. Her mind tracks once more to the drawings and reports on the salon floor, copious and detailed and painful. Caspar's and Otto's air of complicity. The complacency of men. Her fists bunch, and she forces them to relax. She will not be vanquished by drawings of stoves and orchards.

'Will you excuse me, Seigneur?' she says. 'I will leave you to your examination.'

De Vries bows again. 'With pleasure, Madame.'

Out in the hallway, Nella faces Thea. 'What's happened?' she asks, keeping her voice down.

'Nothing's happened,' Thea says, but she looks almost feverish. There are dark circles under her brown eyes, and her eyes themselves are very bright, and there is a restlessness to her movements which isn't normal. 'Are you really selling that painting?'

'We need the money,' Nella whispers, trying, and failing, to hide her accusatory tone.

'It's not my fault,' Thea whispers back. She turns to go, plucking up her cloak and throwing it round her shoulders. 'I'm going to fetch some bream for Cornelia.' Suddenly, she stops. 'What were you arguing about last night?'

'We weren't arguing.'

'Of course you were. I heard your voices.'

For a moment, Nella considers lying. But she cannot be bothered with the effort of it, the elaboration. 'Caspar Witsen was here,' she says. 'Your father invited him when we were out.'

Thea's eyes widen. 'The botanist?'

'It appears that ever since the Sarragon ball, your father and he have been making secret plans.'

'What plans?'

'Perhaps ask your father to explain further. I have no time right now.'

Nella makes to move back into the dining room, but Thea catches her arm. 'Tell me, Aunt Nella. Please.'

There is a long silence between them. The house around them is very still. 'Your father and Caspar Witsen wish to plant pineapples on my land,' Nella says.

'Pineapples?'

'Yes. Stoves, hot-houses, all of it. They wish to set up in business together, I believe. A botanist and a clerk. Great men of industry.'

Nella knows she sounds bitter, that her words are a disservice to Otto, and it is unwise to voice such a feeling to his daughter. 'Except they do not have the money for such a venture,' she says. 'And your father still will not tell me where he plans to get it.'

Thea looks thoughtful. 'In Assendelft? Where your mother drowned?'

Nella feels a pain between her ribs. 'Go and buy the bream. And do not tarry.'

Suddenly, Thea puts her hand on her aunt's forearm. Her touch is warm and strong. It has been a long time since they showed each other any physical affection. 'When I come back,' Thea says quietly, 'will my mother's painting be gone?'

Nella hesitates. 'Thea, how else do you think we'll pay for Cornelia's bream?'

Thea retracts her hand, the softness vanishing from her face. She dissolves into a place she will not let Nella reach.

Nella receives two hundred guilders from de Vries for the Bakhuizen. Not a magisterial sum, but neither is it mean. More than anything, these guilders feel like a talisman against what Nella fears might come next, if Thea doesn't see the sense in pursuing Jacob, if Otto cannot find employment.

De Vries hands her the sum in the form of ready money, not even a promissory note. How many more guilders is he wandering around the city with? She watches him unhook the gilded frame from the wall, his arms stretched to full capacity, holding the roiling seas in his embrace. Imagine being so immune in your wealth that you stride these canals with hundreds of guilders lining your coat, falling from your body like dried leaves.

But there are lots of people like that in this city. For a long time, Nella's own husband was one of their rank. You might be robbed on the Damrak, but the world won't end. Except actually, she thinks, Johannes was robbed, and it did. So she will guard these two hundred guilders ferociously, because it is more altogether than they have seen in a long time.

She stands on the front step, watching de Vries manhandle the painting down to the canal path before he loads it onto the back of his cart. He jumps up to join his driver, who flicks his whip and the horse pulls off.

Cornelia comes out to watch. 'So that's that,' she says. 'Otto won't have expected it.'

'No more than I expected to find Caspar Witsen in the salon last night. Did you know what he was planning?'

'No, Madame.'

Cornelia's expression is so dark that Nella believes her. 'Did you ask Thea to get you some bream?' she says.

Cornelia looks startled. 'No.'

'She said you did.'

Cornelia does not reply, turning her head up and down the canal. 'Who are you looking for?' Nella asks.

'Thea, of course.'

'But she's only just left. Cornelia, is everything all right?'

Cornelia twists her hands together, still scanning both directions of the canal. 'Everything's fine.'

Nella joins her old companion in looking up and down the Herengracht, not in search of a tall young woman, her cap like a perfect onion, coming back with a basket of bream, but for a blonde head, a pair of light-brown eyes, so fiery at times they look almost orange. The miniaturist has to be coming: she has to. Nella feels as if she's running out of time.

'Who are *you* looking for?' Cornelia asks, her eyes narrowing with suspicion.

'Nobody,' Nella says. 'We're just two women standing on a doorstep, Cornelia. Waiting for nobody.'

About an hour later, Nella hears Otto calling for her through the house. She stands in her room, the map of Assendelft covered in the men's annotations spread out on the bed before her, the two hundred guilders from the painting stashed beneath her mattress. Otto's footsteps come up the stairs, a swift knock on her bedroom door. Straightening her cap, she tucks her loose hair away and smooths her skirts.

'Come in.'

Otto appears. 'We need to speak.'

Nella gestures to the map on top of her bed. 'What else is there to say? I will not permit this.'

Otto glances at the map. 'Cornelia tells me you have sold the shipwreck by Bakhuizen.'

'And if I did?'

'You did not consult me.'

'Something of a habit in this house.'

'Two hundred guilders was not enough. He took advantage.'

'I'm used to men doing that.'

'Nella—'

'Two hundred was a good price. The paintings were left to me,' Nella snaps, hating how sulky she sounds, as if they are siblings bickering over what their dead parents have left behind. The truth is, she might have taken any money for it, knowing how it would irritate Otto to have lost that final painting. Her cheeks flush with anger, but also with embarrassment. She feels as if she has no diagrams nor calculations for her future, no one to partner with in planning.

'Has it come to this?' Otto asks, as if he is reading her mind. 'The dividing up of our possessions? We have shared everything for so long.'

Nella prods the papers on her bed. 'And yet you seemed quite happy to divide up mine.'

Otto closes her door quietly and comes to sit on the chair beside her bed. 'Van Loos cannot have Thea,' he says.

'Why can't he? She might want him.'

He ignores this. 'I am looking for other ways out of our mess.'

'By exploiting my childhood home without even asking?'

He looks up. 'I am not exploiting you. And of course we were going to ask.'

'*We.*'

'*I* am asking you now. I wanted to get everything in order, so that any questions you might have, I would have the answers.'

'Here's a question. What do you know of my time in that house? My childhood?'

'As little as you know of mine. But what has childhood got to do with it? It's a house, Petronella. You have not been back for nearly twenty years. Raze it to the ground and start again.'

'When we live on the Herengracht, the centre of the world?'

'You can grow things there,' Otto says. 'You can breathe. You can avoid tedious parties held by Clara Sarragon. Stop searching for unwanted suitors.'

'Thea *needs* suitors. Assendelft is the past.' Nella sighs. 'And it's too much of a risk. That house is a ruin, Otto. Believe me. The structure is unstable. And the land you have drawn upon here has been debased. It's a bog, it's a marsh.'

Otto puts his head in his hands. 'If it's marsh soil, that's what Caspar says we need.'

'The elite have their country houses, because they have staff,' Nella says. 'They have spare money to make their pleasure palaces. You think you will live as a prince, but you will be like a farmer.'

'Better that than a liar.'

Nella waves her hand over the map. 'We do not have the capital for these fantasies of yours. Where are you going to get it?'

Otto looks away, and Nella, sensing a sliver of advantage, persists. 'Otto, this house – Johannes and Marin's house – has held me for eighteen years, and you for even longer. It is not a lie. It is solid. It is one of the grandest addresses—'

'You are a songbird who only knows one tune!' he says. 'What use is this grand address, if you're only using it to tout my daughter to the first man who shows an interest? If you're selling her mother's heirlooms cheap to pay for our appearance?'

Nella tries to control her anger. 'We *must* look to Jacob. This house has underwritten his interest in her, do you not see that?'

'And have you truly considered what that interest is?'

'What do you mean?'

He looks exhausted. 'Why do you think he has chosen Thea?' he asks.

'Because he likes her!'

'He *likes* her. I have seen this happen before, Nella. This interest from men who look like him, in young women who look like Thea. I have seen this *liking* of which you speak, and what happens with it, and I do not trust it. As if my daughter is a butterfly he has never seen before. He will pin her to the wall for his collection, and then forget about her once he sees another pair of shiny wings.'

He is vehement. She looks up at him, and sees with horror that his eyes are filled with tears. Nella feels herself floundering. 'Thea isn't a butterfly,' she says.

'I know that. But you place too much value on his opinion.'

'And you do not place enough. Thea is an Amsterdammer in need of a future, and this house represents what she is! Credible. Dignified. Wealthy. It attracted Jacob's eye, and he saw Thea sitting in the middle of it.'

Otto wipes his eyes. He stares at her, but Nella will not give up. 'And who will see her, Otto, sitting in a barn in the middle of nowhere for the rest of her life, waiting for your pineapples to grow?'

'Our walls are bare. He sees that too. Her dowry is pitiful.'

'Not so pitiful. We have saved for her. And now there is the money from the painting—'

Otto rises to his feet to stand by her window. 'Two hundred guilders? In what world do you live, that you think they will marry?'

'You were not at the playhouse last night. You underestimate your own daughter. And him.'

'And what would van Loos say, if he found out I no longer have my position at the VOC?'

'That is something Jacob does not need to know. Otto,' she says, lowering her voice. 'Do not forget that he has invited us to dinner on Sunday. I believe a proposal is imminent.'

'You are deluded.'

Nella waves her hand at the map. '*I* am deluded?'

'You speak of your own dreams, Nella, not hers. Thea doesn't love him.'

'Love doesn't come into it! You know nothing of what it's like to be a woman. To be powerless.'

Otto turns to face her. 'Believe me, Petronella. I have an inkling of that.'

Nella stares into the gaps between her floorboards, the wood shining and smooth where her feet have trodden so many years. 'You should at least listen to what Caspar Witsen has to say,' Otto goes on, and she can hear the effort he is making to keep his voice light. 'The plans—'

'Our future, in a spiny fruit? My father ran orchards too, you know. Apples for cider. Cherry brandy. Look where that got him. Caspar isn't a merchant, Otto. He isn't Johannes—'

189

'Johannes took risks too, and was rewarded. You forget I worked closely with him for years—'

'Rewarded?' Nella laughs. 'Johannes flew too close to the sun! And look what happened to us all. You would drag us to the ends of the earth, to eke out our existence under a rotting roof with soil beneath our fingernails, for the vision of a former university botanist?'

'Assendelft is not the ends of the earth.'

'You have not been to Assendelft.'

'But I have been to the ends of the earth. And one way or another, I'm going to enter into business with Caspar Witsen.'

They stop, both of them breathless. They have not argued like this before, but on it comes, their frustration with each other, with the situation in which they are stuck. Nella takes a deep breath. 'And I will ask you again: with what money are you going to build these stove-houses?' she says, unable now to keep her voice low. 'These contraptions? These roofs and steam-pipe systems? With what money will you buy the glass panels? The seeds and the bottles, not to mention the wages for the staff? It is a madness, Otto. We are not Clara Sarragon. We cannot afford personal botanists to show them off at balls!'

'No, we are not, and I thank God for it.'

'So, for the last time: how are you going to afford it?'

Otto pauses. 'I will sell this house.'

She stares up at him. '*What?*'

'There's no other way that will make it possible. I have had the house valued.'

'*When?*'

'Never mind when. They told me four hundred thousand guilders.'

A silence falls. Otto stands by the window, staring towards the grandeur of the Herengracht canal. Nella perches on the edge of her bed, her head reeling, her left thigh crumpling the corner of the map. The sum is astronomical, hypothetical: but she feels it like a physical blow. 'You cannot be serious,' she whispers. 'You cannot expect me to move from here, back to *there*?'

'Why not?' Otto says. 'Can you truly say that this city is what it was?'

'This city is an ever-changing thing. It can give us everything. And this house, here, is all we have to make sure we can take it.' Nella feels her panic rising, her life as she knows it morphing beyond her control. 'It signals to the world who we are.'

'It's a hollow show. And you know it.'

'It would be an act of betrayal to the memory of Johannes and Marin. To our own lives here. You haven't even been to Assendelft, and you want to get rid of this majesty?'

'Majesty?' Otto repeats with scorn. 'The majesty of people like Clara Sarragon? Like my employers at the VOC? Like the merchant wives at the guilds, who came to ignore you? I have known a lot of Clara Sarragons in my lifetime. More than you might imagine. And their husbands too. I refuse to know them any longer. This is not a question of parading little pieces of toast around a society party, covered with a condiment I have made in the back of my kitchen.'

'So what is it a question of? Because why do you really want to do this? Is Thea going to be your excuse forever?'

It is his turn to look winded. 'What on earth does that mean? I think only of her. We have a chance to change our destiny.'

Nella rises to her feet. '*Your* destiny,' she says. 'You cannot sell this house. I will not let you have Assendelft.'

'The land, then,' Otto says. Their eyes meet, but neither one of them will budge. 'Let us have the land.'

'No. You will have to find somewhere else to grow your empire.'

Otto looks outraged. 'Empire? This is not about empire.'

'Is it not?'

'Do not sulk, Nella, because you have no better ideas. Do not be petty.'

'Not pettiness. This is common sense!'

'You would rather be held captive by this city, for another eighteen years?' he says. 'Your little life, preserved in aspic? That house, that land, stands empty. Ready. *That* is common sense. The pineapple could be more to us than just a fruit.'

'No,' Nella says. 'You might call it a little life, but it is too much of a risk, and I will not give up on Jacob.'

Otto stalks back towards her bedroom door and thrusts it open. The air between is like a bruise. Before he leaves, he turns to her. 'What will it take?'

'I came from that place,' Nella says. 'It is the past. And I will not let you throw away your daughter's future, like my own parents threw away mine.'

He slams the door behind him. Nella sits for several minutes, forcing herself not to weep.

XV

The third misericord, to the left of the altar, has a carving of a man and a woman. The wooden couple are held in equipoise, their hands and the soles of their feet pressed upon each other but their bodies leaning away. Thea peers down at it. Are their toes and fingers straining to break apart, or to save the other from a fall? The man appears to be grimacing as he turns his head, and the woman, her neat cap carved in a perfect sphere, has her eyes on him, her expression one of hesitancy. They tussle, but they will not let each other go. Thea stares at this little couple, unable to discern their moral. And there *will* be a moral, because this is the Old Church in Amsterdam.

She straightens up and looks around, dreading that she might be being observed, but the Old Church just before midday is not peopled; an elderly man contemplating alone, his hat loose in his hands, a pair of women drifting slowly together across the cold slabs. A couple stands away in the corner, less a religious meeting than a lovers' encounter. None of them notice she's there. Thea has one hundred guilders and the note demanding them tucked inside her skirt, and slowly she takes out the money.

Having finally escaped her aunt under the pretence of buying Cornelia's bream, she had walked to Raamstraat in the Jordaan, the rolled-up map of Africa tucked in the bottom of her basket, to find the cartographer she had selected from *Smit's List*. She had fully expected the man to try to outwit her. She is used to being underestimated, both her sex and the colour of her skin blinkering the men who stand on the other side of apothecary counters, of fish stalls and butchers'. Of map shops. But she has not spent eighteen years at Cornelia's side without learning a thing or two from the marketplace: the bartering, even the flirting, tedious but effective, and sometimes necessary – and the assurance that there are several other dealers she knows who will give her a better price.

Thea knew it was a map of some quality – and indeed, none of the other maps of Africa the cartographer had in his shop were as detailed or as intricate. His eyes widened as she unrolled her treasure, followed swiftly by a simulation of indifference, as if this was a normal sort of map that passed under his eyes every day. In the end, Thea sold it to him for two hundred and fifty guilders. She felt very little regret leaving the map behind; it is, after all, only a piece of paper, and the pieces of paper now in her possession have far more power. Thea has heard her aunt's words too many times. If money can buy you a freedom of sorts, it can also buy silence.

The map, if anything, was a reminder to her of how narrow the circumscription of Thea's life is. And now she has guilders to spare, enough for a betrothed couple to pay a priest for a proper marriage, and run away to Paris. As she wedges the money under the misericord of the warring couple, she muses how much easier it must be in so many ways to be a Catarina or an Eleonor Sarragon. To be wealthy, or a suitable shade of pale, to be passive: to not worry about where money comes from, nor question its sources. To not have to hide yourself, constantly on the alert for looks and rumours about you. It would be something, for one day, to know how that feels. To do what you want, because you want to. To be free.

After checking the money is well hidden, Thea wanders to the far east corner of the church. Here is the spot where her mother is buried. She thinks about her little version in the attic, buried in the dark of the cedar shavings. Thea does not come to visit the grave slab as often as she should; but the truth is it feels as strange to do it as it might be to tiptoe up the attic ladder and peer at the miniature. Her mother feels more present in the way her father and aunt tiptoe round her absence, how their silences build an outline of a woman glimpsed only fleetingly in the corner of a room.

How can Thea stand at a grave and remember, when there are no memories to recall, when they still will not tell her Marin's stories? All Thea feels, when she thinks of her mother, is confusion, a shimmering blank, a compass with a missing point. Even so, she stands at the foot of where her mother's bones lie, the stained-glass windows watering the grey stones with pale yellows and greens, patches of ruby and blueish plum. The only thing to mark Marin Brandt's resting place are three words: *Things can change.*

It is a hopeful message, but this being Amsterdam, of course it's also a warning. Night will come again, so don't be complacent. Feather your nest, but don't love money. Do I look like a dutiful daughter, coming to lay flowers? Thea wonders, staring into the slab. No, I am a dutiful lover, coming to lay money to protect my heart. My mother might understand. Marin might understand how Thea's secret love for Walter will endure, despite these assaults. How Thea will throw money at this to keep scandal at bay, how hard she will work to maintain appearances. Thea has been well trained in that. She will do what it takes. After all, that is what her mother did, loving a man that society wouldn't approve.

I know what you have been doing with Walter Riebeeck. Thea shivers, looking over to the misericords. But no one is there.

Outside in the bright day, the sun encourages. Thea feels pleased she has acted so decisively. For a moment, she thinks about going to the Schouwburg in the hope of finding Walter there, of telling him what has happened, and how quickly she has solved it. She loves to find new ways to show him the lengths she will go to for their love, how she will protect him at all costs. But perhaps that is immature. It is not what Rebecca might do, and there is something pleasing to Thea about managing this herself, to know that she is more than capable of dealing with a foolish blackmail note on her own.

Yet, as Thea hurries through the old part of the city back home, she will admit there is a deeper reason for keeping this note to herself. She doesn't want to frighten Walter off. After his extreme reaction to the sight of his miniature, and his fear that someone is watching them, how might he react to a note calling her a whore, threatening to tell the whole world the secret of their love? He might not want to see her for a while. He might even say the betrothal is a bad idea, and she couldn't bear it. Better he doesn't know, to protect the sweetness of their time together. To keep it stable, and secure.

XVI

Jacob van Loos's house on the Prinsengracht is a wonderland. Nella feels as if she is eighteen years old again, arriving in the city for the first time into Johannes's home. She feels Jacob's house like a jolt in her body, before it absorbs her into its beauty and tranquillity. The sounds of the canal fade away as she is enveloped by its symmetry and taste, its velvets and its wreaths of amber. And then it pierces her, how long they have lived by a thread, a masquerade of a wealthy family. What else are they, but an uncomfortable assemblage of souls, teetering on the edge of disaster?

She tries to contain her staring, but there are fine paintings on every wall. Still lifes of pewter ewers and fine-blown glass, garnished with lifelike lemon peels. Bucolic landscapes, hunting scenes – and shipwrecks, too, although thankfully not the Bakhuizen she has so recently sold. It would be too much to discover that de Vries is van Loos's dealer, that Marin's favourite possession should adorn his wall.

Delft vases and German crystal rest on every surface, and the scent of burning amber incense fills the space. Beautiful side-tables with slim straight legs, inlaid with marquetry and mother-of-pearl. Marble tiles spanning out, jet black, white, and veined with grey. A vast new Turkey rug, in shades of mustard and rusty red – the largest Nella has ever seen – covers a great swathe of the hallway, cushioning her feet, its design woven to intricate, abstract perfection. Through an archway, the invited party can spy another room, high-ceilinged, pale-green walls, elegant chairs and a low table with curved legs. A harpsichord in the corner, covered with music. To think: Thea might become the mistress of all this.

The invited party: Otto Brandt, his daughter, Thea, and Petronella, gratefully accepting the afternoon invitation to a Sunday dinner. Nella is pleased that Otto is here, but wary. Since their argument, they have been civil with each other for Thea's sake. Nella has heard no more of Caspar Witsen and his pineapples, nor the great plans for expansion into her old territory. But Otto's silence, in its own way, worries her. Something has taken root in him, and Nella knows, despite his presence here tonight, how adamant Otto is that Jacob will not have his daughter. *One dinner*, he had bargained, back in January: *And if Thea doesn't like this van Loos fellow, then we never have to see him again, either.*

For Otto, Jacob van Loos is like Clara Sarragon: dangerous and unlikeable, cut from the same expensive cloth. Now it is the middle of February, and he has agreed to come tonight: one dinner more. It seems suspicious to Nella. Is it to lull her into a false sense of security? It cannot be that he has given in.

Other suspicions: in the past week, Thea has appeared sombre, and more than once Nella has caught her watching at the hallway window. 'Thea, is everything quite well?' Nella asks, but her question is brushed off. She's still resistant to Jacob, that's what it will be. Or perhaps she knows there is discord between her father and her aunt. I shouldn't have told her about Caspar and the pineapples, Nella thinks. I shouldn't have been short with her when she asked about the lake. I shouldn't have told her *anything* about my life in Assendelft.

This is what happens when you start telling your story. You become unwieldy, to yourself, to others. They think they understand, that they have the measure of you. But they don't. Maybe Marin had it right, keeping all her cards so close to her chest. And the cold weather doesn't help. The canal ice has melted, true – but the warmth is not here yet, the foods at market have not yet changed. It feels as if they are waiting for something, but none of them know exactly what.

Nella is confident that Jacob van Loos cannot tell any of this. They are a family expert at hiding. They sit with him in his pale-green salon, and they smile. Nella is silenced both by the wealth and by the memory of a house like this. Its owner is wearing a coat of deep-black silk, his small shoulders well accommodated by an excellent tailor. On his feet are a pair of slippers, dark black elaborate leather, long and pointed, with a huge white satin bow on either foot. Nella finds herself staring at them, until Jacob's housekeeper, Mrs Lutgers, a woman who must be over sixty, small, fine-boned and pale, breaks her reverie.

'A pot of tea, Seigneur?' Mrs Lutgers asks. 'Before you eat?'

Jacob gestures. 'Would my guests like a pot of tea?'

Thea says nothing. 'Not for me, but I thank you,' Otto replies.

'Thank you, I will,' Nella says, and out glides Mrs Lutgers, no backwards glance. Well, let us eke out time here, Nella thinks. Let Jacob take in Thea's beauty once again, see her grace. This is one of the most beautiful rooms Nella has ever seen, and in the grey afternoon light diffusing through the windows, Thea looks perfect. This room, like Thea, has not too much gold or pearl upon it. Not too much shimmer, to assuage the Netherlandish dislike of show, but enough to gladden the eye as it tracks the room, from the corner of a fine wood cabinet to the beauty of a picture frame, from the quiet clock ticking on the mantel, to the plump cushion embroidered with ivy, wedged against Nella's spine. Even the air feels pearlescent, rarefied.

Jacob glances at Nella with amusement. 'You were not expecting it,' he says.

'What do you mean, Seigneur?'

'You like this room.'

She smiles. 'How could one not?'

'People assume I do not have an eye.' He looks at Thea. 'That I cannot appreciate delicate things.'

Nella can feel Otto's gaze on her, but she holds her own attention towards Thea, who keeps her eyes upon the lacquered table. Mrs Lutgers returns, setting down the tray before her master. Jacob hands Thea a small china cup on a saucer. 'It is my honour to pour,' he says. 'In London, the lady always does it, but in Amsterdam the men must serve.'

It is not his allusion to servitude in her name that pricks Thea alive, but this mention of London: she looks up at Jacob as if broken from a dream. Nella watches Jacob lift the teapot to pour Thea's cup, the hot liquid falling from the spout, as impossible to push back as a waterfall. Why would he invite them here, if he wasn't truly interested? Otto was making stories where there are none. Jacob hands her a cup too, and like the rest of the room, it is perfectly designed, rimmed with gold. As he pours, the steam rises to Nella's face, dampening her chin and the fine hairs at her temples.

'Have you seen anything at the playhouse since we met there, Mistress Brandt?' Jacob asks.

'No, Seigneur,' Thea replies.

'But your aunt told me that you love the place?'

'Did she?'

Jacob looks confused. 'She says you often go and see the same play more than once.'

Thea regards him blankly. Nella feels an irritation spreading through her body. How can Thea manage to answer him so abruptly, show such indifference over his interest, and imply her own unreliability, with only two words?

'Are there other things you love?' Jacob asks. 'Love is a broad emotion, I know.'

'I think it quite particular,' says Thea.

'Yet one must start somewhere,' Nella interrupts.

Both Jacob and Thea glance at her in surprise, and Nella flushes in her cheeks. She chastises herself: she mustn't push too hard. After all, she was the one who told him he should ask Thea about the things she loves.

'I love pineapples,' Thea announces, suddenly, into the silence. She turns, smiling at her aunt. 'They have a wonderful taste, don't you think? Perhaps there is a future in pineapples.'

Otto looks at his daughter in confusion. 'How odd,' Nella says, returning Thea's smile. 'Because you did not like Clara Sarragon's, when it was turned into a jam.'

'Things can change,' Thea says. She turns to Jacob. 'That is what our family believes.'

Otto walks to the window; Nella feels her irritation prickling further as Thea looks serene. Jacob glances between them, like an astronomer gazing at three stars, studying their bright spots to construct their constellation.

'I must say,' says Jacob, addressing Nella with a swiftness that makes her jump, 'I still think about your cook's saffron and white wine sauce. Cordelia, was it?'

'Cornelia,' says Otto.

'I shall have to poach her.' Jacob laughs. 'An apt verb, for a cook! Or maybe she might come willingly?' He looks meaningfully at Thea.

Thea stares back into the table. Otto reaches for the spare teacup and pours himself some tea. Nella maintains her composure. Would Cornelia ever form part of Thea's marriage contract? she wonders. Would Cornelia leave the house on the Herengracht to be with Thea, a priceless asset to be packed with her ladles in the wedding trousseau?

Cornelia might well do it. She might not bear to be apart from her beloved nurseling. But imagine asking her, offering the assumption that she is a moveable part of the household she has lived in nearly all her life. It would be terrible. Nella would hardly dare to do it.

And yet, overlaying the awful prospect of losing Cornelia to this house, is the realization that for the first time, Jacob has made a hint in front of Thea and Otto of his intentions.

❧

After a dinner of rabbit, that Nella enjoys to a degree, despite finding it much more basic and blander than anything Cornelia might make, and rather suggesting he needs a better cook in his life, they return to the pale-green room. Otto looks as if this is the longest afternoon of his life. Jacob asks Thea if he can show her his harpsichord, and pinioned by the politeness required, Thea acquiesces. Otto and Nella remain on the sofa with their glasses of wine, and for fifteen minutes regard in silence the stilted show across the other side of the room. It could be a lovers' scene, the young woman seated at the instrument, her head inclined, the suggestion of mesmerization by the beautiful keyboard, and the magnificent wooden inlay of the box in which it sits.

'At what point will he realize that she cannot play?' Otto murmurs.

'He didn't ask her over there for that,' Nella murmurs back.

Jacob takes the seat and begins to move his fingers over the keys. The precise twang of the harpsichord fills the room, note after note spiralling to the ceiling. Nella can see her niece's expression of surprise that Jacob is adept and musical: it was not what Thea was expecting. A man interested in dry cases of the law, in accruing money, in fancy leather slippers; by Thea's rigid way of judging people, it should not follow he has talents that bleed into her sphere. It is inconvenient to Thea's argument against him, and Nella feels hopeful.

Jacob plays a few more phrases and stops, abashed. 'After two sons, my mother longed for a daughter,' he says, pressing a key. It echoes through the room. 'I came along, but she trained me anyway in the softer arts.'

'You are very good,' Nella says. 'How pleasing to see that the instrument is not just an ornament.'

'All beautiful things should have a purpose,' says Jacob. He turns to Thea. 'They should not be left in a corner uncelebrated, unseen.'

In the silence that follows, Jacob rises to his feet. 'Mistress Thea, should you ever wish to come and play it, I would be more than obliged. It is no lute, so I cannot carry it over to you on the Herengracht. You would have to come here.'

Thea knows it is her cue; she knows that this is a generous gesture, and a pointed one, made within the sight and earshot of her father. Jacob's offer is legitimate and sanctioned, and if it is accepted, what other offers might follow on its heels?

They all wait to see what Thea will say. She looks with concentration at the harpsichord. 'Thank you, Seigneur,' she says. 'But it is too precious an instrument. I fear my fingers might break it.'

Jacob smiles, closing the lid over the keys. Nella is furious, but she can do nothing about it now, and soon it is time for them to leave. He is going to Leiden for a couple of weeks on business for his mother, he says. But he will return, and when he does, they should all meet again. Yes, says Nella. We absolutely must.

Goodbyes and thank yous, and delicious rabbits, and of course we will repay the favour and have you to our table. Who knows what Cornelia might summon up in another fortnight, when early spring vegetables might be coming from the soil, and the lambs will soon be ready to be slaughtered?

They smile as they leave the house of Jacob van Loos, but walk in silence the five minutes it takes to reach their own. There is much Nella wants to say, to scold, to beg, to ask why they cannot see what she is trying to do, but she is tired, enveloped in her own thoughts. Otto pushes open their heavy door, and Cornelia appears from the shadows to greet them.

Nella looks at their cavernous space, their bare walls, the air of sorrow. 'What is it?' Cornelia says. 'What's wrong?'

Nella's words burst out of her, and she does nothing to stop them. 'Thea is a rude, ungrateful child.'

For a moment, the others stare at her in shock. 'What? She thinks she know how the world works,' Nella goes on. 'How her future will unfold according to her will. But it won't. She is going to live poor. And I will no longer take responsibility for it.'

'Nella,' Otto says, his voice a warning.

'No. I've had enough of all of you.'

'Madame,' Cornelia pleads, wringing her hands.

'You've all done what you wanted to do,' Nella cries. 'You all *do* what you want to do. Johannes pursued his own paths. And because of that, I never could. Otto, you and Marin chased your hearts' desires. And now Thea, stubborn as her mother, talks so impudently to Jacob? Sits there, refusing my help?'

'Do not speak of Marin and her heart,' says Otto.

'I will,' Nella says. 'She abandoned me, to this.'

'She abandoned *you*?' he says, incredulous.

Nella feels so angry, but her words are tumbling, more powerful than she can control. She cannot bear the way they are all looking at her, as if she has lost her senses.

'How do you know what I wanted to do?' Otto asks. 'You know nothing of Marin and me. And when have I ever stopped you from pursuing your own path? When, by God, will you ever stop pitying yourself?'

'Both of you, enough,' Cornelia urges.

Thea stands riveted by the words that shoot between her father and her aunt.

'You could have married,' Otto goes on, ignoring Cornelia's request. 'You never stop speaking of our poverty, as you describe it. You know nothing of the word. And you were eighteen when Johannes died, Nella. Eighteen! Your life had barely begun.'

'Yes,' Nella says, pointing at Thea. 'And then she came along. I had a child to raise, or have you forgotten?'

'She wasn't yours. You didn't have to raise her. In case you've forgotten.'

His words are blows. Nella turns to Thea, who stares at her, wide-eyed. *I wanted to look after you*, she wants to say, but the words won't come.

'One can always start again,' Otto says. 'One way or another. I know that, better than any of you. The truth is, Nella, you didn't want to. You could have left this house. Had children of your own. But you didn't, and now you regret it. And that is why we find ourselves in the salon of Jacob van Loos.'

Cornelia begins to weep. 'Stop it, stop it.'

'No fine words about Johannes after he was murdered paid for firewood to keep us warm,' Nella says, summoning all her strength. 'Nor did they put food in Thea's stomach, nor make clothes to dress her. No guild came to our aid. No neighbours cared. I had a murdered husband and her dead mother, and the only comfort we had was money – real money. And it saved our lives.'

'We saved each other,' Cornelia says.

'Money saved us,' Nella replies. 'Money is a shield. It's a weapon. It's a blessing. And who taught me that? Your *mother*, Thea. Your mother, who in the end took more risks than any of us and left us in this predicament. She took your father for a lover under the cloak of darkness, and the devil take the consequences—'

'Nella,' says Otto. 'Enough.'

'Jacob van Loos doesn't care about the story of Johannes and Marin Brandt, and that is a miracle. How likely is it that a man like him will come along again?'

'If you like Jacob so much,' Thea shouts, the ferocity of her voice shocking them into silence, 'then marry him yourself.'

Silence falls. None of them have ever spoken to each other like this, and Nella feels the horror of it, the coming repercussions, ringing through her blood. Shaken, she walks unsteadily up the stairs, as if retreating to her room will end this, when really it has just begun.

Their faces turn up to her from the dark hallway. Even in the guttering candlelight she can see Otto's anger, Thea's exhilarated expression at speaking her mind; how widely Cornelia's eyes pop in her head.

'Thea,' Nella says, straining with every sinew to keep her voice level: 'your mother conceived you in secret. Birthed you in secret. Died for you, in secret. Your father lived in a cloud of grief so thick that on your birthday he can still barely look at you. He claims he thinks only of your needs, but the truth is he's terrified to lose you, and will hobble your chances without even realizing. If I have learned anything these past eighteen years, it is that there are only two things you can rely on: yourself, and your ledger book. But we have lost our money. The kind of money that never runs out, no matter what you spend or lose? We've lost it. The disgrace of Johannes and your mother is our shame. It's your shame. You will carry it with you for as long as you live. So now you have only yourself.'

They are all frozen rigid, staring up at her as if under a spell. Nella takes a deep breath. 'Marry out of this family, Thea, as I married into it. Get out if you can. There's no other choice.'

XVII

As spring finally appears on the canal, a second winter sets in within the Herengracht house. The skies outside turn bluer as the light within diminishes. The inhabitants stumble in its semi-darkness, the corners deep, the corridors unnavigable. Cornelia packs away the fur collars, the heavy cloaks, and brings out the lighter ones, but there is nowhere they willingly travel together as a family. No menagerie visit, no pleasant garden to see the blossoms, no idle market trip. It is as if something has broken, that there is no way back from the words which were hurled, the ghost of a mother long gone, thrust like a lance to pierce an enemy's heart. And not just those long gone, but those who may never come. The husbands, the children, the bricks that women are told to use to build their lives.

Aunt Nella won't come out of her room. For over two weeks Thea hasn't seen her, which is a relief in its own way. It's a greater relief, however, not to have to see Jacob, but she's barely seen her father either, everybody keeping out of everyone else's way. It's not hard to do, in a house this size. You can listen for closing doors, for the creak of a floorboard, the tread of a foot, and plan your route accordingly: but you have no idea what anyone else is actually doing. Only Cornelia continues on her normal patterns: cooking food that no one seems to want, polishing and scrubbing, baking bread, cutting it, spreading it thick with butter and leaving it on a plate outside Aunt Nella's door. Aunt Nella loves bread and butter, but it's nursery food. Cornelia is feeding Aunt Nella the comforts of childhood.

Well, let her, Thea thinks. Let my aunt eat dry crusts, after the things she said.

But underneath, Thea's heart is in pain – that things should be like this, that everything should feel as if it's falling away. Her only sustenance through these days is her visits to Walter, and she takes advantage of the stultifying atmosphere on the Herengracht and the fact she is being less monitored, to steal time with him at the playhouse.

All through the fateful dinner at Jacob's, Thea had her mind on the third misericord to the left of the Old Church altar. She was exhilarated at what she has done to protect herself and Walter. She had tried to concentrate on the conversations over Jacob's steaming cups of tea, his ample table, his plinking harpsichord – but all she could think about was what she had done for love.

The money Thea left wedged under the carving must have been taken, for she had put it there well before the Sunday. Her actions thrilled her, but they also made her feel a little sick. She could see how angry Aunt Nella was becoming with her at Jacob's house, even before the storm in their own hallway afterwards. But she and Walter are safe now. Surely, they are safe.

'You promise we will marry as soon as the contract's finished?' she asks Walter one day in the painting-room, watching him dab at a Roman arch.

'Thea,' he says. 'Of course. We have already agreed.'

She regrets asking it as soon as she speaks, but she wants so much to tell him what has happened at her home: the awful argument that has left them all stranded from one another, the threat of Jacob, the struggle over money and her aunt's house in the country. This is not how life should be. She thinks of all the plays she has seen, when heroines strike out on their own or with their secret lovers. Why is she so paralysed? But at the same time, she wants to appear light and airy, effortless and easy. She wants to annihilate her whole biography, so that for Walter she exists only in this room, always pleasant, always desirable. He must complete his contract, that much she knows. That fact is immoveable. She has to be patient, and it isn't long, really, is it? Only another month or so. She can wait.

And yet. She and Walter must act on their betrothal before it's too late, before Jacob van Loos and his hints of marriage become too powerful to ignore.

Thea watches Walter's back as he paints the arch, ancient Rome coming back to life. She feels in the pit of her stomach the allure of his concentration, wishing it would turn on her, but also enjoying being a voyeur. Her growing physical desire for Walter overcomes her worry about everything else. She feels constantly hungry for his beauty, his caresses, no more wanting to ruin her stolen moments with him with talk of an expedient marriage than she was with the miniature or the blackmail note. She finds herself looking at his real palette, and notes that it is full of many colours. Whoever sent that doll of him was quite wrong. Walter is not a man who paints the world only red.

'I have a surprise for you,' he says, putting down his palette and wiping his hands, vanishing behind the flat of the Roman arch. He re-emerges, holding a board in his hands. 'Ready?'

Slowly, with some ceremony, Walter turns the board round, and Thea realizes that she is looking at her own face, worked in oils. 'It was just as I said. Like trying to paint the sun.'

For a moment, Thea is speechless. She does, in a way, look beautiful. She does, indeed, look bright. She has been committed into a piece of art. But something makes her hesitate. The fact is, the woman looking back at Thea doesn't look like her, not in the way that Walter's miniature seems to capture him. Her spirit is missing: it hurts to see its lack, because Walter is so smiling and proud, and he thinks he has made her happy. He thinks he has captured his love.

Thea is jarred by the realization that whilst Walter can paint a Roman arch or a coco-nut tree, or a strawberry bush, he has failed to capture her. She had thought such a thing impossible. It is a deeply discomforting moment, but she collects herself, and smiles. 'Oh, Walter,' she says. 'Thank you, sweeting. I've never had someone paint me before.'

'I'm glad that it was me,' he says.

She comes towards him, admiring the brushstrokes, admiring him, kissing between each compliment she offers of how well, how lovingly, he has worked her out, and he takes her kisses gladly.

Still, Thea thinks, when she is making her way home: Walter made the effort. He wanted to do it, to commit me to immortality. And that is all that matters.

When she slips back into the house, she's surprised to hear her aunt's voice down in the working kitchen, talking with Cornelia. It is the first time Thea has heard her aunt speak for more than a fortnight. She creeps to the head of the kitchen stairs: they are working at the table by the sounds of it, a spoon clanking a bowl, the rasp of a knife down lengths of endless carrots.

'Not even one pineapple?' Cornelia is saying.

'I won't allow a single one,' says Aunt Nella. She is silent for a moment, and Thea listens to their knives hitting the wood. 'He was not honest with me.'

'He was going to tell you the truth, Madame,' Cornelia says. 'You just happened to get there before him.'

'But my map, Cornelia. They'd written all over my map.' She pauses. 'I wish he would leave my past alone, given how unwilling he is to share his. There has always been so much he will not tell me.'

'Nor me, Madame. Perhaps that is a good thing. If a person tells another everything about himself, does he not, in a way, disappear?'

'Not at all. I should rather say it's the opposite.'

'But the person *you* have known vanishes before your eyes. I would not want that. I prefer the fragments offered.'

'Yet Thea tells you everything,' Aunt Nella says.

Cornelia is silent for a moment. 'It is strange you think that.'

'Why? It has always been the way.'

'Madame: you do not tell Otto everything, either. You will not tell him why you won't sell Assendelft. If it's such a hovel, and this is your home.'

'This is Otto's home.' Her voice is heavy. She sounds exhausted. 'Johannes left it to him.'

'Oh, come,' says Cornelia. 'Otto's name might be on the

papers, but he was speaking in anger about you leaving. It is your home.' She hesitates. 'Many things were spoken that night that people did not mean.'

Aunt Nella sighs. 'And yet I doubt Otto will forgive me for the things I said.'

'Of course he will. As you should forgive him.'

'He thinks so little of me, Cornelia. He thinks I could have left here, after Thea was born. He says these things, and then expects to take my father's fields.'

'Madame,' Cornelia says gently. 'They are your fields.'

'Yes. And they're the only things that belong to me,' Thea's aunt says. 'In matters such as these, Cornelia, it *is* important whose name is on the paper.'

It has been a long while since Thea has listened in on a conversation such as this. She used to do it all the time. She realizes how much it soothes her to hear their companionable exchanges, however brusque they get. Their deep familiarity can never disappear.

'I truly do think,' her aunt starts again, 'that Jacob is a good match for her.'

'But Thea wants true love,' says Cornelia. Thea's heart swells with gratitude.

'What does that even mean? And where's she going to find it?' says Aunt Nella. 'The only place you find that kind of love is on the stage of the Schouwburg. This idea that Otto has, and Thea too – that I'm trying to get rid of her. I'm not.'

'I know, but—'

'And this way she speaks to me. As if I have much to learn from a young woman who has spent her entire life under one roof, deprived of precisely *nothing*.'

'But perhaps you do,' Cornelia says.

'She hasn't *lived*, Cornelia. Hasn't made a mess of her life, nor tangled herself in the mess of other people's. She has no scars.'

'How do you know?'

'She knows nothing of failed dreams.'

'Do you wish her to be scarred? To fail?'

'No, of course not, but—'

'Because I'm sure the passing of time will make that inevitable.'

'And I am trying to prevent that. Yet she insists on telling me the shape of life. Its points and purposes. How I am failing to take it in my hands. She follows her father in that manner. And her mother. What does she know of my hands? She doesn't even *look* at my hands. Thea is all jug, no stopper.'

Cornelia laughs.

'I don't know why you find it funny. I have always been respectful of my elders.'

Cornelia laughs even harder. 'Is that so? You and Marin were a pair of angels with each other?'

Aunt Nella sighs and falls to silence. The room is filled only by the women's movements, well practised and effortless as their hands knead pastry and mould it into tins.

'Cornelia,' her aunt begins again, and this time there is a strange hesitancy in her voice, a thickness to it that makes Thea lean down the stairs even more. 'Do you ever think about the miniaturist?'

At the mention of this word, Thea goes very still. The air around her seems to condense. 'No,' says Cornelia eventually, but her tone is guarded. 'That was a long time ago.'

'But sometimes it feels like yesterday.'

'Madame, why are you—'

'Don't you *ever* wonder if she might be near?'

'Of course I don't.'

'If she's watching us?'

'Madame—'

'Because at the Sarragon ball – and – no, let me speak, even though I know you'll say I'm mad, or that it's one of my melancholies – but I had the strangest sensation.' Aunt Nella sounds almost enraptured. 'The cold on my back. It was *there*, Cornelia – at my neck, just like it used to be, as if I was being watched. I swear: I heard her say my name.'

'*What?*'

'I swear, I *saw* her.'

In the dark above, her heart thumping, Thea puts her own hand to the back of her neck. She remembers how cold she felt herself to be along the canal, heading for the Schouwburg, the prickling sensation at her nape. Her conviction that perhaps, after all, Walter was right, and there was someone watching her. But who is this person her aunt is speaking of, with such admiration, almost akin to love?

'She isn't here, Madame,' Cornelia says. 'She wasn't at the ball, and she isn't on the canals. She isn't *here*.' Cornelia hesitates. 'And maybe she never was.'

'She *was*,' says Thea's aunt. 'Because who were you really looking for, Cornelia, when Thea went to buy the bream?'

Thea can hear the almost imperceptible intake of Cornelia's breath. She thinks again of her nursemaid's horror at the arrival of the package, the note, her fierce desire to know who they were from, what was inside them. *There are things that have happened in this house, Thea. Before you were born.* She thinks of the miniatures in her bedroom, Walter and the golden house, hidden in her box. Those above them, in the attic: her parents in their frozen, tiny perfection.

'I told you,' says Cornelia. 'I was waiting for Thea.'

'But, Cornelia, how do you know the miniaturist hasn't come back? We could barely keep hold of her the first time she came into our lives.'

There is a clatter as Cornelia throws down her knife. 'I rue the day the Seigneur ever bought you that cabinet house. I rue it with all my heart. Madame Marin was right about those frightening little dolls with their hints and threats: we should have kept them out.'

'I *sense* her, Cornelia. I think she's here.'

'Nonsense. Forgive me, Madame, but that's nonsense. Leave it alone. I thought you wanted to leave the past alone?'

Cornelia takes up her knife again and starts aggressively chopping. Thea dare not move. A thought occurs to her: if the miniaturist is the one who has made all these pieces, then why is Cornelia not telling Aunt Nella about the parcel that arrived?

'Maybe she found out what I did to my wedding cabinet,' says Aunt Nella. 'She knows how I destroyed it. What if she's come back for revenge?'

'Sweet Jesus, Madame. *Enough.*'

'Sometimes,' Thea's aunt says in a quieter voice, 'I have wished, with all my heart, that she would come back.'

'You should not say that. How can you say such a thing, after everything she did?'

'And what was it she did, other than show me myself?

Those pieces she gave me were beautiful,' Aunt Nella goes on. 'Do you remember the lute? The betrothal cup, the box of marzipan? She gave me a life I had lost, a life that I'd been promised.'

'She was a meddler,' says Cornelia. 'A witch.'

'She was a guide. My protector.'

'Your protector,' Cornelia repeats with scorn.

'I didn't listen to her, and look at the price we paid. I wish I'd listened. I wish I'd paid her more attention.'

Cornelia exhales. 'All that is over. You need to make peace with Otto, speak to your niece—'

'There's something I have to tell you,' Aunt Nella says. 'I have a confession.'

'A confession?' Cornelia says, the dread in her voice palpable. Whoever this miniaturist is to Thea's aunt, she is something very different to Cornelia.

'I went into the attic and opened Marin's chest.'

'What?' Cornelia breathes. 'But we're not supposed to. That's for Thea, when she's ready.'

Thea grips the banister as if she is holding on for her life. From down the stairs comes the sound of a lettuce being viciously ripped apart. Thea waits, her breath held, not daring to move as the lettuce segments land on the ancient wood.

Of course the chest was my mother's, Thea thinks, astounded that she did not realize this before. Of course it was. She pictures herself and her aunt, up in the dark of the attic, kneeling before the chest as one might an altar. They have done it without the other knowing, each of them feeling their way through the miscellany of Marin Brandt for comfort and rescue. Now Marin's precious map sits in a cartographer's window in Raamstraat. At least her miniature is in its resting place, next to that of Thea's father.

'I removed the miniature of the baby,' Aunt Nella says.

'Madame.' Cornelia sounds horrified. 'Why did you do such a thing?'

'Because Otto is not the only one who wants to keep Thea close.'

'I don't believe it's just that. Not from you. Did you put it back?'

'No.'

'You want to summon the miniaturist.'

'I can't *summon* her, Cornelia.'

'Then why didn't you put the baby away again?' Cornelia hisses.

'Because I wanted to remember what it felt like to have someone on my side,' Aunt Nella hisses back.

Cornelia gives a mirthless laugh. 'You still believe she will solve all our problems.' She pauses. 'I have to tell Otto.'

'Absolutely not.'

'We need to be alert. Those things are dangerous. They brought us no happiness.'

'They made me happy,' Aunt Nella says. 'I admired them, and I shouldn't have got rid of them. They were mine, Cornelia. My story. Something unique. When she sent them to me, I finally felt that someone understood what was happening to me, that someone truly saw. I long for that feeling again.' She hesitates. 'Because the truth is, I feel so alone.'

Her aunt's voice is full of such sorrow, so full of yearning and pain, that Thea's eyes fill with tears. She rubs them, furiously, as she hears her aunt begin to cry. This is the true confession, and Thea can hardly bear to hear it. She moves backwards up the kitchen stairs, praying to creak no floorboard, that she might escape this conversation unheard.

Up in her room with the door locked, Thea sits before her two miniatures. She holds Walter in her fist and squeezes him, as if to do so might move the man she loves to more decisive action. She touches his hair, missing the way their tendernesses were simpler before the prospect of Jacob, before the threat of the blackmail note, and now, perhaps, the intentions of this miniaturist. She places the small gilded house in the middle of her palm, watching as the March light through the window gives it a faint glow. Whose house is this? Thea wonders, and why has it been sent to me, if it is my aunt who seeks the miniaturist, and not me?

But staring at these pieces whose meanings she cannot penetrate, it is her aunt's loneliness which affects Thea most. The force of it seeps into her blood and up into her head, like strange medicine she's never drunk but which tastes oddly familiar. Aunt Nella had a cabinet house. A wedding gift which she destroyed. *Cornelia, do you ever think about the miniaturist?* Clearly, Aunt Nella does. Her plaintive enquiry, her confession. The baby she has lifted from the past to comfort her in the present.

You only need to look at these miniature pieces to see how they might influence a person, and Thea is sympathetic to Aunt Nella's belief in their importance. She understands her aunt's desire to respect and read them as something greater than the sum of their beauty, as a means of being seen. It surprises Thea to discover that she and her aunt should have such feelings in common. But as Thea looks down at Walter and the little house, she cannot find a lesson in them. She refuses to give way to the idea that within Walter's tiny limbs or on his empty palette, or inside the four walls of an impenetrable, tiny, gilded house, lie any encrypted messages to guide her through this turbulence. But she also refuses Cornelia's belief, that there is malice in these pieces, whoever this miniaturist is. Because surely, Thea thinks, locking her miniatures away in her secret box once more: nothing made this beautiful can be that bad.

XVIII

Thea doesn't see the second blackmail note arrive. She only finds it by chance, opening the front door to let out Lucas, who has begun to test the month of March for sunbathing opportunities. It's a few days since her visit to Walter and his presentation to her of the disorientating portrait, and she's still reeling from the revelations about this miniaturist having made a possible return. Her father and Aunt Nella have now exchanged a few cool words, but there is no sense of a real truce and the atmosphere of unhappiness remains. However, these quandaries evaporate from Thea's mind as soon as she looks down on the doorstep and sees another note, small and square just like the first, and her name across the top.

For a moment, Thea almost hopes it's from Jacob, because then at least she will be able to deal with it. A little letter from Leiden, easy to dismiss. But she knows, looking at the hand-writing, that it's from the same person as before. She feels faint, suffused with dread, but she manages to look up and down the canal to see who might be fleeing. The citizenry of Amsterdam that she can see make unlikely candidates: a herring-seller and her boy lugging a basket; a maid, laden down with four new brooms she must have just bought at market; a priest; a couple with their small child. None of them look the kind of person who might want to make her life hell.

Thea stares down again at the note, not wishing to pick it up, sick at the thought of its contents. But no one else in her family can see this, so she forces herself out of her stupor and slips it in her pocket. Leaving Lucas behind in his optimistic world of cold sunshine, folding herself back into the gloom, she closes the front door as quietly as she can. Heart thumping, she walks up the staircase towards her room, and opens the note as soon as she's locked her door.

Do not believe the love you feel on seeing him is more than the damage I can inflict. This continued boldness does you no service, but one hundred guilders more will keep me silent, or I will tell Clara Sarragon, and all the city will know. By this Sunday, the Old Church, the same place: the third misericord to the left of the altar. No gold dress can cover what you did.

Thea feels as if she's dreaming. It isn't over: how could she ever have believed it would be? The mention of the gold dress chills her, never mind the reference to Clara Sarragon. The tone is overblown, of course, and would be laughable in any other circumstance, but the writer of the note is telling the truth. Revealing to Clara Sarragon about her and Walter's love would indeed ruin Thea and her family irrevocably, however much she herself believes in their betrothal. They have not been properly married in a church yet, and even if they were to be, it would not be a marriage sanctioned by her father and aunt. She would bring scandal yet again to her family.

Thea thinks of her father, finding out. She pictures Cornelia, her disappointment. Her aunt's fury and sorrow. With shaking hands she folds away the paper, tucking it into the secret box with the miniatures and the first note. She wants to keep these awful missives, private proof to mark that something like this has happened to her, that it wasn't just her overwrought imagination. That it isn't just a dream. Her aunt might say that Thea has no scars – but what does Aunt Nella know? Aunt Nella has been so scared of living, for so long, she would never receive a note like this.

Thea lies back on her bed, thinking hard what she can do to protect herself and Walter from this vicious persistence. Reaching into the box, she takes out the miniatures, trying to look at them as if through her aunt's eyes. She examines the doll of Walter, his hands, his arms, his legs, his face – his entire body – for any signs of guidance, as her aunt believes she once received herself. She looks at her lover's palette again, his brush, as if to find there something she might have missed, but Walter is exactly as he arrived on her doorstep in January. He is a fixity. Walter will not change, Walter can be relied upon. And besides, no more miniatures have come for a while. Perhaps the miniaturist does not want her, after all.

And in that moment, Thea knows what she will do. The realization calms her. It's a risk, and it might not work. But no one else will take it for her, and no one should or could. The problem is hers alone.

◈

It's busy inside the Old Church, but mercifully no one is near the misericords. Thea takes out the second batch of guilders she has prepared from her secret box, and tucks it with the carved warring couple. Instead of leaving the church, she hides herself behind a nearby pillar to observe. She will wait here, hidden, all day and all night if she has to. The first note stated that the misericord would be checked daily, and it's still early, so there is every chance someone might come at some point today. And besides, Thea is an Amsterdammer: she knows how patience is supposed to be rewarded. She knows how to watch, unseen.

For hours, she stands, spying on Amsterdam. Watching the citizens who come to pray, to promise God that they will be better this month, this year, this lifetime. Who might be bartering with God that if He will grant them what they wish or need – money, a good harvest, a new employment, a healthy baby – by some miracle, they will transform themselves. What must He think, Thea wonders, of these endless promises that are bound to be unfulfilled? Perhaps He is used to it.

She watches, too, the men who come to broker business deals – secret ones, no doubt, because why else are they here and not at the Bourse, or the guilds? It makes Thea think of her own father, how he too was formulating a secret plan for Assendelft, and how it has backfired. Is he somewhere here, too, praying on his knees for a solution to their problems, whilst yards away, his dead lover lies like dust beneath the slabs?

Thea wonders if she will ever know what went on between her father and Marin Brandt. Cornelia told Aunt Nella that perhaps we are not supposed to know everything about another person, because to do so would make them vanish to themselves. She looks over to the far east corner where her mother lies, unmarked. Perhaps some secrets this family has held on to are better for being nourished and hidden in the dark.

Thea feels a rush of affection for her father, the way his eyes lit up on seeing her on her birthday. Aunt Nella is wrong: he did not avoid looking at his daughter on the death day of Marin Brandt. He opened his arms to her, he told her she was perfect. And Aunt Nella is wrong that he will hobble Thea's future. None of them will.

More hours pass, and Thea loses track of the time. Her legs begin to ache. Her stomach longs for some of Cornelia's fritters. Night falls; a choirboy moves round the church, lighting candle after candle. She longs to slump down, to sit for a while, but she knows that even by candlelight that would make her too visible, so she summons more determination from within herself and keeps waiting. And eventually, after hearing the bell chime eight, and worrying how on earth she will explain this absence to her family, Thea sees a movement by the misericord.

A hem of a cloak, swishing. A woman's back, her hooded head bent over the carved couple, her hand fumbling to see if something's there. Thea feels light-headed, a spark of anger as the woman slips the guilders into her pocket. But her plan is working: Thea has marked every single guilder, and the proof is now in this woman's pocket.

She watches the woman straighten, her back still facing Thea. Her hood falls loose, revealing pale hair which she swiftly conceals. She hurries out of the church into the cold night, and Thea follows her as discreetly as she can. The woman takes Warmoestraat, one of the busier thoroughfares in the old town, and Thea struggles to keep her in view, the only lights in the dark those flickering from the windows, and the flames of the occasional street brazier. The unremarkable cloak helps this woman blend in too easily. But Thea is dogged, and will not lose sight of her.

The woman hurries off Warmoestraat, down over the bridge onto Hartenstraat. Wherever she's heading, she clearly wishes to get there fast. They are heading in the direction of the Schouwburg now, and Thea feels a rising sense of dread – but the woman turns, walking quickly in the direction of the Jordaan, moving deeper and deeper into the warren of narrow streets that form the working quarter. When the woman finally stops in the middle of a street, Thea half-turns, pretending to be absorbed in a closed apothecary's shop window, staring sightlessly into the dim display of dried leaves in jars and seed-pods. The woman vanishes through a door, and Thea darts forward to follow her towards the close-built, narrow facade.

The door, plain, of not particularly thick wood, falls almost closed, but Thea puts out her hand, her heart hammering. She waits, listening as the woman's footsteps move quickly upstairs to the first floor. Another door is opened then closed again, and the ground floor hallway and the corridor above fall silent.

Still on the street, hungry from her hours waiting in the church, exhausted and disorientated, Thea hovers, her hand still stopping the door from closing, fearing that the woman might only be dropping off the guilders to come back outside, that she might walk down the stairs again after realizing she has not locked the front door. They will have to have their confront-ation in the middle of the street, the last thing Thea wants.

But the interior is quiet, and Thea goes in.

It is a dark hallway, cold flagstones underfoot, and the whitewashed walls emanate damp. It's like a murderer's den, Thea thinks, before telling herself not to be ridiculous. There is a locked door to her right, which she assumes is another dwelling, or perhaps a vacant shop front. The atmosphere is claustrophobic. The woman has left no trail of perfume; this corridor smells only of dereliction and unhappiness. Thea's blood is racing through her body; she has never entered another house like this, uninvited, like a thief. But who is the thief here? she asks herself. That woman has my guilders, and she took them without a second thought.

Slowly, she approaches the staircase, a flight of about ten deep stairs leading to an even darker first floor. There are no windows anywhere. It's like the outside world doesn't exist, but Thea listens: upstairs she can hear the sound of murmuring voices, but not how many there are, or whether they belong to a man or woman. She'd had a simple plan, to follow the taker of the envelope and find them out, to confront them, to tell them that she wasn't scared of shame. But now she feels timid, unwilling to burst in.

She takes the first stair, gauging her weight on the wood. Her years tiptoeing around her own house, hoping to hear a titbit or a secret, prove useful. She can balance her weight and move silently, testing each stair for a creak or moan. She makes progress: the fourth step, the fifth, the sixth, and as she reaches the first-floor corridor, she realizes there is only one door, a few steps along to her right. The voices are coming from within. Thea shifts herself along the corridor, her back to the wall. It occurs to her, only now, that these people might be dangerous. What if they're armed? Thea tells herself she is an adventurer, like her family would pretend when she was little: relying only on her wits. I can kick, she thinks. I have my fists. I can give her a fright.

Even so: she wishes Walter was here. Even Aunt Nella would be welcome.

Thea moves towards the keyhole and bends down. The talking within the room has stopped, and she prays that they haven't heard the rustle of her skirts. She needs the advantage of surprise, but there is no sign of anyone; the inhabitants are out of view. The room is small, kept clean, just like Rebecca's at the Schouwburg, but much more sparsely furnished: a simple bed for two, a pair of chairs, a low table graced only in that moment by a single pewter candlestick, whose candle throws shadows across the cracked wall. The floorboards are dark wood, and Thea spies a cradle resting upon them. It is not elaborate, no carvings or runners: if anything it looks like half a beer barrel cut in two with the sides raised and fixed with stilts. It has been pushed longways against the wall, and a pair of tiny fists rise from within, slowly pummelling the fusty air before receding again, as if they had never been there at all.

Suddenly, a woman's skirts come into view. As she seats herself at the table, with Thea's guilders in her hand, her profile lowers into the frame of the keyhole. The woman is about the same age as Aunt Nella, but she has a much softer face, pale blonde hair and a smaller nose, a plump lower lip that juts in concentration as she begins to count Thea's second offering. She looks as exhausted as Thea feels, and as she begins to count the baby in its cradle barrel shows its fists again and starts to cry.

'See to him, will you?' she says, not looking up. When she speaks, her lip is less plump. Her mouth pinches over her words, her voice hard. 'He's your son.'

A pair of boots move across the floorboards towards the table. A man's lower half comes into view and crosses in front of the woman. 'All there?' he says, and when he speaks, Thea feels a disorientation so acute that she has to steady herself against the doorframe.

'Yes,' says the woman. 'Generous, like you said.'

'We've done enough now, Griete. I don't want to do it again.'

Griete. Before Thea can even think about what's happening before her, the man's legs move swiftly to the crib. He leans over it, reaching in, and when Thea sees his face her stomach lurches, sucked up into horrendous realization. Her heart sits on her tongue, a dead toad stoppering her mouth. A wave of nausea rises up and she watches Walter lift the boy into his arms.

She cannot breathe, but she cannot draw herself away from the sickening aperture of this keyhole. It is a picture that makes no sense, but still Thea looks. It is all she can do not to scream, not to kick down the door and put her hands around the woman's throat.

'You said she had money,' the woman continues. 'You said she had pluck? She lives on the Herengracht – what's one more threat?'

Thea clamps her hand over her mouth and bites the insides of her cheeks. How can they not tell she is here, when her whole body is on fire? Surely they will turn to the door? Surely the smoke will be billowing under the bottom of it into their little room, to come and choke them? Surely they can hear her whimpering?

She wants to run, but still she's rooted to the spot. She cannot drag herself from this parallel world. It is the real world, in which she is a fool, a dupe, someone to be tipped upside down, for her pockets to be emptied, someone who could never truly be loved.

Who is this Griete, with Thea's guilders in her hands, so capable, so in control? Thea looks down; her hand is on the doorknob and she's turning it, she's going in. The couple turn in shock to see who it is, Walter's face ghoulish in the shadows, his horror as he clutches the infant, the woman rising to her feet. From the corner of the room, an older child comes toddling towards its mother. Mama, mama, it keeps on saying.

'Who is she?' Thea says, before the woman can say it herself. 'Walter, who is she?'

But it is not Walter who speaks. The woman looks at Thea, her expression almost one of pity. 'Oh, poor girl,' she says. 'You must be Thea.'

'You don't know who I am.'

'Of course I do,' the woman says. 'Because I'm his wife.'

A Wife

XIX

Otto and Nella are at last in agreement over something, wanting to keep Thea safe, to not push her back into the world. Thea has kept to her room for a month. Her fever had broken after five days of torment for them all, but in the weeks that have followed, she's still frail, won't eat much, turning her face to her bedroom wall. Nella feels ashamed about her own confinement in March, all because of an argument with Otto, when here is her niece, truly and mystifyingly unwell, unable to stand on her own two feet. They let her sleep a lot these days.

They'd all been sick with worry when she hadn't come home. Such had been their separate ways of existing since the argument, they hadn't noticed Thea missing until around six in the evening. Finding her room empty, Cornelia had rushed to the playhouse to see if she was there, and when she'd come back empty-handed, they knew something was very wrong. Otto ran to the docks, to check if any of his old VOC colleagues had seen her, and Nella set out searching through the Golden Bend into the Jordaan, for any sign of their precious child.

When they both returned, bleak with worry, they found Cornelia upstairs with Thea shivering, incoherent in her bed. Despite the relief which made them both cry out on seeing her, temporarily reunited in their love, it was horrifying to see the state she was in. They kept asking her what had happened, but Thea wouldn't speak. Cornelia was blanched with fear. 'Stop asking,' she said. 'She's safe at least.'

'We need a physician,' said Nella. 'Now.'

And physicians have come. They have been coming for four weeks. These men have sliced Thea's veins to let out blood. They have placed leeches upon her, and it angers Cornelia to see them do it, and Otto finds it hard to look. Thea, damp and weak, has tossed and turned in her sleep, talking about golden houses and empty palettes, and babies in cradles, and a door she pulled and pulled on and should never have pushed. Her delirium is catching, and listening to her, Nella feels slightly insane. It is a glimpse into her niece's imagination, and not what she was expecting to find. What does Thea know about babies in cradles, or golden houses? What door did she push that led to this disaster?

'No more leeches,' says Otto. 'I'm sending for Witsen.'

'Out of the question,' Nella says. 'He's a gardener, not a doctor.'

Cornelia looks at both of them with disgust, as if she cannot believe, even now, they are managing to disagree.

But the fever has gone now, and it is April, and although spring is really here and the lambs are being slaughtered, and the canals are fully melted and full of boats, there is no normality in this house, no chance of inviting Jacob within its walls to dinner. They will not endanger her recovery.

Nella sends a note to Jacob on the Prinsengracht, explaining in a lie that Thea has gone to visit friends in Antwerp for a small duration, close friends from her schooldays. She worries that it will be Mrs Lutgers who opens it, tossing it on the fire before her master has a chance to read it, that Jacob will be left in the dark as to why they have suddenly withdrawn. But he replies, in his flowing hand, that he looks forward to seeing Thea once she returns. It is one tiny light in the darkness. They have not lost him yet.

Thea now seems, more than anything, exhausted. She will talk to them of little things, but not of what happened to her that night she came back so pulled apart. Most conversation quickly tires her. For now, these men of medicine and scalpels have been sent away, and the family flail as if pushed under-water, terrified that some damage has been done to Thea that cannot be reversed. She spends the mornings sitting at the window, looking out at nothing, absent-mindedly petting Lucas. In the afternoons, she tends to sleep. She even reads a little of Jacob's book, and also the family Bible. She plucks at the lute, but always without spirit.

What has happened to their child? What did she see? Why has this happened to them, they who were having so little luck in the winter, now forced into more unhappiness in spring?

Ever since Thea's collapse, Cornelia has not been able to go to the markets alone. She is uneasy about something, but won't say exactly what, and Nella assumes it is a general worry over Thea. Cornelia begs Otto to go with her to buy fish, but Otto wants to stay with his daughter, in case their child starts to speak of what happened, so he can get to the bottom of it and make it better. He has kept a vigil next to Thea day in, day out, at the expense of his own sleep. He looks care-worn, his clothes crumpled, his face gaunt.

'Be with Cornelia,' Nella says. 'Thea's still asleep. Get some fresh air, you need it. She'll still be here when you return.'

As she says these words, Nella fears they might always be true. Thea will never leave her room, her vibrant niece will exist this way forever, in the heart of this empty house. She wonders if Otto is happy this might be so, that he has got his wish that Thea might never leave his side. She shakes off the uncharitable thought. No father would wish his daughter to be this silent, this inert. They have always loved Thea for her chatter, as infuriating as it has been in recent months. I would do anything to hear her argue with me, Nella thinks, astonished at how quickly feelings change.

She has hoped, in the past four weeks, to hear something from the miniaturist. Some sign must surely come, anything to help her through this hell. But there has been nothing. All she has is the miniature baby, which she clutches secretly in her pocket when she's sure that Cornelia and Otto aren't looking. Nella is certain that the miniaturist was here, and cannot believe she might have tempted her like that, only to abandon her for good.

Otto and Cornelia depart in search of cheap crabs to stew later, and just as Nella is settling in a chair outside Thea's door, she hears a knock. For a whole month, they have been worried about the risk of the news of Thea's collapse spreading along the canals, mutating into vicious gossip. So a knocked door cannot go unanswered, and as nervous as she is, propriety wins out. Exhausted, Nella drags herself to her feet and goes down.

She opens the door, hoping perhaps to see a parcel on the doorstep, or a figure disappearing up the canal, as it was in the old days: but to her dismay, Caspar Witsen stands before her, that old satchel across his chest, and a small, curiously leaved plant cupped in a pot in his hands.

'Madame Brandt,' he says, his expression slightly haunted. 'How is she?'

His fingernails, Nella notices, are pristine, and it appears that he has drawn a comb through his wild tangle. She hesitates. She cannot have this conversation on the doorstep, and neither does she want him in her house, but there is nothing for it. 'Mr Witsen,' she says. 'Come in.'

She shuts him into the hallway. Close up, she has forgotten how tall he is, how spindly. 'I've brought you an aloe, Madame,' he says, proffering it.

Nella cannot hide her surprise. 'For me?'

'A peace-offering.'

When she does not take it, Caspar, embarrassed, squeezes one of the leaves. 'Slice this open and you'll find a cooling concoction. You can apply it to burns and inflammations of the skin. You can also drink it in tea. It has calming, cleansing properties, you see.'

He stops, as if he fears he has been gabbling. She regards him. 'There have been no fires in this house,' she says, but she knows it isn't true.

Caspar looks a little crestfallen, and Nella feels irritably guilty. 'Thank you,' she says to him, sighing, taking the aloe from his hands.

'It's extremely effective,' Caspar says. 'Aloes are astonishing things. Very resilient. The moisture they can hold. The challenging terrain in which they can flourish. We had many aloes at the university garden—'

'Thank you, Mr Witsen.'

Nella rotates the plant in her hands, admiring its deep green spines, its potency. It looks so incongruous against the wooden panelling and the black and white floor. 'The depths of my knowledge are shallow, when it comes to plants,' she says. She looks up. 'But I suppose you knew that already.'

It is meant as a rebuke, a reference to his trespasses weeks earlier, his handwriting all over her childhood house, his plans without permission. But Caspar Witsen smiles. It is the first smile Nella has seen in over a month. 'Ah, Madame Brandt,' he says. 'My knowledge too is in its infancy.'

They stand for a moment. 'Sometimes,' Caspar says, 'I am a thoughtless person.'

The truthfulness of his words meets a tender place under Nella's ribs. She feels her face turning warm.

'I never meant to upset you about your house in Assendelft,' he continues. 'Land is important, I understand that. The house is precious to you.'

Nella stares at the attempt of the combed hair, this green offering in her hands. She has been starved of conversation for too long, and men's conversation at that. His apology feels heartfelt. It is her turn to feel a little embarrassed. 'Join me in the kitchen,' she says. 'Thea's asleep, and I do not wish to wake her.' She pauses. 'Perhaps we can try this aloe tea.'

❧

At the kitchen table, Caspar sits like a scarecrow brought in from the garden. 'This house is enormous,' he says. 'I would lay down my pair of shoes in this house and not know where to find them.'

'It does happen,' Nella replies over her shoulder, fixing the kettle on the hook to boil water for tea. 'When I was Thea's age, I used to have a miniature version of it. That made it easier to see where everything was.'

'How enchanting.'

'That is one word for it. It was a wedding gift from my husband. I had it all in miniature, fitted into a cabinet.'

'Do you still have it? That would be a wonder to look at.'

'No longer in my possession,' she says. 'Too small to live in.'

Witsen smiles again. 'Too big, or too small. Like a tale for a child. A house like this would be very expensive to maintain. You should have kept the miniature one.'

'We manage,' says Nella shortly.

'Of course you do,' Witsen replies, his cheeks flushing. 'Shall I cut a leaf?'

'Will it not maim the plant?'

'It will grow again. That is the beauty of these living things.' He pauses. 'And besides: better a leaf than a vein.'

Leaving the kettle hanging over the fire, Nella comes to sit opposite him. A shaft of April sunlight from the street-level window drops between them on the table, illuminating the scars made by Cornelia's knives, carved over decades into the wood. 'Otto has told you that Thea is unwell,' says Nella.

Witsen looks grave. 'I was most distressed to hear it. It's partly why I'm here.'

'Partly?'

'Why, yes. I came to give you the aloe.'

'You keep in correspondence with Otto?'

Caspar glances through the window, and looks uncomfortable. 'I do consider him a friend, Madame Brandt.'

The kettle begins to whistle. He pulls out a small knife from his satchel, and expertly slices off one of the aloe spines from the base. 'See,' he says, drawing another incision down the middle. As the leaf bisects, a clear, thick liquid rises to the surface.

'It looks like glue,' Nella says.

But Caspar Witsen is concentrating and does not reply, and Nella has to admit it is mesmerizing to watch him lift a slug-like length of sap onto his blade before dropping it into the teapot. She begins to understand Clara Sarragon's fascination with Caspar's particular expertise, and a little bud of satisfaction blooms inside her to know that he has abandoned Sarragon, despite her wealth.

'Now the water,' he says.

She fetches the kettle and pours the water into the pot. The aloe sap melts away and Caspar stirs it with a spoon. 'It's good for the digestion.' He hesitates. 'Also for restoring lost appetite and melancholy.'

She narrows her eyes. 'Do you make allusions to my weight, or to the condition of my mind?'

Caspar looks caught, as if he doesn't know what the right answer might be.

'Does Otto talk to you of me?' she asks. 'Of us? Of Thea, Cornelia?'

'Sometimes.'

'And what does he say?'

'Nothing I am sure that he does not say to you.'

It is a clever evasion. Nella does not reply, but she feels Witsen absorbing her silence, and it unnerves her, leaving her as exposed as the leaf of the bisected aloe, as if he will press his knife to her own side and cut open the secrets of her green heart.

She hadn't noticed her lost weight herself. It was Cornelia

who came to tell it, by the looseness of her skirts. Cornelia was disapproving. 'It's not as if we can afford just to throw food away, Madame, or give it to the orphans,' she said.

'We can give it to the orphans, and we should,' Nella had replied, picking over half-eaten pufferts, cold vegetable *hutspots*, wondering what they were going to do, now they had reached this impasse, Thea in her room, and the rest of them drifting round, lost. Lucas might be happy with scraps of egg, but they cannot do this for another eighteen years.

'Shall we?' says Caspar, breaking her thoughts. He lifts the teapot and pours the liquid into two cups.

'How do I know you aren't poisoning me?'

Caspar laughs. 'I would never do that.' He blows on the surface of his cup, takes a sip first.

Nella follows his lead. 'It doesn't taste of anything.'

'That's good,' he says. 'Some of these preparations can be disgusting.'

They blow and sip, blow and sip. Nella is grateful for the cup: she can use it as a prop, a little shield to keep this man at bay. He has an insistence to him, a sort of fizzing energy. There is nothing languid about Caspar Witsen. 'I have always believed that whenever one feels melancholy, it is a matter of filling one's stomach,' he says.

'I am not melancholy.'

Their eyes meet but Caspar does not look away; it is Nella who glances down. 'Fasting presents delirium, Madame,' he says. 'We should drink sweet milk, eat fresh bread, good mutton and beef.'

'I wonder where you put it.'

He grins, taking another sip. 'Aloe tea. The beauty of

balance. The Amsterdammer's dream. I believe in looking after the body,' he says. 'Perhaps more than I believe in God.'

The hairs on the back of Nella's neck rise up. 'That's a bold statement.'

'Well, no one can hear us, Madame Brandt. Unless you're planning on reporting me to the nearest pastor?'

Nella laughs, and it feels so good, so freeing. It has been a long time since she laughed. 'So you do not believe in God's plan?' she says. 'In destiny?'

Caspar Witsen takes this question into himself, eyes shining with the philosophical pleasure of it. 'I believe our fates are more in our own hands than we are prepared to accept.'

Now her cup has cooled, Nella drinks deep. 'It's funny you think that. Because I often feel the opposite. As if my fate is in the hands of others.'

He nods. 'It is a common complaint.'

'As yours was in the hands of Clara Sarragon?'

'Indeed.'

What is she doing, sitting down here in the bowels of the house, with a man she barely knows? Nella bends forward, placing her cup down, and the crown of her head catches a beam of sun.

'Sunlight,' says Caspar. '*That* would be good for you.'

She meets his eye. 'You prescribe the sun to me as if I were a plant.'

He laughs. 'Perhaps I will come back to find you bursting into leaf. Your hair a sheaf of grass. Your eyes a pair of lilacs.'

'A disappearance into green,' Nella says, feeling disorientated inside his poetic speech.

He smiles, but he looks uncertainly at her, as if she is a

book whose words, for all his cleverness, he cannot understand. Has she struck the wrong chord – a minor note, to speak of vanishing, of being consumed by the foliage he reveres so much? 'My mother liked plants,' she says suddenly. The words almost take her by surprise. She never talks about her mother.

Witsen looks interested. 'At Assendelft?'

'Yes. She had a garden. She had a lot of dangerous herbs. *Her* knowledge was not shallow,' Nella says, smiling. 'But I can remember their names perfectly. Like a bad child's book of letters.'

Caspar laughs, and shy, but encouraged, Nella continues. 'Belladonna, pennyroyal, milk thistle, comfrey – which my mother told me never to pluck, or even touch.' She looks at her fingers. 'Women would come to her sometimes. Have hushed conversations by the kitchen back door, a pouch passed from hand to hand. I'd always ask what the women were doing there, but my mother would never tell.'

'She sounds like a wise person.'

'She could be.'

Momentarily, Nella is transported back to the site of her mother's most focused concentration. There was always a lot growing in their gardens. Carrots like slender orange fingers plucked backwards from the soil, the misshapen globes of potatoes and onions, lying in the dark for months. Leek and garlic, pea and bean.

'Did much flourish there?' Caspar asks.

'A lot. We would sell it. And the strange thing was, none of us could cook. My mother liked the planting stage, the growing stage, the sense of expectation. But never the execution. Perhaps she didn't want to ruin the bounty.'

'I understand that.'

'Says the man who incised a precious aloe with such relish.' Nella pauses. 'It's why I have always been in awe of Cornelia's abilities, given how far they exist from my own. Cornelia will chop and sever, stew and fry with abandon. She will bend nature to her will.'

'I understand that, also. But you do yourself a disservice, I am sure.'

'Oh, I'm telling you the truth.' Nella sighs. 'But the one thing I was very good at was looking after the chickens. We had their huts among the foxgloves. I always made sure they had their grains and clean roosts to sleep in.'

'There is nothing like the pleasure of an egg.'

'Indeed. They were always to me like small promises revealed in the morning straw, perfect yolks sizzling in a pan. By the age of eight, I'd devised excellent defences against foxes and cats. Various natural repellents from my mother. Fences staked deep in the ground. But sometimes, we would sacrifice a chicken. We would roast it in rosemary and thyme, and my brother and sister and I would sit outside, chewing on its thighs.'

He looks mesmerized by these recollections, and Nella can hear her tenderness, her truthfulness. It makes her feel suddenly vulnerable. 'You wish to see Thea,' she says, trying to pull him back from the past.

Caspar busies himself with the satchel he has placed at his feet. 'I've brought things. But no need to disturb her now.' He sits up straight. 'I do not know what has happened to your niece, Madame Brandt. But I am certainly not here to find it out, and spread it round the city.'

Nella flushes. 'I did not—'

'I understand your caution. Why you did not want me standing out on the doorstep like that. Beware a man bearing aloes.'

Suddenly, Nella feels herself give in. She just wants to stop everything. The worrying, the pretending that Thea is in Antwerp and not upstairs, locked in a world of her own. 'It's all so . . . terrible,' she whispers.

'I can only imagine.'

'Not knowing what's wrong with her. I don't know what to do.'

'These will help.' Caspar opens his satchel and brings out a row of tiny bottles. 'Tinctures. Valerian. Belladonna, like your mother's. Ginger, aniseed. There are others too.' He holds up a bottle, his expression unusually serious. 'This one will help you all sleep. This one will revive the spirits. A few drops, in a glass of wine, or put in Thea's porridge. And there are tinctures for melancholy, Madame. In case.' He hesitates. 'I have prepared them myself. The very best distillations.'

'You are thorough.'

'Nothing but the best for the family Brandt. Some of these plants are miracle-workers, Madame, as I'm sure you know. They can be the one thing that stands between death and life. They come from everywhere – the Cape of Good Hope, Brazil, Surinam. West Africa, Ethiopia, the Moluccas. Java, Jakarta, Mauritius.' Caspar opens his arms wide, as if to take in the scale of the world. 'The university garden in the corner of Amsterdam houses over three thousand plants.'

Nella considers this enormous number, his shining eyes, the picture in her mind of a jungle, spilling out from the walls of the garden onto the cobbles. 'Many more than in Assendelft, then,' she says.

He looks away. 'I was not trying to diminish your mother's garden.'

'And I did not think you were. Did you work at the university long, before Clara Sarragon plucked you?'

'Clara Sarragon does seem to think I grew there from a bulb.' He pauses. 'But I had other lives before that. I worked for a while in the East Indies. For the VOC, in fact, as a physician.'

'Does Otto know that?'

'Of course. I did not like the position, but the one thing I did gain from that employment was a deep understanding of quite how extraordinary a plant can be. How varied they are, in their own parts, and across the world. I brought that knowledge back to Amsterdam, but these days I don't care to employ it unless the circumstances are vital.'

'And do you consider our situation to be vital?'

'I do. They will help her,' he says gently. He hesitates. 'And you.'

'How did you find the plants, when you were in the Indies?'

'With the help of local people.'

'And of slaves?'

'Yes,' he says. 'Of slaves, too.'

Nella wonders what, exactly, Otto has told this man about his own life in Surinam. It is quite possible that Caspar Witsen knows more about Otto than any member of his own family. 'They showed me their gardens,' Caspar goes on. 'Their vegetable patches. Their jungles and fruit trees. They explained to me what the plants could do.'

'Did you plant your seeds in those lands, too?'

Caspar takes a sip of tea. 'Yes. We sent for our native plants, to see if they would survive in new soil. Different rain levels, exposure to sun, and so on. Plants from Java, all the way to the Caribbean, to see how they fared. Then the other way round. I know some men at the botanical garden are trying to grow a coffee bean. Of course, a lot of the plants die en route. One feels personally responsible. So much care has been put into the undertaking. A false move extinguishes the story.'

'But what is the point of it?'

'The point?' says Caspar Witsen, with a bemused expression. 'For the pleasure, of course.'

'Mr Witsen, this is Amsterdam,' Nella says. 'I am a merchant's widow. I can assure you, no one does anything in this city just for the sheer pleasure of it.'

He smiles. 'Knowledge, then. We do it for knowledge, because knowledge is power.'

Nella pictures these men at their desks and their flowerbeds, in humid heat, a trowel or quill in hand: annotating, cultivating, waiting. 'But what do you hope to know?' she says. 'To what end do you want that knowledge?'

'So that people may defend their health. That we may feed ourselves more variously, to flavour our dishes. We want Mother Nature to reveal to us her secrets, so that we may use them accordingly.'

'And sell them accordingly.'

'People in this city go on about the guilds and the Bourse holding power, and the Church and the docks. But the most powerful patch of land in Amsterdam is the peaty two acres on the city's edge, Madame. That garden is everything we are, and everything we could be. The world, connected by the flesh and silver leaves of the pineapple. It is the future. You ask me if I believe in destiny. Well, in one way I do. That little jar of jam you left on your mantelpiece holds it in spoonfuls.'

'But whose destiny?'

'Everyone's,' replies Caspar. 'Eventually.'

'And Thea?'

Caspar Witsen rises to his feet and gestures to his tinctures. 'Thea just needs rest, Madame. Her privacy to recover. Good food. And you.'

Nella feels tears in her eyes, and she wills them away. She hates to cry in front of people.

He sighs. 'I wouldn't be eighteen again, for all the world.'

'Nor I, Mr Witsen,' she says. 'Nor I.'

How long is it since she has had such kindness, such time spent with her in conversation? She is glad to have invited him in. When she looks up, Caspar Witsen is waiting, ready to meet her gaze.

XX

It is her father who comes with small beakers of warm milk, laced with Witsen's tinctures. 'I'm like Juliet,' Thea says, but Otto Brandt has never read this particular tragedy. He does not know about the heroine who drinks potions to mimic death, liquids that freeze her insides for a while so that she might escape her unhappy fate, and soon meet her true love. Thea does not care to elaborate for him, because that will make him worry even more. The difference between Thea and Juliet, of course, is that Thea's Romeo is now a curdled idol, a disappointment, now, at times, a horror. She looks away from her father's concerned gaze.

'Are they making you feel any better?' he asks, reaching for her hand.

'They are,' Thea says, squeezing his hand back, and it's true. She's sleeping these days, not just tossing and turning, every time closing her eyes and seeing Walter, shamefaced, surrounded by his wife and children. She has never known such humiliation, nor felt such shock. She hopes she never will again.

'You do look brighter,' says Thea's father. 'I *knew* it was a better idea asking Caspar than all those city quacks who charge ten guilders for nothing.'

'He will have to bring more,' says Thea. 'Even Aunt Nella is drinking the valerian.'

Her father looks grave. He takes a deep breath, and Thea knows he is going to ask her again what happened on that evening she didn't come home, an evening that she keeps swearing to them that she can't remember. He wants so very much to save her, but it's too late for that, and Thea cannot bear to tell him.

She can remember everything about that night. It's come back to her in bits and pieces over the last four weeks. Griete Riebeeck, her tired face and her two little children. Griete Riebeeck and her husband, Walter. Thea remembers somehow staggering out of the poky lodging on Bloemstraat, bumping into people who shouted at her as she fled through the Jordaan back to her home, feeling as blurred in herself, as disorientated, as the portrait of her that Walter had painted. Cornelia, pulling open the door, the look of utter relief upon the nursemaid's face, her tears which quickly turned to terror as Thea collapsed at her feet, dizzy not just from hunger but from something deeper, something which she knows is grief. Heartbreak is agony, Thea realizes. It is far worse than how it feels in plays.

How could she have been so mistaken? Did he pick her because he saw something in her that was easy to prey on? Thea had given him her heart as effortlessly as breath, and Walter has soiled it, handing it back to her like a dead thing. She closes her eyes and thinks of Rebecca; how sourly she has treated a good friend. She has lost so much and doesn't know how to get it back.

'Thea,' her father says gently. 'You were talking in your fever.'

Thea grips the cup of milk. 'I was?'

'You were speaking of empty palettes. A door you shouldn't have pushed.'

A chill runs up her back. 'I don't remember, Papa. I'm sure I made no sense. It will have been something I saw at the playhouse.'

'Well,' he says, reluctantly dropping the matter, 'I'm glad you're starting to feel better.'

'Aunt Nella told me Jacob wrote a note,' she says, watching her father's face cloud at the mention of their suitor.

'So he did. Your aunt lied and told him you were in Antwerp.'

'She was only doing it to protect me.'

He sighs. Thea looks out of the window and thinks about Aunt Nella, always harping on about money as a shield, about needing to bolster oneself against the vicissitudes of this city. Thea had never thought much of it until now, scorning everything her aunt believed in. But she closes her eyes and sees Griete's hard, envious stare.

What if Griete isn't finished? What if she writes again, asking for more? Before Thea burst into that hole on Bloemstraat, that was exactly what she was proposing. *What's one more threat?* There is always that possibility: the danger is still there.

Her father begins to move to the door, to leave her to rest. 'Papa?' she says, as he pulls the door open. 'Papa, do you believe in love?'

He turns, frowning. 'Of course.'

'What does it feel like, for you?'

He looks poleaxed. He clears his throat. 'What does it feel like?'

He thinks. 'It feels like sunlight. But darkness too.'

Love as the sun, love as the moon: Thea feels her father's words like a truth in her bones. 'And . . . did you love my mother?'

'Your mother?'

He looks slightly dazed. Thea doesn't know whether it's the fortifying effects of Witsen's draughts, or the residue of the fever which has lowered her defences and loosened her tongue. Maybe it is the miniatures of her parents, up in the attic, resting in the cedar wood. Maybe it is how humbled she feels, how ignorant and foolish, in the face of her humiliation over what she thought was true love. But she longs to hear that there is some part of her history, at least, that has been touched by the kind of passion and affection that she so ardently needs to believe exists. She longs for her father to give her that gift.

He still hovers at the threshold of her room. He gazes at his daughter, and then out to the canal through the window. It looks at first as if he wants to speak, then as if he doesn't, and then, as if he simply has no words.

'It doesn't matter,' Thea sighs. 'I was only—'

'Your uncle told me about her first,' he says. 'He told me, as we were coming away from Surinam, that his sister was the cleverest person he had ever met. Far cleverer than him. But that I should be aware of one thing: she was not very good at making friends.'

Thea stares up at him. She cannot believe that finally, after all these years of waiting and wondering, her father is conjuring the times before. It has taken her own broken heart, and a fever, a brush with death, a plea for love, to make it happen.

'And was it true?'

Her father does not move from the threshold. 'It was not true. She was a solitary woman. But that did not mean she was not good at being a friend.'

He might be staring out towards the opposite canal houses, to Thea it's as if he's looking at a horizon she cannot see. An ocean of memory, light catching silver on its surface, the sun moving away to leave the water pitch dark.

'She would break into her brother's study,' he says quietly. 'She would read his ledger books when he was in the city.' He takes a deep breath, turning back to her. 'I did not look at your mother much, Thea. Not much. At first. But what I failed to realize was that your mother was looking at me. One night, after I'd been in this house about a year, she spoke to me. I was in the hallway, putting on my coat, to go and see your uncle in his office at the VOC. Your mother's voice in the darkness stopped me.'

'What did she say?' Thea whispers.

Her father hesitates. 'She said: *I admire you.*' He pauses. 'It was the first thing she'd ever said to me directly, out of the company of others. She walked out of the shadows, only half her face illuminated.'

'And what happened then?'

'I looked at her, for the first time. Properly. She had a slim face, like you. And grey eyes, like her brother. You get your eyes from me. But you've got her serious mouth. Her cap, always pristine. She looked as if she was waiting for me to say something. I wanted very much to speak.'

'But you didn't?'

'No.'

'Because you were Uncle Johannes's manservant?'

'Yes. I wanted to tell her I thought the same of her. I wanted to ask her why she admired me. But instead I opened the front door. Her cheeks had turned pink, you see, and I thought she might like the cool air, and she looked down at the floor, knowing that her mystery was falling away. As if, perhaps, she'd never wanted it in the first place. *Otto*, she said to me, as if she knew my mind. *I admire you, because you know how to begin again.*'

There is a long silence. Her father's and mother's words hang over her like mist. Her father has spoken with a tenderness that Thea has never heard before, and which she realizes she has never heard from Walter.

'And you do too, Thea,' her father says.

'What do you mean?'

'I don't know why you are so unhappy, my love. I cannot bear to see it, to think that someone might have hurt you.'

Thea thinks of the painting-room, the stained gold dress. Her mother's map, the misericord, Griete Riebeeck and the room on Bloemstraat where everything changed. All these dizzying pieces. She is trapped in a nightmare of her own making, but the idea of telling her father is unthinkable. The idea of telling any of them is impossible. 'No one has hurt me, Papa. I just took unwell, that's all.'

'You are my daughter,' he says. 'And you are more special than you could ever imagine.' He makes to leave. 'And Thea?'

'Yes?'

'You do know how to begin again.'

The door closes. Thea feels the breath still trapped in her throat. She has waited for longer than she can remember for a moment like this. For her mother to come truly alive, not a little doll but a real person, spoken into being in the mouth of her father. Someone who chose her friends carefully, standing with pink cheeks and a pristine cap, trying to offer a compliment. Trying, perhaps, to express her feelings.

Better than a doll perhaps, but all the same, Thea thinks of the miniatures of her mother and her father, kept all this time by Aunt Nella. A summoning, a sign; it's all Aunt Nella's ever wanted since she was left with a newborn baby that wasn't hers. But it's Thea who, unearthing her parents' miniatures in the attic, is hearing a story about her mother. This gift her father has given her, this gift she has perhaps taken for herself. This strange gift of a couple's early story. Nothing but a brief moment in a hallway, but everything she needs to know.

Thea reaches under her bed and takes out her secret box. She can hardly bear to acknowledge the blackmail notes, but still she doesn't destroy them. She lifts out the doll of Walter and places him on the bed before her. The ferocity of the love she has felt for Walter will probably never be repeated. How could it be? She will never love another man the way she has loved him. No man will ever make her feel as Walter Riebeeck did. And no man will ever hurt her that way, either.

Recalling the way her father described her mother's flushed cheek, her murmured admiration across those hallway tiles, Thea wonders if that is what she has known with Walter. She cannot claim such a quality of recollection. She thinks of Walter's demurrals about their wedding, which now make perfect sense. She thinks about his boasts of where he was going to work, but then remembers how poor the painting of her was. But even if Walter couldn't capture her, he still looked at her. He still admired her, spent time with her. The whole affair cannot all have been Griete's idea. Maybe he did reallly love her, but was found out, and confessed, and felt helpless to stop his wife? The look on his face in the room on Bloemstraat was like a man watching a planetary collision.

Although Thea yearns to know if Walter planned this all along, part of her hopes she never will. She thinks again of what Cornelia had said: *I prefer the fragments offered.* Thea has wanted to know all of Walter. When she'd first met him, she'd fantasized about entering his lodgings, herself inside them. She wanted to find as many contexts for him as possible, locked as they were in that painting-room. She wanted to live in his world. She will never tell him now how she walked, aged seventeen, up and down narrow streets, imagining she might spot him at a window or see him coming home after a day's work. If she had known where he lived, then everything would have been so different.

And yet. Griete might write again. Why would she not, unless Walter stops her? Maybe it is beyond Walter now; Thea cannot tell. But as long as Griete knows where she lives, and who she is, she might still be in danger.

Thea tips the rest of Caspar Witsen's tincture into her cup of milk, and drinks it down. As she feels it take effect, she holds the small gilded house in her hand. The door still won't open. The windows remain blank. It is a shining thing, nevertheless. Impassable, covetous. A bastion of security. As Thea stares into this golden house, this perfect, symmetrical, harmonious little dwelling, it comes to her, before her eyes close, what she will do.

XXI

'You're eating well again, Madame,' Cornelia says at breakfast, a tease in her voice. 'Have you been drinking Witsen's potions?'

'I may have,' says Nella.

'Good, aren't they?' says Otto.

'Passable.'

Cornelia grins. 'So, are you two friends again?'

Nella and Otto eye each other. 'Of course we are,' she says.

He lifts his glass. 'Of course.'

As long as he doesn't talk about pineapples, and she doesn't bring up the matter of Thea's future. They still don't know what they're going to do. Thea's much brighter now, and Cornelia is happy about it, Nella can tell. So is Otto. Their beloved is safe, and eating, and under their watchful eye. But this impasse cannot last forever.

She wonders every day about the night that Thea collapsed, and why it happened. Otto and Cornelia claim to be in the dark about it too, and Nella has no reason to disbelieve them. None of them know, but none of them dare speculate with each other, for fear of shattering the fragile peace. All Thea will say is that she took ill on one of her walks, and managed to get home. But what was this talk of palettes and gold houses, and cradles, and doors she shouldn't be touching? It makes no sense.

If Witsen's medicines are working for Nella's ability to sleep and eat better, they are not quite as effective for her melancholy. That mood is more resistant. She still has that watery feeling in the day, as if she is flowing too fast through her own life, attaching to nothing, the current too strong to do anything else but spiral on. Early summer balls are beginning, but she doesn't have the energy to court Clara Sarragon or any of her ilk. Instead, she sits many nights alone with the miniature baby in her room, turning it over by the light of a candle to check for some sign or change she might have missed. But the little swaddled figurine remains just as it was when she first found it.

She yearns for her wedding cabinet, for its stability, for the way it rooted her to her life in this house. It gave her more security than Johannes ever did. How could I have destroyed it? she thinks. She'd hewed it like a tree, the tortoiseshell enamel splitting, the pewter inlay bending out of shape forever, the oak and elm beneath it ruined. I wasted my chance, she thinks. The miniaturist chose me, and I wasted my chance.

If she goes for a walk along the canal, Nella waits for another coldness on her neck, a prickling sensation to let her know that she is being observed, guarded, *anything* – but there is no such feeling. She is alone in the street as much as she is at home. She wonders if Witsen will visit. She wonders whether to write to Jacob and tell him that Thea has returned from Antwerp, but it feels like an uneasy thing to do, a falsehood, something she should not be doing any more, especially as they do not know the fragility of Thea's mind compared with the robustness of her body. So she wonders and does nothing, and still the money dwindles, and Otto has no work, and all their energy is spent on Thea, to make her better, to make her as she was.

'Thea's asked if she could come with me to market today,' Cornelia says.

'Really?' says Otto.

'She's getting ready now.'

'Do you think it's wise?'

'It's a good thing,' Nella says. 'It's good she gets out of the house.'

'I'm glad you think so,' says a voice.

The three of them turn in surprise, as if they have been caught gossiping. Nella cannot believe her eyes. Thea is fully dressed, her cap pristine, her skirts dark, perfectly black, not a cat hair on them. Her collar is starched and stiff against the cotton of her spring jacket. She gazes down from the kitchen stair upon her family, and they are mesmerized. It is hard to recall the sweating, delirious, childlike young woman who only five weeks ago lay in her bed as if the sheets were a shroud. She looks older, and she is very still, like a chess piece waiting to move herself. She hasn't quite regained her normal weight, and the thinness to her face reminds Nella of Marin.

'Would you like something to eat?' Cornelia says. 'Some—'

'No, thank you,' Thea interrupts. She does not move from the stair. 'But there is something I wish to tell you all.'

Now it comes, the confession, the revelation: the thing they've all been waiting for ever since they feared that she was gone. Nella feels her heart creeping up the insides of her throat. Otto's fingers grip tight around his porridge spoon, and Cornelia shifts on her feet.

Thea takes a deep breath. She almost falters. 'Tell us,' Nella says. 'I promise. We're ready.'

Thea's father bows his head. Thea clutches her hands together, then lets them drop. 'I have had much time to consider this,' she announces, her voice wavering, 'but I am content with my decision.'

'Your . . . decision?' says Nella.

Thea tips her chin into the air. 'My decision.'

'What is it, Teapot?' Cornelia asks. 'What have you decided?'

Thea takes a look around the kitchen, as if for a final time. She turns and meets her aunt's gaze. 'I have decided that if he will have me, you can arrange the marriage with Jacob van Loos.'

Absolute silence. Thea looks relieved that the words are out of her mouth, and a little pleased with their effect. She blinks, waiting for reactions that do not come. Behind her, Nella can tell that Cornelia hasn't moved. Otto is motionless, staring at his daughter. Nella cannot believe what she's hearing. After all these months, everything she's planned for, hoped for, might really come true. From this pile of ashes, they will rise again. Thea's words reverberate in her body, a shock tiding which moves the responsibility for Thea's life out of Nella's hands inexorably into Thea's own.

Suddenly, Nella feels far from this house, her watery mind turning from these old shadows, upwards from their earthy cellar, outwards through the panes of the salon windows, to another life that is nearing their reach. It is Thea's life that they are reaching for, of course, Thea's life that will change – life as a wife, with a full purse and new clothes. But it feels as if their lives too are shifting shape, losing definition, turning into something new. She wants to run to Thea and hold her in her arms.

'Jacob van Loos?' Otto says.

'But you do not love him,' says Cornelia. 'Do you?'

'Of course she doesn't,' says Otto. He looks at his daughter desperately.

'Before we begin,' Nella says, holding her voice calm, 'are you quite certain that that is what you want?' She wants to be sure, before she can give herself to this extraordinary development.

Thea laughs. 'Aunt Nella, you looked shocked. You have wanted this for many months. Surely you should be the happiest of all of us.'

'I have thought such a match to be prudent, yes.'

'Do you think he won't have me?'

'I am sure he will have you.'

'No, wait. Why this change of mind?' Otto says. 'I know it isn't a change of heart. Or is it? Thea,' he says pleadingly. 'Thea, my love: when I said you knew how to begin again, this is not what I meant. This is absolutely not – what on earth has happened?'

Thea inhales deeply and lets out a long breath. 'Aunt Nella told me that love takes practice. Patience. Time.'

Otto and Cornelia look at Nella with barely disguised irritation. 'So I did,' Nella says slowly, 'but—'

'She told me I would learn how to love. She *told* me that it might not take the form I had originally expected, but that I should be adaptable.'

'Indeed, I—'

'That marriage was the only way I could get out.'

Nella feels her own statements wash back over her. They are surprisingly cynical to her, heard from the mouth of another.

'No,' says Otto. 'I forbid this.'

'Papa,' says Thea. She rests her serious gaze upon him. 'I have heard a little about what true love is. It's a rare thing. But there are other forms of love, that can be learned.' She hesitates. 'And if they can be learned . . . then the man I learn them with might as well be rich.'

'I don't want you to be any part of that world,' he says.

'There is only one world,' Thea replies. 'And we're in it.'

Otto looks devastated. He stares at his daughter as if he has no idea who she is.

'We have no money,' Thea says. 'Papa has no work. There are no more paintings left to sell. Are these things not true? With a marriage like this, our family can leave its shame behind.'

No one speaks. Thea begins to look impatient. And well she might, Nella thinks. For have we – have I – not impressed upon her, time and again, the importance of safety in money and status? The Madeira wine for her eighteenth birthday, only purchased because it was half-price? The selling of the last painting, the cutting back on meat; the lack of new clothes; the campaigning for an invitation to the Sarragon ball? Back and back it goes, past the anonymity of Marin's grave, the bemoaning of their fate and history, and beyond even that, to a lake in Assendelft. And Thea is going to do something about it. She is going to solve all their problems in one wedding.

'You don't have to do this,' Otto says.

Thea turns to him. 'I do. And very soon. This marriage will protect us. It will be a new beginning. And it will set us free.'

There is a sound, halfway between a sob and gasp. It has come from Cornelia, sitting on the end of the kitchen bench, hunched over. She looks up. 'You're going to leave us,' she says. 'You're really going to leave?'

'Only if he agrees to marry me,' says Thea.

'She'll just be on the Prinsengracht,' Nella says, but even as she speaks the words, she knows that Jacob's house, its pale-green walls, its harpsichord and perfect china cups, is a world away: a destination that Cornelia may not easily, or willingly, navigate.

Cornelia stares at her in fury, but Nella feels defiant. She believes in Thea's strength. She has no idea what has caused this reversal of intention, but what does it matter? They finally have a plan.

'We didn't have a feast when Thea was born,' she says. 'We made no ceremony. We claimed no fuss. We hid in the shadows. But not this time. This time we will be proud.' She turns to her niece. 'I will go to Jacob,' she says.

Thea's eyes widen with gratitude. 'You will? And soon?'

'Of course. I will speak with him,' Nella says, avoiding Otto's accusing eyes, Cornelia's vibrating anger. 'I will make this marriage for you, Thea. And then the world will see.'

XXII

The effect of words on the body can be fast: pledges to marry a man can turn into a brisk walk from the Herengracht to the Prinsengracht. Thea, her stomach churning, trots to keep up with her aunt's stride, all thought of her going to the market with Cornelia forgotten. Today is a fine day, if slightly blustery. Gulls wheel and plunge, the sky is bright over the roof tiles opposite. She herself feels vigorous, filled with a strange purpose, a restless nervousness. 'Should we not have written to Jacob first?' she asks her aunt.

'We have lost much time already,' Aunt Nella replies. 'You have been unwell for over a month, Thea. And besides—' She lifts up the basket of Cornelia's sweet walnut wafers on her arm. 'We come with a gift! I won't launch into the topic of marriage immediately. I'll speak to Jacob first, test the temperature of the waters, and then invite you in. If it goes well, these matters don't take long.'

Thea looks at her in mystification. 'How do you know?'

'My mother's arrangements for me were all done by letter to your mother. So in person, this will surely be quicker. We can be at home in time for supper.'

Hard to tell, whether Aunt Nella's matter-of-factness is covering up her own nerves, or whether she really thinks arranging a marriage of this nature could be so easy. Thea has to admire the spirit, the boldness – but then again, Aunt Nella has laid much groundwork for this moment over the past few months. In many ways, this is not exactly a cold visit. In many ways, she has been coiled like a spring for this.

Aunt Nella stops in the middle of the path. 'Is my collar neat?' she says, pulling at it. 'My cap?'

'Yes. Perfect as usual.'

They reach the steps of Jacob's house. As they ascend the neat, clean stone stairs and Aunt Nella reaches for the horseshoe knocker, looking more determined than Thea has ever seen, Thea puts her arm out, touching her aunt's sleeve. She stares at the solidity of Jacob's door and thinks about what lies beyond it. The serenity of pale green. The harpsichord. The rooms above, whose dimensions she doesn't yet know. The endless sets of slippers, concealed in a cupboard. And in the centre of this house, the man himself. Jacob: with his narrow shoulders and pointed slippers, who smokes a pipe, who plays music better than she thought he might, but whose talent is not enough to banish Walter's imprint from her body or her mind.

'Aunt Nella. It is true I do not love Jacob.'

Her aunt touches her hand, her basket pressing into Thea's skirts. Inside, the wafers slide from side to side. 'I know that, sweeting. We all know that. Jacob probably knows it too. It is not a cause for alarm.'

Thea looks up at Jacob's house. 'I suppose love is not a guarantee of anything.'

'It is not.'

'You taught me that.'

'I admit it's a strange lesson,' says Aunt Nella, but she seems to hesitate. 'Thea, do you truly want to continue with this? Is this all too much after the last few weeks? Because we can go home, if that's what you want.'

Thea thinks about what waits for her at home. Bare walls and empty coffers, a pair of blackmail notes threatening her with ruin and the possibility of more to follow. Cornelia, banging pans. Her father, wishing she was eight years old. And in the city, the threat of Griete Riebeeck. She thinks about the tiny gilded house underneath her bed, how she had held it in her fist, how she is trying to find a different ending to her story.

'No,' she says. 'That is not what I want. But I hate how angry Papa is.'

Her aunt's expression softens. 'He will come to understand. If you want to go out into the world, marriage to a man like Jacob will protect you from the Clara Sarragons that populate it. That is my hope, at least. Marriage is a contract, Thea. If Jacob signs it then fails to honour it, and you, we will still be close by, and you will be free to leave.'

'I will?'

'Of course. It is the law of this land. A woman can walk away from a marriage with what she came with, and what came after, including children.'

For a moment, Thea's head reels. Children, with Jacob? Such a prospect seems like foreign land, hitherto unmarked on any map.

Aunt Nella puts the basket on the step and takes her by the arms. 'But listen to me, Thea. If you do want this, you can learn to respect and admire a man, even if at first he is unfamiliar. And he you. It's what I did. In fact, the learning is everything. It is continual. And although it's true I only had three months to practise it, I do know that you can adapt. Marriage is adaptation, because life is adaptation.'

'Were you surprised by my announcement?'

Her aunt smiles. 'Oh yes. I did not think you would ever agree with my cold philosophy of love.'

'Perhaps it is still a little cold. But it is sensible.' Thea leans forward and lifts the horseshoe knocker.

After a minute, Mrs Lutgers opens the door, only wide enough that her face is visible, a perfect moon, pallid in the sun. She surveys the two women. 'We've come to speak with Seigneur van Loos,' Aunt Nella says. 'I am Petronella Brandt, and this is Thea. We've brought your master some sweet wafers.'

'I know who you are,' Mrs Lutgers replies, but she pulls the door back in a surprisingly expansive gesture, although her expression remains unreadable. 'Come in.'

In the huge hallway, the housekeeper gestures to a set of chairs that they can use whilst she goes in search of Jacob. 'So friendly,' whispers Thea, as the woman disappears.

'It's a good sign,' Aunt Nella whispers back. 'She knows we mean something to him.'

Thea almost can't believe this day is happening, even though she is the one who has set it all in motion.

'Be serene in your answers to Jacob,' her aunt says quietly, taking a seat. 'Intelligent, of course, but perhaps not too . . . exuberant.'

'Exuberant? I am not exuberant. Am I?'

Her aunt looks at her. 'Just – if he wishes to speak, then let him.'

Thea shifts uncomfortably on her chair as they continue to wait. There is an excess of flowers everywhere. How has Jacob managed to acquire such blooms, this time of year? She cannot taste fresh air for their perfume. How big can this house be, she wonders, that it takes the housekeeper this long to locate him?

'What if he says no?' she whispers. 'What if he looks at us as if we're mad? As if such a notion to marry me is disgusting to him?'

Picturing his rejection, Thea suddenly realizes how much she needs Jacob and his willingness to hook her out of the swamp she's sinking into over on the Herengracht. She hates that her future, her family's security and reputation, should pivot on the whim and desire of a man she barely knows. But then again: the same could be said to have happened with Walter. She'd pivoted her life on him too, and at least Jacob lives here and not in some one-room hovel in Bloemstraat.

If Jacob says yes, then his money, and therefore his status, will elevate Thea away from the grubbiness of that Jordaan lodging. No child of hers will ever go without food, nor wear a stained smock, while its father commits adultery with unsuspecting young women and its mother extorts money for their pleasure.

Suddenly, Aunt Nella startles her out of her thoughts, taking Thea's hand to squeeze it tight. 'If Jacob says any such thing, then I will take you out of here without a backward glance.'

Mrs Lutgers comes to tell them that Seigneur van Loos is happy to receive them in his salon. She probably knew he was there all along, Thea thinks. She just wanted us to sit here and simmer.

As planned, her aunt goes in alone. Thea waits, taking in the beautiful still-life paintings on the hallway walls. She walks along the vases of flowers, fingering the petals as if to find reassurance in their velvet tongues. The robust tulips, with their bulbous little heads, in split colours of red, pink and white. The roses, expertly cultivated, because some have heads the size of small cabbages, floury to the touch. They remind her of Caspar Witsen and his botanical tinctures. It must take a lot of work to turn a plant into a tincture, she supposes, and she has no idea how one might ever begin.

I will write to him, she thinks. I will write and thank him, and ask him how it's done.

'They'll fall apart if you touch them too much,' says a voice, and Thea looks up. Mrs Lutgers is standing in the shadow of the main staircase, watching. How long has she been there?

Thea withdraws her hand, annoyed with herself for being so intimidated. She is used to the sort of scrutiny Mrs Lutgers is subjecting her to; that close kind of look, as if this woman wants to get under Thea's skin to see her bones. She wonders how long it would take her, as a new bride, to remove Mrs Lutgers from her position in this house. How persuadable might Jacob really be to bringing Cornelia in her place, and maybe, with his money, a couple of servants more?

'Would you care for refreshment?' Mrs Lutgers asks.

'No, thank you.'

Mrs Lutgers clasps her hands, her face rigid and apprehensive, her fingers coming apart again. 'As you wish.' The housekeeper balls her hands into fists and presses them to her side, as if restraining herself. Then she bursts to life, marching off back to her domain.

A few minutes later, the door to Jacob's salon opens and Aunt Nella comes out, closing it behind her. She is wearing one of her public smiles. Thea goes to speak with her, but her aunt moves her away from the door, taking up Thea's hands.

'If you want him,' she says quietly, 'then he's yours.'

Thea stares at her aunt. It's as if neither of them can believe it. It's as if they've caught a strange creature and locked him in a room, and they are uncertain of his qualities, his proclivities, how much he needs to feed, what it is exactly that he feeds on. But still, they will keep him. What dowry figure, what savings and offerings has Aunt Nella brokered in that green-walled salon, to make a union with the Brandt family appealing to Jacob van Loos?

Thea stands there with her hands still clasped inside her aunt's, as if they are about to begin a dance over these marble tiles, so much brighter than their own. She feels the quality of air shift around her, seep into her, her life beginning to change. There will be no more paper chains on the window, no more birthday puffers. She thinks of Rebecca playing Lavinia in *Titus*. Lavinia, her tongue cut off, her hands lopped, still telling her story regardless.

Thea pulls her own hands out of her aunt's grasp, and turns to meet her fate.

❧

Jacob is standing by the mantelpiece, stuffing tobacco into his pipe. The basket of Cornelia's walnut wafers lies untouched on the low lacquered table. He turns to her, bows and smiles. Thea manages a curtsey. As she closes the door she sees Aunt

Nella, sinking into the chair Thea had occupied, putting her head into her hands as if she's been carrying a heavy stone.

Thea shuts the door quickly and turns back to Jacob. She feels as if she is not the protagonist in this scene at all, as if she could be watching it unfold from the mantelpiece, from behind a thick jar of pulped pineapple.

'The Old Church,' Jacob says to her, by means of a beginning. 'That is the place where your aunt says you might wish to be married?' He waits for her to say something. 'It is a venerable building.'

Usually Thea is ready with some words. But this time she is mute. She and her aunt have not discussed churches at all. She takes a deep breath, rallying her strength. 'The Old Church would suit. It is to happen then, Seigneur,' she says. 'We are to be married.'

Jacob smiles again. He takes a deep drag. 'We are. And you must call me Jacob.'

Thea feels rooted to the spot.

'From the moment I saw you . . .' Jacob begins, laying his hand on the mantel. He moves over to the wafer basket and lifts the cloth. 'Thea, you are not like other girls.'

'I am not?'

'You are infinitely superior.'

Thea wants him to enumerate her so-called superiority, to parcel it out in understandable blocks. She thinks of the Eleonors and Catarinas of this city, and why exactly Jacob thinks her to be so different. She suspects that she might dread his answer, that it is rooted in unforgiving soil.

'Come, sit,' he says, all authority.

She makes her way to the sofa and perches on the end, the

imprint of her aunt beside her, a depression in the velvet.

'I think we shall be happy,' Jacob said. 'In fact, I wrote to my mother about you.'

She turns in surprise. 'You did?'

'I told her about a motherless, beautiful young woman I had met, who was the only highlight of a tedious ball. She was fascinated. She wanted to know everything about you.'

'And have you told her?'

Jacob reaches to relight his pipe. 'Not everything. Some things are best left to a meeting in person.'

Thea wonders how much Madame van Loos will consider her a superior being, compared to the opinions of her son. 'Will she attend the wedding?'

'I certainly hope so.' Jacob blows out a plume of blue smoke. 'I will write to her, presently. She has waited a long time for me to find a bride, and now finally the moment has come.'

Madame van Loos looms into Thea's imagination. She had not even considered her before now. She grips the side of the sofa. What has she done?

'When were you hoping for our marriage to be sanctified?' Jacob asks.

Thea does not like the word *sanctified*. She does not want the saints in the stained glass, watching. 'Very soon, I hope.'

'I think three weeks will be sufficient for all the papers to be drawn up, for us to announce our *ondertrouw*. I plight my fidelity to you, and you to me, and the pastor will be engaged.' He pauses. 'The ninth of June is a propitious day.'

'It is?'

'My mother's birthday.'

'Would you not rather marry on another day, Jacob?'

'She's had a lot of birthdays. Why not – a present to her: to see me finally wived.'

Thea smiles over her spike of discomfort. 'And afterwards, will we live in this house?'

'We can live here, if it pleases you,' Jacob replies. 'Or in Leiden.'

'Or maybe further away?' Jacob looks surprised, and Thea falters. 'At the playhouse, did you not say that you dreamed of seeing hot lands?'

Jacob drags on his pipe again and blows out the smoke. Despite the grand proportions of the room, the air around the sofa is beginning to grow thick. 'I did. But did *you* not say that you had no need of them, because you had seen those palm trees in your heart?'

His finger hovers, closely, above this area on Thea's dress. She swallows, unsure whether to be more disturbed that Jacob has remembered her veiled declaration of love for Walter, or by the close insistence of his hand. She thinks of the tips of Walter's fingers, caressing along her body, up and down his canvases, making another world so real that she could step inside it. Walter would look so out of place in this perfect room, with his smock, with that blond hair, those paint-encrusted fingernails. She thinks of his tongue between her legs, and under her skirts she moves her thighs closer together. She thinks of him leaning over the cradle of his child.

'I have changed my opinion since then,' she says. 'I am very happy to go away.'

'Well,' Jacob replies. 'I know many people who could help us. Eventually, I would like to be near my mother. She is ageing, and will need our help. But there are many places we can travel to, before that necessity manifests.'

'Excellent,' Thea says, although she was not prepared for an ageing mother. She thinks of her own who is ageless, and wonders if there are other maps up in the attic, inside that chest of Marin Brandt. There might be more to pore over – no need to sell them now – and a real ship voyage to be had. There might be a real shipwreck, not one simply painted to be hung on a wall. Jacob might go down with it. She smiles at him. Her thoughts are everywhere.

Jacob clears his throat. 'You are not the bride every man in this city might choose.'

This brings her back sharply. She says nothing. Even with the haze-applying effects of his tobacco smoke, Jacob is not handsome. He does not excite her nor repulse her. He is just a man with money and connections, whom Aunt Nella believes Thea might come to admire and respect.

Thea keeps her mouth closed. She keeps her tongue hidden against her teeth. She does not say the same thing in reply, but the thought is blazoned across the inside of her eyes in Walter's red paint: Well, Jacob Someone: *you* are not the groom every woman in this city might choose.

People have said worse to her. But not in this context, the building of a partnership, a future. Thea looks out of Jacob's huge salon windows, and thinks about Griete and her threats, about her father's lack of work, her aunt's increasingly thread-bare attempts at dignity and wealth. She thinks about Cornelia, complaining how she is constantly having to make do with cheaper cuts of meat. She thinks about Walter, and how much it still hurts.

What does Jacob want from her exactly, for being the bride not all men might choose? Her gratitude? About that, she will have to wait and see.

She says: 'Jacob, I will never make you question your decision.'

Jacob smiles. 'And I will never question it myself.'

This isn't true, of course, Thea thinks: because that's exactly what you did.

XXIII

The end of May offers true warmth, the sun rising higher over rooftops, turning gables chalk white on cerulean. Cornelia's marjoram, her sorrel and chive, sprout abundant in her kitchen window, and Lucas begins his proper annual sun baths on the doorstep, lolling on his side from early morning to late in the afternoon. Bright yachts and barges are taken out of sheds, given new licks of paint. Sails are freshly rigged, seat cushions re-stuffed, re-stitched, grateful Amsterdammers taking to their vessels to feel God's beneficence. The days are stretching. Spring coats are put in trunks and sleeves are rolled up to the elbow. The fruit and vegetables at the markets change again in anticipation of summer recipes; lamb's lettuce and radishes, precocious cherries – and all the maids and cooks at the markets agree with Cornelia how the salmon and the rabbits seem chubbier. *More flesh off the bone when you put your knife to it!* Winter pickles of quince and cucumbers are taken out of pantries and paraded on tables, another proof of the rewards to be reaped when you do your preparation. When you employ patience and foresight, and think of your future soul with love, enduring privations, knowing that the time to bloom will come again.

The *ondertrouw* has been noted down in the Old Church, the pastor has been consulted. The bride is readying herself, resolute for her future, and her family rise up with her to the challenge. It is Nella who seeks out a florist under *F* in *Smit's List*, a man called Hendrickson, whose great-grandfather made a fortune in the tulip fever some ninety years before. The Hendricksons still trade in the market of flowers, because the descendants who came after let the money fall through their fingers – 'like soup through a skimming spoon, Madame'.

Hendrickson, who comes to the house with a painted volume of the flowers he possesses, suggests honeysuckle for the bonds of love, and peonies and roses, because the ones he has are very beautiful this time of year, he force-grows them under heat, and they will look well gathered in the bride's hands. He says this looking down at Thea's fists, bunched together like a pair of winter bulbs.

And what Hendrickson doesn't say, but which Nella wonders, is that the vibrancy of their colours – blush pinks, blood reds – will hopefully detract from Thea's un-sunned face, her continued thinness, and the fact that there is no money to buy new bolts of fabric for a wedding dress. Thea will be in her best old dress of deep ruby, still short in the sleeves. Nella wonders whether they should pay for the expense of a betrothal cup.

'A betrothal cup?' says Cornelia. 'Won't any cup do, if it's being drunk from by betrotheds?'

Nella thinks of her own wedding and the lack of a cup, how she had written to the miniaturist to supply her one so she could at least live out her fantasy in tiny form, and how the miniaturist had obliged. 'They're important, Cornelia. It will be an heirloom.'

'That Thea will have to sell off in twenty years?'

'Cornelia, enough. History is not going to repeat itself.'

Cornelia is still begrudging this wedding, but before fury comes pride. Four days after Nella and Thea's visit to his house, the future bridegroom comes to dine, and Cornelia makes a feast even more elaborate than the first she laboured over. She produces an enormous whole salmon, stewed in butter with a crushed mace and nutmeg crumb, young eels in sorrel and chervil finished with a creamy egg sauce, asparagus in butter and pepper, a celery salad, and currant pancakes, washed down with the last of the Madeira saved from Thea's birthday.

'He *wants* to marry me, Cornelia,' says Thea. 'You didn't need to spend all my dowry at the market.'

Privately, Nella wonders if Cornelia is trying to kill the man with an excess of butter.

When Jacob arrives for the dinner, Otto receives him civilly, but without warmth. Nella senses her niece's apprehension. Thea's fear of disappointing her father is a fear that Nella once knew too well, but she also understands Thea's desire to leave this house on the Herengracht, where for so long its inhabitants have only looked back.

Thea thinks her aunt knows nothing of what it is like to be young, to be desirous for your life to begin, but as her niece stands nervously in the hall while Jacob removes his hat and makes a sweeping bow, Nella feels pinioned by the memory of her own past. She, too, had once stood in this very hallway, calling after her husband, yearning for him to start her life.

There has been no argument, no denial from Thea's father over the coming nuptials, and though the reception he gives the husband-to-be is not effusive, neither is it wholly hostile.

Otto has cast about for solutions to this wedding, and found none from any quarter, and now he is grimly accepting that it is going ahead, mostly because Thea wants it. The last thing he desires is for his daughter to turn away from him, and Nella sees his struggle, the momentary glimpses of disbelief that he masks with practised skill. There are days when she feels responsible for his unhappiness, but then she thinks of everything that is to come Thea's way, and remains convinced that they are doing exactly what Marin would have wished.

At first, the conversation at the dinner is stilted, mainly steered by Nella. Cornelia unceremoniously presents dishes onto the tablecloth as if she were throwing dough. If Jacob notices, he makes no comment. They talk of the coming slew of Amsterdam society parties, the follies of summer boating in the vicinity of gulls, and of what might be happening down at the Bourse. They do not correct Jacob when he enquires with Otto as to how life at the VOC is treating him. Nella comments on Pastor Becker at the Old Church, his newness to the post, his relative youth, and when they should go and speak to him. When she suggests she could go tomorrow, Jacob says that is an excellent idea.

But what Nella really wants to speak of is other things. *Why Thea? Why us? What do you think of us, please?* But it is not safe to, not yet. She cannot ask these things until after the wedding. She tells herself that she wants to know all this because there is much that is unorthodox about this situation, and she wants to be sure, once and for all, that Jacob is a man with a sensible head. But there is something murkier inside herself which she cares not to examine: she wants this young man's approval. She wants to be inside his circle, whatever that is, but the whole point of this dinner is to behave as if that is where she already resides.

In Jacob's pale-green salon, she had been frank. 'We do not have the wealth of a family like Sarragon,' she'd said, thinking of the savings they had made for Thea's inheritance, eaten away by the costs of running the mansion, and Otto's lack of work. 'We will not embarrass you,' she had continued, 'but . . .'

'Material wealth is not everything, Madame,' he'd replied. 'Conversation, youth, beauty, intelligence. These are also commodities a man might prize.'

Nella had felt uncomfortable, then: focusing as she had so much on the lack of financial worth her niece possessed, she had perhaps spent too little time on Thea's personal charms. It was a reversal of her behaviour in the box at the Schouwburg, but this time she had been more nervous. She had not been able to stop thinking about Thea's statement, whispered just before they knocked on Jacob's door: *It is true I do not love Jacob.* Thea has long been obsessed by love, and Nella has chided her for it. But perhaps it is a wise obsession? Perhaps it is a voicing of a deeper doubt, and one that Nella herself should be apprised of?

But there is no time left for such meditations, and certainly not across this tablecloth, covered in flecks of salmon juice and eel. Marriage hovers now, and money too. If only there was a tincture Caspar could make, Nella thinks, to conjure true love.

After the pancakes have been eaten, the two men lock themselves away in Otto's study to work out the details of the contract. They are in there for an hour, far longer than Nella and Thea's interviews with Jacob.

As time ticks, Thea is clearly agitated. 'What if Papa is telling him no? What if he says he can't have me?'

'He will not say that.'

Cornelia, clearing the plates, stacking them onto her arm with a clatter: 'Maybe he will?'

'And then what?' Nella replies tightly. 'Then we are back to where we started. January, all over again?'

Cornelia huffs, carrying off the smeared remnants of her impressive offering, downstairs to a waiting Lucas. Thea plays with her soiled napkin in her fingers, over and over. Nella wants to say something to reassure, but words fail her. She is tired. There is still a wedding posy to pay for, a pastor to see, another feast to prepare, so quickly on the heels of this one.

The women hear the door open, and rise as one, moving into the hallway. Jacob's face is not so easy now; he looks serious, as if he has been charged with great responsibility. He bows. 'Ladies, it is late, and I have kept you too long.'

'But we will see you tomorrow?' Nella says. 'To visit the pastor?'

Jacob looks surprised; she knows she sounds more plaintive than she would have liked. He glances at Thea. 'Of course,' he says, taking his bride's hand; Thea, demure as a wax doll to receive this ministration.

Nella opens the front door onto the balmy air. Jacob bids them farewell, and they listen to his steps diminishing into the night. After he has gone, Thea excuses herself to join Cornelia in the working kitchen. 'I need to talk to you,' Otto says quietly. 'In the study.'

'What is it?'

'Follow me.'

Nella rarely enters the study. It doesn't hold happy memories, for it was here that Johannes used to squirrel himself away, avoiding his duties as a husband. It was here that she tried to make him love her. A small room, Otto keeps it neat, the household books piled up in towers, the grate always brushed and clean.

He ushers her in, closing the door. He moves towards his chair on the other side of the desk, and sits heavily. He gestures for Nella to take the remaining empty chair. 'He wants more,' he says.

'More what?'

'More money, Petronella.'

Nella, still standing on the threshold, stares at him. Her cheeks burn. Was Jacob always going to throw down this financial gauntlet?

'You were not expecting it?' Otto says, an edge of triumph in his voice.

This is Amsterdam, so perhaps she has been naive: Jacob was only going to discuss serious figures once he stepped into Otto's counting room. Their conversation in his salon was a milked-down taster of what was to come, a condescension to her sex.

'Jacob is a lawyer, with his own new house on the Prinsengracht,' she says, as lightly as she can manage. 'He has a life to build for himself. You can hardly be surprised.'

'On the contrary,' Otto replies. 'Given the glowing portrait you insist on painting of him, I am in fact extremely surprised. You gave me the impression that Thea had no price for him. That he would take her with a set of Cornelia's pewter pans. That is patently untrue.'

'I told him what we had. He said that was enough.'

'He was lying.'

'He wasn't lying. What did you say to him, Otto? What did you say?'

'All I asked was how serious he really was about Thea. And now we know.'

Nella feels her panic rising. 'Thea wants this marriage. I will do everything in my power to make it happen.'

'That was what I was worried about,' Otto says.

'Jacob is merely being a sensible businessman.'

'Ah. A sensible businessman.'

Nella comes to sit in the chair opposite him. 'How much does he want?'

Otto leans forward on the desk, pressing the tips of his fingers together. 'What he wants, what he asked for, is a hundred thousand guilders.'

Nella feels winded. '*What?*'

'Payable before the wedding ceremony.'

'It cannot be true.'

'I assure you. Quite true.'

'One hundred thousand guilders?' She takes a deep breath. 'We have got this far,' she says. 'We are so close. We will have to sell this house.'

He sits back. 'Ah. Now you wish to sell the house.'

'You told me you'd had it valued, and that was for a pineapple. *This* is for your daughter. It's our last chance. I know you see it.'

'The house is in my name,' Otto says, 'and I will do as I see fit. The ninth of June is just round the corner, Nella. How quickly do you think I can sell a mansion on the Herengracht?'

'By securing Jacob as a son-in-law, we will be obtaining an even more illustrious address. One mansion for another. Thea might even possibly enjoy a share of an estate in Leiden.'

'But where will *we* live? You and I and Cornelia? In van Loos's attic on the Prinsengracht? In a hut in the corner of Madame van Loos's field?'

'We'll find somewhere. Somewhere smaller. Not so covered in dust and bad memories.'

'No,' Otto says. 'I want to be in this house. But –' he draws a hand down one side of his face – ' I have offered your young man another option.'

Nella begins to feel herself bristle, dreading that Otto will bring up Assendelft, after telling him time and again that it was not to be touched. 'Otto—'

'It isn't Assendelft,' he sighs.

She stares at him, mystified, fearful as to what they could possibly possess that might mollify Jacob's appetite for acquisition.

'I do not want to leave this house whilst I am living,' Otto says. 'But upon my death, I have proposed that this house transfers to him.'

Nella is stunned. Her mind races to understand the implications of this. There is something about Otto's proposed transaction that astonishes her even more than the sum requested by Jacob. 'But what will happen to me, to Cornelia, if we outlive you—'

Otto holds up his hand for her silence. 'Jacob wants this house, Nella. Don't tell me you didn't see it in his eyes, the moment he walked into it. He might wait twenty years to own it. Maybe longer, maybe less: but I think he knows that patience will be rewarded.' He folds his arms, looking sardonic. 'Surely you are willing to vacate it if I predecease you, in the name of this glorious marriage?'

Nella recalls the first time Jacob came here, his eyes taking in the proportions of the rooms. *I declare*, Jacob had said: *this is one of the most wonderful houses in the city. A hidden gem.* Otto was paying closer attention than she had assumed.

'I think you will be persuaded when you hear more,' Otto continues, absorbed in his plan: 'To secure both this promised inheritance, and the guarantee of a marriage for Thea, Thea's dowry is reduced to twenty thousand guilders.'

'He will accept just a fifth of what he asked for, upfront?'

'This house is worth a lot of money, Petronella. For his part, Jacob will pay a monthly stipend to us, starting immediately after the wedding, of two hundred guilders, and to Cornelia, a retaining sum of thirty guilders. This will be accrued by us, and I envisage it will cover your expenses after the occurrence of my death. I have also persuaded Jacob to consider it as wise contribution to the upkeep of his future inheritance: namely, our floors and walls and insulation, everything to keep this house intact.'

'You have been thorough.'

'She is my daughter. He is easy to read. If he wants all this, he's going to have to pay for it. He only has the rights to this inheritance – this house – once they are married, and only then in actuality once I am dead. I have agreed to pay the twenty thousand before the wedding takes place. But this way, both parties feel they are gaining something.' Otto pauses, giving his old friend a long look. 'Which I assume was one of your main ambitions in arranging this marriage in the first place.'

Nella is stunned. 'It is the way of this city.'

'So it is. One day, Jacob will have a house worth well over half a million guilders, and Thea will benefit from its value, and his prior investments in it. And you, I hope, will have many guilders to bolster you in old age.'

'And – where do we procure twenty thousand guilders?' she asks.

'We take out a loan, with this house underwritten as guarantee.'

'This house?' She cannot believe Otto will take such a risk to give Thea what she wants. 'Surely Jacob would object?'

'It is mine to deal with until I die.'

'But how would we ever pay such a loan back? What terms would they offer? What stretch of time? It's twenty thousand guilders.'

'We will pay it back in instalments. We can negotiate terms. We can use the stipend he will be giving us.'

She does the arithmetic in her head. 'But even if we used all of Jacob's stipend money, that would take us nine years to pay back twenty thousand, and that's without interest.'

He shrugs. 'We would not pay it so quickly. We would stretch it out. Years, maybe. We would take on the debt.'

'But—'

'It is not a perfect solution, Nella. But at least when I am dead, the problem can be Jacob's.' He sighs. 'In the interim, perhaps I will find a new job?'

'Jacob could sue us. If anything happens, Otto, this will cripple us. You have no work, where will we—'

'Nella. I have decided. I'm not losing this house if I can help it. The grandsons of the men Johannes and I dealt with are still in their moneylending businesses. I will do my best to negotiate a fair rate of interest.'

Nella feels tears in her eyes. It is such a risk. She feels backed into a corner, out-played, but when she looks at Otto she can tell he feels the same way about her too. They are bound together again by this secret, and it feels like the old days, when Johannes was lost, and then Marin followed him, and things for them felt desperate.

'Thea can never know about this,' she whispers.

'Never,' he says. 'Well, I have no intention of telling her. And we keep it from Cornelia too.'

'Agreed.' She hesitates. 'I know you are angry with me.'

Otto looks down at his desk. 'I am more tired than anything. If this is what Thea wants, and it appears to be so, then this is what we will do. A house for a daughter. Bricks, measured and priced, for Thea's future.' He looks up at Nella and holds her gaze. 'Perhaps it was always going to come to this?'

XXIV

The little parcel on the doorstep is unmarked. It terrifies Thea to see it, but it's the early morning of the eighth of June, the day before her wedding, and she wants to see Rebecca. She knows the actress goes to the playhouse on a Monday to practise her lines alone, and it's been too long since she's seen her friend. There's not much time left to say sorry, to ask Rebecca to be at the Old Church tomorrow to witness the ceremony with Jacob. Before anyone can come and ask her where she's going, Thea scoops up the delivery and takes it with her, opening it as she goes.

As she hurries along, tugging the string, pulling at the paper, she thinks about her aunt's longing for the miniaturist. Perhaps I should have left this where it was, she thinks. My name was not written on this parcel. It might not be for me.

But it's too late, Thea decides. And besides, everything else that's turned up has been for her. As she turns the corner of Leidsegracht, she stops dead. Looking at what rests in her hand, she makes an audible gasp. A few people around her turn, but Thea is oblivious. In the centre of the paper lies the most perfect, breathtakingly real-seeming, but very tiny pineapple.

Its leaves, deep green shot through with silver streaks, fountain out from the top. In size it is no larger than a small almond, but much more rotund. Stout and sturdy, its outer skin feels as rough as the real fruit from Caspar, its flesh only mildly yielding to the touch. It is not easy for Thea's fingernail to pierce it, and neither does she want to. She doesn't know what it's made from, but she's sure it's not edible, however much she'd like to try. It's a strange jewel a lady might have set inside a ring, never to be seen elsewhere, the sort of thing the ladies of Amsterdam would covet. Thea holds it up, running it round her thumb and forefinger in wonder.

And then she feels it: the cold on her neck, the hairs on her nape rising, that prickling sensation that Aunt Nella mentioned when she spoke of the miniaturist: that feeling of being acutely observed. She hears someone calling her name. She snaps her head up, not even knowing what she's looking for. There is nobody she can see who is watching her now: after her initial gasp, everybody is busy again, on their way to work.

Footsteps come up fast behind her. Thea clenches her fists, ready for anything. Her fear intensifies; she cannot bear to turn. Cornelia called this woman a witch. She waits almost cat like, ready to spring.

'It *is* you,' says a woman's voice. A swish of skirts, and a face looms before her, of Eleonor Sarragon.

Immediately, the sensation of cold on Thea's neck disappears. She folds her fingers round the pineapple and keeps it safe in her palm. She notices a page hovering, waiting for his mistress to be done with this encounter. He is black, and their eyes meet, before he breaks his gaze away to look at his toes. His coat is too big for him, and his wrists are swamped by too-large cuffs. But it is Thea who feels suddenly self-conscious – that the boy will not come forward too, with any of Eleonor's – or her – boldness. That clearly he is so young, that he might not wish to talk to her. It has always been rare for Thea to be close to the dark-skinned children she sees in the city, and an old longing rises up in her to hear this child speak. Just to speak of the day they find themselves in, but perhaps to show him the treasure in her closed hand, and to ask questions too: Why can't they find a coat that fits you? Who crops your hair so close? The two of them are locked in a silent moment, and to Thea's astonishment, the little boy sticks his tongue out at her. But then Eleonor speaks, and the spell is broken.

'Why did you not stop?' Eleonor demands, wrinkling her nose. 'I called your name.'

'Eleonor. I thought you were someone else.'

'We haven't seen you for a long time. You're never at the playhouse. And we've had several parties when you haven't been.'

'I wasn't invited.'

'Oh.' Eleanor takes a step back, her eye travelling down Thea's gown. 'I am on the way to my silk merchant,' she says. She hesitates. 'Accompany me, if you like?'

Thea does not reply. She cannot trust these offerings, and nor does she want them.

Eleonor's eyes narrow, then light upon Thea's clenched fist. 'What's that in your hand?'

'Nothing.'

Eleonor looks surprised. 'If it's nothing, then you can show me.'

'No.'

'What are you hiding, Thea Brandt? You are very rude, do you know? You are not good at making friends.'

'That depends on who I meet.'

Eleonor draws herself up. 'Then I'll be on my way.'

'It's a pineapple,' Thea says.

Eleonor laughs. 'What a strange fabricator you are. Don't you know anything? No pineapple could be that small.' Eleonor sighs, and Thea has a moment of realization, how bad Eleonor herself is at making friends. Eleonor shakes her head, as if Thea is a lost cause, as if Thea might be a little mad, and she begins to move up the Leidsegracht. 'Albert, come,' she says, and the page turns immediately in his too-large coat, not looking back as he joins with his mistress.

But then Eleonor stops again and turns around. 'Is it true?' she asks.

'About the pineapple?'

Eleonor stares at Thea. 'No. Is it *true* that you're marrying Jacob van Loos? I heard that the *ondertrouw* had been applied. I could scarcely believe it.'

It never ceases to astonish Thea how words run like water in this city, how her and Jacob's names in ink have crept out of the Old Church, rising up in people's imaginations. She studies the other girl's face. Eleonor, so well practised at pleasantry, releases the sourness of her person in a smirk.

'I am,' Thea replies. 'We are. Tomorrow morning.'

She sees the little boy's eyes widen. 'Well,' says Eleonor. 'I pity him.'

'I beg your pardon?'

'Indeed. I hope *someone* at least has taught you how to make him happy.'

Stunned, Thea watches Eleonor and Albert disappear over

the bridge. For a moment, she wants to run after them, to shake Eleonor till her teeth rattle. But she opens her palm again, to check that she wasn't dreaming, that she isn't a little mad, that it really was a tiny pineapple that was left on their doorstep.

And there it is. Of course it is, almost glowing from within. Thea stares at it, fascination mingling with fear – for is it really possible that the miniaturist knows that Caspar Witsen brought them a pineapple, that her father probably dreams of these things, and that her aunt would rather let the one they have moulder in their house on the Herengracht?

She thinks about her wedding, the posy prepared by Hendrickson the florist: the promised blood red and pinks of peonies and roses, honeysuckle for the bonds of love. *The bonds of love*, as if there are chains to it, heavy chains that are prone to rust. The posy is waiting in a jar of spring water on her bedroom shelf, timed perfectly to be the plumpest it can be for the Old Church tomorrow morning, all colours intent to triumph over the ancient glass windows. She has been told to practise holding it well, how not to crush the stems. Imagine, to be marrying next to the bones of your mother. The puzzle of her skeleton under the puzzle of a daughter.

At home, there is much to do. Last-minute dress alterations, hair preparations, lavender baths to soak in so she is as fragrant for tomorrow as she can be. Cornelia, fretting over rosewater wafers and sugar flowers, salads and meats, pastries and puddings. The Brandt family have invited the van Loos family back to the Herengracht after the ceremony, and according to Jacob, the invitation has been readily received. Thea's father's outfit hangs sombrely on the back of a door, and so does her

aunt's, in shades of deepest black. There will perhaps be argu-
ments over whether Lucas should wear a wedding ruff. Old
times and new times, for running underneath all this is the
sense of a goodbye, of one life ending so a harder, tougher
one might replace it. And underneath that, a hole in their
hearts. A hole the size of Thea.

Thea tucks the tiny fruit into her pocket and continues on
her way to the playhouse.

Our stories can end only one way, that's what Aunt Nella
has often said. We like to think there are many outcomes, she
says: but our fates are out of our hands, and may never have
been ours in the first place.

But Thea is not so sure. Because who can tell? As the thread
of her life as she has known it unspools, at times so golden,
and at others, like now, so frayed – there might be different
stories, still clustered close, ready to be made. Chances, those
missed and those embraced, still might lead to new ends. Thea,
now walking along the Keizersgracht, almost sees them in the
air. Here is Walter, a single man, in love with her simply. Her
aunt, a happier woman. Her father, rewarded. Beyond this
June morning, there is another waiting. The curtain will be
pulled back and everything will be different. If she can only
put her mind to it, and find the curtain.

Perhaps, thinks Thea, it is simply the unreality of the situation. To find myself betrothed, where love is not apparent.
Shakespeare, were he still living, would have done well to pay
attention to this plot. How, in order to avoid the vengeance
of her lover's wife, tomorrow Thea will marry a man she does
not love. Her family, in their costumes and props, have
concealed the truth of their genteel decline, and duped a

wealthy young lawyer who has declared his interest in their daughter. Yet none of it has the sense of frayed and funny ends being tied up to a round of applause. Their plot feels freewheeling, chaotic and strange, and yet it is Thea's life. And step by stolid step she's walking through it, operating its strings, being pushed along by it too. She feels both in control of the wedding tomorrow, and completely at its mercy.

At the backstage door of the Schouwburg, Thea is relieved to discover that she has arrived earlier than the guard. But the door has been unlocked and she slips in, unnoticed. She hurtles through the corridors until she reaches Rebecca's door, dreading she might see Walter, taking the opportunity of a quiet day to work on his canvases. Knocking on it, praying that the room is occupied, she whispers, 'Rebecca, it's Thea. It's Thea. Let me in.'

Within seconds, the door opens, and Rebecca is standing before her. Thea rushes into Rebecca's arms and buries her face in her shoulder. 'I'm sorry,' she mumbles. 'Oh, I'm sorry, I'm so sorry.'

Rebecca holds her tight, and then at arm's length, not letting her go. 'You don't need to say sorry.'

'I do. It's been months since I've come to see you.'

'Thea, it's all right. What's happened? What's the matter?'

'I didn't even know if I could come here. I didn't know if he would be here.'

Rebecca frowns. 'Walter?'

'It's all gone wrong. It's all gone horribly wrong.'

Rebecca closes her door, and guides Thea to the little table. In the corner of the room, Emerald the dog wakes from her slumber, and promptly rests her head back down. 'I've not warmed any coffee yet,' Rebecca says, lifting up a crystal decanter, 'so you'll have to make do with wine.' She glances at Thea. 'Which might be a better choice, in the circumstance.'

Thea takes the glass tumbler from Rebecca's hand, sitting in one of the chairs by the script-covered table, and drinks the wine down. It's fiery and strong, and it burns her gut. 'Is he here?' she says.

The actress makes a face. 'This early? Forget it.' She looks at Thea carefully. 'But why are you asking me?'

Thea takes a deep breath. It has been so many weeks since she's been able to talk about this to anyone, she's not sure if she knows how to find the words. She decides to go to the heart of it, the horrible heart. He's married,' she says.

Rebecca slides heavily into one of the other chairs. 'Sweet Jesus. Are you sure?'

'Oh, as sure as I'd like to be.'

'Thea,' Rebecca says. 'I truly had no idea. I did not think he deserved you, but this is worse than I thought.'

Thea stares into the dregs of her glass. 'His wife knew about me, all along.'

Rebecca turns pale. 'What?'

'How could he do it? When I loved him. I only ever loved him.'

Tears that have been waiting weeks begin to fall. Thea lets out a low moan of pain, of rage, and Rebecca takes her in her arms, and Thea soaks her sleeves until eventually the sobbing stops. She extricates herself, her face blotchy and red, drained, but calmer.

'Have you told your family this?' Rebecca asks.

Thea looks at her in horror. 'Do you jest? Of course I haven't.'

'You should.'

'I will never tell them.'

Rebecca sighs. 'If I were you, I would. They will not punish you.'

'You don't know my family. And anyway, if you were me, you would never have put yourself into this mess in the first place.'

Rebecca smiles. 'Do not be so sure. Why do you think I was trying to warn you? I know how it feels.'

It seems impossible to Thea that someone so self-possessed, so powerful and generous as Rebecca is, could ever have let herself be used like this, could ever have got something so wrong.

'I was horrible to you,' Thea whispers.

Rebecca takes Thea's hand, and with her other wipes her tears away with cool and delicate fingers.

'You are not going to forget him, Thea,' she says. 'I can't promise you forgetfulness. But in the years to come, you will think of him with a quiet bemusement. You will treat yourself with a softness that at the moment you do not believe you deserve.'

Thea feels exhausted by the relief of their reunion. 'You're such a great friend to me. I nearly lost you.'

'Never. I didn't go anywhere.'

Thea takes a deep breath and reaches into her skirt pocket. Her fingers brush the petite solidity of the pineapple, and for a moment she considers showing Rebecca this curiosity, of sharing with her this half-finished tale of the miniaturist, and the pieces in her secret box, her aunt's yearning for meaning, for one more meeting with this mysterious woman. But it's not the time, or the place. It seems like something she needs to keep between herself and her family.

Instead, she pulls out the two blackmail notes and slides them over the table towards Rebecca. 'I want to show you these. His wife wrote them,' she says. 'Her name is Griete. She's blackmailed me.'

Rebecca stares down at the two notes, reading them rapidly. 'Oh, God.'

'I had to pay her to keep quiet about Walter. As you can see, if I didn't, she'd tell people like Clara Sarragon about us. My reputation would be ruined.'

For a moment, Rebecca says nothing. She places the notes face down on the table, and leans back in her chair. 'And did Walter know she'd been writing these?'

Thea pauses. 'He did.'

Rebecca's curls her lip. 'Scum.'

'You should see where they live, Rebecca. He's very poor, and they've two children, and—'

'Thea, no. You cannot defend him. What he did was weak and cruel.' She hits the tabletop with the edge of her fist. 'I knew there was something about him. I saw it. I knew it. I should have done more.'

'And I never would have let you.'

'But I allowed you to meet him here—'

'I'm an adult.'

'I should have been a better friend!'

'I would just have met him somewhere else if I could,' Thea says, her heart heavy. 'It's entirely my fault.'

'None of this is your fault.'

'But partly it is. I saw what I wanted to see. And I wanted him so much.'

Thea closes her eyes, thinking about all her times in the

painting-room, that locked-away world so detached from reality. Walter's hand on her skin, the touch of his lips, the giddy tessellation of his canvases spinning around their heads as they melted into each other's bodies.

In such moments of recollection, in the warmth of the presence of Rebecca, she wonders if the heartbreak to come was almost worth it. But then the disappointment of her happiness and her fear of Griete pursues her, until she thinks she might be sick. She opens her eyes and pours herself another glass of wine.

'Are you all right?' Rebecca asks.

'Griete might threaten me again. They need the money. But it was hard enough for me to pay her the first two times.'

'I thought you were rich?'

'We have the appearance of it. I paid her in secret from money my family don't know about.'

'How?'

'I sold my mother's map of Africa.'

'Thea, this is terrible,' Rebecca says, her face shadowed by worry. 'You cannot continue like this. What are you going to do?'

'Well,' Thea says, 'come to the Old Church, tomorrow at ten in the morning. I would like very much for you to be there.'

'The Old Church?' Rebecca looks wary. 'Why?'

'To witness my marriage.'

'Your *marriage*?'

'Yes.'

Rebecca's eyes widen. 'To *whom*?'

'To Jacob van Loos. The man my aunt met at the Sarragon ball. Do you remember? He lives on the Prinsengracht. Maybe you were right, after all. I did find a good young man. Or at least, my aunt did.'

Rebecca looks panicked. 'But—'

'Jacob is eligible. Rich. And he will marry me.'

Rebecca takes Thea's hand. 'Do you want to marry him?'

'I started it, Rebecca. I was the one who said I wanted him. And it is not without its advantages. Jacob will offer me protection, and my family, for the rest of our lives.'

'But what if Griete hears of your wedding? What if she starts writing to Thea van Loos on the Prinsengracht, demanding more money? You would have to conceal the truth from him as well as your own family. What if it never ends? You should tell them the truth.'

The thought of this momentarily silences Thea. A wave of nausea rises into her throat. 'My father has not worked since Epiphany. Our savings have gone. It's a risk I am going to take, because I am their only hope.'

'You may think that,' Rebecca says, sounding desperate. 'But it doesn't mean it's true.'

'They have raised me and cared for me, and all I have done in the last few months, ever since meeting Walter, is to act with great selfishness.'

'Oh, come. I do not think—'

'The time has come for me to repay them.'

'There is no debt to being their child, Thea. And what is *his* family like?'

'I haven't met them. They're coming from Leiden tonight, to stay with him, but I won't meet them until tomorrow morning.'

'Is he a good man?'

Thea stares into the empty glass. 'I do not know.' Rebecca

looks miserable. 'You will not come tomorrow?' Thea says. 'You do not agree with my actions?'

'I understand them, Thea. I do. I myself encouraged you to find a young man.' Rebecca puts her head in her hands. 'And now I wonder if that was such a good plan.'

Thea smiles at her. 'I often dream of being like you. I have always wanted to be like you. You have no husband, no obligations. But unlike my aunt, you do as you wish, and people love you for it.'

'Thea, I am an actress because there was nothing else I was good at. I needed the money. I didn't have a family who loved me.'

'I don't believe they're the only reasons. I've seen you on that stage.'

Rebecca pours herself a second glass. 'I've been doing this since I was six years old, and I never know whether the play I'm in will be my last. I'm ageing. The parts available are thinning out. Soon, it will be just old crones and witches, and even those will stop. And one day, no one will want to see me, and I will look in the mirror and not know who I am. And then what? What then for me and my blank reflection, and doing as we wish?'

'Freedom,' says Thea.

Rebecca laughs. 'Oh. That.'

Thea rises to her feet. 'I'd like to leave those notes with you. Will you look after them for me? I can't have my family or Jacob see them.'

Rebecca looks up at her. 'If that's what you wish,' she says. She closes her eyes and rubs her temples, and Thea can tell she is distressed. 'Stay here today.'

'I can't, there's so much—'

'Stay. Watch the afternoon play.'

Thea hesitates. 'What is it? It's a while since I've been.'

'You won't believe it when I tell you.'

'From you, I'll believe anything.'

Rebecca smiles. 'It's *The Taming of the Shrew*.'

Tell me, Thea Brandt: why do you come to the playhouse? Months ago, Rebecca had posed her that question in this very room, and Thea had told her she came in the name of Walter.

It wasn't strictly true, Thea realizes that now. It sounded like the right thing for a young woman in love to say. The truth is, she also came because she loved to watch plays. But today, it occurs to Thea to wonder whether it is wise to stay and watch a story about a woman who is bullied and cajoled into submission by a man who should know better, however ironically her friend embodies the role. In the name of Jacob, Thea should leave.

But she stays. Here is her second home, after all, with a true friend who lives on the margins of her Herengracht life. Here is the make-believe that Thea has always believed in more than life. And who is to say that after tomorrow, her new husband will let her come to the playhouse? He did buy her that book warning against it: unlike her, he has not hidden himself. Who is to say that Thea might ever enjoy such freedom again, to sit here, with another woman and her little dog, and her wine decanter, and her piles of scripts and sense of humour and of care, in a small warm room where the rules do not apply?

So Thea stays, and they talk and laugh over nothings, and when the time comes, she does not sit in the auditorium, but for the first time in her life, and maybe her last, Thea watches her friend from the wings. Not a crone or a hag, or a witch or a miniaturist. But Rebecca as Katherine: the actress supreme.

XXV

Many times, Nella will look back on the morning of Thea's wedding to Jacob and wonder what she missed. Not just on that day, of course, but all the days that came before it, leading to the moment that she walked into Thea's bedroom as the sun began to rise. Within the days and months and years of her life with Thea, within Thea herself – was there a hint or sign that might have prepared her for what unfolded? They had worked so hard for this day, all of them. Putting aside the pains in their hearts and the doubts in their minds, hammering away their fears with the same diligence and hope with which the silversmith hammered the figurines of a bride and groom into Thea's full-sized betrothal cup. True, they had not yet met Jacob's family; true, they had had to raise a loan of twenty thousand guilders and promise this house away in order to push this wedding into being. But the pastor was waiting at the Old Church, and the money, in the form of a thick pile of banknotes, had been sent to Jacob. Life was an act of adaptation, and Thea had seemed set to adapt.

On that morning, Nella wakes earlier than the sun. Caspar Witsen's tinctures have run out, and she has not slept well, for too many worries about what might go wrong – a groom who doesn't appear, a father of the bride who will not let Thea speak her vows. As she tosses in her sheets, these images run in Nella's mind, together with her memories of waiting to be married at home in Assendelft, listening out for the sound of horses to signal Johannes's arrival. There was no father in her life by then, to forbid the ceremony to go ahead. Indeed, Geert Oortman's profligacy and love of drinking were the prime reasons the wedding of his eldest daughter was taking place at all. A rushed marriage: no guests, no cup, no feast or dancing. At least, with Cornelia's cooking, and the posy from Hendrickson, they are putting on a better show for Thea.

In the dawn dark, dreaming, it is almost as if Nella's father is in the room with her: the first man in her life, dead for over twenty years. There he is, sitting in the corner on the chair by her linen cupboard. He is in the soft kid breeches he always wore, the ones with oily patches, scuffed black boots, coat too baggy, that unkempt hair. He would barely look presentable in a tanner's workshop, let alone a house on the Golden Bend. You would never know he came from a line of aristocrats. The Oortmans had possessed land all round Assendelft for over two hundred years. Aggressive strivers always, until Geert Oortman came of age and ruined everything.

What happened? he keeps saying to her, and Nella doesn't know if he's asking for himself, for his daughter, or for Thea. She tries to speak, but she cannot, and she wakes, disconcerted. *I am not like him,* she thinks. *I haven't ruined everything.*

If her father hadn't died. If her husband. If Marin. If her mother, her sister. If the dead hadn't crowded in. Well, they wouldn't be going to the Old Church today at all. If her father hadn't been a drinker, Nella is sure her life would have been different, less rushed, less contingent, and fuller. He sold off manors to fund his habit until only the house with its orchards and lake were left. Always a glass between his fingers. Even now, on this happy wedding morning, Nella can hear his cuff buttons dragging on the kitchen table in Assendelft, the thud of his skull on the wood, his boot soles scraping the flagstones as she is called to help Carel and her mother carry him to bed. His was a body that was always restless, wanting more excitement for its life than his wife and children ever brought.

Well: Nella addresses him silently in her bedroom, listening to the city gulls outside: *you left us nothing but excitement.*

She left the village of Assendelft to marry Johannes, but her mother refused to leave the crumbling Oortman house, where in winter the ceilings leaked on their heads and water dripped through the floor. *It's all I have left*, she would say, clinging to those rooms with defiance. It had once been a beautiful house, and in Mrs Oortman's eyes it still was. Arabella, the child left behind, would write to her sister in Amsterdam, letters Nella never replied to. She told her older sister how their mother swore she heard voices in the high-ceilinged rooms. *She will converse with them*, Arabella wrote: *speaking to the air.*

Nella's mother would run her fingers over the grimy rosewood panelling, as if it was newly waxed. She smiled in the kitchen, as if it billowed lovely scents. Her senses created a house which no longer existed, but which housed her nevertheless. As her grip on reason loosened, Nella's mother never saw a lake of weeds. Instead, for her, sparkling water, bisected by a family of ducks. Its surface was as still and crystalline as a mirror, and she walked into it to see herself.

And still Nella never went back. Nella was married to Johannes, ensconced in her new Amsterdam home, dry and expensive, perfectly situated on the Golden Bend. She had rubbed her slate clean. But it is always there, that house, those people, the place where she began. Nella closes her eyes again. She thinks about Caspar, drawing over her childhood in black lines of conquest. The plans to build glass-houses on her soil, the anger she felt. She thinks of this house around them, the way the plaster is succumbing to the damp of the city. Otto has put this house, his life, in the hands of the moneylenders, toasting the future of Jacob and Thea van Loos. It seems unbelievable to Nella that it should be possible to place their hulking monument on such a thin line. In her mind's eye she sees it teetering, and she cannot bear to think what might happen if any of them make a wrong move, to see the home that has held them for so many years come crashing down.

Nella rouses herself: just the usual spiralling of her mind, thinking too much. She focuses on the day to come, how soon it will be time to rouse the bride, to feed and dress and escort her to the church. By half past the hour of ten, Thea Brandt will be a wife.

⁕

As soon as Nella knocks on Thea's door and steps inside, she senses that something is wrong. There is a shape in the bed, and the room is still. The shutters are closed, a long finger of light stretching itself through a crack, spreading towards Nella's feet. Dust motes swirl inside the single band of illumination. Thea's wedding dress, pressed and spritzed, stitched and embellished, has been draped over the chair where before it was hanging in her cupboard. In the shadows, the dress reaches its arms over the seat, its wide skirts tipped up: the boning inside the bodice and the stiff quality of the fabric making it look like a full woman, throwing herself head-forward to her fate. The wedding posy sits on a shelf behind it, as still and perfect as one of Jacob's flower paintings, next to his gift of the playhouse book. Nella feels a growing horror as she stares at the dress's handless arms, as if its sleeves are pathetically reaching for those plump petals, those severed stems, drinking the last of their water. Her mouth is dry. She dare not turn her head back towards the bed.

But from the bed, a movement. So she looks, expecting to see Thea stir. Thea, tousled, sleep-drenched, sitting up, throwing open her shutters to let in the light. But it is Lucas, stretching awake in the sheets, arching his long back in the blue shadows. Immediately, he jumps off the bed and comes to Nella, pushing at her skirts. And she just knows, like this cat also knows. Nella runs to the bed, pulling at the bulk where Lucas has been sleeping, fear pushing her blood so hard through her body she feels like her heart is stuck inside her throat.

She fights with those sheets to reveal the pillows that have made a body underneath, her niece now two sacks of feathers, soft but sinister, as headless and armless as the dress she has abandoned.

Nella falls across the body of pillows, clambering to reach the shutter clasps. She calls Thea's name. She calls it, again and again. She manages to open the shutters, her eyes flooded with a greenish gold as she squints onto the canal. There is no one down there – not a single soul – except, just as she goes to move away from the window, someone is standing on the distant corner of their junction with Vijzelstraat, in the shadow of the building opposite, their hood up, staring in the direction of their house.

When Nella manages to focus her panicked gaze on the spot, looking for a head of bright hair beneath the hood, all she can make out is a fleeing foot, vanishing to nothingness up Vijzelstraat. It could have been anyone. Anything, a dog, a trick of her eye. She feels torn – should she flee from this house after the vanishing figure? By the time she has rushed out to where they may have been standing, she will never catch up.

Her fear rising to breaking point, Nella wheels around the room, searching for an answer. She staggers over to Thea's cupboard. Boots, skirts, shirts: they are no longer there, just blank spaces where clothes used to be. The dawn has revealed only these truths: Thea is not in her bed. Her clothes are missing. She is not on the street outside.

Thea, she says. Thea. There is no reply, only the sounds of doors opening, feet running along the corridor.

As Cornelia and Otto burst into Thea's bedroom, Nella turns to them, crying out what she has known, long before she checked the bed. Cornelia is frozen by the sight of Nella's distress.

'Where's Thea?' Otto says.

'She's gone.'

He stops dead. 'What do you mean, *gone*?'

Nella gestures to the empty bed. 'My girl,' she says, barely able to get the words out. 'My girl has gone.'

The Vanishing Girl

XXVI

They have only a few hours to change the story that is unravelling. It seems unbelievable that across these canals, in his house on the Prinsengracht, Jacob van Loos remains under the impression that everything is as it should be, that soon he will be married to Thea, and become wealthier by some margin, whilst they are swirling in this living hell. There are two realities: the story of the world outside these four walls, and the story within this house. Grey faces and gnawing worry, whilst a normal day, insulting in its sunny banality, carries on.

Otto looks as if his daughter's disappearance has vaporized part of his soul. Haggard, he paces around the house, going through empty room after empty room, calling her name, his voice falling unanswered on the floorboards. Nella calculates. Jacob and his family will be getting ready to leave their house soon. She has no idea what to do. She and Cornelia stand staring at the unmade bed. Cornelia goes towards it, kneeling down as if to summon her beloved nurseling back by prayer. She puts her head on the mattress, her arms outstretched, and Nella, helpless, looks on.

'Oh, God,' Cornelia says suddenly, her voice dull and husky. 'Oh, no. Oh, God.'

Nella feels a sick thump in her guts. 'What is it?'

Cornelia has been rummaging in the sheets. She pulls out

her hand and turns round, scrabbling to her feet. Slowly, fearfully, she opens her palm, looking up at her mistress with fevered eyes.

'Look, Madame,' Cornelia whispers in horror. 'Oh, sweet Jesus, *look*.'

On Cornelia's palm sits a tiny, shining golden house. Meticulously, beautifully made, its gold leaf glints in the morning light. As the women gaze at it, time, for a moment, stands still. Nella feels that cold thrill of recognition, that sense of things beginning to slot into place just out of her reach. Otto comes back, standing at the threshold of his daughter's room. He looks at the glowing miniature on Cornelia's palm, as if catching sight of something he hoped never to see again, as if it is something which might blind him. But Nella comes towards Cornelia's trembling hand, and lifts the house between her fingers.

It's the miniaturist's work. Nella is sure of it, just as Otto is sure and Cornelia too. Nothing else draws them in like this, sucking their fear and attention into itself. They are paralysed by its presence, here in Thea's room, so unexplained and potent.

Nella thinks she might cry – from recognition, relief or terror, she isn't sure. For eighteen years she has waited for a sign, and now it comes to her on one of the worst mornings of her life. As Otto and Cornelia look on, she runs her fingers over these minuscule windows, these chimneys. She tries the front door, and it opens easily, so she peers inside. But there's nothing there, just an empty house with two floors. How long has Thea had this, and why has she left it behind? Nella can feel the power of this miniature thrumming under her fingers.

Suddenly, she is back in this very room, weeks ago in April, Thea in her fever, turning in damp sheets, muttering under her breath about a golden house. Is *this* the house Thea had been referring to, and if so, whose house is it? Has Thea been writing to the miniaturist, or vice versa? Nella casts her gaze around the walls. *I was right*, she thinks. *I knew it. The miniaturist came back.* Are there more pieces hidden in this room, or upon Thea's person, that might explain all this? All Nella knows is that Thea is gone, and this tiny gold house has been left behind.

She looks up to see Cornelia staring at her. *Say nothing*, Nella tries to communicate silently. Otto cannot know what she has yearned for all these months. He cannot know that Nella has crept into the attic and taken out his doll and Marin's, yearning for intervention from the miniaturist to help them with their fate. He cannot know how Nella has prayed for this moment, for material proof of the miniaturist's return, and now his daughter is gone.

But Cornelia seems preoccupied with her own worries. She rushes to the window, as if looking out for a bright head of hair under a hood. Nella is sure there is nothing there, not now – but when Cornelia turns back to face them her expression is rigid.

'Is that . . . what I think it is?' Otto says. 'I don't believe it. Except looking at that house, I think I do.'

'Otto—' Cornelia begins, but he interrupts her.

'The miniaturist,' he says, and his voice is laced with dread, his movements slow and heavy as he comes towards the miniature house, as if he is wading underwater to face a foe he cannot vanquish. 'I would know that handiwork anywhere.'

Nella grips the house tightly, wanting to protect the miniaturist from his scrutiny. 'We don't know where Thea got it from,' she says. Slowly, she opens her fist again. The house sits, expertly carved, expectant. 'She could have bought this at a market.'

'Nothing like that sells at a market,' says Otto. 'And why was it hidden in her bed? Why has she kept it close?' He swipes the tiny house from Nella's palm.

'Otto, no!'

'Tell me the truth, Nella, or so help me God, I will go and throw this in the fire. Have you been having dealings with the miniaturist?'

Nella feels struck dumb. 'Of course I haven't. She left this city years ago. I haven't seen or heard from her since.'

Cornelia puts her head in her hands and sinks onto the bed.

'If you're lying to me—'

'Otto, I haven't seen that woman for eighteen years.'

'She's taken her!' Cornelia cries.

They turn to her in horror. Nella reaches forward and takes the house back from Otto's fingers. He looks astonished but she moves a step away from both of them, shielding the miniature with her other hand. She feels safer when it's in her possession, believing him more than capable of turning it to a cinder. Cornelia would probably encourage him to do it.

Otto turns back to Cornelia. 'What do you mean, she's taken her?'

Cornelia looks stricken. 'Why would Thea run away?' she says. 'And where would she go? Thea was ready for the wedding.' She jumps up, begins to pace. 'Thea was *ready*. Then that witch came back to take our child.'

They stare at Cornelia in stupefaction. She's just speculating, Nella thinks. She doesn't really know. At the bedroom door, Lucas sits watching, cleaning his paws.

'No,' Nella says to them, trying to collect herself. 'Look at Thea's bed. Look at her empty cupboard. Thea planned this. Maybe she's at the playhouse? Maybe she's at the church already, with her luggage? The miniaturist isn't *back*. The miniaturist does not involve herself like this—'

Otto makes a noise of scorn. 'Please, do not pretend to be an expert. Most of our problems started with your obsession with her in the first place. Your gross misunderstanding of her purpose.'

Nella feels like snapping. She wants to ask Otto if he truly considers her, or the miniaturist, responsible for Johannes's affairs. For Marin's secrecy with Otto himself, for the poverty they are sliding into. But she bites her tongue. She wants to keep the miniaturist within her reach. 'We must think logically,' she says. 'The front door hasn't been forced. Thea has done this of her own accord—'

'Listen to me,' says Cornelia. 'You don't understand.' The maid's breaths are ragged, her face as pale as Nella has ever seen it. 'A parcel came.'

Nella feels dizzy. 'A parcel? When?'

'Some months ago,' Cornelia says. It's costing her an effort to make this confession, Nella can tell. It is a betrayal of Thea's confidence, and it goes against the fibres of Cornelia's being. 'After the Sarragon ball. It looked – it looked just like they used to. Just like when you were eighteen.' She hesitates. 'And there may have been more.'

For a moment, no one speaks. 'And . . . Thea took this package?' Nella asks.

'She did,' Cornelia says miserably.

'And it looked like it was from the miniaturist?'

'It did.'

'And you didn't tell me about it?' says Otto.

'Or me?' adds Nella.

'Thea isn't a little girl any more!' Cornelia cries. 'And I didn't want to think about it. I tried asking her! I tried warning her, but I couldn't explain it all, not properly. How could I even begin to try and tell her what happened before she was born? You always want me to keep quiet. She told me the parcel was a present from Eleonor Sarragon. A ring, of all things, and I wanted to believe her. I wanted it to be true.'

Nella looks at the house in her hand. 'It may have been true. There is every possibility that Eleonor Sarragon—'

'No. Stop it, Madame! Stop trying to pretend those people care about us. And stop trying to protect that witch!' Cornelia says. Her eyes fill with tears. She sits back on the bed in anguish.

'How could you not tell me about this?' Nella says. 'After everything I said to you—'

Cornelia looks up, suddenly furious. 'I wasn't the one who tried to summon the witch in the first place. Going up to the attic, into Madame Marin's chest, disturbing the past, getting out those cursed little dolls.'

'What?' says Otto. He looks in disbelief at Nella. 'You opened Marin's chest? You tried to *summon* the miniaturist?'

'Of course not—'

'It wasn't you she wanted,' Cornelia races on. 'It was Thea.

318

Thea's not at the playhouse. She's not at the church. She's *gone*. And the miniaturist has taken her.'

Otto sits heavily in Thea's chair. Nella wants the floor to swallow her up. It seems impossible that Thea might be with the miniaturist. But looking at this golden house – maybe, just maybe, it might be true.

'We will find her,' she says. 'Wherever she is, I promise we will find her.'

About fifteen minutes later, Nella, still in her nightclothes, and Otto, fully dressed, stand alone in the cool shadows of the hallway. Beyond their front door, the day is now fully alive. The citizens of Amsterdam bustle past the giant windows of their house, completely unaware of the decimation behind them. Thea has dissolved like the day's early mist. She thinks with a queasy horror of the scene that awaits her at the Old Church. It will be she who goes to Jacob van Loos. She began all this, and she must end it.

She thinks, with a pounding heart, about the twenty thousand guilders they have handed over to Jacob, of the fact they have pledged him this house. She thinks about what Marin would say to her. How disappointed she would be. In the shadows of Otto's face, Nella assumes he's had the same thoughts.

'We can't do this alone,' he says. 'We will need to summon the militia.'

'The *militia*?'

'We will catch this meddling woman once and for all.'

'You dislike the militia. As do I. They took away Johannes, they came after you. And now you wish to rely on them?'

'What other choice do we have?' he says, his voice catching. 'I have to speak with them. Knocking doors can be their first plan.'

Nella rubs her temples. Soon, everyone will know their business. These militiamen always seem to have nothing better to do than parade the streets for a bag of money, in armour that has never seen a battlefield, gripping pikes that have never pierced a deer, let alone a criminal. If someone does have Thea, they will hear them clanking a mile off. 'We should go to the docks,' she says.

Otto looks as if he has seen a ghost. 'The docks?'

'She could easily be on a ship.'

They fall to silence, thinking of the mighty Amsterdam dockyard, and how easily one girl could slip away unseen. A giant bay, pier after pier spanning east to west, along which hundreds of ships await. Ships like houses shifting on water, unstable mirrors of the stable city, spanning towards the horizon. Nella imagines Thea, earlier this very morning, perhaps talking her way onto one of the English trading ships, or a *fluit*, the largest vessels that would travel fastest. The sun would have been out by the time she was far from that monumental basin of water. The air lifting the edges of her jacket, riming her cheeks with coolness and the taste of salt for the first time, the sea glinting its surface into a mosaic of shattered gold. *I should like to see Paris and London. To go to Drury Lane. I should like to visit the Opéra.*

'If she's on a ship,' Otto says, voicing her thoughts, 'then we will never find her.'

Nella cannot answer this. She will not admit such defeat out loud. 'I will go to the Old Church,' she says. 'And tell Jacob the wedding is cancelled.'

Otto glances at her. 'His family will be there. Are you sure you can do it?'

'I am quite capable of withstanding the humiliation.'

'I wonder if you are,' he says. 'I wonder if any of us are, and that's why we're in this predicament.'

'Otto,' Nella says tentatively. 'Remember that Thea's clothes are gone. She was not . . . snatched, even if she is with the miniaturist.' She puts her hands up, sensing his anger with her. 'I know Cornelia is convinced. I know you're both angry with me about getting the miniatures out of Marin's chest. But there is still the possibility Thea did this for herself.'

For a moment, he looks as if he is going to say something, but then thinks better of it. He looks down at his palms, exhaling deeply. 'Thea asked me about her mother,' he says. 'How she and I met.'

'And . . . did you tell her?'

'Not everything. But what I told her was the truth.'

Nella feels sick with worry. Did something he said to Thea make her want to run? The thought of Thea, out there on this bright anonymous day, moving away from them, grips Nella with a terror she can hardly withstand.

'Otto, I have been the architect of this marriage, before I even set eyes upon Jacob van Loos,' she says. 'I have moved all the parts around, without a second thought. Thea did not love Jacob. I knew that. And yet I persisted.'

'Actually,' he says. 'You have done it with much thought.'

'Either way. It is my responsibility.'

'I suggested giving him this house, Nella. And I signed for the loan,' he says, his voice hoarse. 'My only other solution was to grow pineapples.'

'A more benign solution than mine. A pineapple doesn't demand a hundred thousand guilders at the beginning of a marriage negotiation.'

'No, but I'm as much to blame. And a pineapple is still expensive.' He moves towards the front door, restless to go out into the day and search for his daughter.

'Otto – do you remember what Marin told you about the baby she was going to have?' Nella says.

Otto turns back. Today, there is no clamming up on the matter of Marin. He smiles faintly. 'Of course. *His life must be what he makes of it*. Marin was sure that Thea was a boy.'

'Well, at least she was right about Thea making her own life.'

'What do you mean?'

Nella takes a deep breath. 'I trust Thea. And I do not think she would put herself in danger.'

But Otto's expression is bleak. He opens the front door and the sunlight floods in. 'Then you do not remember being eighteen.'

XXVII

On the contrary, Nella thinks: half the problem is I remember being eighteen too well, and remembering has been a curse too long. Otto has left, and she stands in the hallway with Cornelia, in the dress she had planned for the wedding. As Cornelia pulls hastily at the stays at the back of the bodice and the ties on the skirt, Nella feels as if the air is being squeezed out of her. Deep in the pocket, she has stored the golden house.

'Not too tight,' she says. 'I need to be able to move fast.'

'I don't know why you're insisting on wearing this,' Cornelia mutters.

'Because impressions matter.'

'Even now, it still matters what van Loos thinks?'

'Perhaps it matters even more.'

But maybe Cornelia is right: it doesn't matter. Not really, not any more. But if they are going to slide down the social scale, then Nella intends to do it in style. 'Marin would have gone looking immaculate,' she says.

Cornelia makes a small grunt of assent. She can hardly deny it. 'Finish those, Madame,' she orders, indicating the plate of toast crusts balancing on the hallway seat.

Nella reaches over and stuffs the buttered ends into her mouth. Her nerves have pushed hunger away, but she needs the fortification. There is something ghoulish about this, the solo walk to the church, the wrong bride, an aunt coming empty-handed, bearing nothing but ill news.

'What are you actually going to tell him?' asks Cornelia. 'That she's ill? That she's changed her mind?'

It is a good question. What can she say? What story can she piece together, since Cornelia found the tiny house in the tangle of Thea's sheets? To tell Jacob that Thea is ill is merely to postpone the painful inevitable. To say that she has vanished feels insupportable. It will make them look careless, or Thea unstable. To say she has been stolen is a scandal too far.

'I don't know,' she says weakly. 'I'll decide when I see him.'

Cornelia sighs. 'I hope Otto gets the militia searching soon.'

'As soon as the militia are looking for her, Cornelia – that is, if they agree to such a request – Jacob van Loos and his family will hear of Thea's disappearance anyway. There is no escape from the truth. It will be just as when Johannes died, and everyone knew our business. I have to go,' she says. 'The ceremony is due to start in fifteen minutes.'

Suddenly, Cornelia grasps her arms. 'They may say displeasing things to you.'

'I know. But I'm ready.'

'I'll come with you.'

Nella pictures it: Cornelia, at the altar of the Old Church, a frying pan braced in her hand. 'No. Stay here, in case she comes back.'

They stare at each other for a brief moment, sharing a hope that perhaps it is all a joke, that Thea will return to laugh and tell them she has been for her last ramble as an unmarried woman. But it seems as likely as Johannes walking back through the door. Whatever Thea has done, she has done it in seriousness. Cornelia, pale-faced, nods.

'But thank you for the offer,' Nella says, taking Cornelia's hand and squeezing it. 'As always. Thank you.'

'Well,' says Cornelia. 'Well.' She brushes her free hand down her apron, embarrassed, but she doesn't let go.

❦

Nella moves across the flagstones of the Old Church, her heart thumping. She cannot believe the group that has assembled by Marin's grave to bear witness to this wedding. Clara Sarragon is here, her daughters too. Who invited them? They have simply decided to attend, no doubt, to harvest the gossip and gawp. Sweet Jesu: what they will have to gawp at now. What wickedness and laughter they will channel around the salons and gaming rooms, the tea-tasting parties of Amsterdam, repeating for anyone who will listen, how they saw it all unravel with their own eyes: the bride who never was, the angry van Loos. A sea-sickness threatens to overwhelm her, but Nella keeps her head high. And there is Rebecca Bosman, her neat, short figure dressed soberly for the occasion, her face turning towards the church door.

Instinctively, as Nella so often does whenever she comes to the Old Church, she casts her own gaze quickly around the expansive space, hoping to catch sight of a bared blonde head by a pillar, a piercing gaze, to feel the cold at the back of her neck. But the only cold Nella feels is from the largeness of the church. For all that she has the golden house in her pocket, Nella knows the miniaturist is not here. Maybe Cornelia is right. Maybe she really is with Thea.

Her eyes turn back to the wedding party, where she spies Caspar Witsen. Today, he has failed to comb his hair. Otto must have told him Thea was to be married, but why would Caspar want to be here, given his old employer is on the other side of the half-circle, her looks a dagger? He catches sight of Nella, and smiles, but seeing she is alone, and noticing her expression, the smile dies on his lips.

Here is Pastor Becker, so new and young. Has he ever had to manage a case of a missing bride? Now is the time to see. Nella keeps moving ever closer. And by the pastor is the groom himself, Nella's problem, Nella's target, perfect in black, his velvet slippers brushed, his face neither beautiful nor plain, his shirt starched stiff, his beard barbered with mathematical neatness. A face of money and security, turning to her with complacent expectation that the ceremony will be conducted with elegance, like the rest of his life. He sees she is alone, and frowns. Nella takes a deep breath, and continues towards them.

Jacob has brought his mother. It has to be Madame van Loos, for they share the same quizzical stare. His brothers do not appear to be in attendance, for which Nella feels a deep relief. Too many van Loos in this circumstance would be untenable. Madame van Loos is also dressed in rich black, her face framed by an out-dated but impressive circular collar, giving the impression that her head is the sole delicacy on offer in the middle of a pristine plate. She turns to see what has caught her son's eye, and with Nella in her sights, she tilts her head to one side. Small black eyes and a small dark mouth, a nose like a little beak: she looks more like a finch than a hawk. And here is Mrs Lutgers, close by her master, standing nearer to Jacob than his own mother.

By now, they have all noticed Nella. They are all looking at her. Only the pastor is smiling. She has no idea what speech will come from her mouth when the moment calls for it. She pats her pocket, feeling the solidity of the little house through the lining of her skirt. But the wedding party already know that something is wrong. A few frowns, some barely concealed grimaces of satisfaction. Rebecca is wide-eyed, her mouth slightly ajar as she guesses at the plot. Nella finally attempts a smile. It doesn't feel right on her face, and she lets it fall. She takes a deep breath. She has never spoken so vulnerably in public before.

'Good morning,' she says, offering them a curtsey.

Pastor Becker, clutching his small Bible, inclines his head in lieu of a bow. Jacob takes a step back. Nella sees his eye travel over her shoulder, as if behind it Thea will materialize, clutching her perfect wedding posy, her face golden on the morning of such change. He looks back at Nella and she forces herself to hold his gaze. She wills him to understand her silently: *It isn't happening. It's over. Take your mother and your housekeeper and go home.* But stubbornly, Jacob waits. He wants her to spell it out.

'As you see,' she says, 'I come alone.'

'Is the bride delayed?' asks Pastor Becker with a stab at tolerance, a patrician smile that doesn't suit him. 'I am sure we can wait a little longer. On such occasions, the mercurial nature of the female sex can surely be allowed.'

He can be no older than twenty-three. Nella ignores him, turning to Jacob, studiously avoiding the eyeline of his mother. 'Seigneur, may I speak with you alone?'

For a moment, she thinks he will acquiesce. But as his foot

moves, his mother reaches out and puts her hand on his arm. Jacob turns to her. She speaks to him with her eyes and Nella understands. She would do the same. In a city like this, the more witnesses the better, otherwise the truth gets twisted. The little finch wants to force Nella to declare the reason for Thea's absence publicly. Let there be no mistake as to who has let down whom, which side of the contract has proven its players to be frauds and weaklings. Nella fantasizes turning on her heel right now, running to Jacob's house and pulling the twenty thousand guilders from his desk whilst his residence lies unattended.

As the Sarragon girls begin whispering to each other behind their hands, Nella knows she will have to speak. 'Very well,' she says. She keeps her focus on Jacob, but she can feel all their eyes boring into her. They hold one collective breath, waiting for the hammer to fall.

'Thea has absconded,' she says.

For a few seconds: silence. 'She has *what*?' says Madame van Loos. Somewhere behind her, a distinctly Sarragon titter. Out of the corner of her eye, Nella sees Rebecca Bosman step forward, think better of it, then step back again into the gathered crowd.

'Mother,' Jacob interrupts, with a warning in his voice.

'I told you,' his mother hisses to him. 'Didn't I *tell* you?'

Jacob comes closer to Nella, his voice low. 'What do you mean, "absconded"? She is supposed to be marrying me.'

This close to him, Nella can smell the apple pomade applied to his hair, the odd metallic scent of the starch on his collar. His pale-brown eyes the colour of a dried leaf, his eyelashes so very short. He stares at her, unblinking. Her throat is dry, her hands threaten to tremble. She wishes that Cornelia had indeed come, clutching a ladle or a pan. She wants to wield them in front of this man, to make him step back with those eyes of his, with his cloud of choking hair oil. She makes a single fist of her fingers, and clasps it in front of herself in an effort to control her nerves.

'The wedding is cancelled,' she says.

'Absolutely not,' replies Jacob. 'You must go and find her. I will not be humiliated like this.'

'I am very sorry, Seigneur, but we are looking for her. And so far we have not found her.'

'Then you are very careless,' he says.

Nella tips her chin and meets his gaze. She takes a deep breath. 'Or perhaps my niece has done the right thing?'

He narrows his eyes, rubbing his hand over his beard. 'What she has done is nothing to be proud of. It belies an instability that I have, at times, believed runs through your family's blood.'

'I beg your pardon?'

'My son is quite correct,' says Madame van Loos. 'She is a very headstrong, disobedient and thoughtless girl, to depart her house alone. To reject such a future. To leave us standing here.'

Nella looks to Jacob, hoping he might defend his bride. But his face is frighteningly devoid of warmth. 'I've been a fool,' he says.

'Jacobus, you are not to blame,' his mother replies.

'I gave you the benefit of my doubts, Madame Brandt. The Lord alone knows, I had enough of them.'

'If you had doubts, Seigneur van Loos, you were prepared to put them aside for the right price.'

His cheeks flame. 'And what else should he have done?' his mother interrupts. 'A little brown girl? Yes, he told me the truth about her, Madame Brandt. I got it out of him. My son is too kind-hearted a soul. So easy to exploit.'

'If you wish to talk about exploitation, then let us discuss the hundred thousand guilders you first demanded,' Nella says. 'You have taken our money without a hesitation. Our *house*. You were the one who exploited *her*. As if she was your whim.'

Jacob flushes, but Madame van Loos smiles. 'But that is why we asked for such a guarantee,' she says. 'Because of this very . . . instability. You types, you have such wiles.'

Nella feels the ground shift beneath her. 'We request that you return the sum.'

There is a silence. 'The terms of the contract were that I keep the money if the wedding does not take place,' Jacob says.

'That is impossible,' Nella whispers.

'Otto Brandt signed it.'

Her head reels. Otto kept that part of it from her. 'You must at least return us half,' she says, struggling to keep the desperation from her voice.

Jacob looks away, readjusting the cuffs of his coat. 'We are at church. I will not discuss this here.'

From one side of the semicircle, Rebecca and Caspar move closer, and from the other, Clara Sarragon and her daughters inch near. Nella feels her panic rising sharply. How little she wants all this overheard, how eternally damaging it could be for Thea and for them all. But now here comes Becker, with his shining pastor face and his protruding ears, his eyes glued to her. All of them, waiting to hear her defence.

Nella stares back at them, unable to speak. She thinks about what Jacob said to her at the ball the first time they met: *Your husband did not receive a fair trial.* Jacob had wanted to impress upon her that he, alone of everyone, knew that Johannes had been betrayed by the city. And she had wanted to believe so much that he understood their situation, how unique it was, how difficult yet precious. But she sees it now: how it had thrilled this young fool to side hypothetically with a sodomite, to flirt with scandal, and to plan to marry Thea. Wherever Thea is right now, Nella is beyond glad that she isn't here, clutching her posy. She cannot believe how narrow Thea's escape has been.

'I dismissed the city's censure of your husband,' Jacob says.

'You are a hypocrite. You only read that trial on paper. You did not sit on a hard bench in the court room, looking at his crippled body.'

His face clouds, taking on a sour expression. 'I also offered you security. I also accepted the unanswered questions over Thea's parentage.'

From out of the corner of her eye, Nella sees Clara Sarragon edging ever closer. 'You *accepted* them?' Nella says. 'You professed interest in what you perceived to exist outside the norm, but you did not really wish to join with it. And as for security: I do not call taking our house away from us a gesture of *security*. You are a coward.'

His cheeks go red again. 'A girl who grows up without a mother, even if it is on the Herengracht, is an almost impossible prospect. You should be grateful she only cost you what she did.'

Nella cannot believe her ears. She wants to fly at him.

She has never before been so overwhelmed by the desire to physically harm.

'Allying yourself to such a girl was hardly to your advantage,' Clara says to Jacob. 'Her terrible behaviour. Marrying a woman like that . . .' She trails off.

'A woman like *what*?' Nella says.

Pastor Becker steps in. 'I think we should stop this now. We are not in the house of God for petty squabbles and accusations.'

'This is not a petty squabble,' Nella says.

Pastor Becker twitches the corners of his mouth. Nella knows he doesn't like her. She has brought disorder to his door. She can see how the morning sun has moved on Marin's grave slab. The light pours in through a pane of yellow glass onto her unmarked stone, and glows like gold.

'The bride is not coming,' says the priest. 'So there is no wedding. Go home, all of you. Go, and think on the time you have wasted.'

No one moves. No one wants to be the first to leave. Nella thinks of Marin's majesty. Nella will be the last to leave this scene, if she has to stand here five hours more.

Clara Sarragon approaches Jacob, touching him gently at the elbow, leading him away towards her daughters. 'Come,' she says. 'And you too, if you please, Madame van Loos. You have both had a very distressing morning. We live close by you on the Prinsengracht. Come to our house for a while. I have the most superior new botanist. He comes from England,' she adds, throwing a look at Caspar. 'You will taste my new mango compote and declare yourself in heaven.'

Pastor Becker clears his throat.

'Come, Madame Brandt,' murmurs Caspar, attempting to lead Nella away by the elbow. 'Let me take you home.'

'No,' she says, shaking him off. 'I'm quite capable.'

'I know you are. That is not the point.'

And so in the end, it is the lure of a tropical dessert that lifts Jacob van Loos from Nella's life. The pastor walks back to the *kerkmeester* office behind the organ, shaking his head. Nella stands with Rebecca and Caspar, watching as Jacob moves away across the flagstones, richer by twenty thousand guilders, flanked by Clara Sarragon and her girls on one side, and his mother and Mrs Lutgers on the other.

He will be married to one of them in a month, Nella wagers silently. She doesn't know which party to feel sorrier for. Go, with your Sarragon girls, she thinks. Grow old and jealous with them. Let your horizons shrink even more.

She thinks of Thea, out there somewhere, and feels such a pull to find her that it almost overwhelms her. For the first time, she has experienced a weak version of what Otto and Thea must have experienced on uncountable occasions. The easy right that people feel, to insult you. To try and diminish you to your face, without a single repercussion.

She feels exhausted. She has spent so many hours, weeks and months planning for a day like this. She thinks about Pastor Becker's admonishment: *Go, and think on the time you have wasted.* She is the biggest squanderer of them all.

'Madame Brandt,' says Rebecca, breaking into Nella's thoughts. 'We have not met.'

Nella turns to her. 'But I have seen you perform. And now you have probably seen everything about me that you need to know.'

Rebecca smiles. 'Very unlikely. But Thea talked about you a lot.'

'Really?'

'Oh yes.'

Nella sighs. 'My niece has always been my worst critic. And it would appear that she had good reason.' She smiles at both Rebecca and Caspar. 'I thank you both for coming today, truly: but you will have to excuse me. It is no lie that Thea is missing, and it's my fault. Her father is summoning the militia and I cannot waste a minute more.'

She turns to move, but Rebecca puts a hand on her arm. 'Madame, wait. There's something I need to show you.'

The actress looks so worried that a dread creeps into Nella's blood. Rebecca glances at Caspar. 'It's . . . delicate.'

Caspar bows. 'I will – with your permission, Madame Brandt – but also without it, I must confess – join the search. Thea must be found.'

Nella feels such a strong rush of gratitude towards him that tears begin to prick her eyes. He is always making me cry, she thinks, brushing her fingers quickly over her eyes. 'Thank you, Mr Witsen. Anything you can do.'

'Try not to worry,' he says. 'I believe that Thea wishes to be found.'

'How do you know?'

'Because she loves you,' he says.

Nella feels so astonished by this, that she cannot speak. By the time she has gathered herself, Caspar has hurried off.

The women watch him go. 'There was a man,' Rebecca murmurs.

Nella's stomach plummets. 'A man?'

Rebecca sees her looking in the direction that Caspar has fled. 'Oh, not him,' she says. She pauses. 'This man is called Walter Riebeeck.'

'Go on.'

'He worked at the theatre. Chief set-painter.' Rebecca takes a deep breath. 'Thea was in love with him.' She lowers her voice. 'She . . . considered herself to be betrothed to him.'

'Miss Bosman, that is—'

'And I believe that they were lovers.'

Nella stares at the actress's plaintive expression. The sense of the flagstones moving beneath her like water returns. She wishes she could sit down, before she falls. 'What did you say?' she whispers.

Rebecca grimaces. This is discomforting her, to spill the secrets of a friendship, and such secrets too. Thea, with a lover. Thea, who knew all along what it felt like to be in love—

'Do not be angry,' the actress says.

Nella begins to move off. 'Is she with him? Is that where she is—?'

Rebecca holds her lightly by the elbow. 'Wait, Madame. I do not think she is with him. But I do believe that he has hurt her very badly.'

Nella looks wildly around the Old Church, her head pounding, the words the actress is speaking to her making no sense at all. 'How has he hurt her?' she manages to say. 'What has he done? You're wrong, he must have taken her—'

'No,' says Rebecca, with more authority, reaching into her pocket and pulling out two pieces of paper. 'Walter was married,' she whispers.

Nella stares at her. 'Did you know that he was married? Did you—'

'No, Madame, of course I didn't. He never made mention of it.' Rebecca hesitates. 'Thea discovered that he and his wife were blackmailing her.' She hands the papers to Nella, who struggles to keep her hand from shaking. 'Read them, Madame,' she says gently. 'Thea asked me to keep them safe, but maybe she couldn't bear to be near them any more. But there is also the possibility that she was planning to run away even then, and didn't want them destroyed. I don't think she wanted you to find them. But after what I've seen this morning, I cannot keep them to myself.'

Nella looks down at the vicious words. She imagines Thea receiving them, reading them alone, worrying how best to remedy her awful situation. A sadness so acute washes up her body that she has to put her hand on Rebecca's arm. 'How long has this –' she struggles for the right word – she cannot bring herself to call it courtship, or a true betrothal – '*business* been going on?'

'Months. Since before last Christmas. But the blackmail I think is more recent.'

Nella might crawl to Marin's grave to lay her cheek on the bright stone. To whisper, *I'm sorry*. She thinks again about the night of Thea's collapse. How Thea had insisted again and again that all that had happened was a bad turn. But it was a fever of heartbreak, a fever of such pain. Nella's own heart aches at the thought of it.

Thea suffered it all alone, whilst she just kept on talking about money and marriage and Jacob. Thea must have been moving further and further from them, more secretive and scared, until one day, she turned around and said: *You can arrange the marriage with Jacob van Loos*. In the face of being blackmailed, in search of safety, Thea became Jacob's bride. A monetary protection that her own family have broken themselves to provide – to Jacob. Nella thinks she might be sick.

'Did she pay this couple?' she asks, her voice hoarse.

'I believe so.'

'With what money?'

'She told me that she sold a map,' Rebecca says. 'Belonging to her mother.'

So Thea has been in the attic, too, has dug up her inheritance. Nella imagines Thea lifting the doll of her mother out of the cedar shavings, seeing her lifelike face for the first time. Did she take her miniature mother with her when she left? As soon as she shares all this to Otto and Cornelia, they will be even more convinced that the miniaturist has her.

'That man is right,' Rebecca says, indicating the direction Caspar took. 'Thea loves you. I think she agreed to this wedding because she believed it would protect her whole family. But she couldn't do it, and now she has panicked. She's frightened about what you will say. She hates to disappoint you.'

'You know her very well,' Nella says. She looks down at the notes. 'I feel as if I hardly know her at all.'

'There are things she has told me, true. But believe me, Madame Brandt, I feel to blame. I should have done more to discourage her from a man like Walter. I may not have known he was married, but I could tell the sort of man he was, and I should have been a better friend.'

Nella rubs her temples. 'Miss Bosman, I encouraged her to

pursue a man like Jacob van Loos. So I would not punish yourself too severely on my account.'

The women regard each other. Rebecca looks genuinely miserable. Nella can sense their shared guilt and sorrow. She and I are of a similar age, Nella thinks. Strange, how Rebecca should be Thea's closest friend.

'And is this man – this Riebeeck – still working at the playhouse?' she asks.

Rebecca looks grim. 'He's not. I checked. He's gone to another city, and taken his family.'

'But . . . Thea wouldn't have followed him, do you think?'

Rebecca frowns, considering the possibility. 'Truly, I don't think so. When we last spoke, it seemed that although she felt strongly for him, she also wanted nothing more to do with him.'

Nella sighs. 'I suppose that can only be a good thing.'

'Do *you* have any idea where she might be, Madame Brandt?'

Nella shakes her head. 'I don't.'

'If I hear anything, I will tell you.'

'Thank you. I'll keep these notes, if you don't mind?'

'Thea will be angry with me that I've showed them to you.'

'When I find her – and I *will* find her, Miss Bosman – I shall tell her the fault is all mine. She will understand.' Nella crumples the hateful notes into her pocket, praying that her words are more than just empty promises, that there will indeed be a time when Thea is back with them, angry, but able to forgive.

As her hand brushes the little house, Nella hesitates. 'One last thing. Did Thea ever mention to you that she was receiving miniatures? Miniatures like this?'

Nella takes the golden house out of her pocket and watches the effect it has on Rebecca. The other woman looks enchanted by its tiny perfection. 'What *is* that?' Rebecca whispers.

'I don't precisely know,' Nella says. 'But did she mention anything?'

'No,' says Rebecca. 'I would have remembered something like that.'

Nella puts the house back in her pocket. 'Please forget I asked. A foolish thing. Thank you, Miss Bosman: for your care of my niece, and your candour.'

Before the actress can reply, Nella curtseys and moves away. She has been gone too long already.

XXVIII

'We need to tell Otto,' Cornelia says.

'Absolutely not,' Nella replies. She's hurried back to the Herengracht, and finding Cornelia still alone, in even more of a state of torture, has felt no other choice but to sit at the kitchen table and relay everything that has unfolded over the gravestones. 'Cornelia, the existence of Walter Riebeeck is Thea's secret to tell. I forbid it.'

'But the militia need to know about him!'

'Rebecca Bosman said that he and his wife had gone! We should not be pursuing him. We must trust Thea. And can you imagine if it came to light? Our Thea, tangled up with some petty blackmailer couple? We cannot do it to her. I will not do it. Think of how it would damage her reputation, even more than breaking a wedding to Jacob.'

Cornelia blanches. 'Show me the notes again.'

'You'll only get upset.'

Cornelia looks desperate. 'The actress could be lying.'

'Why would she be? She isn't, Cornelia. You weren't there.' Nella sighs, laying her head on the table and pushing the notes across the wood. 'No. I regret to say that Walter Riebeeck is very real.'

'But Otto—'

'Cornelia.' Nella raises her head. 'How do you think he will respond to the news of a lover? A married one, at that? This Riebeeck has gone, let us not involve Otto in it. Thea might never speak to you again.'

'That's if we ever find her.' Cornelia slumps down. 'We're no closer to finding her than we were this morning.'

'No.'

'No child is safe,' Cornelia says miserably. 'From the minute they're born.'

We've all been suffocating Thea for so long, Nella thinks. Either by being too protective, not schooling her in the ways of the world – or, by making too many assumptions about her future. I would have run away too. I would have flown over the rooftops. I might have found a Walter of my own, pouring my fantasies into his undeserving and beloved body.

But then again: look at what can happen when you break away. You leave behind such devastation.

How has she managed it? Nella wonders. How have we missed all this? It is astounding to her, to realize that Thea might have experienced things Nella had wanted for herself with Johannes, when she was so firmly and painfully rebuffed. A thing she has wondered about ever since: how it might feel to know the touch of a man who wants her.

She thinks of Thea, sitting in Jacob's box at the playhouse, announcing how the painted palm trees of the Schouwburg sets lived in her heart, meaning more to her than any real tree. Thea, shining brilliantly at the Sarragon ball, unfazed by the barely veiled criticisms of the other girls. She was limned with a sort of confidence that perhaps only comes from feeling loved, and Nella couldn't understand it.

But the terrible thing is, perhaps Thea couldn't understand

it properly either. She was happy, because she had offered her heart, and thought the offering had been accepted. And then it had gone wrong.

Nella could kill this Walter Riebeeck, whatever she preaches to Cornelia. She could rip his stupid painted palm trees into shreds.

'Are you angry with her?' Cornelia asks, breaking her thoughts.

She sighs. 'I'm angry with *him*.'

'I know that. But what about Thea?'

Nella considers this. 'It would be easy to say I am angry. In many quarters of this city, what Thea has done would be considered unpardonable – the casual dismissal of virtue in the pursuit of love? But those quarters have never much approved of this family anyway.' Nella once more moves through the scene at the Old Church this morning: the imperious Madame van Loos, smug in her verdict and richer in pocket; her son Jacob, the coward; the Sarragon women, scenting an opportunity to crush an outsider. Her anger renews, coursing through her veins. The van Loos family and the Sarragons don't know the whole truth, but if they did . . . it is so easy to prize virtue, it is useful to so many parties to do so: but perhaps not at all costs. It cannot be possible that all young people in this city manage to get to eighteen without some compromises here or there. We just don't talk about it.

'No,' she says. 'I'm not angry with her. I just want her to come home.'

Nella considers briefly telling Cornelia about the marriage contract, the twenty thousand guilders, the stipends promised, the house to be handed over at Otto's death. Surely they will not be giving Jacob the house now? Impossible, as the marriage has not taken place. Still: it is bad enough that they are in debt for twenty thousand. It would be a relief to unburden herself, but Cornelia can hardly solve an issue that will only agitate her further. Why tell her today that the place she has lived in since she was a little girl has turned to water, running through their fingers?

It seems outrageous, that people who are so wealthy already should be able to keep such a sum. But I was so desperate for it, Nella thinks. I wanted Thea married so much. I wanted that safety. And Otto wanted what Thea wanted. And Thea didn't even know what that was.

There's a knock at the door and the women jump. Cornelia rushes up the stairs, Nella following close on her heels. They pull open the door to find Caspar Witsen. He looks tired. 'I've been everywhere,' he says. 'I couldn't find her.'

'Come in,' Nella says.

'I cannot.'

'You should eat something. Drink something,' says Cornelia.

'Please,' Nella adds.

Caspar allows himself to be brought inside. He seems to be wrestling with something, pacing before them, running his fingers through his mane of hair. 'Thea wrote to me,' he says. 'Asking me about flowers.'

Nella and Cornelia exchange a glance. 'She wrote to you?'

'It was after the announcement of her *ondertrouw*. At first I thought it might be something to do with her wedding, but she wrote asking about how one makes tinctures of one's own. She said she was very grateful for the ones I had brought, and interested.'

'Tinctures?' For a moment, Nella has flashes in her mind of poisons, of belladonna and hemlock, of too much valerian. 'And . . . did you reply?'

Caspar's face crumples. 'I was so busy. I hadn't yet had the time.' He reaches into his pocket and hands over the letter.

I feel as if I'm putting my niece back together through bits of paper, Nella thinks, reading the letter. A new Thea, one I had no idea existed.

It is Thea's handwriting, unmistakable. *The tinctures have proven so helpful to us all, but I am sure the process is complicated,* she has written to Witsen. *I can think of little better than watching a seed grow from nothing. To stand in the middle of an orchard and see one's hard work flourish.*

It is dated from a week ago. Nella hands the letter back. 'You must keep this. It is yours.'

Clearly distressed, Caspar takes the letter. 'Madame, I would do anything to make this easier for you.'

'You have done enough already, Mr Witsen. We are so grateful. You helped so much when she was unwell.'

'And if you ever need anything, Otto has the address of my lodgings.'

'Be assured,' Nella says soothingly, putting her hand on his arm. He looks at her, seemingly to say something further, but he thinks better of it.

'We will write to you as soon as we know where she is,' she says. They watch him go. No tincture, Nella thinks, can summon back a vanished girl.

❧

By ten o'clock that night, thirty men from the St George militia and a few others, including some serving women from the houses nearby their own on the Golden Bend, are still on the hunt for Thea. There has been no luck, and her state of absence is declared.

When Otto does come back, he is accompanied by an officer, and Nella lets the two men in. Cornelia is down in the kitchen, reheating a chicken pie for the moment of Otto's return, to strengthen his resolve.

'Seigneur Kobell, Madame,' says the officer.

He is young, Nella thinks – but then again these days, so many people are younger than her. 'We've been looking for hours,' Kobell says. 'And have been thorough. My men are going to need to rest.'

'But the money I paid,' says Otto.

'Let them sleep a while, Seigneur Brandt,' says Kobell. 'And then when they're refreshed, they will spend tomorrow looking anew.'

'But by then we shall never reach her.'

Kobell rubs his hand up the side of his face as if to massage it out of a stupor. 'We will find her.' He hesitates. 'But you must prepare yourselves for a longer search. As long as she wishes not to be found, our task is made the harder.'

'How do you know that she does not wish to be found?' Nella asks, remembering what Caspar had said in the Old Church this morning, a conversation that feels about a fortnight old.

Kobell frowns. 'But if she wishes to be found, then why would she run away?'

Nella sighs inwardly at the limit of his understanding. He

is too young, but it is as Caspar said. There is always a sliver of hope in a person who has run away, that someone will come and save them from themselves. Nella knows the feeling herself. She holds on to the hope that Thea does not want this to last for ever. She wants them to find her.

Nella notices Otto's own exhaustion, and she thinks about Walter Riebeeck: the viciousness of those notes, the revelation of a broken heart. She feels a pang of guilt that even now, even under such awful circumstances, they are making new secrets to keep from each other. Does he really believe that Thea is with the miniaturist? If she isn't with Riebeeck, then maybe she is?

Nella wonders if he has mentioned the miniaturist to Kobell. No, he would not do such a thing, because he has barely any proof, and prefers to be taken seriously. The miniaturist, for now, must be their own, private preoccupation. She feels more tired in her bones than she has ever felt in her entire life.

'Enough,' says Otto, breaking into her thoughts. 'These hours are crucial. We must not stop.'

But Cornelia is coming up the basement stairs, proffering her chicken pie. It smells delicious, so hot and homely, so at odds with the fear coursing through them all. Kobell turns his head.

'You must have some, Seigneur Kobell,' Nella says. She, like Cornelia, sees the advantage of food in this moment, even if Otto cannot.

'It's night,' Otto persists. 'It's *night*, and we still haven't found her. She is my daughter. She is my life. No one in the city has offered up a single crumb!'

'And the stables? The docks?' Nella asks. She looks over at

Cornelia, hollow-eyed, but still with fire in her irises. Cornelia has always been used to less sleep.

'We went there. Reports back from the docks,' Kobell says, looking at a piece of paper he has taken from his pocket. 'This morning, fifty ships were due out. Of the ones we caught before they sailed past Texel, not a single captain or purser has reported a girl or a boy of Thea's build, looks and age, looking for a berth.'

'Of the ones you caught,' echoes Nella. Kobell acknowledges this with an apologetic shrug. 'What time was the morning tide?'

'Just after seven.'

'So there was plenty of time for her to get onto the water if she was desperate enough.'

'Thea wouldn't go on the water,' says Cornelia, spooning the pie onto plates. 'She's has never set foot on a ship. She is still in the city. I *feel* it.'

'Not necessarily,' says Nella. 'What of the stables?'

'Nothing there, either,' says Kobell.

'Have you tried the convents?' Cornelia asks.

'The convents said they hadn't got her.'

'They could be protecting her.'

'Body of Christ!' Otto exclaims. 'A convent?'

'Thea wouldn't go to the nuns,' Nella says. 'And even if she did, she couldn't stay there forever.'

Kobell declines the pie, and opens their door again. Cornelia stands surprised, his plate still proffered in her hand. 'Rest now,' he says. 'I assure you, Seigneur, Mesdames: the night guard is still out there, looking, and I will return in a few hours.'

Before Otto can protest, he offers them a quick bow of his head, and vanishes into the dark. The three of them are left alone.

'He's right,' Nella says. 'We need to sleep. We're no good like this. Thea is probably sleeping too.'

But where Thea is sleeping, and who with, are questions none of them can bear to think about. Otto will not concede going up to his bed. It is impossible for him to conceive of slumber when he has no idea what has happened to his daughter. Nella understands it: he wishes to sit vigil in the hallway, for a couple of hours at most. Upright in a chair with a cushion at his head, the pie turning cold beside him.

❧

Alone in her room, wide awake, Nella lies on her bed, fully clothed. The St George militia, however little she likes the memory of their involvement with Johannes's arrest, do sound as if they have been thorough. Cornelia has it wrong: Thea is not in the city. But equally, it seems impossible to imagine Thea on the water. Nella closes her eyes, her mind hopping from image to image. The sight of Thea's empty bed. Cornelia, pulling out the miniature house with that look of horror on her face. Jacob at the church, Caspar's dying smile; Rebecca, an actress out of role, handing her the truths about Thea's heart.

Nella turns on her side and looks at Caspar's aloe which she has placed by her bed, reaching out to feel the stump where he sliced a leaf to make her calming tea. *I can think of little better than watching a seed grow from nothing*. She thinks about why Thea might have left the miniature house in the tumble of her sheets: was it by error, or with a desire to tell her family that she, too, knows about the miniaturist? Nella closes her eyes again. Whether or not Thea is alone or with the miniaturist, she wants Thea back.

She feels a gnawing pain in her ribs when she thinks that she might be the reason, not Walter Riebeeck, why Thea might have gone away. All those times they have argued. All those times Nella has told her niece that she doesn't understand the world. All these days she has spent, pushing Thea towards Jacob, letting Thea hear her endless complaints about money, about the sacrifices she's made. She imagines Thea in the attic, taking out her mother's doll, her unanswered questions being poured into a miniature that never gives an inch.

Marin, who also hated the restrictions of this house, loved it in equal measure. She had been so proud of it. The first day that Nella was here, eighteen years ago, before Thea was even born, Marin had asked: *Your grand ancestral Assendelft seat: is it warm and dry?*

It can be damp, Nella had replied.

But now see, Marin, Nella thinks: it is this house that might fall from our hands, into the murky waters of the Heren canal. And your daughter has freed herself from it, before me.

She puts her hand in her pocket and feels where the miniature baby rubs against the tiny gilded house. *Come back to me*, she murmurs – not to the miniaturist this time, but to the one person she has treasured most of all.

Do you hear me, Thea? she whispers. *Come back.*

෴

It is just before dawn when Nella realizes what has happened. She sits up, rigid in her bed. The idea of it is suddenly so obvious, that she cannot believe they didn't think of it. In the midst of their immediate panic about Thea's vanishing, the miniaturist, the ordeal at the Old Church, followed by the revelation of Walter and the self-importance of the militia, the most obvious solution has passed them by. It has taken Nella these hours alone, her mind a spiralling shell. It has taken Caspar Witsen with Thea's letter, and that little golden house, to make her see.

Nella rises from her bed, her heart in her mouth. She senses inside herself an ending and a beginning, two stories meeting each other to make an eternal circle. She knows where Thea is, and that she must go alone to find her. She will not take a barge – not the way she left, eighteen years ago. She will rent a horse from a stable. Yes, a horse; because however much of a nightmare this might turn out to be, Nella has never forgotten how a country girl rides.

Green Gold

XXIX

On the morning of her wedding to Jacob van Loos, before dawn, and before anyone else in the house is awake, Thea sits up in bed. She looks around the same room she has slept in her entire life. The white walls. The dark, bare floorboards. The long shelf, upon which she has left the book given to her by her future husband, and the wedding posy waiting in its water. It is just as Hendrickson said it would be: the petals are now at their fullest, bright and colourful even by the light of the solitary candle. They look innocent, not seeming to know that their stems have been cut, how even by tomorrow they will have begun to wilt.

Thea has barely slept. The box of the three miniatures lies open on her lap. She stares into it, her sense of desperation rising. Here is Walter and his empty palette. Here the golden house with its sealed door. And here, the tiny pineapple. She looks at them as hard as she can, trying to understand their language. But what Thea wants, more than anything, is to stop this day.

She cannot begin to imagine how it might feel to be laced into her wedding gown, to be accompanied along the canals towards the Old Church to see Jacob, to stand before Pastor Becker and make her vows. And then, to walk back here again with Jacob's hand in hers, a married woman. To drink from the betrothal cup. To feast, then leave.

But it is something Thea has promised to do. It will save her family's future; securing them once more within the confines of acceptability. It is something she is on the cusp of making real, and yet it feels so dreadful to her, so impossible and wrong. She thinks of all the food Cornelia has prepared. She thinks of her father, in this very room, telling her she can begin again. And then she remembers Rebecca's warning – how the attentions of Griete Riebeeck may never end. She had thought she would be escaping into this marriage, that she could put up barriers to keep the world out. But it might make things even worse. This was Thea's new beginning: life as a wife. And she cannot do it.

Rising from the bed, Thea dresses quickly in an everyday skirt and blouse. She puts the doll of Walter and the pineapple in her pocket, glancing at the one miniature she has not touched. Her first impulse is to leave the golden house inside her box, and to place the box under her bed. But she hesitates, taking the tiny dwelling between her fingers once more, holding it by the candle's light. She tries the tiny door again: still locked. There must be something inside this house, if only she knew how to open it, to coax its secrets to her.

On the day she announced to her family that they should make plans to approach Jacob for a marriage contract, she had believed this house had been sent to her as a sign. It was a portrait of Jacob's house, a message to her that she should seek his golden security and leave this tarnished place where she's spent her entire life. She was trying to see these miniatures how her aunt sees them, as pieces of guidance. But now, she doesn't want this little mansion. It is a reminder to Thea of her failure, a herald of a future that is not hers.

Thea places it on the small table by her bed. She wants her aunt to see it, to leave behind something that tells Aunt Nella she knows about the miniaturist too. But as for Walter, and the pineapple, they are Thea's. Imagine her father, seeing the doll of Walter! It represents everything about Thea's life that she wishes to hide. Or her aunt, seeing the pineapple she hates so much. Even now, Thea wants to protect her family. In her hurry and distraction she does not notice, tossing her pillows and sheets, arranging her bed so as to make a simulacrum of her own sleeping body, how the little house gets caught, enfolded into the warmth of the nest she's left behind.

Emptying her clothes cupboard and the rest of the guilders from the map sale into a linen sack, Thea leaves her room without a backwards glance, slipping down the main stairs, avoiding every creak of the wood which might reveal her. She tiptoes deeper into the house, to Cornelia's store, taking a loaf, a small disc of Edam, a large flask of ale, some cold slices and cinnamon cakes. She can barely tolerate being in that little room, surrounded by so much preparation for her wedding feast. Back up the kitchen stairs and across the hallway, Thea stuffs the goods on top of her clothes bag and draws back the bolts of the front door as slowly as she possibly can, wincing every time there's a grating sound. Cornelia will be awake very soon.

This is for the best, she tells herself. You have disappointed everyone enough.

Her skirts move, and she looks down to see Lucas staring up at her, circling her legs. 'I'm sorry,' she whispers. 'I wish I could take you too.'

Lucas sits on a white marble square and continues to watch

her, but Thea cannot bear his attentive affection. She can't imagine never seeing him again. She looks out to the blueish dawn, and then to the salon, thinking about all the birthdays she has had in that room, sitting on that rug. The fluffy eggs, the rosewater pufferts: the adventurers who never went beyond the Herengracht. There is a bruise on her heart, another, another. She wants to stop the sensation but she can't. She wants to be five again, delighting in games of exploration that go nowhere. To be encircled by their love.

Enough, she tells herself. You squandered all that. It's in the past.

But it's as if Thea is under a spell, and she cannot force herself to step into the day. She bends down to kiss Lucas, forcing herself to think again about Jacob as a husband, of Eleonor Sarragon and her mocking eyes. She thinks about Griete Riebeeck, and above all, Walter and his betrayal, his words of love – his promises: the worst part. There is no future in this city for her. Thea must make one somewhere else.

And yet, even though she manages to get out of the house, closing the door quietly behind her, she stands at the corner of the Herengracht with Vijzelstraat, waiting to see what her family might do. Will someone look down from her bedroom window once they notice she has gone?

If they do, Thea thinks, I'll go back.

She almost longs for them to throw up the windows and call for her, to burst outside, to drop to their knees in supplication and say sorry, we're so sorry, our baby: we will never make you do such things again. Because the truth is, Thea is scared of what she is about to do. This isn't a play. Gentlewomen of the Herengracht do not simply disappear. She will go back through that door, and marry Jacob, and become a wife on the Prinsengracht.

But when the small face of Aunt Nella does appear at the window, she looks to Thea like a little scared moon. A real gentlewoman of the Herengracht, scanning the canal path, her hand upon the pane like a frozen gesture of farewell. She looks like a prisoner, hoping someone might come and release her too. Thea knows she cannot go back through that door.

Waiting on a bridge on the outskirts of the Jordaan are many daily cart-men, taking payments for ad-hoc journeys, hauling whatever is required – potatoes, slaughtered cuts, linen sacks full of a young woman's life. The sky is breaking now into pink bands over the canals, the sun tinging the clouds with gold. One old man agrees to take her out of the city for a guilder to where she wants to go, but they do not speak on the journey, Thea remaining in the cart behind rather than up with him by the horse. It's still so early and he seems unwilling to talk, and she's glad of it. Alone with her sack: early practice for the life of solitude to come.

The house fronts of Amsterdam pass them by as the city wakes up, the maids and manservants on their way to early market, the shop owners expertly removing their boards, the clerks skittering over cobbles to be in the office before their masters. All this activity, so familiar to Thea, and she is leaving it behind. One hour passes, then another. The fields grow in number but the dwellings dwindle. The old man asks her if she's sure of where she wants to go, and all Thea can say is yes, because to say no is to go back, and she can't do that, not now.

357

The sun beats through her cap, the horse flicks flies towards her with its tail. The cart wheels are noisy, mesmeric, and Amsterdam seems nothing but a dream. Thea feels sick with fear that she is moving further and further from what she knows, that she could be riding slowly on to nothingness. Even so, she dares not look back the way they've come, as if, were she were to turn around, the path would have dissolved with no return. Any moment, the land either side might tumble away into infinity, and the cart, the horse, the man might tumble too, and she will realize how she has left herself unaided, unnoticed, without a future or a past.

She thinks of the moment that Cornelia will realize that she's gone, and her tears well up and threaten to spill, but she cannot cry on this cart. She must keep it all inside, or her tears might never stop.

Judging by the position of the sun, her wedding is about to start. Thea imagines Jacob standing in the Old Church, his family, the pastor, maybe even Rebecca: all of them waiting for the bride to show. Thea looks at the back of the old man's head, his grey wisps, the rolls of his neck, two moles at his collar. This is her view instead, and she begins to feel the enormity of her actions, this lack of planning. She wonders if it will be Aunt Nella who goes to the church to tell them the news that she has disappeared.

Of course it will. Only Aunt Nella has the strength.

The cart rolls on. Deep in her pocket Thea touches the doll of Walter and the little pineapple, these signs of her life that still confuse her. She has shed Griete Riebeeck's blackmail notes into Rebecca's care, and now she has rid her family's house of these two talismans. A strange sort of housekeeping, and Thea hates that she still has Walter with her. She could not leave him to be found, but still she cannot bring herself to destroy him. As for the pineapple, it is now to her the most beautiful of the three miniatures. Checking that the carter has his eyes on the road, Thea lifts the tiny fruit from her pocket, rolling it between her forefinger and thumb. To her astonishment, it appears that the fruit has grown a little bigger.

Surely not, Thea thinks, rubbing her eyes to refocus. It must be the sunlight: in a bright mid-morning and not by dawn candlelight, its true size will be more clearly seen. Impossible to think it might have grown – it must be from her fiddling with it, and the material has swelled up. But the pineapple has not lost its pigment: if anything it looks more vivid and plump. Its allure reminds Thea of Caspar Witsen's enthusiasm for his pineapple jam, his offered knowledge in the form of his tinctures. Her aunt will be calling on those sleeping tinctures now, Thea supposes.

When Aunt Nella realizes I've gone, Thea thinks, she'll want to put the whole city to sleep for a hundred years. She sighs, pushing the little pineapple back into the dark of her pocket. The bells of the Old Church would have rung out by now. Thea would have been a wife. Aunt Nella is going to be so angry.

Further into the countryside they travel. The dwellings vanish, the horse trots past blackcurrant bushes which open up onto more fields, the sun burning them into shades of emerald and mustard, topaz, gold. It feels as if Thea is moving through one of Walter's perfect sets, his bucolic scenes that the playhouse always used for comedies. But she cannot feel the comedy in any of this.

'Are you *sure* this is where you want to go?' the old carter says over his shoulder.

Thea looks around, equally uncertainly. 'Yes,' she says, but how can she be sure, when she has never been here?

The old man pulls up the reins and looks around. All that can be heard below is the buzz of insects in the verges, and above, a great volume of birds. No city gulls here, but a chorus of calls that Thea cannot name. There is no sign of human life. Just sky and sky, and unspooling land, majestic clouds, a light breeze that lifts her cap strings.

'I'm a city man,' he says. 'I don't like this silence.'

It isn't silent, Thea wants to say. Can't you hear the birds?

'They say pirates come this far inland to hide their hoards,' he goes on, looking around, as if half-expecting one to jump out from behind a hedge and hold a knife upon his throat.

Oddly, the old carter's own fear expressed like this makes Thea calmer. She imagines sea-grizzled men, men like her uncle, coming out of the water to bury pearls and ingots underneath the hedgerows. It seems preposterous, but the space around them is huge, and open to possibility. She thinks the land is beautiful.

'I'm not going any further,' the old man says, invading her thoughts. 'I'm turning round. I think it's about a mile further. But you'll have to walk.'

'Why? You said—'

'This is as far as a guilder will take you.' He peers at her. 'Unless you've got more?'

Thea hesitates, thinking about the many guilders from the last of the map sale wedged in her bag. She could keep him on, but she has no idea how long that money is going to have to last. 'You can let me down.'

But the carter finally seems to pause. 'You've got kin here?'

Thea jumps out of the cart and drags her bag behind her. 'In a manner of speaking.'

He squints down. 'What's that supposed to mean?' The realization dawns on his face. 'You're running away,' he says. 'Are the militia after you?'

'The militia?'

'If you think you're the first girl I've had in my cart, running away—'

'I have family nearby,' Thea says, her voice faltering. His mention of the militia is more disturbing to her than the idea of any pirate.

'They always regret it,' the man says. 'Think they can cope on their own.'

'Who do?'

'The *girls*,' he says, 'who run away.' He looks at her as if she is soft in the head.

'I'm not—'

'What makes you think you're any different?'

Before Thea can reply to this, the carter lifts his whip to the horse's flank. The crack is a sour note in the bird-drenched morning. He moves off, turning his cart in the wide road. Thea watches as it begins to grow smaller, disappearing the way they came. Never has she felt so alone.

She begins to walk the last mile in the other direction. The sky is enormous. The dew has already burned off the grass. As she keeps walking, her bulky linen sack bashes the side of her thigh. Sweat pools under her cap, the base of her back aches, her neck is burning, and the burden is heavier than she anticipated. She wants to stop but fears to do it, a young woman alone on a country path. Even though there is no one around, to stop here feels exposing in a way she has never understood it to be in the city. The old man's scornful parting words still smart. *What makes you think you're any different?*

Right now, Thea thinks, I could be the only woman alive.

It would be all right to cry now, she supposes, swatting away a drowsy fly, the heat on the path ahead beginning to shimmer. It would be all right to let out the sob that has been threatening like thunder since the moment she walked out of her home, away from the fate she never wanted. She could sob, she could scream, and no one would know.

Thea looks around, the huge blue sky, the low and endless land. So this is Assendelft. To think, that this is where her aunt grew up.

How much did Aunt Nella scream, out here? Or did she keep it all inside?

You've got this far, Thea tells herself, stumbling a little. Just keep going. But she is frightened now that the house at Assendelft might simply be a story her aunt concocted, to explain away her own escape into the dream of Amsterdam, to justify her bitternesses over the years as that dream went wrong.

Perhaps there was never a father who drank, nor a mother who walked into a lake. There was never a brother or a sister. There was never a house so terrible that Aunt Nella didn't go back. It was all a lie, and Thea has walked into it, nothing but a bag of clothes and a pair of miniatures to help her out of it again.

She had thought to come to Assendelft because she knew her father would not think her capable of such a journey, and

Cornelia would not imagine that Thea would want to make it. Her aunt will never come here to find her, because it is the place that haunts her dreams; and she has sworn never to return. Thea has come to a no-place, where she thought she would be safe. But now, mere hours later, all she wants is to be found.

Just as Thea thinks she might cry from the impossibility and the scale of her situation, she sees it. It is not a made-up place, not just a figment of her aunt's imagination, but a real thing. A speck of a house in the distance, its chimneys still tiny, rising to the sky. It has to be Aunt Nella's childhood house, for there is no other house nearby. The June sun illuminates it like a brick jewel, framed by the clouds which tower over it, heralding the fact of its existence, as if a hand has dropped it capriciously from a great height in this expanse, to see how it might fare.

Thea feels her heart race harder. Her feet begin to pound along the path of earth. The world feels alight with colour. She keeps running. The house grows bigger, its two broad, thick-walled storeys, its brickwork the colour of dried blood. She draws even closer, breathless to see an enormous hole in its roof, how several of the chimneys are missing bricks, and those that are still upright look soon to crumble. She stops at the rotten fence, panting, her head light. Every window is boarded up. Sightless, bound and bandaged, across its front door several sturdy planks have been secured with nails. Vines of ivy snake out from under the ground-floor windows, and the large front garden is wild.

Thea slips through a gap between the rotten fence poles. Despite the house's strange muteness, it is hard not to feel as if someone is watching her. Could someone be peering at her from behind one of the planks? She watches, waits. But all she hears is the hum of bees, the wind through the leaves, the plaintive music of the birds inside them, whose names she does not know. There are no cows. No chickens. No sheep, no wild horses. There are the fruit trees, as Aunt Nella described them, some gnarled, some sprightly. Poppies, shooting up through the overgrown grass, red shocks inside the green.

But the house of Aunt Nella's childhood is not what it once was. Thea looks up at those ancient walls, and just as she is drawn to them, she feels fear in her heart. A trap, waiting to spring.

XXX

Dawn is breaking over Amsterdam, but there are still stars pricking the sky as Nella puts together her underthings, a pair of blouses and a few cotton caps in a leather bag, no travelling trunk this time, no parakeet in a bulky cage, as on the occasion that she made the mirror of this journey. She adds to the bag the money from the sale of Marin's shipwreck. Before she changes her mind, she folds up the plan of her childhood home, a place that has been winnowing in and out of her thoughts ever since she realized where Thea might have gone, and stuffs it in too. Kissing the miniature baby, she puts it in her pocket. She scribbles a note to Otto and Cornelia, because whilst she knows her disappearance will not raise as many concerns as Thea's, Nella understands she cannot simply vanish too. She hopes they can read her scrawl, and understand her flight.

Down in the hallway Otto is still asleep on the chair, rigid with exhaustion. His slice of chicken pie has been eaten, but by the looks of the crusts tumbled on the tiles, by Lucas, and not by him. Nella cannot imagine the fatigue that enables such an uncomfortable repose, but for a moment, in the shadows, she fears Otto is only pretending to be asleep, that he will insist on coming when she wants to do this alone. Nella waits, her breath held, but for now Otto is not in this world. She hopes he's somewhere that is giving him respite before he wakes up and remembers the day in which he lives. He might well be angry with her for doing this without him, but Nella remains resolute, tiptoeing down to the working kitchen where she leaves her note. She scoops as much of the wrapped wedding food and some simpler fare from Cornelia's pantry into her bag as she can, and taking a sharp paring knife from the cutlery box, she slips it into her boot. Quietly, she unlocks the front door they use for deliveries, ascending the steep flight of steps up to the Herengracht.

Nella rushes along the canal path, as Thea must have done the morning previously, and she wonders if Otto and Cornelia will assume that she, too, is running away. But they will have to trust her. She is certain that their future is marooned in Assendelft, mingling with her past.

Nella sees herself on this canal, eighteen years ago, before she was a widow, stepping off Johannes's second-best barge. *You're not offended?* Marin had asked. *Second-best in this house still means new paint and a cabin lined in Bengal silk.* Nella had thought that new paint and Bengal silk were signs of his love, but they were words of pride and glamour, papering the cracks. She thinks of the widows she has watched along the canals all these years, their expensive lives and mysterious existences. For so long she aspired to such richness, but it was a dream she could never turn into a life.

She is heading for the stables on Reestraat in the Jordaan, at the sign of the four horseshoes, adjacent to an inn of the same name. The hire of the horse is simply done. Nella tells the ostler at the stables that she'll take his chestnut mare for a day and a night, and then she stops herself, and says, *Three days. Actually: five.* The house in Assendelft is beginning to rise up, brick by brick inside her breast, and with it comes dread and excitement. She will need time there, more than just a day and a night. She finds herself checking the mare's eyes and nostrils, all four hooves, her fingers gentle on the creature's body, old reflexes which surprise the ostler. Here is a gentlewoman of the Golden Bend, leaning over the handsome flank of a beast, scrutinizing the health of a foot for rot. But the ostler is a good one; his animals are well looked after, glossy on top with good muscle underneath. This chestnut is pliant but strong, a beauty.

Nella can hear from the inn the locked-in, leftover men who have been drinking through the night. She remembers where this horse might be taking her, and holds the reins tighter. 'How much to keep her?' she asks.

The ostler raises his eyebrows. Early in the day for a negotiation, but he's an Amsterdammer, used to dawn transactions and morning flits. 'I'll give you twenty,' Nella says, before he can dictate the price. 'Including the saddle and hardware.'

'Thirty.'

'Twenty-five. But that's my best offer.'

The chestnut is worth forty at least, but the ostler takes Nella's money. 'She'll last you wherever you're going,' he says. 'And bring you back, after.'

Nella leads the mare out by the reins, and walks her for a mile through the edge of the city before the road widens out. Perhaps one should never go back, she thinks, her hand gentle on the mare's velvet muzzle. But what might be waiting for her at Assendelft has nothing to do with what came before, and everything to do with what will come hereafter.

The earth is dry, there is a light breeze, and the sun is not yet punishing. It amazes her how well she remembers how to ride. It would astonish Cornelia and Otto, and Thea too. Amsterdammers do not ride horses when one can walk to places, or sit in a carriage, or take the waterways. But how could she have forgotten how wonderful this feels? As Amsterdam begins to vanish, and Nella feels herself unwatched by any disapproving gaze, she spurs her mare across fields and the creature opens her lungs, letting loose her legs upon the land. She feels as if she could be flying, as if this mare is not a quick purchase from a tired ostler who has worked through the night serving ale to sad old men, but as if she is Pegasus itself, born from the split body of Medusa.

Any moment, Nella thinks, I am going to throw my rage upon the skies.

However, she slows down, aware that she does not know this horse well, and it would not do either of them any good to push too hard, too quickly. Dropping to a trot, Nella feels exhilarated. She turns to her right and sees she is running the route of the waterway, one of the many barge systems that lead out of the city, along canals both natural and man-made. There are low-slung barges upon the water, and it almost pains Nella to see them; how redolent they are of her own voyage to Amsterdam, eighteen years ago. She pulls the reins and returns to the road. It has to be different this time. If it isn't, then all of them are lost.

As she comes closer to the landscape of her childhood, she can tell it by the height of the skies, how the land seems to depress deeper into the horizon, the clouds congregating higher and higher in the deepening blue. Nella grew up inside this almost spherical sensation of space, pushing it away to fit into neat rooms and neater cabinets, serried house fronts and mathematical waterways. The contrast of it now is shocking to her. You did so well, she tells herself. You took to confinement like a duck to water.

And then she feels it. It creeps up the back of her neck: that cold, familiar sensation of being watched. It isn't just in her mind, because the mare seems to feel something too. Despite her pliancy until this moment, she rears up, letting out a noise that sets Nella's teeth on edge. She coaxes the mare down and settles her, facing straight ahead. The creature snickers, moving her hooves uncertainly. The road in front is empty: it is behind them that something waits.

Nella waits. Still, she does not turn. A breeze whips the loose strands of her hair. The birds are louder here: blackbird, chaffinch, pigeon. The far-off screech of a peregrine, soaring beyond her sight. The trill of a linnet, hiding in the hedge. She feels in her pocket for the miniature baby and pictures herself, turning, offering back the tiny infant from her outstretched palm. She almost does it – but what is it, really, waiting in the road behind her? It isn't love. It isn't clarity. It might be nothing more than a grey figure blurred at the edges, almost too far away to be sure it was even a person at all. A mirage, moving in the heat.

To see that uncertain sight would break Nella's momentum. To succumb to the yearning to see who was there, to ride this mare back to where she has come from, would ruin the trajectory of this story. You cannot have two stories. You can end with only one.

Nella looks once more down the road ahead of her, to where

she knows her mother waits. And her sister, too – both dead for years but their passing so unacknowledged, it's like they're coming back to life. On the road behind her, she pictures Marin and Johannes, the miniaturist too. She feels her chest tighten, her fingers gripping the sure solidity of the miniature baby that has been hers for so many years. She wonders if she will always be thinking of these ghosts.

She will. She might always sense them somewhere on the road, because that's what love is. Behind her, desire shimmers in the distance. Let another woman claim the miniaturist, Nella thinks. Let Marin and Johannes go. You've managed without them for eighteen years. And there is one person waiting up ahead, who has needed you every day.

So Nella does not turn. She puts the baby back in her pocket, she spurs her mare and rides. And then she sees them, after eighteen years away. The chimneys of Assendelft, far on the horizon.

XXXI

Nella shuts her eyes and lets the horse lead. She wants to listen before she sees, to remember how it was before a new chapter begins. How beautiful this breeze always was! She had forgotten. How unusual the absence of gulls, when the sky had filled itself with larks. She wants to smell the dog rose in the hedges, and the wild garlic. The hooves make a hypnotic, even rhythm on the earth, and Nella steadies the beat of her own heart to the creature's music. She is outside time, she is fifteen, she is five. She is sixty, an older woman, knowing the earth from which she came. She has always insisted to Otto that the land around Assendelft is bog and marsh, all year unchanging. On this preternatural morning, such a claim could not be farther from the truth. Did she have Junes like this, before she was eighteen? You so often drench your childhood in sun, but she never remembers it like this.

She hears the distant dip and rise of bumblebees, dancing over lavender. Her mother's honey bees will be wild by now, their hives rotten and empty. Her mother was a good bee-keeper, talking to bees better than she talked to people. She never once thought to say to her mother: You are very good with bees. You are good with the soil, so teach me too. What once would have felt like rocks on her tongue now seem like simple comments. Nella never once gave her mother a word of admiration, because she had decided that Mrs Oortman did not deserve it, seemingly content as she was to immerse herself in those neat and ordered hexagons of sweet syrup, closing her mind to the chaos that reigned in the house. The drunkenness, the rages that slid into despair.

But maybe it was not contentment? Maybe it was resignation, or helplessness? When Nella had asked her mother whether she would love Johannes, her mother had thrown her hands up. *She wants the peaches and the cream*, her mother had said, as if such a combination were impossible, an example not of her daughter's greed, but her naivety. *The girl wants love!*

Nella opens her eyes and pulls lightly on the reins. She knows something about resignation and helplessness. She doesn't wish to know about it any more. She slips off the mare, tying her loosely to a tree, feeding her a couple of oat biscuits from Cornelia's store.

Taking her bag and moving through the field, Nella comes suddenly upon the far edge of her mother's lake. She stops where she is, standing before it as one might a grave. And yet, she does not feel any of the repulsion that she feared. The expanse of water is smaller than she remembers. In her mind it was vast, but now it looks circumnavigable in a quarter-hour. The surface glints in the sun like a sheet of jewelled metal, mesmerizing, beautiful. Nella had forgotten quite how beautiful it is, but she remembers what she told Thea about her mother – how, by the end of her life, Mrs Oortman had found it hard to hold on to what was real.

Maybe the true problem, Nella thinks, staring at the water, was that my mother saw what was real far too easily. On a day like this, under a sky so blue, the land biblical in its vibrant abundance, it would perhaps be easy to slip under that jewelled sheet, to meet the trout and pike that live beneath, to choose never to return.

A sorrow threatens to bubble up. Nella moves on, towards the main part of her family's land, forcing herself not to dwell, keeping Thea foremost in her mind. Thea has to be here, somewhere – because if she isn't, then Nella is at a loss, and it seems quite possible that they will never see each other again. Up ahead is the line where the orchards begin. And beyond the orchards, the house itself. Nella can hardly look at it. She realizes that she's been holding her breath.

The house disappears again behind the thickness of the orchards, and she breathes out, steadying herself, for she is nearing the apple trees, and the past is exerting itself once again. Nella remembers exactly where her father's stone is laid, beneath his favourite tree, and she moves towards it as if pulled by an unnameable force. Eighteen years have matured many of the trees she remembers as saplings, but her father's is sturdy, the grave slab covered with lichen, slug trails, his name still visible.

Nella stands before it, seeing her father in two pictures: how bloated he was the day he died, and several years before that, how he would take his three children into this grove, lugging giant willow baskets, setting them to gather up the windfall, the fruit turned to cider. He would stand watching with amusement, praising them for the capacity of their bony little arms. If Nella turns round she might even see him, the rays of the sun throwing him into light and shadow, three small figures running around, hurling apples into the baskets.

Her mother's grave is beside his. And next to hers is Arabella's, three flat farewells that spell out nothing but their names and dates. She notes with curiosity that her brother, Carel, does not seem to have a marker. It makes her feel guilty that his passing has gone unmemorialized, and there is no one left to explain to her as to why this might be.

She kneels before the bones of her family, thinking she should say something – a prayer, perhaps – but she is out of practice when it comes to speaking to these dead people, or offering thanks for their lives that were. They have lain here so long without a greeting from her, it feels wrong to try and talk.

Nella places her hand on the grass at the foot of her mother's grave.

Maybe tomorrow, she thinks. Maybe I will come back tomorrow, and tell them where I have been. And where is that, exactly? Despite only having been in one place, she wouldn't even know how to begin to describe the years that have formed the backbone of her life. She never told them anything about Amsterdam. The loss of Johannes, the death of Marin, the birth of Thea. She left Assendelft and pretended it didn't exist, and it was a way of pretending that the life she'd had here had never existed here either.

She leaves the grave slabs and walks on through the orchards, row after row of pear and plum, damson and quince, their branches a canopy of shade against the sun. On the borders, the gooseberries and blackcurrants are beginning to show. She is surprised to see how much is flourishing, considering the dead land the agent had described. Did he come in the winter? It's possible; right now, walking through the middle of it, Nella cannot recall. Now, everything is a promise of riches, which no one has been here to attend for years, to pluck and put into a pie before the excess fruit rots once more into the ground. She passes the lavender fields on her right, extended wildly beyond her mother's neatest borders. Mrs Oortman would cut the stalks and dry them out, sewing the seeds into cotton pouches for the children to tuck under their pillows, three small heads breaking open the scent throughout the night.

Sleep could be fragrant here, Nella will concede that. It wasn't always broken and worried.

But as she walks towards the house, past the protective fruit wall that used to let the peaches grow, her heart begins to thump harder. Her throat constricts, she finds it hard to swallow. Out here in the fresh air, Nella can just about control the overpowering associations, but the house will be a different matter. The agent was right about the herb and vegetable gardens, she notes, her mind fixing to these details in order not to picture what might lie ahead. Gone are the mint and rosemary, the tarragon and sage. The belladonna, the pennyroyal, all of it. She thinks of Caspar Witsen, how she told him about this place, her mother's garden. She didn't tell him it was beautiful, but despite its emptiness, it still holds a pleasing quality to the eye.

☙ ❧

The house is the same place she remembers leaving, and it is not. Around its old bricks and windows, the shrubs and vines were never so tangled, the paint on the sealed shutters was not so peeling. It seems so derelict, as if no human has touched this place for a hundred years. It looks forlorn, those boarded-

375

up windows, the scraggy honeysuckle, the dead strawberry bushes skirting the building. This is far from the gilded house that Thea has been holding in the palm of her hand.

That miniature house, left tumbled in Thea's bed: perhaps without her realizing it, the sight of it had made Nella first wonder about Thea being in Assendelft. Later, alone in her own bed, she had thought that maybe – just maybe – it was a sign from the miniaturist, a means to send both of them to a place of memory, to make it real again. Memory has led Nella here, but could the golden house have led Thea here, too?

But no: Nella's thinking is just another example of her fantastical tendency to wish for things that are not there, making plots and plans, where there will always be uncertainty. Has coming here been a terrible mistake?

The front of the house is equally forbidding. The main door has several planks nailed across it and Nella stumbles along the perimeter, part of her resistant to the house's pull, but another part certain that she needs to get inside, regardless of the truths that lie within. Then, in the corner window, she sees where the planks have been wrenched away, the rotten wood snapped. The glass has been smashed, and a dark hole stands gaping. Her heart hammering, she stares into the wound, big enough for a sizeable person to have jumped through, not just a woodland animal crawling in for a place to nest. It is shocking to see this forced entry, this invasion. But then again: not even Nella has a key, so what does she expect?

For a moment, she hesitates. To go within, whether through a door or a window, is to open a box she has kept closed for many years. If she does, she may never be able to get out again. She had sworn to herself she would never go back.

She thinks of Cornelia and Otto in Amsterdam, how frightened and worried they must be. She thinks about the debt they have created with the moneylenders of that enormous city, and how it might destroy the way they have lived. And above all, Nella thinks of Thea, running before the dawn, to a future she cannot know how to control, pursued by blackmail and a broken heart.

Nella throws her bag through the window and climbs after it, a stray piece of glass ripping her skirt. This is no golden house, not yet, Nella thinks, cursing under her breath. It is a dark, strange house. I will need to pull off all those planks, those little shards. I will need to find a proper key.

Struggling to adjust to the lack of light, the first thing that hits her is the smell. She had been fearing worse, animal carcasses, rot – but it's a damp scent of age, a place that has seen no air, cool and dark compared to the harsh sun of the growing June day. Everything is silent in here, compared to the patchwork of birdsong, the bees and the insects in the grass outside. It is like a tomb.

'Thea?' she calls. Her voice echoes back to her. 'Thea, are you here?'

There is no reply. Trying not to fear the worst, Nella peers around, using the minimal sunlight coming through the broken window to gauge her surroundings. These flagstones, huge and cold, greet the pressure of her feet like an old friend. She's in the playroom. There are still shapeless bulks of furniture covered in dust sheets, paintings propped against the walls, their canvases nibbled in places. In the corner stands a spinet. Seeing this deserted instrument, Nella cannot help but recall the shining harpsichord in Jacob's perfect salon, his fingers moving deftly, such deceptive sounds. It is as if she has walked through a mirror to this sister room, the old, tired, abandoned version, where no one should be.

She tries to imagine how it was for Arabella, living here alone with their mother. What did the two women do every day, before Arabella found Mrs Oortman in the lake and was left to grow up here alone? Did she long for her sister to return? Arabella might have sat in this very room, looking out over the fields, watching the flat and endless horizon for the sign of her vanished sister.

Do not think of it, Nella tells herself, for she has come back too late now, with her tales of the city.

Leaving her bag behind, she carries on, swallowing down tears and a strange nausea, moving towards the entrance hall along the front corridor. Her father's deer-heads still protrude from the walls, their glassy eyes draped in cobwebs. The sun makes its way where it can through the nailed planks, giving Nella the sense that she is walking through threads of golden light, breaking up the dark. She turns to check the parlour, the receiving room. Still no sign of Thea.

The corridor opens onto the hall, and Nella sees the old enormous fireplace, its blackened bricks, the lintel with her family's crest, 'O' for Oortman in the centre, criss-crossed with vines and wildflowers. The long trestle table, around which they ran, and fought, and joked, still stands. It almost seems to Nella as if she can see them all, sitting here as they used to. As if her family have carried on without her, and it is she who is the ghost. She runs her finger over the table. Thick yellowish dust, untouched for years.

'Thea?' she says. Still, there is no reply.

Just as Nella makes to move through the hall, on through the other side corridor to the north stairs, she spies something in the shadows on the table. Reaching for it in the semi-darkness, the tips of her fingers meet something rough and slightly spiny, and she instantly recoils. What was she thinking, trying to touch a long-dead mouse? But when she peers forward in the shadows, it isn't a mouse. Tentatively, Nella touches it again, unyielding, perfectly compact.

She knows the quality of this object, its textures and perfection. She can sense the hand that made it. Her panic rising, Nella collects the object in her hand and moves to a front window in order to see it better. She freezes.

On her palm, illuminated in one of the few slats of light, sits a miniature pineapple.

The fruit's dimensions, its sense of promise, otherness, radiate from its little body, a spray of leaves shooting from its top. Nella holds it still, looking out between the planks over the window, straining her eyes to see the land beyond. She turns back to the north staircase. 'Thea?' she calls, her fear rising. 'Thea, are you here?'

Nothing comes. Nella slips the pineapple into her skirt pocket, and moves swiftly through the semi-darkness, locating the stairs with ease. Up on the top corridor, she opens door after door, but each room is shrouded in dark. 'Thea, I'm here,' she calls. 'I've come.'

But still Thea does not reply. Why is she not answering me? Nella wonders, and a cold, sick fear starts spreading through her body. There is only one room left: Nella's own. She approaches the old door, her heart beating hard, the miniatures of the pineapple and the baby deep in her pocket.

The last time Nella was in this room, she was so young and hopeful. She had played her lute to success. She had secured a city husband, a man from Amsterdam, his family, on the Herengracht, waiting. She had packed her chest herself, putting her parakeet in a cage for the very first time. She was so ignorant.

As she puts her hand on the doorknob, Nella thinks of Johannes, and the man called Walter Riebeeck. Thea's lover, hidden from them all, this man who took Thea's heart. Is it worse to have a Walter or a Johannes in your life? Two extremes of a man; one who took everything he could, or the other, who wished to take nothing?

Nella takes a breath and turns the doorknob. The shutters are closed. The bed is exactly where she left it. The curtains on its posts are shut. She stands on the threshold and closes her eyes. She hears her father singing, her mother calling out. The scuffle of Carel's feet on the flagstones. Arabella's laugh. Then she moves towards the curtains and everything is silence. She takes the curtains in her hands and pulls them apart.

XXXII

The horse in Thea's dream shakes the ground, jarring the rim of her skull, its hooves louder than anything she has ever known in the city, louder than the storm that ravaged the roofs when she was little. In her sleep this creature comes, pounding across the fields towards her aunt's house, flattening flowers and plants in its wake. Round this house it races, mane flying, riderless. Thea cannot tell whether it is fleeing from something, or coming to rest. She wakes with a loud start. She half-opens her eyes and looks up.

Her aunt sinks to the side of the bed, her head in her hands. 'Oh, Thea,' she says. 'Thank God.'

Aunt Nella. It seems almost inevitable to Thea, and longed-for, that Aunt Nella is here, that it should be she who has first discovered her.

'You found my old room,' her aunt says.

'Did you bring a horse?' Thea murmurs, still half-asleep. She reaches out her hand and her aunt takes it, fingers interlocking. 'I swear I heard a horse.'

'Well, I left it some way off.'

Thea opens her eyes fully. She almost lifts her head off the pillow. 'You rode here?'

'I did,' says Aunt Nella. To Thea's astonishment, she is wiping a tear from her cheek. Thea cannot remember ever seeing her aunt cry.

'All the way?' Thea asks.

But Aunt Nella rises from the bed and opens the shutters. Behind the planks on the outside of the building, long fingers of sun make their way in. 'These rooms face east,' she says. 'The sun simply pierces your face in the morning.'

Thea sits up against the fusty pillows. It might just be her morning stupor, or the dizziness of the sun after the velvet cloister of this bed, but Aunt Nella looks different. It's not her tears, nor her expressions of relief. She looks brighter. There is colour in her cheeks. Her hair is untidy, which is unusual. As her aunt comes to sit on the side of the bed again, Thea can sense the exertion she has gone to. She braces herself for her aunt's recriminations, which must surely come, now she has been found alive, now Aunt Nella has ridden so far.

But Aunt Nella doesn't seem angry at all. In fact, she's behaving as if Thea always absconds to her childhood house, to sleep all night in a giant bed that really belongs to her. 'How did you know I was here?' Thea says.

'You left a clue, of course.' They stare at one another. 'The little gold house? And then I read what you wrote to Caspar Witsen.'

Thea cannot hide her surprise. 'He showed you my letter?'

'He did. He came to tell me about it, when we realized that you'd gone. You wrote to him about orchards, Thea. I was convinced that you were not writing because you were interested in wedding posies, or even tinctures. You were thinking of a place like this.'

Thea chews her lip. 'Perhaps.'

'And you left another clue for me, here, downstairs in the entrance hall. First a golden house, and then a pineapple.'

'I thought you might understand them,' Thea says. 'Better than anyone else.'

Her aunt gazes at her steadily, and reaches into her skirt pocket to bring out the little pineapple. 'How long have you been receiving these?' she asks.

'Since January.'

Now it is her aunt's turn to look surprised. 'So long, and I didn't know! How did you find out about her? From *Smit's List*? Did you write to her?'

'Her?' Thea feels momentarily daunted by her aunt's intensity.

Aunt Nella holds the pineapple aloft. 'The woman who makes these things. Her name is Petronella Windelbreke. But I have always called her the miniaturist.'

For a moment, they say nothing, just staring at the perfect pineapple.

'They just arrived,' Thea says, 'I never wrote her a thing. I don't know about her. Have you . . . met her?'

Aunt Nella sighs. 'Nearly. Once.'

Thea waits to hear more, but nothing comes. 'I did overhear Cornelia and you talking about her.'

'Eavesdropping?'

'I didn't mean to!'

Her aunt raises her eyebrows, but Thea barrels on. 'I understood that this person meant something to you when you were my age, that maybe she still did. You said to Cornelia that you thought she might have come back. So I wondered if it was the same person sending things to me. But I was never entirely sure.'

'I think it is her.' Her aunt's eyes shine as she examines the miniature fruit. 'This pineapple is extraordinary.'

Thea almost wants to say how she thinks the pineapple might have got bigger, but she remembers how angry her aunt was when Cornelia suggested that the miniaturist was a witch.

'It looks so harmless,' Thea says.

Her aunt turns. 'What makes you think it could be anything else?'

'Well . . . Cornelia doesn't seem to trust her.'

'And you?'

Thea studies the petite, plump item. 'It seems ridiculous to me that there might be any worry over what its meaning is.'

Her aunt sighs. 'Did you go looking for the miniaturist, after you received the pieces?'

'Not once. Do *you* think she's come back?'

Aunt Nella reaches into her pocket again and, slowly, she opens her hand. What Thea sees lying there stops the breath in her throat.

'What *is* that?' she whispers, leaning over to look even more closely, but she knows what it is, of course. It is a perfect, miniature baby. It is her own miniature, purloined from her mother's chest, the baby that Aunt Nella confessed that she took for herself, a decision which so infuriated Cornelia.

'It's you,' says her aunt. 'Or rather, a symbol of you. It does look a little like you did, when you were born. I took it from the miniaturist's workshop, and I've kept it close, all these years.' She pauses. 'Thea, did you go into the attic, into your mother's chest?'

Their eyes meet. Now is the time for truths. 'I did,' Thea

says. 'I saw my parents, but I didn't take them. I left them where they were.'

'Wise,' says her aunt. 'Whereas I stole this when you were born. Still: it has given me great comfort over the years.'

'You thought the miniaturist was at the Sarragon ball, didn't you?'

'I did. I so wanted her to come back. But I was perhaps mistaken in that desire. I don't think she was ever going to come back for me. And then we all started to worry that maybe she'd come back to claim *you*.' Her aunt smiles. 'But we were wrong.'

'You were?'

'Of course we were. I don't see her anywhere, do you? You have come to claim yourself.'

They sit in silence for a moment. 'Aunt Nella, are you angry with me about the wedding?'

Her aunt takes a deep breath. 'No. I'm just glad you're safe.'

'And . . . do Papa and Cornelia know where I am?'

Her aunt gives her a harder look. 'I wouldn't leave without telling them where I was going. I left them a note. But Cornelia, and perhaps even your father by this point, are still convinced that you've been taken by the miniaturist.'

'I don't think I would ever let that happen.'

'Then you are a stronger character than me,' her aunt says. 'I think I would have let her take me wherever she was going.'

'But how does she know about our lives?'

'My eternal question,' her aunt replies. 'I liked to think she was my north star, an instructor in my life, but Cornelia and your father believe her to be a meddling spy. And I do think she watched us, from afar. I think she wanted to offer us our lives, as they simply already were.' She pauses. 'Your father has employed the St George militia to scour the city for you. To take you from her clutches.'

'The militia?' Thea covers her face with her hands. She will not cry.

'But they won't find the miniaturist. And they won't pursue her, or you, of course. Now that I've found you.'

'Jacob,' Thea murmurs, feeling a beat of old dread. His name falls dully on the sheets. Walter and Griete rise up in her mind, threatening to overwhelm her. 'Aunt Nella, I'm sorry: I couldn't do it.'

Her aunt reaches out for Thea's arm. 'I understand. And I'm sorry that you felt you had to marry him in the first place.'

'Did you speak to him?'

'I did.'

'What did you say?'

'I told him the truth. That we couldn't find you.'

'You didn't make something up?'

'I did not.'

'And did he—'

'Jacob will survive,' her aunt says shortly. 'As will you.' She gets off the bed, once more drawn to the window.

'But I have brought great shame on the family.'

'No more than is traditional.'

'Although I do believe, Aunt Nella, that he might have treated me rather like his harpsichord. Or his hot-house flowers, grown out of season. An unusual object to parade in his rooms.'

Her aunt turns to face her. 'You're right. He never deserved you, Thea.' She gestures to her old room, the tatty velvet bed curtains, the pineapple and the swaddled baby, resting on the sheets. 'I am only sorry it took me this long to realize.'

A sob rises up in Thea's throat, but she pushes it back down.

'I should send a message to the Herengracht, to tell them you're safe,' Aunt Nella goes on. 'They'll be sick with worry. There's an inn about a mile on. There used to be messengers passing through it. I'll go and see.'

'And if you can't send word?'

'We have to let them know you're safe.' Aunt Nella pauses. 'Thea, do you want to go back to Amsterdam?'

They regard each other. Thea waits. It feels to her as if there is no way on this Earth she can go back to that city. Not now. Not yet. Maybe never.

Her aunt looks at Thea with a sudden, extraordinary tenderness. Her silhouette is haloed by the gold of the morning outside. 'Thea,' she says. 'I know about Walter Riebeeck.'

There is a long silence. To hear his name on her aunt's lips makes her stomach shift, her mouth go dry. Feeling nauseous, Thea stares into the bedsheets, unable to lift her gaze. What, exactly, does her aunt know? Is she going to demand information, accounts and detail? She has tried to run away from Walter, but her aunt has brought him with her from the city and laid him on her broken heart.

But there is also relief. To talk about it, to unburden herself of his weight. Slowly, Thea reaches into the linen sack by the bed. Fumbling for a moment, she takes a deep breath and brings out the doll of Walter, holding it out to her aunt. 'I can't go back,' she whispers. 'I won't.'

Her aunt goes very still, unable to draw her eyes away from the exquisite doll in Thea's hand. But then she collects herself and takes it. 'Ah,' she says, surveying the man. 'I see your problem.'

Thea closes her eyes and thinks of the painting-room. There is no possibility that she can talk about that. 'I loved him, Aunt Nella,' she says, her voice catching. 'I really loved him.'

'I am sure of it,' says her aunt quietly. 'Or I doubt you would have carried him here, after all he did.' She frowns at Walter's beauty. 'I never thought I'd see one of these again. When did you receive it?'

'It was the first thing she sent me. Aunt Nella – how – *how* do you know about Walter?'

Aunt Nella hesitates. 'Rebecca Bosman was waiting at your wedding. She told me.'

Thea feels a sharp, jagged moment of indignation. 'She told you?'

'After what she saw unfold between myself and Jacob, I dare say she felt she had no choice. I'm glad she did. She cares about you greatly.'

Aunt Nella comes to sit on the bed, still holding Walter. Thea wants to take him from Aunt Nella's hands, but she also never wants to touch him again.

'Rebecca also told me about his wife,' Aunt Nella says.

Where is Griete, right now? Thea wonders. Is she looking for me? It seems, being here now in Assendelft, very unlikely. It's almost as if Thea had wanted the woman to pursue her, as much as she has claimed to herself that that was the last thing she desired. It is a revelation to her. Griete has more to contend with than Thea Brandt.

'Rebecca also showed me the notes,' Aunt Nella continues. She takes Thea's hand. 'I am truly sorry that you've had to manage this on your own.'

Thea feels a rising wave of exhaustion. 'Does Papa know?'

'He doesn't. That's not my story to tell.'

'Thank you,' Thea whispers. She pauses. 'I don't think I'll ever tell him.'

Her aunt considers this. 'Well, we don't need to know everything about each other.'

Thea smiles. 'But I always said that was part of our problem. Too many secrets.'

'Some secrets are all right. Others are not.'

Thea looks towards the windows. 'Being here, in Assendelft, I think I'm finally starting to know a bit more about you.'

Her aunt looks sardonic. 'Tell me: is it the dust? The withered herb garden?'

Thea laughs. 'No. The freedom you had.'

'Ah, my freedom.'

'No, I can feel it. Before it was taken away.'

Her aunt runs a hand down the side of her face. 'I should have done better for you. If I'd been a better guardian, if I'd shared more with you, then maybe Walter Riebeeck and his wife would never have happened.' She pauses. 'It's my fault, but I wish you'd felt that you could tell me.'

'I thought I knew what I was doing.'

'None of us know what we're doing.'

Coming from her aunt, this surprises Thea. 'Except the miniaturist?' she asks. 'Who seems to know everything.'

Her aunt regards the miniatures on the sheets. 'She does seem to know more than most. But I'm talking about *us*. Not her.' She takes a deep breath. 'Thea, I've never had my heart broken in the way that you have. But I have known unease and sorrow, for different reasons. I've known what it's like to love someone, to have them turn out to be a different person to who you thought.' She bites her lip. 'It's a peculiar pain, the realization, the letting go. The pain that you feel can make you doubt your own life. But I promise you: things change. They do. The pain will ease. And you will, in time, forget how sharp it felt.'

'But how long?' Thea says. The tears are coming now: she cannot stop them. 'How long will it be?'

'I cannot tell you,' says Aunt Nella. 'But I do know that the day will come when you do not think of him. It will be as if Walter is a figment. As if he happened to a different person. As if he were nothing but a doll.'

'Can we bury him?' Thea says suddenly.

Her aunt looks surprised. 'Bury him?'

'Yes. Can we bury him in the orchard?'

Aunt Nella smiles. 'That's a good idea. Of course we can.'

Thea is so grateful to be taken seriously. So mesmerized by how radiant Aunt Nella looks in the striped gold light of this Assendelft morning. Whoever Aunt Nella was when she herself was eighteen and in this room, and whoever she might become in the years to follow, she has ridden from Amsterdam to find Thea. She has come. She has drawn back a pair of curtains that perhaps she never wished to touch again, to wrench Thea from the nightmare in which she was enveloped.

'Thank you,' Thea whispers, and finally she lets herself cry. Big, heavy, sobbing tears, gouts of air catching in and out of her lungs. Her aunt holds her, and for a good long while, longer than Thea can ever remember, neither of them lets go.

XXXIII

They decide on an early outside breakfast of cheese rolls from Nella's supplies, to be eaten by the lavender bushes, on an old blanket rescued from the playroom. 'No table,' she says to her niece. 'Not exactly Amsterdam manners.'

'I don't mind,' Thea says. 'It's beautiful out there.'

'Do you know what your mother used to say about the countryside?' Nella asks, as she climbs back out of the hole in the window that Thea made to get in. 'There's nothing to do in it.' She laughs, jumping down, shading her eyes to look towards the house. 'But there is a lot to do.'

The morning sky is still a pale blue, dew on the grass everywhere. Nella watches as Thea nimbly removes herself from the empty window frame. 'That was just after I'd found out about you,' she says. 'I suggested to Marin that she could have her confinement here. Or, if you were born in the city, we could still bring you to Assendelft.'

Thea, brushing down her skirts, looks up at her in astonishment. 'You suggested bringing me here?'

'I did. I told her that there'd be no prying eyes. You could live in peace.'

'That doesn't sound like you. You're always telling me how wonderful the city is.'

Nella says nothing to this, and they search for a spot by

the lavender, the hems of their skirts wet. 'What will Cornelia think when she sees all the food we took?' Thea says.

'She'll probably be glad to know we're eating.'

'It will serve as crumbs for her to follow. Like the clues you found.'

Nella smiles. 'I follow miniatures, Cornelia follows bread rolls? Don't tell her you said that.'

Chewing her roll for a while, Thea says: 'You are wedded to the city, aren't you? You think it's the only place I can be.'

Nella considers. 'It's true I've said that for many years. There's still sense in such a statement. The city is so many things.'

'But not yet. Not now.'

Feeling restless, not wanting to contradict herself any more, Nella rises to her feet. 'I need to go and fetch the mare from the fence. I'll be half an hour. Will you be all right?'

Thea closes her eyes and leans back into the sun. 'I'll be fine.'

❧

Nella walks past her mother's lavender fields and the fruit wall, through the orchards and along the lake, out into the fields. The mare is waiting patiently, and Nella leads her slowly back to graze by the apple trees. As she stands in the dappled shade, her attention is caught by the sound of splintering wood. She looks up. Through the trees, Nella sees that Thea has found an axe – from Geert Oortman's tool cupboard, most likely – and Nella watches her niece move methodically around the outside ground-floor windows, bringing the axe head up and down against the rotten planks, over and over, breaking them away in order that the shutters might be opened.

The wood is so weak it snaps easily, as if willing to be broken. Nella is rooted to the spot, the slow reveal of the place reminding her of old uncertainties, her dread of it not quite vanquished. It looks to Nella as if the house is opening its eyes towards her. As if, for the first time in a long time, it's waking up. As she stands before it, it feels as if a part of her, too, that has been lying dormant for so many years, is also coming back to life. She is not sure of this side to herself. Its qualities, its strengths and flaws. It has been a very long time. Perhaps this house has always been waiting, weathered by rain and sun, for her return. But the question is, does that mean she should have come back?

Nella keeps walking towards the house. By now, Thea has removed the planks over the front door, and moved along the periphery. Unnoticed by her niece, deeply absorbed in her job of stripping away the bandages the house has been wrapped in, Nella walks freely into the entrance hall, through into the kitchen, and imagines Cornelia bustling around in here, reaching for her pans, tutting, tasting, shooing Lucas off the surfaces. She imagines Otto, sitting at the table, reading where her father once sat.

At the thought of Otto, Nella listens to check that Thea is still absorbed with her chopping. She reaches for her leather bag. She pulls out the old plan of Assendelft, annotated on all corners by Caspar Witsen. How angry she had been when she saw it; how hurt! But then she pictures Caspar's aloe, sitting by her bed. She thinks of his worry over Thea, his determination to help them find her. She thinks of his tinctures, of how easily they had talked, how she had told him of her mother's skill with herbs, something she had never told anyone before. Nella's eyes travel up to the kitchen door. For a moment, it is as if her mother is standing there, talking with the women she would help – right there at the threshold, their eyes turned to Mrs Oortman with gratitude for her discretion and skill.

Nella shakes these ghosts away, and looks down at the map. Here are Caspar's drawings, of an extension off the back of the kitchen to make a stove-house. Here are his points about heating, his numbers and annotations. None of it enrages or pains Nella now. Perhaps, these are lines of promise. What was it Caspar had said to her, sitting at the Herengracht kitchen table? *That garden is everything we are and everything we could be.*

Otto has written something, too: *Brandt and Witsen Co*, a note in his handwriting at the side of the sketched building: *Purveyors of Pineapple, from Amsterdam to the World.*

Nella straightens up. How easily they both missed off her name, even though the property upon which they draw their dreams belongs to her.

Nella thinks of Thea, outside. Radiant in the sun and framed by the symmetry of the old house, holding the axe that belonged to Nella's father. It is a potent scene. She thinks again of what Thea said, of likening Jacob's attitude to his marriage to her as to the acquisition of another harpsichord. I nearly saw it too late, she thinks.

But this place is not perfect either. She knows that. The sun won't always shine like this. Other things won't fall away so easily. The past always comes to meet the present, and there are only ever small moments of perfection, of happiness. How you navigate the rest is more important. Nella has lived in this paradise before. She understands its limits, far more than Otto or Caspar, or Thea, could. Those bright small moments pass, and you're left wondering when the next might come along.

But there is a difference now, Nella supposes, because she knows that the next moment of happiness *will* come. Before, in this house, and later in Amsterdam, she could never be sure, and then she was trapped in the knot of her own doubt.

It could be different, she thinks. It has to be. They must consider the likely possibility that Jacob van Loos will never give them back those guilders from the marriage contract. Thanks to the efforts of Clara Sarragon, their reputation in certain Amsterdam circles might have moved beyond repair. At least, given that Jacob and Thea did not actually marry, the house on the Herengracht remains Otto's, to do with as he wishes. Yes, they will receive no stipend to help pay back the loan, and keep the house in repair. But if Otto chooses to sell, and if Nella says he can work on Assendelft – then this time everything might be different.

And they have other things, apart from guilders: the mind of Caspar Witsen, and Nella's will, and Otto's courage, and Cornelia, always the heart of Cornelia. And they will have Thea. The baby who was perhaps supposed to live here, after all.

With the rest of the money, Nella thinks, we will make a future. *Oortman, Brandt & Witsen*. It has a ring.

She imagines the lintel in the entrance hall fireplace, carved by a new stonemason. *O.B.W.*, garlanded with pineapple leaves. At this point, there's nothing to lose. Why fight Amsterdam any longer? *Drain part of the lake*, Caspar has written, *to irrigate the seeds.* She looks out of the window. What might her mother have had to say about that? And what might Marin have said, to know her once warm, dry house on the Herengracht was being sold to shore up a ruin? Her daughter, a pineapple-farmer?

Johannes would enjoy all this, Nella thinks. He really would. He'd be amused at the prospect of such a challenge, of the human capacity for hope, a little bit of folly. He came here once, to hear her play the lute, and said that the prospect to the lake was beautiful.

'Cheese might be cheaper here without the city mark-up,' says Thea, startling Nella out of her thoughts. 'But will that be enough to convince Cornelia?'

Nella's been so absorbed, that she hasn't noticed Thea coming back in. She turns: her niece, the axe hanging loosely in her hand, sweat at her brow. She watches Nella carefully. There is no point now trying to squirrel away Witsen's diagram.

'These are Papa's plans,' Thea says, coming close.

'Strictly speaking, they're mine.'

Thea narrows her eyes, reading Caspar's writing. 'Am I really the reason you came back?'

'Of course you are.'

'So why did you bring it with you, if it made you so angry?'

'Thea: it wasn't your father, and it wasn't Caspar Witsen, and it wasn't the miniaturist who brought me back here. It was *you*.' Nella pauses. 'And after all: you were the one who brought the pineapple.'

Thea takes a seat and looks more closely at what her father

and Caspar have written. How much she needs me to love her, Nella thinks. How could I never see it before?

'These are ambitious,' Thea says.

'Well, so am I. And so is your father.' Nella hesitates. 'And perhaps we have spent too long in Amsterdam.'

Thea looks up, comprehending, her eyes wide. 'Are you really going to do this? After everything you said?'

Nella takes a deep breath. 'I think we all deserve a new beginning, don't you?'

Thea doesn't respond immediately. She will not be so near the playhouse now, Nella supposes. There will be no Rebecca to call on. No grandeur to enjoy, the likes of which Jacob van Loos might once have offered. But then again – none of that ever really seemed to impress Thea. That was me.

Instead of answering her, Thea turns the question back to her aunt. 'But isn't this an old beginning for you?' she says. 'To come back here?'

'To return to live where I was a child?' Nella sighs. 'Some might see it as a failure. I tried for so long, before you were even born, to flee it. But now I'm back, I see it's not the place I left. How can it be? My parents are gone. My sister, my brother. It can be what we want it to be.'

'So you're not going to run away from it any more?'

Nella traces her fingers over Caspar's handwriting. 'I'm not.'

'So we can stay?'

'We can.' As she says these words, Nella feels her heart rise inside herself in a way she hasn't felt for years. 'Thea?'

'Yes, Aunt Nella?'

'Let's go and bury Walter.'

◈

The burial is quick, for Walter's body is small. Thea has selected an old walnut tree for her lover's resting place. She kneels down and lays him in the shallow bed of earth they have dug with Mrs Oortman's rusty hoe.

'Aunt Nella? You said that if you'd been a better guardian, then Walter might never have happened.' Thea pauses, and Nella watches her niece exhaling slowly, shaking off the excess earth as she rises from her knees. 'But I don't know if I want Walter *never* to have happened. Because if he hadn't – if none of it had – then I might never have come here. And you might not. And nothing that is going to happen next would ever have taken place.'

'It's possible. But maybe you would have come here, regardless?' Nella says. 'You cannot ever be certain that lying within a person is the only seed of your life's next chapter. However neatly you would like to think of it.' She pauses. 'But I do know I would punch Walter, if I met him.'

'Aunt *Nella*.'

'Right in his pretty face.'

'Those are not words for a funeral.'

They both laugh. Thea bends over the grave for the last time, to cover Walter's face with earth.

They begin to meander back towards the house, garlanded with mid-morning birdsong, surveying the pyre of rotting planks that Thea has built. The trees vibrate with the birds' noise, the leaves almost lifting themselves within their chorus. Nella is struck by the realization that she may never live in the house on the Herengracht again, that their fate as a family hangs in the balance. They are taking steps towards something, but still they don't know exactly what. The power from the birds is louder than anything from nature Nella has heard in years – a hundred, maybe two hundred voices, singing and trilling and talking, as if they and their trees are the only things to exist in this world, as if she and Thea are tiny shapes moving like shadows beneath them. It stuns Nella, as if all the birds are inside her head, and her mind is shining again, hopeful again, as it has not been for so long.

And then they hear it, beneath the birdsong. The sound of horses' hooves.

Thea runs back down to the front fence of the house, through the long grass. She turns, beckoning to her aunt, and Nella joins her at the gate, waiting, their eyes on the horizon, the city and their old life somewhere beyond, the sky radiating into gold and an ever deeper blue.

In the distance, the women see two figures, one smaller than the other, being jolted atop the high seat of a horse-drawn cart. As the horse makes its way along the track, Nella is sure that the smaller figure steadies a wicker cage, which holds within it the upright silhouette of a large cat. The cart appears to be piled with boxes. Nella's mare, who has been roaming around the inside fences, lifts her head at the wheels' interruption of the birdsong. Her ears pricked, she gives a little snicker.

Up on the seat, the smaller figure turns to the larger. Something is said. An arm lifted, a finger pointed, and Nella's spirits rise higher as Thea waves her hand. A hand waves back. Thea turns to Nella, her face aglow, this day now fully broken into blue. Nella and her niece look to the path. Closer and closer come Otto and Cornelia, and Lucas in his wicker cage.

'I wonder if she's given him a ruff for the occasion?' Nella says, putting her arm round Thea's shoulders.

Thea laughs. 'Imagine. He'll probably be sick.'

Soon they will know if there's to be a quarrel over their cat's neck, Nella supposes. But what will it matter if there is? There is always a quarrel, and always a peace. The four of them, waving, smiling, on their feet. Ready, in this wilderness, to begin again.

Acknowledgements

My deepest gratitude:

to my wonderful literary agent, Juliet Mushens,
for her unswerving support, care and advice during
the writing of this book and always; and to Jenny Bent
for navigating its fortunes in America.

to my editor, Sophie Jonathan, for guiding this
story with particular attention and heart, and to
Kate Green for being such a thoughtful person.

to the design team at Picador, and Line Lunnemann
Andersen, Martin Andersen and Dave Hopkins,
for such a gorgeous, detailed cover.

to everyone else at Picador, for their
hard work and imagination.

to Helen Gould, for her generosity in
helping me think in sensitive ways.

JESSIE BURTON

to my copy editor, Nick Blake, for conversations
about medlar trees and indoor lambs.

to my foreign editors and translators, who have welcomed
Nella once more into their own languages.

to the booksellers and bloggers, who, in a
daily sea of books, have given time and enthusiasm
to my writing for nearly a decade.

to the readers who have enjoyed my books, and have
shared their enjoyment both with me and with others.
Nothing compares!

to my beloved family and friends, who never waver.

And:

to S., who makes everything possible, and always better:

and to little I.B., who we love more than we can begin to tell.